ALL ABOUT WOMEN

"Greeley writes with style, delicacy, and sympathy."

— *Newsday*

"I enjoy reading Andrew Greeley. He spins wondrous romances, and he has an admirable ideal for what his church should become."

— *New York Times Book Review*

"He writes of love and passion, risks and pursuits, high adventure and the generosity of winning."

— *Pittsburgh Press*

"He is an expert on the emotions that make us human."

— *Minneapolis Star*

"Greeley is a first-rate storyteller."

— *Miami Herald*

"Wonderful ... virtually impossible to put down until the warm and satisfactory ending."

— *Rave Reviews*

Also by Andrew M. Greeley
Available from Tor Books

Angel Fire
Faithful Attraction
The Final Planet
God Game

For Roy

All About Women

Juliette

Stories By

Andrew M. Greeley

Andrew Greeley (signature)

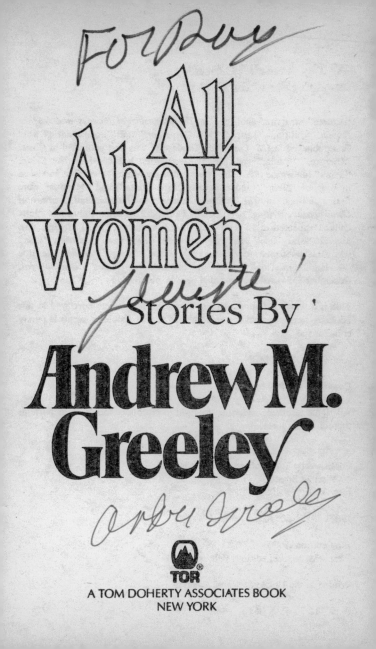

TOR®

A TOM DOHERTY ASSOCIATES BOOK
NEW YORK

"Andrea" was first published in *The Magazine of Fantasy and Science Fiction;* "Caitlin," "Laura," "Ms. Carpenter," and "Sionna Marie" were first published in *U.S. Catholic;* "Cindasoo" was first published in *Clues;* "Dierdre," "Paula," and "Peggy" were first published in *The Critic;* "Jenny" (under the title "The Priest and Jenny Martin") was first published in *Redbook;* "Julie" (under the title "Julie Quinn") and "Martina" were first published in *The Literary Review: An International Journal of Contemporary Writing,* published by Fairleigh Dickinson University. "Julie Quinn" appeared in 26 (Fall '82): 12–22; "Martina" in 31 (Spring '88): 333–42. "Mary Jane" was first published in *The Arizona Quarterly;* "Lisa" was first published in *Woman's Day;* and "Marge" (under the title "A Handful of Tinsel") was first published in *Ladies' Home Journal,* December 1984. All are reprinted here by permission.

ALL ABOUT WOMEN

A TOR Book
Published by Tom Doherty Associates, Inc.
49 West 24 Street
New York, NY 10010

ISBN: 0-812-50570-0

First edition: 1990
First mass market edition: February 1991

Printed in the United States of America

0 9 8 7 6 5 4 3

For Marilyn James who knows some of the
worlds of these stories

A still life in my memory aflame,
As a Van Gogh blossom, radiantly fresh,
Unfaded by the claims of age and pain
And the first quiet hints of lurking death.
Girl and woman in delicate suspension,
Deft painting in blue and golden glow,
Perfection, promise in one dimension
And a self that has only begun to grow.

Now wife, mother widow, forty years have fled.
Does your story, just begun, approach its end?
Are your bright grace and promise already dead?
Hope remains, distant rival, do not bend,
By God's love at fourteen you were not misled,
We shall be young once more, we shall laugh again!

Contents

Since the beginning of man the hours between the coming of night and the coming of sleep have belonged to the tellers of tales and the makers of music.

—Anon.

God made us because He likes stories.

—Elie Weisel

Our lives are the stories God tells.

—John Shea

❧In the❧ Beginning

To begin with, the title is a pun.

If you have to explain a pun, you are already in trouble, as I learned from the title of my first novel. Some folks see in a pun some sort of dark conspiracy, and an explanation does not cure them of their suspicions.

However, several of my friends and colleagues were baffled by the title. So, fully aware of the risk, I will essay an explanation:

I do not purport to know "all about women." I merely purport to have collected a group of my short stories, sixteen of which have been published in magazines with such disparate terms as "Women's," "Catholic," "Mystery," "Fantasy," "Science Fiction," and "Literary" in their names. Each story is about a woman, either as the protagonist or the antagonist of the story.

I had thought of calling the collection *Sacraments of Grace* or *Moments of Grace* because in each story a woman either is or creates an opportunity of grace for another person or is visited by an offer of grace in the form of another person.

The narrator in the last story, "Gilberte," insists that stories are not video replays of reality but bits and pieces of life rearranged and combined not to tell what actually happened, or even what ought to have happened, but what might have happened. His observation is true especially of the story about himself and of the story he intends to write at the end of his story.

The storyteller modifies the real in order to make it Real, that is to say, to tell a story which says something, however slight, about the meaning of the Real.

As Frank McConnell puts it:

> *You are the hero of your own life story. The kind of story you weren't to tell yourself about yourself has a lot to do with the kind of person you are and can become. You can listen to (or read in books or watch in films) stories about other people. But that is only because you know, at some basic level, that you are—or could be—the hero of those stories too. You are Ahab in* Moby Dick, *you are Michael Corleone in* The Godfather, *you are Ric in* Casablanca, *Jim in* Lord Jim *or the tramp in* City Lights. *And out of these make-believe selves, all of them versions of your own self-in-the-making, you learn, if you are lucky and canny enough, to invent a better you than you could have before the story was told.*

Or to express the same notion in different words, as Kathryn Morton wrote some years ago in *The New York Times Book Review,* "Narrative is the only art that exists in all human cultures. It is by narrative that we experience our lives. I would propose that . . . imaginative narrative . . . was decisive in the creation of our species and is still essential in the development of each human individual and necessary to the maintenance of his health and the pursuit of his purposes" (December 23, 1984).

Narrative puts order into the chaos of life and meaning into its seeming absurdity.

> *More than just showing us order in hypothetical existences, novelists give us demonstration classes in what is the ultimate work of us all, for by the days and the years we must create the narratives of our own lives . . . so you say reading a novel is a way to kill time when the real world needs tending to. I tell you that the only world I know is the world as I know it and I am still learning how to comprehend that. These books are showing me ways of being I could never have managed alone. I am not killing time. I'm trying to make a life.*

So to the question of whether my stories are autobiographical I always reply that they are pieced together out of the experiences of my life but do not replicate or merely re-present those experiences. Even those two classic authors of autobiographical fiction, James Joyce and Marcel Proust, notably rewrote the stories of their lives in order to tell a story about what they thought their lives meant.

Many young writers fresh out of creative writing programs do not grasp the difference between the real and the Real. Hence they write autobiography in which, they hope, nothing has been changed. Thus they settle scores with parents, siblings, and lovers and hope for publication in *The New Yorker*. The only problem is that rarely is a videotaped replay of a young writer's life experiences until twenty-five sufficiently compelling to hold a reader's attention. That is frequently a blessing, because if the young writer should by some mischance write a story which would compel the attention of an ordinary reader, then s/he might become popular and thus be denounced routinely by book reviewers (frequently copy editors at the journal publishing the review) for whom popularity is a sign of failure.

Novels and short stories are compulsively gleaned for traces of details of the author's secret lives and loves, a rather bizarre form of voyeurism, it seems to me. One reviewer, basing his view on a dedication of a book (not the one he was supposed to be reviewing) to "Erika," announced to the world that I had a sweetheart when I was growing up named Erika. On the west side of Chicago in the 1930s and 40s, an Erika? Come on. Mary Lous and Betty Janes and Margaret Annes, maybe.

Or Rosemaries and Jennys and Julies and Lauras and Peggys.

But Erikas? You gotta be out of your mind!

(The real Erika was a colleague of mine at the University of Chicago, a professor emerita of human development, a German-Jewish refugee from the Holocaust, and a psycho-analytic hypnotist.)

You will learn much about my attitudes toward women in these stories, should that subject interest you more than the stories themselves, which it shouldn't. But you won't learn much about the facts of my life. Did I sit on the pier of my family's house at Lake Geneva with a young woman like Laura?

We didn't have a house at Lake Geneva. Was there a woman like Laura? Sure, but only in the world of my imagination.

More or less.

As a certain cardinal of Chicago who will remain nameless said to me when I told him that another character (Ellen in *The Cardinal Sins*) of mine was not real, "That's a shame."

There was a child with a smile like Jenny's but the woman in the story is a creature of my imagination made up to go with the memory of the smile.

The Gray Ghost really lived and died, but Julie Quinn is

a figment composed on a Sunday afternoon at Port Dickson, where, for some reason I cannot explain, I thought of him. Perhaps the narrator's absolution is self-directed—healing his own guilt for the death of the Ghost.

(When Roberta read the story, she was displeased with me: "Greels, why didn't you introduce her to us?" Me: "Roberta, she was there only in my imagination." I'm not sure I convinced her.)

Monsignor Martin Branigan is based on Monsignor Daniel "Diggy" Cunningham, God be good to him, who was immensely proud, the funeral homilist said, of his fictional portrait. The people from his parish of "Saint Ursula," however are products of my world, not God's. They represent, if I am forced to say it in prose, the possibilities of Catholic life—as does the Clan Ryan.

I hope Ms. Carpenter is like I imagine her.

Even the real-life counterpart of Shanny Nolan, drawn more from life than most of the others, is necessarily abridged, edited, and transformed for the purpose of converting the real into the Real.

While the real life Shanny and Ed are like all humans larger than life, these two young people are even larger. Hence their legitimate protest, "Father Greeley, why not a novel?"

"Why not a library?"

"That would be all right, too."

Is their story true? Are the other stories true? Only if you spell the word with a capital T. They are all True in the sense that they are told, like every story, to say something about what life means and about what possibilities for life are open to all of us.

Tucson
January 1989

❧ Jenny ❧

For most of my life Jenny Martin has been the memory of a smile. It begins slowly, hesitantly, a skier at the beginning of a run, not sure that it is safe to plunge over the edge. Then it picks up momentum, as the skier races down the slope. Then it explodes as though the skier spins in snow and sends up a cloud of white crystal that transiently harnesses all the sunlight of a cloudless day.

Fragile and uncertain at the beginning, Jenny Martin's smiles always ended in an explosion of white light and laughter, as on the day when our tricycles collided in front of the Baptist church and I met Jenny for the first time, a little girl who was amused, not offended, by a show-off little boy trying to bang up her tricycle.

Or so it seems to my memory.

"Hi," said the girl who went with the smile. "I'm Jenny."

I will never believe that children don't fall in love. I did. That very moment.

Several years ago I was glancing through an album of childhood pictures my sister had assembled. One of the photos was of a birthday party when I was about ten years old. I'm sure that Jenny Martin was one of the little girls at the party. But I was not able to pick her out of the crowd of solemn-faced little girls with braided hair, none of them as pretty as I remembered Jenny. Such is the magic of dreams.

I have supposed for decades that the smile I remember is more a creature of my memory than the smile of a real-life child. When we return to the neighborhoods in which we were raised, everything is appallingly small. Tiny patches of front yard confront our memories of vast lawns. Modest two-story houses like Jenny's replace our imagination of gigantic, Victorian mansions. At first sight of the scrawny front yard and the decaying old house, we think that our neighborhood has changed. Then we realize that it is older but essentially the same. The neighborhood hasn't changed. We have.

So it must be, I have told myself oftentimes, with Jenny Martin's smile. Just a little girl's pleasant facial expression, nothing spectacular. But because it was the first girl's smile that was ever directed at me, it has lingered in my memory and been transmuted into the dazzling smiles I see in movies or in television advertisements.

Of course I knew Jenny when she was something more than just a little girl. Nonetheless, I assumed that my memory of Jenny's smile on Garden Boulevard in the 1930s has been imposed on my memory of a troubled young woman with whom I spoke in the late 1940s. No, there could have been nothing all that special about Jenny's smile.

A few weeks ago I saw this smile again on two different women. If my memory played any tricks at all, it was to picture Jenny Martin's smile as less than the reality.

For many years Jenny Martin's smile lingered on the periphery of my consciousness, not quite forgotten—it would never be forgotten—but still among my conscious reflections. Then, about five years ago, I encountered Betty Regan, the president of our grammar-school class, in the Old Ground Hotel in Ennis, County Clare, Ireland. To be candid, I did not recognize her. Affluence, motherhood, and age had not deprived Betty of all her attractiveness. She was someone's cheerful, good-natured grandmother bubbling as she had so long ago, but not the dazzling brown-haired, brown-eyed beauty of our school days.

Our reunion in the lounge bar of the Old Ground made its pilgrimage from enthusiasm to melancholy very quickly. Life had not been kind to many of our classmates. Divorces, suicides, alcoholism, financial failure, sons killed in Vietnam, others become drug addicts, a long litany of heartbreaks, disappointments, and frustrations. Life does not seem to have many happy endings.

"Gosh," Betty said, the bubbles gone out of her champagne. "I didn't realize there was so much unhappiness. I'm not looking forward to our fortieth reunion anymore."

"It was a hard time to grow up," I said. "A big leap from depression to prosperity and an even bigger leap from prosperity to the 1960s. We felt we were unlucky when we were growing up and then when we made our money and moved to the suburbs we thought we were very lucky, and then when our children turned against us, we realized how hollow our success was."

"Well, at least you don't have any convicts in your class," said her husband. "Two of my law-school classmates have done time at Lexington."

"We had one of those, too," said Betty, with a faintly ironic laugh. "Remember her, Father? Jenny Martin? I think she was the dumbest kid I ever knew."

"As I remember her, she had a hard time. Stern old German grandparents, a father that played around, all kinds of trouble in the house."

Betty nodded thoughtfully. "Do you remember that time Sister Cunnegunda tore her apart? Wasn't that a show and a half?"

Well did I remember it. It was history class in eighth grade, the first year since the beginning of grammar school that Jenny and I were in the same room. We had moved away from her end of the parish four years before and she and her smile had drifted out of my young life. The subject was the history of Chicago and Jenny, as was her habit, was staring vacantly out the window, presumably watching the snowflakes fall.

"Jenny Martin," snapped Sister Cunnegunda, "you're not paying attention."

"Yes, Sister."

"When was the city of Chicago founded?"

"I'm sorry, I don't know, Sister."

Sister Cunnegunda bore down on her like a battleship ramming a PT boat. I suppose she only asked Jenny a dozen or so questions but it seemed like a hundred. The last one was "Who's the mayor of Chicago now?"

Everyone knew, of course, that it was Edward J. Kelly.

"I'm sorry, Sister, I don't know."

"Do you know your own name?"

"Yes, Sister."

"Then go to Sister Superior's office and tell her your name and tell her how you behaved in this class."

"Yes, Sister." Jenny slipped out of her seat and rushed towards the door, her face crimson, tears streaming down her cheeks.

"She may be the most stupid child I've ever had in my classroom," Cunnegunda thundered after her.

We reveled in Jenny's humiliation. Every class needs a target, a class fool, a class clown, a class scapegoat. Usually it is an inarticulate boy who may make up for it by his skills on the football field. Poor Jenny couldn't even jump rope well.

And God help me, I laughed with the rest of them. Sister Cunnegunda tore her up and threw her to the sharks down in the principal's office, and I laughed at my Jenny.

As I try to recall her anguished face that day, it seems to me that she was pretty. Pretty girls are not usually targets of fury and classmate laughter.

"Of course," Betty bubbled on. "She was a *nice* kid. She

always wanted to belong to the gang but never quite knew how. She flunked out of Providence in her sophomore year and never even managed to graduate from Austin High. You really had to be dumb to flunk out of a public high school."

"Dumb or scared," said her husband, earning considerable respect from me for the observation.

I knew that she had taken courses in reform school and finally won her high-school diploma after she was released. But I saw no point in admitting that I was at all interested in Jenny Martin.

"Whatever happened to her?" I asked, in a neutral tone of voice.

"Oh, she lives in California now. I think I have her address somewhere back home, so we can send her an invitation to the fortieth next year."

"Married?" I asked casually.

Betty shook her head in disapproval. "She married, from what I hear, some sort of gangster type. I don't suppose she'll come to the reunion anyway."

Not many of us fall in love at six and stay in love with that person for the rest of our lives. So the love relationships of those whose age is still in single digits do not seem to interest psychologists. After all, such loves are shallow and transient, as one psychologist remarked to me when I asked him about single-digit love.

But that ignores the point of view of a six-year-old for whom the experience of loving and being loved by someone your own age who is not a member of your family is the most intense phenomenon that's happened in your life. You've forgotten or repressed the very early experiences with your mother and your father and have begun to tentatively probe the world beyond your house where there is a lot of rivalry, hostility, competition, and cruelty. Then you find somebody who just plain likes you and whom you like in return. If that person is a member of the other sex, mutual affection becomes, for a time, the most important

11

reality in your life. You don't even know that the name of what you're experiencing is love, but you do know that the other person is on your mind always and you can hardly wait to see her when the new day begins.

Because of my vivid memory of Jenny's smile, I've carefully watched kids in the single-digit years and noted how powerfully they're attracted to one another. Love is a dangerous, messy, demanding, unruly emotion at any age, even six. There must have been something special between Jenny and me. Most adults forget their single-digit love affairs, but I've never forgotten Jenny or rather the smile that my memory has created to remind me of her.

For a couple of years all the time that we were not in school or doing homework or sleeping, Jenny and I were together. There were other kids around playing with us, but they were not important. Jenny and I raced both on foot and on our tricycles and then on our bicycles (she won, usually). She watched when I played softball in the alley and I watched when she jumped rope with her friends. When we moved out of the neighborhood at the end of third grade, I didn't miss her at all. Perhaps the relationship was coming to an end. We were about at the age when kids swarm with their own sex anyway. When we moved back into the parish two years later—at the opposite end from where Jenny lived—I had no particular inclination to seek her out. Although we were in the same grade in grammar school, I don't think we were ever in the same classroom until in the eighth grade when we sat at the feet of Queen Kong, as we lovingly called Sister Cunnegunda, with a notable lack of fairness, it seems to me, to the ape. By then I had forgotten how much I had loved Jenny. So I laughed at her with the rest, although with a troubled conscience.

By the time we arrived at Queen Kong's jungle we were living in different worlds—she in the world of "fast girls" and I in the world of the future seminarians. From a distance she seemed, with her blossoming young woman's body, to be remarkably attractive, but my mother, who was almost as fond of Jenny as I was, said sorrowfully that she was afraid that Jenny was beginning to be "cheap."

My mother meant makeup, dyed hair, provocative clothes, gum chewing, and cigarette smoking. Jenny, she told me, had been a very sweet little girl and somehow the sweetness had been lost. "It would be awfully hard to stay sweet in such a sour house," she remarked.

I think, after that remark about Jenny, my guilt would have made me forget Jenny completely if I had not made a fool out of myself the last time we met. It was on the Washington Boulevard bus during the winter vacation from the seminary in 1949.

I had heard her story the summer before, while playing basketball, ineptly of course, in the parish school yard. Danny Daley, the son of a police captain and a grammar-school classmate, was sitting with me on the ledge of the outside wall of the parish gym drinking Coke and discussing his future. Like so many of my other classmates, Danny had discovered two years out of high school that it was a mistake not to have gone to college and was trying to figure out a way to combine a full-time job and full-time school the coming fall. (Later Danny was wounded in Korea and came home to finish college and medical school on a government scholarship.)

"It's much easier for the girls," he complained morosely. "They don't have to go to college to be a success in life. They just have to marry a man who has gone to college." (Ah, Daniel, you married a woman psychologist and your three daughters are all doctors, too. You lucked out in the changes, one of a fortunate few.)

"Some of our girls have gone to college, haven't they?" I asked, now thoroughly out of contact with my classmates.

"A couple, though I don't know why." He laughed. "And of course Jenny Martin is in a special kind of school."

"Oh? I didn't know Jenny went to college?"

"She didn't," Danny said sardonically. "She's in reform

13

school. An accessory after the fact in a robbery. Some guys she was hanging around knocked over a delicatessen down on Taylor Street and she was in the car. Trust to Jenny to get caught."

"She's in jail?" I asked in amazement.

"A year and a day," Dan said, losing interest. "My father says if her parents had stuck with her and got her a good lawyer, they'd have been able to cop a plea and she'd have ended up on probation, but they dumped her. If you ask me, they're even more stupid than Jenny."

I'm sure that I had not thought of her since the warm spring evening on which we had graduated from grammar school and like so many of the other girls in the class she had wept through tears. I remembered my mother saying she was cheap and our laughter in eighth grade and the smile when we raced on our tricycles. I felt that I had to do something to help her and consoled myself with the cheap grace that Jenny and I had gone our separate ways, were traveling down very different paths, and that was that.

On the Washington Boulevard bus, I would not have known that the young woman who said hello to me was Jenny if she had not smiled. Perhaps I romanticize that smile, too. A firestorm smile on a dark afternoon during a winter vacation from the seminary can be as easily mythologized as a smile in the early years of grammar school. But I am certain that the young woman next to me was very lovely, no longer cheap, certainly not a depraved ex-convict. Indeed, if Jenny seemed to be anything at all that day in her knit gloves and shabby cloth coat and light blue scarf, it was a prim, docile, and, yes, intelligent young postulant in a religious order.

She assumed that I knew her story. She did not seem ashamed or defensive. "It was a terrible place," she said lightly. "People do terrible things to each other in jail, but I did manage to almost finish up my high school, which I wouldn't have done on the outside."

I had no idea then what terrible things women might do

to one another in jail. Now I know all too well and shudder for Jenny's humiliation as well as admire her bravery for going back to the classroom.

"You graduated from high school?" I asked. I realized how easy it would be to fall in love with this sad, brave, pretty young woman. Fall in love again, that is.

"Yes, and I'm even taking junior-college courses at Wright at night. I live at home, and pay room and board, but it's cheaper than if I lived on my own. I work in Carson's basement during the day and go to school three nights a week. It kind of keeps me out of trouble." And she smiled again, this time laughing at herself.

"Are you doing well in college?"

"Going into the exams last semester," she said, smiling for the third time, "I had grades as good as those that you would get. Then I blew the exams and was lucky to end up with a *C*." She sighed. "That's better than the *D*'s and *F*'s at Prov."

I knew enough about psychology by then to understand that you turned *A*'s into *C*'s because you wanted to.

"What's it like at home?" I asked, I hope gently.

And then all her anger and pain and frustration came tumbling out and a little stream of tears rolled softly down her cheeks. Home had been hell as long as she could remember. Her grandparents and her aunt insisted that she was a stupid wicked little girl. "Don't you remember?"

I didn't remember.

Jenny had lived up to their prediction, becoming first stupid and then wicked. Her father had left home, her mother had a serious heart condition, and the old folks seemed as strong as ever and now triumphant because Jenny had proved their prophecies right.

"There was a counselor in the reform school," she said thoughtfully, "who helped me to understand how all these things fit together. She was a wonderful woman. I'm sure I wouldn't even be getting *C*'s now if it wasn't for her."

"You ought to escape from that house, Jenny," I said with

all the brash confidence of a seminarian or young priest who knows the book answers to all problems and the human sufferings of none of them. It would be years before I understood that there are no answers.

"I've thought of that." She brushed a lock of hair back from her forehead. I noticed for the first time that her eyes were blue. Why had I not seen that before? "But I don't know where to go or what to study or where to get the money."

"If you had *A*'s going into your finals," I rushed on nervously, realizing now how much of a jackass I was, "then you're not stupid, Jenny."

"I think that's true." She frowned as though searching for a word to complete a crossword puzzle. "I also think I'm pretty mixed up. My counselor in the reform school said I should see a psychiatrist when I went home. They'd throw me out of the house if I did that."

"I don't know any of the answers, Jenny." I stumbled badly over the words. "But you have to leave home and move away from Chicago, as far away as you possibly can."

The wisdom of Solomon, huh?

She considered very thoughtfully, her blue eyes remarkably serene. "I want to be a counselor like Mrs. Holmgren, the woman who helped me. But how can I be that working in Carson's basement and taking two courses in night school every semester, and without a penny left over after I pay my room and board?"

"You can do it, Jenny, if you really want to badly enough."

Her blue eyes examined my face with unwavering curiosity. "I suppose you're right," she agreed.

In those days we were taught at the seminary to avoid appealing and fragile young women and not to even think about bestowing upon them reassurance and affection. Not that I would have known how.

When it came time for my first Mass, I tried, not too vigorously, to find out where she was living so that we could send her an invitation. Of course she didn't come. Why should she, even if she had received the invitation.

So the story of Jenny Martin and her magic smile ought to end, banished from my life and from our neighborhood without a trace, save a vague rumor that she was married to a West Coast criminal.

Only the story doesn't end there. I'll tell you the rest of it without any attempt to find meaning. For in the life of Jenny Martin, God did not draw straight with crooked lines. He drew reckless comedy with madcap lines. I saw her smile just the other day as I was walking out of a university lecture hall in the San Francisco area. A tall, slender young woman with long honey-blond hair, a stack of books cradled in her arms, was waiting outside the doorway of the lecture hall, hesitantly, as though she wanted to say something to me but was afraid to do so.

The young woman fit very nicely into the beige skirts and sweaters of a couple of decades ago that were in fashion again.

"Nice talk, Father," she said in the tones of hesitancy that indicate not the absence of poise but its presence.

"Thank you very much," I said. "I'm glad you liked it."

And then she smiled.

"Jenny . . ." I stammered.

The kid was delighted. "Actually, Jennifer, Father. My mother is Jenny. She says they didn't have any Jennifers in her day. Will you come have supper with us?"

I really can't, Jennifer. I have to catch an airplane. I don't want to intrude on your family. You must give my best to your mother. Tell her you smile just like she used to. No, I really can't. Maybe the next time I'm in San Francisco . . .

"Yes."

Her last name, it turned out, was O'Malley. We were to drive home in her Ford Escort. I remembered Betty's story that Jenny's husband was a criminal. What kind of a situation was I headed for? Jennifer admitted that her parents did not send her to invite me to supper but she seemed quite unconcerned about upsetting them. But would Jenny want me to meet her criminal husband?

I regretted my impulsive *yes*. There had to be some way to back out, I thought as Jennifer unlocked the door of her cream-colored car.

And then I realized this very self-possessed law student did not look or act like a daughter of a criminal family. She had Jenny's smile but she was older and far more sophisticated than Jenny was the last time I saw the smile—less fragile, perhaps, than her mother as a young woman, but also more innocent. Betty's information had to be wrong.

"Are there other children in the family?" I asked Jennifer, trying to sound innocent.

"You want all the poop before you get in the house, huh? That's a good social scientist at work. *Well,* there's my older sister Laura who's an M.D. married to another M.D. and living across the bay and there's my brother Bart who's a lawyer working in my father's firm and there's me and there's Petey who's sixteen—my mom says he's the only planned birth in the family—and then there's my brother Joe who's five years older than me; he's the third child and sort of the black sheep in the family."

"Black sheep?" I asked.

Jennifer giggled. "He really went wrong, Father. I don't know what we're going to do about him."

"What is he, Jennifer?" I asked, suspecting I was being put on and having a pretty good idea what Joe was.

"Go on, you *know* what he is," insisted Jennifer.

"This archdiocese or a Jesuit?"

Jennifer rolled her eyes in mock dismay. "My brother a *Jesuit*? No way, José." She giggled yet again. "I mean some of my best friends are Jesuits, but would you want your sister to marry a Jesuit? Actually, he's in the San José diocese with Bishop Pierre."

Jennifer parked her Escort in the driveway of an enormous old house on the fringes of Nob Hill, built after the fire. Her grandparents had lived here, she told me. "Petey and I are at home now and Bart and Susie, his wife, live down the street."

"Your father's a lawyer, then?"

"My father—no, that's all right, I can carry the books myself—is a professional commissioner. After he stopped being U.S. attorney here he did a couple of terms in the state senate and then he decided he didn't like that kind of politics anymore so now he serves on commissions for the governor and even two for the president. That's why Bart and I have to go to law school." She sighed in mock exasperation. "Someone has to keep the money coming in."

"And your mother?"

She sighed again. "Mostly my mother is on committees. They're both professional do-gooders, Father. She's chairman of the Opera Board this season and on the acquisitions committee at the museum. Of course, she still does her counseling."

"I see." But I didn't see anything at all. The woman who presided over this enormous and elegant house which I was rapidly approaching could scarcely be my Jenny. Who was she? What would she look like? No way, José, would there be any connection between her and the little girl who used to beat me in tricycle races.

"Was it bad, Father?" Jennifer asked, suddenly very serious.

I wasn't going to pretend that I didn't know what she meant. "It was terrible, Jennifer. Worse than you could possibly imagine."

Jennifer nodded, as though she understood. "She's one hell of a strong woman. Did the people who grew up with her realize that?"

"I knew she was special, Jennifer," I said truthfully enough.

From the moment I had entered Jennifer's Escort, I

wondered what time had done to my Jenny. How had a half century changed her?

"Hi, I'm Jenny," said the smiling woman who threw open the door before her daughter put the key in the lock.

As she embraced me, I knew the answer to my foolish question. Jenny hadn't changed at all. Her hair was gray now, but the lines on her pretty face said character and laughter. And her body was trim, elegant, and a delight to hold, however briefly. She glowed with the radiant serenity that in women of our years always means both frequent exercise and frequent, satisfying sex. Her glow was especially brilliant in the penetrating blue eyes that I'd noticed for the first time on the Washington Avenue bus, and in the slowly exploding smile that I'd loved for decades. My imagination had not begun to do it justice.

"First time I've ever hugged you. I hope it won't be the last. No way will it be the last! Jennifer, call your father and tell him to come home right now. We have an important guest for supper."

"He'll geek out," Jennifer sniffed.

"I hope you don't mind my coming unannounced . . . Jennifer said . . ." I mumbled.

"Don't be ridiculous." Jenny kissed me again. "I'm glad she invited you. If I had any nerve at all, I would have invited you myself, fifteen years ago."

You touch the wellsprings of past memories very gingerly because there's always the possibility that the elaborate house you've carefully built for yourself will fall apart. Of course, when the past reappears without warning and the house survives, you celebrate.

So it was a festive dinner that night. Jenny, Bart, her strapping silver-haired handsome black-Irish husband (who had played football for USF in the old days when they were a power), Jennifer, vibrant and intense like her mother, and sixteen-year-old Petey, a young man with sparkling eyes and an even disposition, who looked like a carbon copy of his father. There was a cook and a maid and vintage Napa Valley wines and Abstract Expressionist paintings hanging in the dining room. Like her daughter, Jenny was wearing sweater and skirt, hers light blue, carefully calculated to match the color of her eyes. My Jenny had become a great lady, an authentic grande dame, an inhabitant of a totally different world from that of our west-side Irish parish in the 1940s but also totally different from the bastions of the west-side Irish even today.

She entertained us while we ate with a comedy routine about the art museum, the opera, and "my son the priest." The family had heard it all before but they laughed anyway. I had forgotten that Jenny made me laugh when we were children. At the end of the day I would recount to my mother the funny things Jenny had said and done and mom would say what a sweet little girl she was.

"It sounds like you have an intense and intricate relationship with your son the priest, Jenny."

"Mom's the psychologist, Father," said Jennifer. "Mustn't stop her in midflight with your theories."

Jenny enveloped me with a smile, warm and soft this time. "It's made more intricate because poor Joe is invested with residual memories of my relationship with my childhood sweetheart the priest."

General amusement from those present. Except me.

With her family's laughing consent, Jenny was defining me, claiming me, challenging me.

The steel doors clanked shut.

The laughing woman sitting across the table from me, hand held by her adoring husband, was a literate, urbane woman of the world. A long time ago we had exchanged a few sentences on the Washington Boulevard bus and an even longer time ago we had raced each other down Garden Boulevard. Two worlds, yet one person and one spectacular smile; slow, fragile, and then white heat.

This poised, cultivated matron had decided that I amused her. Easy to walk back into her life and very difficult

21

to walk out, even if I wanted to. How was I living up to her memories of me?

"You realize it was all your doing, Father, " Jenny said, guessing my thoughts and reminding me that she had done that when we were both six. How could I have forgotten?

"No," I said dimly.

"Of course it was," Bart insisted. "If you hadn't told her to leave Chicago, she would not have come to California and we would never have met. I could say thanks for the rest of my life and not even begin to catch up."

If I was entitled to my selective memories, so was she.

"After I talked to you on the bus, I saved my money." Yes, at six she was a delightful babbler, too. "Then when I had enough money for a one-way ticket to San Francisco, I sneaked out of the house and rode the Washington Boulevard bus to Union Station. I must have said fifty decades of the Rosary to keep up my courage. It was a terrible train ride. I wanted to quit before we reached Iowa. It was the middle of summer and the air-conditioning wasn't working. I rode in the coach, got off at Berkeley, found myself a job as a waitress in an all-night food place, talked my way into a junior college, and ended up as a Ph.D. candidate doing my internship working in the probation office for himself"— she tilted her head in mock disrespect toward her husband —"when he was the assistant U.S. attorney. That was before he became the head honcho."

"And we fought from the first day she walked into the office," Bart continued the story. "I was a stern guardian of justice and she was a gentle proponent of compassion. But she shouted at me and I talked softly to her and after six months brought her home to meet my mother and father."

"The nerd fell in love with me," Jenny said, her eyes misting. "So I had to dump him real quick."

"She's around teenagers so much she talks like them," said Petey with a wink, clearly relishing a story he must have heard a thousand times.

"She wouldn't talk to me, wouldn't answer my phone

calls, avoided me in the office, asked for a transfer to Los Angeles. I didn't know what to make of it because I thought she had fallen for me, too."

"He always was too vain for his own good." Jenny's smile when she looked at her husband would have lighted the entire Sierra Nevada mountain range.

"So one Saturday morning I violated all my professional ethics and looked in her file. Then I understood. My parents are the quintessence of aristocratic San Francisco Irish respectability, pillars of the church and the community. I was aimed at a life of public service before I was conceived. I could not have a wife with a prison record. So I drank too much at lunch, went up to the twin peaks, listened to the army/McCarthy hearings on my car radio, mooned for the rest of the day, and then drove down at ten-thirty that night, walked into this dining room where my mother and father were sipping the same Courvoisier we're drinking now, and told them the story."

The brandy, I might note, was superb and doubtless sinfully expensive.

"You'd never believe what they told him, " Jenny said, grinning impishly and still pleased at her triumph.

"What they told me," Bart went on, "was that Jenny was the nicest girl I ever dated and if I let her slip away because of a silly nine-month prison sentence, they would be terribly disappointed in me. So I went to her apartment, dragged her out of bed—and then, as now, Father, she was very impressive in a thin nightgown—carried her bodily down the steps and dumped her in my car."

"A Packard, would you believe?" Jennifer giggled. "Who spirits away their true love in a *Packard*?"

"Hush, dear," said her mother. "They didn't do Ferraris in those days or I would have held out for one."

"And carried her back to this house." Bart continued the oft-told tale as though there were no female interruptions. "We've never let her out since."

"It wasn't laughs all the time," Jenny added. "But there's been more laughs than anything else."

"We could have gone back to Chicago and wiped the slate clean," Bart said. "Her trial was a farce and her lawyer a dunderhead, but we somehow thought it was better this way."

"You stand on the past," Jenny said, dead serious for the first time that evening. "Instead of running from it. I never went back to the neighborhood. We've stopped at O'Hare lots of times, of course, and even gone downtown. . . ."

"Jenny was never accepted there when she was growing up, Father, except by you and a couple of others. She was the stupid little girl who flunked out of school and got in trouble with the law. Hurt from those injuries never quite goes away. I think she ought to go back and let them see who she is now, but she's still afraid."

My God, Jenny, that terrible day in Queen Kong's class I laughed at you with everyone else. And you've forgotten all about it because you need me to explain your own courage. So you're signing me on as an occasional part time chaplain because your memories are much less objective than mine.

"The neighborhood isn't there anymore," I said. "Everybody's moved out further west."

"It's wrong of me to want to go back and impress them," she said thoughtfully. "They've probably forgotten about me and they wouldn't be impressed anyhow."

I sipped my brandy and felt the doors lock, the alarms activate, the guards take up their posts. Another memory of the young Jenny: she always won the arguments.

Yes, Jenny. You win of course.

And it's not your story, is it? Not the story of a woman who turned death into life. Rather it's the story of a priest who didn't believe strongly enough in the power of life. If anyone rises full of grace today, it's your childhood sweetheart the priest.

"So what does my childhood sweetheart the priest

think?" She was beaming happily, knowing that I would never escape from her again.

"You really have to come back for the fortieth next year, both of you," I said. "And with some of the kids, including the one that Jennifer said was the black sheep. Don't do it for yourself, Jenny; you don't need it. But I think we do."

"See?" said Bart, embracing her.

"Nerd," she said, pretending to try to push him away.

Oh yes, it's going to be a wonderful fortieth anniversary/reunion. Jenny will sail in with her handsome husband and her handsome family and wisps of the opera company and the museum and her Ph.D. trailing behind her, and rub everyone's nose into the ground.

She'll be smiling the way she did so long ago and still does. Jenny Martin will be grace for all of us.

❧ Sionna Marie ❧

My name is Ed Nolan and I'm almost seventeen. Edmund Burke Nolan, if you want to be supercilious. (Our priest says I like to use big words and I get them about ninety percent right.) Everything in my life is okay except I have this terrible problem with my sister Shannon.

I'm spelling her name the way most people would. She spells it Sionna ever since the priest told us that's the real Irish way to spell it. It's the name of a river and a goddess. Shanny doesn't think she's a river.

She's really Shannon Marie. Or Sionna Marie. She pronounces her second name the Irish way, "the right way" according to her—Marie pronounced like you have a bad cold which has settled in your sinuses sounds like "Maura."

"Shanny Maura," says the priest. "That sounds like it might be the name of the woman who held the milk can when Mrs. O'Leary's cow kicked over the lantern to start the Chicago fire!"

My sister is quite ineffable. And I looked that word up in the dictionary to make sure I had it right before I typed it into my Apple Macintosh. It's the right word, for sure.

Shanny is ineffable. Not infallible (though she thinks she is), but ineffable.

I've always had problems with Shanny. Mostly it was keeping her out of fights. Now . . . well, that's what this story is about and my teacher says I'll ruin it all if I tell you the end now.

Shanny and I are Irish twins, which means I was born eleven months and twenty-nine days after she was. The priest says it wouldn't make any difference if it had been one year and a day, we'd still be Irish twins.

Mostly Shanny and I get along all right, more like real twins than like teenage siblings. That's because she's always been one of the guys, not afraid to climb fences or play basketball or things like that. Now that she's getting ready to go to college next year she says she's given up being a tomboy in public. But she'd still rather hang out with the guys than with the girls her age.

I mean, how many big sisters do you know who come around to watch their little brother practice with the other guys on the wrestling team?

The other guys noticed her, of course. Shanny is the kind you notice.

"Hey, Nolan, is that chick your girl?"

"Nah."

"Then why does she always show up for your matches?"

"She's my sibling?"

"Your *what*?"

"It's nothing dirty. It means brother or sister."

"She's no brother."

"You're putting us on, Nolan, that chick isn't your kid sister."

"You're right, I'm her kid brother."

"No way."

"Really."

"No way!"

"Hey, sis, you want to meet the guys?"

She came down the steps of the gym grandstand in two

bounds. Sure she wanted to meet the guys. I mean that was a substantial component of why she was there in the first place.

You like that? "Substantial component"?

Well, most girls would have been gross about it and become good friends with one or two of the guys. Not Shanny. She took over the whole team. All of them would come to the house to see her or even up to our place at the lake in the summer. Bother Shanny to be friends with the whole wrestling team?

Not an iota. She loved every second of it.

She sings and dances and acts, too. All the guys in the casts think she's cute, though I'm not sure about the kind of guys who go out for drama.

So how come I have to get her out of fights? Guys make passes and that sort of thing?

No way. Shanny can take care of herself in that arena. I mean since she's been lifting weights, she's built, in both connotations of that word. Not muscle-bound or anything like that but strong and tough.

When she water-skis (and she's the best chick on the beach at skiing) she doesn't so much skim the water as attack it.

As you've probably guessed, she is totally bossy. Extremely so. The priest says that Shanny is rarely in error and never in doubt. He asked her once if she ever lost an argument. She thought about it for a moment and then said, "*Well*, sometimes my Dad thinks he wins an argument with me. It's good for his morale."

The priest says that in another age she would have been a pirate queen or a mitred abbess ordaining priests no matter what Rome said, or maybe even an Irish goddess.

"But," he says ruefully (don't bother looking that one up, I got it right), "it's the 1980s, and she thinks she's an Irish goddess, regardless."

Tell me about it.

She's also very thoughtful. Well, like my mom goes, more

of the time than a lot of teenage girls. Like once last summer up at the lake I was really bummed out because my current chick's mother had put the quietus on her spending the weekend at our house—like there was enough privacy in our place to do anything wrong even if we wanted to!

Well, Shanny knew I was bummed out and knew why and knew that I might demolish a large complement of six-packs, so she organized a surprise birthday party for me—only five weeks late!

So what about the fights I used to have to get her out of. (I know that's two prepositions at the end of a sentence, but you expect me to say, "fights out of which I got her"?)

See, you have to know about our little brother Jimmy to understand that. Jimmy was born when Shanny was five and I was four. The poor little guy had just about everything wrong with him. The doctors said he'd only live a couple of months and maybe Mom shouldn't even bring him home from the hospital.

Mom, who is a lot like Shanny, goes, "No way. He's our kid and we love him, no matter what's wrong with him, right?"

I don't remember what he looked like then, though I guess he never changed much. He certainly couldn't see and probably couldn't hear and never learned to walk. In fact, even at twelve years old he was no bigger than a baby. And to be objective about it, the little guy did look kind of different. But he was ours and we loved him, you know?

I guess Mom and Dad were a little nervous when they brought him home, not sure how the rest of us would react. Mom said that Jimmy was sick and probably would never get better, but God loved him and so would we as long as we had him. So there were, according to family mythology, two little kids standing around staring down at this strange-looking baby, wondering what we were supposed to do.

Then Shanny took him in her arms and began to sing a lullaby. I don't remember exactly and I guess I'm superimposing what happened later, but poor little Jimmy would kind of smile whenever Shanny would sing to him.

The doctors said Jimmy wouldn't last a year at the most. We kept him alive for twelve years. They used to bring all of us kids over to the hospital every couple of months to ask us dumb questions. The priest said later that we were probably somewhere in an article in a medical journal about how families can cope.

Don't bother hunting up the article because me and Shanny made up funny answers to their dumb questions. Well, Shanny made them up and I regurgitated them.

Mom says that we could have never kept Jimmy with us so long unless all the kids had helped. But all of us know that Shanny was the one who worked the hardest. She told me that she could never remember a time when she didn't get up in the morning and bathe and dress and feed Jimmy. She wasn't complaining (when Shanny complains it's mostly about school being *boring!* and you can hear her all the way to Comiskey Park) she was merely stating a fact.

I guess the doctors who asked the stupid questions were worried about what the effects of having Jimmy around the house would be on the rest of us. Well, as you can tell, I'm a real misfit, right? I mean I'd be okay if the chicks didn't dig me so much I had to fight them off by the dozens. And Shanny sounds deprived, too, doesn't she?

I don't know what would have happened in other families, but Mom doesn't exaggerate when she says that Jimmy brought us all together and made us a family.

The problem was other people—kids, grown-ups, well-meaning friends, and not so well-meaning strangers, as the priest said.

That's where the fights come in.

I mean we walk into a restaurant on a trip somewhere and people would take one look at Jimmy and start complaining in whispers which were just loud enough to hear.

"That child is disgusting."

I suppose he did look disgusting. He never did grow much

after Mom brought him home. His body was misshapen, his face twisted. After a while we didn't notice. It didn't matter to us. He was ours and we loved him.

"They should put him away."

"Why was he permitted to live?"

"How can we eat with *him* in here?"

My parents would usually try to ignore them. Not Shanny. She would dash over to the table and scream at them, "He's my brother and I love him and you just shut up."

Like, *wow,* huh?

Usually they'd shut up. Occasionally some airhead would go, like, "You poor little thing; you shouldn't have to put up with that monster."

That's when Shanny would start punching and I'd have to pull her off. Mom and Dad would tell her she shouldn't fight that way, but I think they were really proud of her. So was I, but I was always the one who had to drag her away.

See what I mean, Shanny was always a problem.

It was worse with kids. Grown-ups would usually keep their smart-mouth ideas to themselves. When Shanny got a little older and people would complain about Jimmy being down on the beach, she'd chew them out verbally instead of punching them out.

She'd go, "You're so uneducated that you make me sick. Don't you understand that God wants us to love little people like Jimmy?"

For starters.

That would shut them up. Some people would even apologize and ask about Jimmy. Shanny is, like the priest says, nothing if not flexible, so she'd turn on all her "sweet little girl" charm and maybe even make them think a little. She got pretty good at her "canned" lecture after a while.

Kids were harder, especially when, like we were in third and fourth grade, and fifth- and sixth- and seventh-graders —mostly boys but some girls, too—would make fun of

Jimmy in the playground or when Shanny would take him out in the stroller.

Well, Shanny didn't put up with it and it didn't make any difference how big the kids were. She'd charge them like she was Richard Dent, right?

And who'd have to pull her off before she killed the big kid?

You got it. Little Eddie Nolan.

I was a little punk then. But quick.

I had to be.

'Course if the big punk caught up with me, Shanny would charge back into the fray. Two against one, we Irish twins were pretty good.

Kind of violent, huh?

Well, you see what the priest meant when he said pirate queen. But you know, it worked. The word went out to leave Jimmy alone and people sure did.

And pretty soon parents were telling their kids what a wonderful girl that sweet little brown-eyed Nolan child is. She loves her handicapped little brother almost as though he were a real child.

Lucky they never said it that way when Shanny was around because Jimmy *was* a real child as far as she was concerned.

And all the rest of us, too.

I found him dead in the bedroom in our house at the lake on Easter Monday morning. The priest goes that no time is a good time to die but Easter is the least bad time. He also goes that we must now think of Jimmy as more alive and more mature than any of us. Why, he's like, he even knows more than Shannon does.

We all laughed, but I'm not sure Shanny thought it was as funny as the rest of us.

It was hard at the wake and funeral because a lot of people would go how fortunate we were to be free of Jimmy. Shanny, acting real grown-up now, would respond that we thought we were fortunate to have him with as long as we did.

"I was so mature," she's like to me later, "that I'm disgusted with myself."

"I guess we're growing up, sis."

"Gross!"

The priest told us that we would mourn for about a year just as we would if any member of our family died. I guess some of us did some pretty odd things that year. But we're all right.

Mom and Dad were pretty worried about Shanny, which shows how geeky parents can be.

"Maybe it was too much a burden for such a little kid to carry."

"Ha," the priest goes. "No way Shanny gets points for a deprived childhood. Not with the wrestling team still hanging around."

"But what will happen to her?"

"She'll find some lucky guy at whom to direct all that passionate affection."

And to Shanny he's like, "And the guy better be at least as strong-willed as you are."

"No way I'm going to marry a creep or a wimp."

"That guy you had around last summer . . ."

"Well, I got rid of him, didn't I?"

So how's Shanny a problem to me now?

If you have to ask that question, you don't understand my story. You totally don't understand it.

I'm going to Shanny's college next year, right?

And she has this need to take care of someone, until she finds Mr. Strong Will, right?

So who's she going to take care of and protect from all the six-packs and all the chicks who will throw themselves at his feet?

You got it, folks.

Everyone's favorite Irish twin: poor little Eddie Nolan!

✤ Martina ✤

Martina, I thought as I considered her latest victim's tearstained face, needed periodic fixes of hate the way a vampire needs blood.

"It isn't fair, Father. I'm innocent," the victim pleaded. "I didn't do it."

Ah, but she did, you see; there was no appeal from Martina Condon's guilty verdict.

"Joe Condon says they will be forced to pull Coady Anne out of Regina and send her away to boarding school for her senior year. Your remarks on her sex life make it impossible, Joe says, for the poor kid to show her face either at school or here in the neighborhood."

"It isn't true," Linda sobbed, "I never said a word."

I had to put the charge on the record. I would have to face the Condons later in the day. I wanted Linda's explicit denial of the allegation that she had conspired to prevent Coady Condon from becoming president of the parish High Club.

It all sounded vaguely like an FBI scam—"allegation,"

"conspire." Such is the Catholic Church as the twentieth century lurches toward an uncertain conclusion.

Linda Meehan, our youth minister, was an intense, stringy young woman in her middle twenties. She would have been an intense stringy young nun thirty years ago. But in these days, dedicated young people calculate, reasonably enough, that the Church can lay valid claim to only part of their lives. Linda was not completely unattractive and doubtless would leave us in another year or two to begin the process of creating future teenagers who would harass another generation of youth ministers. On the whole a much better outcome for the Church than that she should stay in a religious order all her life, a bitter woman who had burned out in the teenage ministry at twenty-seven.

"Even if you had conspired to keep Coady Condon from being elected president of the teen club, it would not have necessarily been wrong. Why I remember . . ." I cut short my recollections of rigged parish elections in ages past. First of all, pastors ought not to indulge in too much reminiscing or they will be thought on the high road to senility. Secondly, in the new, nonclericalist, democratic Church of the era after the Vatican Council, one did not rig parish elections.

Or at least one did not admit it, not even, as the Scripture says, in the quiet of the closet.

"I would have been perfectly happy to work with her. She's a sweet girl. There never was much chance of her winning. Even if I didn't want her as president, I would not have had to say a word against her. I certainly wouldn't have raised any questions about her . . . her sexual behavior. There isn't any, Father, I'm certain of that."

"So her mother tells me," I replied dryly.

"What did I do wrong, Father?" She dabbed at her eyes with a crumpled tissue. "Martina and I were such good friends. How could she possibly suspect I would conspire against poor Coady?"

Somewhere far beyond the boundaries of the parish and beyond the knowledge but not the curiosity of the members of the teen-club, there was a boy whom Linda allegedly dated with some regularity. ("George" by name if you were to believe the teen-club gossip.) Linda was not slaking all her needs to love and be loved with the parish adolescents.

"I'm afraid that was your mistake," I said as gently as I could.

"Martina didn't seem to make any demands."

"That's part of her game."

It might not seem like a very important game. Is there a church in the country without mothers who push their children beyond the kids' competence or popularity? All right, there were some special twists to Martina's game. But after one term as a pastor in a modern Catholic suburban parish, the demitasse tempest of *l'affaire* Coady Condon should be no challenge to me.

True enough, if I were willing to offer Martina the head of our youth minister on a silver platter.

Penny ante? Especially since Linda was not likely to want to renew her contract a year from now? Couldn't the pastor have a nice little talk with her and suggest that she might want to take a sabbatical after Christmas—with pay, of course?

Sure it would be easy—if the pastor had no character at all (like a bishop). But, while I can compromise with people till the day before the Last Judgment, I was not about to let Tina Condon win this one.

So much time has to be spent fending off disaster, even if it's only one small disaster.

"Mr. Condon . . ." Linda began.

"Always agrees with her. Tell me about it. What kind of a father is it who won't stand up for the rights of his children?"

"He's such a nice man."

"Nice men are especially likely to believe their wives. . . .

Tell me, Linda"—I don't think I sighed too loudly—"have you become good friends with another couple in the parish lately? Not that there's anything wrong with that."

In the old days when I was a curate (*not* an associate) only the pastor was permitted to have friends in the parish.

"No, Father, not that I can . . . well, there's the Kellys, but Tina introduced me to them."

"That figures. You see"—I did not want to sound like a cleric whose two courses in counseling at Loyola cause him to think he's as qualified as Freud—"the Kellys were a test. If you liked them more than the Condons, you were already on the way to disloyalty."

"But I don't . . ."

"You don't understand the game, Linda; you were certain to like them more, no matter what you did."

"I couldn't win?"

"You've got it. . . . Is that boy we never see really called George?"

"No." She flushed an appealing shade of crimson, which persuaded me that whatever his name might be, he was a lucky young man. "That's the kids' name for him. I won't tell them his real name. It protects a part of me from their curiosity. His real name is . . ."

"Consider me one of the kids. Call him and tell him he owes you a supper tonight. Okay?"

"Sure." She continued her appealing crimson blush. "No problem."

"I'll worry about it for a while. We're not going to feed you to the wolves, Linda."

When I had come as a new pastor, I was not well received. Some of the old-timers resented the fact that I had replaced the founder (one of the better prelates of the middle nineteenth century). I was also an uncertain quantity to most everyone else. Martina Condon quickly made her move to "adopt" me. Since she was intelligent and generous with her energy and her concern, and her husband was likable and fun to argue with, I was tempted. Some residual instincts of Irish political sophistication, inherited from both sides of the family, made me hold back from the obvious offer of support, consolation, and admiration.

"Wait and see" was my mother's favorite expression. I waited, I saw, and I decided that I would get along much better with the Condons if I kept a wary distance from them. It was a wise choice. I had not quite made it sufficiently into her orbit to be accused later of disloyalty.

Her hates were not ideological but maternal. Her mother love was a ticking bomb. She did not feel that she was a good mother unless she were hacking with her broadsword those who were seeking to assault her children. Since, despite an M.A. and considerable intelligence, she had elected to define motherhood as a career and the source of her worth as a person, it was necessary to swing the broadsword, early and often, as we used to say in Chicago politics.

So, while I was the boss (which along with a dollar will get you a ride on Mayor Harold's subway) and held the cards and while I would not sacrifice poor Linda, who had more than earned her keep, I looked forward to a battle with Martina Condon much as I would to combat with a saber-toothed tiger whose cubs I had carried off.

Some of the junior boys were at the parish basketball court, a place they could be found during the autumn months at any hour of the day or night. I offered to engage them in a game of twenty-one. They dared not refuse. After all, I *am* the pastor, and as I told them, if I couldn't play I'd take up my court and go home.

You have to be either dedicated or unbalanced to enjoy teenagers, especially junior boys. Whether I am either or whether it is merely flattering to my morale to rout them at twenty-one (standing six feet three helps) is a matter which need not detain us at the moment. I was on an intelligence mission.

38

"I hear the High Club election is disputed," I said as I missed a jump shot that ten, well, no, twenty years ago would have been little more than a lay-up.

"Goofy Mrs. Condon," said one of the animals, hitting a shot which was deliberately fired from the same spot where I had shot and missed.

"Is George really a nice guy, Father?" The second animal fed the ball for a lay-up to his fellow. "I mean, poor Linda, she doesn't need a geek boyfriend when she has to put up with Mrs. Condon, and"—his voice turned into a fair imitation of Tina's—"poor sweet little Coady Anne."

"George," I said firmly, tossing the rebound to the second animal, "is no geek."

Their blood drenched with reproductive juices, these animals were normally capable of considering a girl only in the most explicitly clinical aspects of her body. Concern for Linda Meehan as a person demonstrated that (a) emotional maturity was catching up with the reproductive juices in this collection of barely domesticated beasts, and that (b) Linda had succeeded in her mission with them, maybe better than she realized.

"Mrs. Condon," continued the other, "is an airhead."

"But still, Coady had the same right to run as anyone else."

"Poor sweet little Coady"—he sank his third jump shot—"couldn't attract freshmen to a strip show."

"Really major," agreed the other.

"I mean she's all right, kinda cute, if you like them little, but no way she's going to win a High Club election."

"The sophomore animals would run all over her, poor kid."

"So why should Linda bother? Everyone thought it was a joke, like Mrs. Condon pushing poor sweet little Coady into running when she's going to get creamed. Right? Patty O'Hara would win by tons of votes if she was running against Miss America. Right?"

Right, indeed.

39

Patty O'Hara would cream the Archangel Raphael in an election.

They would have denied an anti-Coady fix in any event. Linda was one of their own, and like Mafia dons, priests, and surgeons, teenagers stood by their own. A solemn high and serious denial would have confirmed Tina's charge. The denial I heard, touched with ridicule and cruelty, supported Linda's story. As I had expected. Did Linda with maybe a twitch of her lips at the mention of Coady's candidacy (perhaps at the thought of poor sweet Coady confronting our sophomore animals, who were especially animalistic this year) give perhaps a basis, as thin as angel-hair pasta, for the charge?

Maybe. But finally so what? In Tina Condon's world Coady would be cute as teen-club president, just as she was cute in the designer clothes that she wore when she was ten. In the world of the electorate only a space cadet would think that Coady had a chance to win. Her candidacy deserved to be treated respectfully but not seriously. No one can be held responsible for an occasional twist of the lips or a functional equivalent thereof.

Back in the store, that is, the rectory, I turned on the evening news. There were problems in South Africa, Lebanon, Yemen, and city hall. And I was barely restraining the forces of chaos in my neighborhood over a teen-club election.

There is no proportion, a wise person (tell you the truth, I don't remember who it was) once remarked, between the importance of a prize and the passion with which it is sought.

When Joe Condon had phoned me before my conversation with the youth minister, his tone had been sad and troubled—not angry or reproachful. Indeed, his posture was that it was all over and the die had been cast.

"We've decided that the best thing to do, Father, is to pull poor Coady out of Regina and send her for her senior year to a boarding school in California. I've spoken to the nuns out there, and they tell me she should have no trouble catching up with the work."

The call was my first hint of the controversy. But by assuming that I was well informed, Joe was indicating that he took for granted my acquiescence in the injustice and calumny. He was demonstrating that he and Tina were prepared to be good sports about it all, even though their hearts were breaking.

"Well, after what Linda Meehan did, it seems to be the best choice for everyone; Coady, Linda, you, everybody else. We certainly don't want to be a parish problem all year long."

You betcha.

I had been through annual sessions with the Condons and knew the scenario by heart.

The first time it had been the O'Connells. Joe and Tina appeared at the rectory door, a solemn if mismatched couple: Joe, tall and lean, in sport clothes perhaps more suitable for spring than for mid-September; Tina, as slight as an injured sparrow, in subdued colors appropriate for a sparrow.

Tina was well named, a little woman with a small body and small bones, doubtless cute like her daughter when she was young, and hardly ugly now—a kind of well-groomed, well-turned mouse at first impression.

Okay, as the animals had said on the court, if you like them small, which, to be honest, I didn't.

The conversation about the O'Connells was not hard to remember because I had heard it several more times, with minor variations, since the first episode.

Joe: We're worried about the O'Connell children, Father. There's nothing much we can do about it, since we're not friends with them anymore, but maybe you can have a talk with them about the kids.

Me: (knowing the O'Connells had been good friends of the Condons, maybe even gone on a vacation with them) Oh?

41

Joe: I don't understand much about such things, I didn't graduate from college, you understand, but when kids grow up in an atmosphere of constant deceit, you have to worry about whether there's any chance for the kids to achieve full maturity.

Me: Oh?

Tina: What does an atmosphere of deception do to children, Father?

I went along with the game, explaining about psychopathic personalities and their impact on children. It was a mistake, because I had permitted myself to be dragged down a long, intricate, and convoluted path at the end of which it was assumed that I had accepted their diagnosis of the O'Connell family: Mrs. O'Connell was a psychopathic personality and her husband was afraid of her.

I was never told exactly what the O'Connells had done. It was somehow assumed that I knew the whole story before Tina and Joe showed up at the rectory and thus it was unnecessary to provide me with the details.

"What exactly did they say about your boy?"

"We wouldn't want to repeat it, Father." Tina was always calm, cool, rational—the utterly self-possessed mother dealing sadly but realistically with betrayal and attack.

What was I supposed to do?

The explicit agenda was that maybe I could have a talk with the O'Connells—not about reestablishing the friendship (the O'Connells had already tried and been briskly rebuffed, without ever, I would learn, being given a formal description of the charges against them)—but about the dangers of deceit, described always in the abstract, to their children.

"They can do so much harm, Father, to their own children, too, without even realizing it, can't they?"

Having thus transferred the burden of their terrible knowledge about the O'Connells to their pastor's shoulders, Joe and Tina could return home with clear, if still worried, consciences.

Then there were the Murrays, who were guilty of some sort of terrible public discussion of sexual intercourse in front of the children, and the Ryans, who had turned all the other children against the Condon children.

I carefully checked out the stories each time. There was never any basis in fact. "Father, it all exists in her head, poor woman," Jean Ryan said with a sigh. "And she's such a nice friend until she goes haywire. You know it's happened to others but you can't believe that it's going to happen to you."

"Catch-22, Kafka's trial," Steve Ryan, a professor of literature at Chicago Circle, added, "and Wonderland all rolled into one. Out of sight."

So when I opened the door and admitted Joe and Tina to the rectory (suspecting that the nosy teenage porteress who was on duty that night ought to be kept out of the picture), I knew the general story line that was to be played out. I wasn't sure, however, what nuances would be added now that I was, to some extent, responsible for the assault on poor sweet little Coady (who was indeed little and sweet and emotionally impoverished now, if any senior girl in the parish was—and utterly beyond help now from anyone but God).

I resolved that however difficult it might be, I had to stand for reality. Linda had not conspired against Coady. The latter had lost the election. She had finished fifth among five candidates because, as Richard Daley observed of Hubert Humphrey, she didn't have the votes. No way, José, as the animals would say, was Linda to be replaced.

Brave words.

They were both tense, solemn, preoccupied—like the people you see in hospital waiting rooms outside of surgery. Tina's eyes were red from weeping.

"It looks like we're going to have to move, Father," Joe began, his thin, black-Irish face knotted in a fierce scowl. "If you think that's what's best, just say the word and we'll put the house on the market tomorrow. Change every fifteen years is good for a family anyway."

"I've investigated the matter," I said, sounding a bit like the United States attorney at the daily press conference in which he confirms the leaks from the day before by apparently denying them. "And there is no evidence that Ms. Meehan ever spoke a word against Coady. If you could tell me what it was exactly that she is supposed to have said, I'll be happy to look into it further. . . ."

You'll note I did not say "alleged." Pastor, not United States attorney.

"I feel so sorry for poor Linda." As always, and despite her red eyes, Tina was cool, self-possessed, and reasonable. "What will it do to her own children? I mean how can you grow up to be normal and healthy if your mother feels that popularity is more important than integrity? And makes up stories about another person's sex life just so she can be popular? What are the effects of that kind of home environment, Father?"

Tina was wearing a simple, and expensive, brown tailored suit, the mother as professional woman.

"As best as I can determine," I continued on my truth-telling tack, "Patty O'Hara would not have lost to the Blessed Mother should she have been a candidate. Patty received three times as many votes as all the other candidates put together. There's no need to rig an election in favor of such an accomplished politician and certainly no disgrace in losing to her."

Truth to tell, if Patty O'Hara was set down in Rome two weeks before the cardinals went into conclave, she would be elected pope. By about the same margin. On the first ballot.

"She's been very good with the kids; we were all fond of her," Joe plowed on, his left eyelid twitching nervously, "and we understand that she's close to getting engaged to George . . ."

"His name is not George."

"But you really have to worry about a girl with that kind of character defect, don't you, Father?"

"There are different talents given to different people. Patty is a great politician, but she can't sing a note or play the piano. Coady has the makings of a concert soprano, I am told."

"And, of course, there is the problem"—Tina was resolutely thoughtful, objective, dispassionate—"of the influence such an antisocial character defect might have on the young people with whom she is working today, not that it's our responsibility to worry about that."

"I have complete confidence in Linda."

"We really are concerned about her, Father." Joe shifted uneasily on one of the hard chairs we keep in rectory parlors even in the post-conciliar era because they discourage parishioners from staying too long. "Maybe if she spent some time in an institution, a few weeks, anyway, it would help." He grinned. "I kind of feel sorry for poor George."

"His name is not George!"

Tina leaned forward, fingertips under her tiny firm chin, a whiff of expensive scent easing its way discreetly across the parlor. "I suppose that there's no way, is there, Father, that you can screen for those character defects, before you hire a youth minister? I know they screen young men in the seminary."

"When her contract expires, Linda tells me that she may go back to school for her doctorate, but I would have no problem renewing it."

Well, that should have made things clear enough, shouldn't it?

"The whole thing is unfortunate." Joe was now playing with his Cadillac key chain as his eyelid twitched violently. "Mind you, it's not your fault, Father. Everyone says you're doing a great job here under the circumstances."

"Poor sweet little Coady didn't want to run." Martina shook her head, baffled over an insoluble puzzle. "But all her little friends insisted. And Linda encouraged her, which

45

was her business, she certainly didn't have to do it. And I said to her, I said, 'Coady, Patty O'Hara is a formidable candidate.' And she said, poor little tyke, 'I don't have to win, Mummy; I only want to see what it's like to run.' That's why the outcome is so unfortunate."

"What outcome?" I shouted, angry at myself that I was angry and angry that again I had been pulled into their Wonderland scenario.

"We'll do whatever you think best, Padre." Joe put the Caddy keys into his blue sport coat (ideal for dinner at the country club after golf). "We understand that we've become something of a parish problem. We're sorry, but we feel we have to stand by our kids, especially when there are sexual innuendos. What else," he added with a slight choke in his voice, "do you have if you don't have your kids, right? And if you don't stand by them, who will you stand by?"

"So . . ." Tina took over for him, as if rescuing him from the incoherence his strong emotions had created. "If you really think it would be better for us to move, we'll do it, without any ill feelings."

"I don't think you ought to move," I exploded. "There's no reason for that."

"It'll be hard." Joe had actually pulled out his handkerchief and was wiping his eyes. "We've always thought of this parish as home."

"For the love of heaven, what do you want me to do?" I shouted so loud that the associate pastor told me later he could hear me above the TV (before which he sat with the same religious fervor, day and night, as the junior boys manifested at the basketball courts).

"Poor sweet Coady will be all right, of course. She has a family to stand by her. She feels fine, actually." Tina arranged the folds of her skirt. "Really it's Linda we're concerned about, Father. Her parents are both dead, you know."

"Will you both shut up and listen!" I rose to my full six feet three inches of slightly moth-eaten dignity. "I don't want you to leave the parish. There is no reason to do so. Linda did not interfere in the election against Coady. There is no conspiracy against you. This whole crisis is a product of your imaginations."

I promised myself a double shot of Bushmill's Black Label when I would later sneak by the curate and the TV. Protestant ministers have wives on whom to dump this sort of crap. Black Bush is a harmless substitute, not so pleasurable but not so demanding either.

"Maybe you could have a talk with her, Father," Tina murmured softly.

"Coady?" I was girding my loins for a full-scale attack on Martina's game—demolish the whole thing in one fell pastoral swoop. Act like a monsignor even though they were an extinct species.

"Oh, no, she's fine. I mean Linda. Maybe if she went into therapy before she was married . . ."

"I'll think about it," I muttered, wanting them to walk out the front door before I was trapped in Wonderland with them.

Those magic, if quite dishonest, words were enough. They had discharged their responsibility.

We shook hands, they thanked me, and after assurances that everyone thought I was doing a great job "under the circumstances," they left the rectory, walking briskly down the steps into the warm, caressing Indian-summer night— brave, mature Christians, coping well with intense personal pain.

My heart unaccountably heavy despite my victory, I went to the office instead of the parlor. Paying no attention to the red-haired sixteen-year-old porteress who was dying for information, I glanced out the window.

Joe had his arm around Martina, a protective, reassuring husband standing by his wife in her grief. She was sobbing hysterically, her body shaking like that of a widow at a graveside.

"Is Coady Anne *really* going away for the rest of her

senior year?" The redhead's curiosity had finally torn its bonds asunder. An Irish biddy in training.

"I don't know, Jackie." I turned away from the window. "Maybe."

"Poor kid. Everyone likes her. She has tons of friends. Really."

"I know."

"I feel sorry for Mr. and Mrs. Condon, too."

Also a gentle Irish mother in the making.

"I feel sorry for everyone, Jackie."

"Yes, Father."

You give up a family of your own and you dedicate yourself to a life of compassion for the least of the brothers and sisters. Fine. But my compassion reared its hesitant head only after Joe and Tina Condon left the rectory. It probably would not have healed their pain, but how did I know that? What sort of compassion is it that excludes those who are strangling on their own hate?

The saints would judge Linda innocent of betrayal. As I sipped my Bushmill's, what would they think of me?

⸙ Mary Jane ⸙

I didn't like the look of Arnie's rectory the first time I saw it five years ago; a sinister place, I thought. My reaction, I suppose, was not psychic sensitivity but a romantic tendency to think that all late-nineteenth-century homes with turrets and gables look sinister. Still, I was right, as it turned out.

"Wow," I said, "that's a big place, especially with no curates. . . ."

Arnie took my flight bag out of the trunk of his Datsun and glanced up at the old gray house outlined against the twilight. "It used to be the bishop's house in Sander's time. When the city spread in this direction, they built a church next to it and had a ready-made parish. Hell of a place to heat in the winter . . ."

He met me at the United flight at the airport. He was easily recognizable despite the twenty years since we had been together in the seminary—tall, thin, with fair hair, not as much of it at the temples, more at the earlobes. He still looked like a plainsman, wiry toughness, far-seeing blue eyes. Same old Arnie, yet something indefinably different, not just the lines around his eyes—a look of abstraction, preoccupation. Arnie was a monsignor and a rural dean, former president of the parish senate. He wore gray slacks, a parish baseball-team jacket, and no Roman collar.

We drove through brown and desolate frost-touched cornfields as the gray sky turned dark. Next week it would be night at this hour as we reluctantly traded in daylight saving time to salvage some early-morning sunlight for our ride to work. The plane was late, the lecture was at seven; there would be time for a hamburger before I went through my act.

"Sorry to schedule it so early," Arnie said as we left the farm country and entered the fringes of his parish. "We Iowans go to bed early, though. . . . Then the Friday housekeeper got sick, so I had to cancel the supper. I hope you don't mind my hamburgers."

I assured him that I was used to cooking my own meals. Arnie and I had not been particularly close at the seminary. He was a solid, quiet kind, his family from the land where Poland and Germany meet, whose members star on the athletic field, perform competently in the classroom, and keep their own counsel—hardly a soul mate for a Mick with more flair than sense. He had worn well, better than many of us, I thought as we drove up to the old rectory. He used the language of the new Church with practiced ease, parish council, school budget, servant church, religious education team, charismatic renewal . . . no identity crisis here . . . only those deep-set eyes intently scanning the prairie, even though there weren't any prairies around. I was glad I had accepted his invitation to talk, though you wouldn't refuse a classmate; I wanted to see how one of my generation handled the post-Conciliar Church on the fringes on a small Iowa city.

My momentary unease vanished when we went into the house. It was as warmly and as tastefully decorated as any Lake Shore Drive apartment—light, creamy pastels banishing all hint of Victorian gloominess. "You've got a good interior decorator, Arnie," I told him as he led me up the staircase to my room. He turned toward me and smiled the same faint plainsman smile I had known in the seminary. "Hell, I did it myself. Didn't dare risk hiring one firm over the others; we've got all the interior decorators in the city in this parish."

My room was a pleasant light green with a thick, quilted comforter doubling as a spread and an extra blanket for the Iowa winters. "You gotta be careful about such things in a place like this," he went on, flipping the thermostat up to sixty-eight and closing the drapes on the gloomy night sky. "I have three different housekeepers. Each one comes in two days a week—keeps the parish happy; no family gets too much power with the pastor."

"A big house for just one man to live in," I said, rummaging through my briefcase for the quotes I'd use in my lecture.

"Cheaper to live in it alone than build a new one." Arnie shrugged as he stood in the doorway. "We use it for priests from the out-counties when we have meetings in the city. Anyhow, it's a lot easier to keep places clean here than it is in Chicago." The faint plainsman grin again. "See you in the kitchen in a few moments."

I put the thermostat up to seventy-two, arranged my things for the morning, even though I was breaking a rule and staying around till midafternoon, and checked out the room: small, airy, comfortable; an easy chair made for sitting in, a mirror which was not scratched, an ivory-colored dresser with big drawers, a shower which worked. The combination of taste and efficient concern for comfort was not what I would have expected of my plainsman friend.

I was hungry, so I wasted no more time on reveries about the past. As I hurried down the thickly carpeted steps something happened which I barely noticed then, but which made a lot of sense—if any of it made sense—later.

Halfway down the stairs I smelled scent, a powerful and unfamiliar perfume, though I confess to no great familiarity with scents. It was strong enough to make me stop and sniff. Where was it coming from? But then it disappeared suddenly. I forgot about it by the time I entered Arnie's flawlessly equipped, ultramodern kitchen.

"No complaints from your housekeepers about the equipment." I laughed, sinking my teeth into a hamburger which was light-years better than my own pseudo-McDonald's efforts.

"All they complain about"—he grinned back at me—"is that the other housekeepers don't keep it clean enough. You can't win with women. . . ."

We talked about the years in the seminary, the tragedy in Chicago after Meyer's death, the possibilities of the next papal election, the peculiarities of Arnie's bishop—a relatively straight man by my standards. I sipped a cup of tea and Arnie carefully nursed a bottle of Heineken's. There were a few minutes before it would be time to greet the lecture audience. We went to his parlor—another stunning room—light blue and white, soft and restful but still masculine—no TV—a piano in the corner with a Mozart sonata open on the music rack.

"Cooking, interior decorating, and Mozart, Arnie," I said in astonishment. "We never would have guessed any of it twenty years ago."

Arnie's fair skin colored. "The Mozart's just part of the theme; I don't play it."

I ran my fingers over the keyboard, pounding out with my terribly inept technique the first few bars of the Mozart; the piano was in perfect tune.

Arnie leaned back in his vast couch and smiled contentedly. "I'm not the only one who has learned something since seminary days."

"The difference," I responded, "is that you're a good cook and interior decorator and I'm a rotten pianist."

I thought to myself that there were lots of other differences. I had become more transparent; publicly so, God help me, Arnie more opaque. I was eager to get on with the lecture and go home.

The school hall was already filled with people when we got there five minutes before kickoff time, and the cars were still pouring into the parking lot. Lecture crowds are influenced not by the quality of the speaker but by the promotional efficiency of the sponsoring organization. Arnie's was very efficient indeed. You could tell from the faces lighting up in smiles when Arnie appeared that his people liked him, flinty plainsman personality and all. The talk went well enough; the people were friendly and courteous. I could have talked in Sanskrit and gotten away with it, I think; I was a classmate of their pastor and that settled it.

At the reception afterward I got a chance to size up Arnie's congregation, mostly college-educated professionals, a lot of them from out of the state. Iowa produces more manufactured goods than it does agriculture, I was told, and the factories in the city were staffed by young managers and technicians from all over the country, smart, articulate men and women who knew what they wanted from their church. They were getting it from Arnie, who seemed to know all about the families of each of them. He even found one young man who had grown up in my parish in Chicago, though I barely remembered him.

"Quite a fella, Arnie," he said to me when the pastor went on to another knot of people, "the plainspoken-Iowa-farmer bit, and not a lot of what you'd call charisma, but he's got us eating out of his hands because he's so concerned about each one of us; love pays off, doesn't it, Father?" he blurted, embarrassed by his show of piety.

"I'm sure it does," I said, sipping my punch and wondering about the impact of this basically frosty man on his sophisticated parishioners, most of whom were better educated and smarter than he. They called him "Arnie" to his face, too; there weren't many places around the country even then where you could get away with that when your pastor was a monsignor—though he didn't look much like a monsignor in his baseball jacket.

I don't mind questions after lectures, and I can tolerate receptions; but I warned Arnie before I came to omit the clerical bull session in the rectory afterward. I'm usually exhausted by that time and require one Librium (prescribed by my doctor for such occasions), a warm shower, and a comfortable bed. Arnie didn't argue. The parish Mass was at noon, sleep as late as I want, we'd grab a bit of breakfast and see some of the country before my two o'clock plane back to Chicago.

I felt soothed and relaxed in the shower, more than usual after a lecture. It was, I told myself, pleasure over Arnie's success with his people . . . something missing in his style, though . . . he was good with his parishioners, but still the faraway look in his eye . . . you're faking it with them, Arnie . . . you're so good at faking that they don't realize you're going through an act . . . your mind is someplace else. It was very cold when I stepped out of the water onto the thick bathroom carpet, like getting out of a heated pool in zero weather. Shivering underneath my towel, I checked the bathroom thermostat. It was at seventy-five, where I had put it earlier. Why the hell was it so cold? I climbed quickly into bed and fell asleep almost at once, basking in a sensation of warmth and peace after the postshower shock; the Librium was working quicker than usual . . . maybe the light supper.

Later, a little after midnight I guess, I experienced a vague unease in my sleep. I struggled to locate the unease: music. In the distance, barely audible, a piano was being played. I was in that state of mostly sleep—slightly awake —where you debate whether something is a dream or not. . . . I was imagining a Mozart sonata, I told myself groggily, because I had seen the music on Arnie's piano. Reassured, I sank back into deep sleep. As the sound of the piano faded away, the judgment center in my brain decided that it was not dream music, but the Librium had done its work. I postponed till morning any questions about the piano player.

The next time I woke, my passage from deep sleep to full, if confused, consciousness, was abrupt and rapid. I was tense, wide-awake, and cold. Someone had turned the light on in my room. I sat up with a start. There was another person in the room with me.

She was sitting in the chair watching me. When I sat up, she rose from the chair and began walking toward the bed, bare arms outstretched. There was nothing ethereal or misty about her. She was as solid as the bed, the chair, the dresser; a slender graceful woman with a lovely figure and a sweet smile, clad in nineteenth-century undergarments. As she drew near the bed, hardly a foot away from me, I saw she was no longer young . . . in her late thirties or early forties . . . her beauty, the durable charm of a mature and sophisticated woman. I also realized that behind the sweetness of her smile she was sinister and threatening. She looked down at me with an expression of affectionate tenderness. Sexually attractive and inviting, but dangerous. An artery in her throat was pulsating, her nipples were outlined against the thin vest. Sadness blended with the gentleness in her face . . . she had suffered much. I almost forgot that she wanted to entrap me as she had entrapped Arnie. Then I saw her eyes and was conscious for the first time of my fear . . . a wild vacant stare . . . madness. . . . On impulse I made the sign of the cross.

Instantly, she vanished, the light went out. I turned on the bed lamp—a different light from the one in which she appeared. The room was empty, but bitter cold. The thermostat next to the bed had been turned down to sixty-five, but it was much colder than that. I pushed it back up to seventy, and huddled under the thick comforter. Was any of it real? Then, as if to answer my question, I noticed the aroma of perfume that pervaded my room; it had been there since I awoke but I had not been paying attention to it. This time the scent—her scent?—faded slowly.

Failing to win me to her cause, she wanted to be rid of me. Well, you win on that one, lady. I won't spend another night in this damned haunted rectory of yours.

I lay there in bed, light on, trying to think. My mind was clouded by the Librium and numbed by surprise. I was no longer afraid, though I should have been. I thought about haunted rectories. The English have no monopoly on them, though they get all the publicity. Bishop Muldoon walked the old St. Charles Borromeo rectory in Chicago until it was urban-renewed out of existence. Holy Family, next to St. Ignatius High School, teems with psychic disturbances. A haunted rectory in Iowa? How very interesting. Was she the reason for Arnie's preoccupation? I calmed down slowly; next week would be a hard week: a report due; I needed my sleep; she had been given the signal I wasn't interested in whatever she had to offer . . . to hell with it . . . I turned off the light and went back to sleep.

It was warmth not cold which awakened me the next time . . . overpowering but not suffocating warmth . . . tender, protective, reassuring. . . . It pervaded my being and excited feelings of peace, security, love. . . . I was a child in the arms of a skilled mother . . . the reaction was not sexual, not in the usual sense of the word, at any rate, but it was enticing, attractive, demanding. I found myself yielding to it, slipping under, embracing its endearments. . . . At the last minute some dim instinct of self-preservation acted independently of conscious decision . . . I pushed the warmth away, mentally and physically, and turned on the light.

There had been no glow this time and there was no lingering fragrance, but the room was frigid again, the thermostat was down to fifty-five. "Bitch," I muttered as I put it back to seventy.

I looked at my Seiko: 4:00 A.M. Damn the woman—damn Arnie—inviting me to stay the night in a haunted rectory. I put on some of my clothes and stormed out of the room; I was not going to spend another moment in his cotton-picking . . .

Arnie's room, which it occurred to me for the first time I had never seen, was at the end of the corridor. There was light coming from under the door . . . the same kind of glow in which she had walked. I hurried down the hallway and stood at the doorway listening . . . no sound . . . I was within a millimeter of breaking in on my classmate and his ghostly lover. Then something . . . delicacy? . . . I don't know . . . anyhow, I walked slowly back to my room, got into bed, noted that the thermostat was where it belonged, turned off the light, pulled up the comforter, and fell promptly to sleep.

I was in the kitchen eating breakfast (you got your own because there was no "Saturday housekeeper") when Arnie showed up. "Hell, man," he said, smiling, "you're up early . . . sleep well?"

"Wonderfully," I replied evasively. His flinty plainsman eyes were curious. Let him wait till after my first cup of tea.

"Who is she, Arnie?" I asked as soon as the first sip of the second cup was on my lips.

My classmate sighed heavily. "I was hoping she would leave you alone; I'm sorry." He looked away from me, putting his coffee cup on the table.

"She didn't," I said flatly, "but to repeat my question: who is she?"

"I'll be back in a minute," said Arnie, rising from his chair and leaving the kitchen. He was back shortly with an old book; he opened it and put it on the table in front of my toast, covering with his hand the legend at the bottom of the page. A picture of a beautiful young woman. "That her?"

"Younger in the picture, and more clothes on, but yeah, Arnie, that's her all right. Now who is she?" I was losing my temper; you don't like to be assaulted in the middle of the night by a lovely spook who is a complete stranger.

Arnie removed his hand from the page. "Mary Jane

Rafferty Alonso, 1860–1903" it read. I closed the book and looked at its cover: *The Life and Times of James Michael Richard Sander, 1845–1903*. Sander had been the second bishop of Arnie's diocese and one of the brightest lights of late-nineteenth-century Catholic hierarchy—one which unlike its successors had shone with many luminaries—James Gibbons, Lancaster Spaulding, John Ireland. On the frontispiece there was a picture of Sander, a tall handsome man with high forehead and iron-gray hair; the genes of his convert Anglo-Saxon ancestors were dominant in that face, no ham-handed son of the Irish working class.

"They died the same year," I said.

"Hell, man, the same day," Arnie exploded. "Do you know any of the story?"

"Not much." I closed the book and went back to my tea. "There's nothing in writing on it, but I've heard rumors on the church history grapevine. Something like the Spaulding-Caldwell affair, wasn't it?"

His plainsman eyes were glowing: a fire on the prairies. "Except that Spaulding and Mary Gwendolyn had half a continent between them; these two lived in the same Iowa town for ten years before she finally gave up and married her Italian count; and they kept it a secret for every day of those ten years."

"So that's why Sander refused promotions to larger cities," I mused.

"That's part of the reason." Arnie was pacing with the same restlessness he used to display patrolling left field on the seminary villa baseball teams. "Hell, man, bring your tea and rolls and come into the parlor."

I trailed along behind him, noting that the Mozart music had been replaced by a Bach variation on the piano. Arnie reached behind a stack of books and pulled out a bulging manila folder. "Here it is, the whole story of the Rafferty-Sander love." He shoved the folder at me enthusiastically. "Maguire, the man who did that book, found the letters. He was too good a historian to throw them out and too pious a churchman to print the story. When I moved in here and things began to happen, I dug through the archives and found them: ten years, most of the time within two miles of one another, except when one or the other was in Europe, and they wrote love letters every week . . . almost five hundred of them."

"How did you get the letters out of the chancery?"

"I'm the vicar general, remember?" He sank wearily into his favored sofa, the file now on his lap. "Hell, man, I could steal the Peter's Pence collection and poor dumb Micky"—his bishop—"wouldn't know the difference."

"Tell me about it," I said, adopting my best Rogerian counseling style.

"Picture the situation." His enthusiasm was returning. "Jimmy Micky Dicky, as the Irish called him, shows up here at the age of thirty-four, a few years after the end of Vatican One, a handsome, arrogant, ambitious genius, part of the same generation which produced Keane, Spaulding, Ireland, Jimmy Gibbons. He is a poet, a theologian, a skilled politician with a Roman education at the propaganda college, and superb contacts in the papal nobility. Everyone thinks he's bound for Chicago or New York and the red hat, maybe the first in America. He takes this cow town by storm, especially since we're making money by then and trying to appreciate the finer things. . . . He knows all about the finer things. No one is more impressed than Mary Jane Rafferty, the twenty-one-year-old beauty who has just inherited her father's money and her mother's piety . . . the richest woman west of the Mississippi . . . and according to some of the newspapers, the most beautiful. . . . But hell, man, you've see her."

"I've seen her picture, Arnie."

He looked startled but plunged on with his story. "Anyway, Jim Sander launched a vast construction program to put this diocese on the map and push his career, of course: schools, hospitals, a college, a seminary; you can guess who picks up the tab. It's Rafferty Memorial Hospital and

Rafferty Hall at the seminary even now." The faraway look was back in his eye. Arnie saw the drama he was describing. "Within six months they were lovers; I don't know how they kept it a secret in such a small place but they did. Sander turns down promotion after promotion, sits out all the great battles of the eighties, becomes almost a forgotten man in the American hierarchy."

"Living all the time in this old house. . . ."

"She gave it to him the first month he was here. Anyhow, they have a big quarrel about 1890, she goes off to Italy and marries her count, he visits them in Como a year later, and they patch it up; there are some letters afterward, pretty tame by comparison. Here, you want to read these?" He passed the dossier in my direction.

I reached out to take it, heard a warning bell, and pulled back my hand. "I don't think so, Arnie, not now, but tell me more of the story. Why doesn't Sander accept promotion now, or have they forgotten about him?"

"Jimmy comes back here and rots." There was a tinge of sadness in Arnie's voice. "He stops writing, doesn't answer mail from his friends Ireland or Spaulding. I often wonder whether he and Spaulding compared notes. . . . He ignores letters from Rome . . . is dead silent through the 'Americanism' heresy thing. . . . Mary Jane has a couple of kids and enjoys the life of the European noblewoman; the letters go quite domestic now. You wouldn't know that they were lovers. Then, in 1896, Sander goes back to Europe. He's fifty-one, an ecclesiastical recluse whom history has passed by. He stops at Como to see the D'Alonsos; she's thirty-seven, the mother of three kids. Something happens . . . he continues the rest of his tour in the company of Baronessa Maria D'Alonso . . . she throws a party for him in Rome with half the sacred college in attendance. . . . Again they seem to fool everyone because I can't find a hint of any gossip. Jimmy Micky Dicky begins to preach and speak again . . . he's the toast of Europe, like Spaulding was the year before and John Ireland the decade before that . . . he goes home, and prose and poetry pour out like someone broke a dam . . . four books in two years—"

"The best stuff he ever wrote," I cut in. "Some of it's still relevant."

"Hell, man, he anticipated the Vatican Council." Arnie was sitting on the edge of his couch waving the dossier again. "No more letters, not a word between them. In 1898 he is offered . . . well, a very big archdiocese; one of the letters from a new Roman patron hints at a red hat shortly after; then she denounces him to the propaganda . . . apparently shows them some of her letters: end of Jimmy Micky Dicky." He slumped back into the couch, exhausted.

"Hell hath no fury . . ."

"I guess, I guess . . . no trace of why, though . . . anyhow Rome wants to ease him out and he obligingly has a stroke in 1900; they send an administrator with right of succession; and he spends the last three years of his life crippled, never leaving this house. He has another bad stroke in 1903; everyone knows that he only has a few months to live; she sails to America when she hears. Well, I'm speculating about her reasons, but she's traveling without her husband and children. She dies just outside of New York harbor, October sixth, 1903, of a stroke—two hours after he dies of the same thing—the feast of the holy rosary," he added irrelevantly.

"Awfully young to die of a stroke." I opened the drapes to brilliant autumn sunshine, clear blue sky, perfect weather for a trip back to Chicago.

"Not too young to die of a broken heart," murmured Arnie with more sentiment than I could imagine he possessed.

"So she comes back to the old house anyhow"—I walked over to the piano—"still trying to reach her lover before it's too late. . . ."

He had slumped down, his head in his hands. "Trying to expiate what she did to him. Doesn't it make sense?"

It didn't make sense at all. "Have you tried exorcism,

Arnie?" I asked, touching the keyboard. I don't particularly believe in exorcism, but I suspected he might.

He looked up at me, his lean, hard face twisted with pain. "You've seen her. Does she look like an evil spirit? Besides, where would she go if we did get rid of her?"

I picked out the opening bars of the Mozart sonata; Arnie didn't notice what I was playing. "Arnie," I said evenly, "Mary Jane Rafferty is dead; she died on a steamer in the Narrows almost three-quarters of a century ago. You and I believe that she is still alive, but not here. You're contending with psychic energy, either the memories of the past or projections from your own deep involvement in the story. It's not good." I sat on the piano bench, knowing I was talking to a stone wall.

"Hell, man, you saw her; does she look like psychic energy? Besides, I didn't know about any of this stuff until after . . ." His voice trailed off momentarily. "I didn't read Maguire's book, I'd never seen her picture; you remember I didn't give a damn about history."

"Do you talk with her?" I asked, now half believing it myself.

"I . . . I won't answer that question," he said sullenly, retreating behind his frosty plainsman mask.

"What's she doing here?" I persisted.

His jaw dropped in astonishment. "Why, she's taking care of me. Isn't that obvious?"

Arnie was on the edge of madness. A woman dead for more than seven decades was taking care of him; he had fallen in love with the ghost in his haunted rectory. I wanted, like I've wanted few things in my life, to be on that United Airlines flight back to Chicago.

"It's bad for you, Arnie," I insisted weakly. "You've got to get away from this place or that thing will destroy you."

"Destroy me?" said Arnie unbelievingly. "Hell, man, she's saving me. I've wanted to leave the priesthood for four years. She won't let me do it."

I gave up.

A couple of hours later we were riding to the airport after a quiet tour of the city in which, to tell the truth, there was not much to see. "One more question, Arnie," I said tentatively. "You said at breakfast this morning that you had hoped that . . . the . . . phenomenon wouldn't happen last night while I was in the house. Why didn't you play it safe and put me up in a motel? You wanted it to happen, didn't you? She wouldn't have appeared unless she knew you wanted her to, would she?"

Arnie didn't take his eyes off the highway. "I guess I did . . . maybe I wanted you to hear my side of the story . . . in case . . . well, I figured maybe you'd write it down and people in the future might understand. . . ."

As I walked up the stairs to the 737 I wondered how someone could grow up in the city and be a priest for a couple of decades and not see pictures of Mary Jane Rafferty. I guess they were in the hospital and the college anyway. Chancellor of the diocese, vicar general, president of the priests' senate; he must have read some history books or at least have heard stories. When he moved into Jimmy Sander's old house, he would have stored up a lot of imagery, only Arnie didn't seem to be the kind with that sort of imagination. Still . . .

I read in the paper last week that the old rectory had burned down on a cold winter night. The pastor escaped with minor burns and was in Rafferty Memorial Hospital recovering from "exhaustion." It wasn't Arnie, of course. He's a bishop in the southwest. A lot of people think that when St. Louis comes open next year Arnie will get it . . . and the red hat shortly thereafter.

❧ Julie ❧

"Roberta, who's that woman by the table at the end of the pool?"

"You mean the handsome one with the red hair and the green swimsuit?"

"Um."

"That's Julie Lyons. Her husband is an oil-company vice-president type up at Kuala. They have a cottage on the strait and usually come down on weekends. Lovely woman."

"Um."

We were at the Port Dickson Yacht Club, once the symbol of white imperialism and now as racially mixed a place as you could find anywhere in the world. Indians, Malays, Chinese, Dutch, English, Swedes, and an occasional south-side Chicago exile like Roberta bumped elbows at the bar without a second thought. Under the clear tropical sky, children of black, brown, and white colors and lots of mixed hues jumped in and out of the delightfully cool waters of the pool. Others scampered across the wide beach to watch the scores of shining sails crisscross the gleaming blue wavelets of the Straits of Malacca. British imperialism was gone, but the good life on a Sunday afternoon at Port Dickson was better than it had ever been in the days of the empire, if, of course, you had the money to join the club. Almost as good as an American country club, I reflected, and a lot more colorful.

Roberta sipped her gin and bitter lemon and noticed that my eyes were still fixed on Julie Lyons. "Would you like an introduction?" There was a frown in her voice.

"Not necessary, Berts, the lady and I have known each other for a long time."

"Old friends?"

"I didn't say that."

I saw Julie against a very different waterside background, much less romantic than the carnival colors of the Straits of Malacca: a small Wisconsin lake, a tiny fringe of beach, an old pier, a few drab trees. She was wearing a green swimsuit then, to match her eyes, I guess, and with her was Terry Dunn. For one frightening moment I saw Terry Dunn standing beside her now, here at Port Dickson, then that disorienting mixture of past and present quickly faded away.

We were sophomores in high school; Terry and Julie were recounting with great glee his religious experience at the Baptist church the previous week. In that pre-ecumenical era our Protestant neighbors were fair targets for anything. The little redhead was no longer little and now filled her swimsuit quite adequately. Even though we had a big fight that day, I felt kind of sorry for her. She would soon leave Terry behind. It was the end of her childhood. She and Terry came to a parting of ways in September, she insisting that it was time for her to "grow up" and Terry solemnly swearing that he would never grow up.

Terry Dunn. Terry Dunn. How can I make him real for you? His lightness, his grace, his contagious laughter, his manic imagination. We used to say of him with some defensiveness that he didn't have a mean bone in his body.

65

His mischief, we argued, never really hurt anyone, not so long as you didn't mind an occasional broken window or a couple of hours rearranging your house after you were a victim of one of Terry's raids. Our parents thought he was terrible, but even they had to laugh at the "Gray Ghost's" exploits. Terry Dunn, at that age, was the kind of person who made you laugh even when you wanted to be angry at him.

His pranks started in the last year of grammar school when we had tired of summer softball. He suggested to the rest of us that it might be fun to break into Kraus's grocery store on Division Street and "rearrange" the place. I resisted, but the others went along. When Herr Kraus, as Terry called him, came in the next morning, he saw that his canned goods were as neatly arranged on shelves as they were the previous night but on different shelves. The poor man thought he was losing his mind, sat down at his counter, and wept for an hour. Then he got furious, and then Herr Kraus, who was a good guy, laughed for three straight days.

On his cash register, he found a neatly printed card: "Compliments of the Gray Ghost." The era of the Gray Ghost and his band had begun.

They took dangerous chances. "Breaking and entering" was a crime; however benign their intent, they could have all ended up in reform school. They never were caught. The victims were not people who would be told by those of us who knew.

Apartments were raided and furniture rearranged. Vacationers came home to find that clothes had moved to different closets and drawers. Statues from the church appeared in the vestibules of private homes. The pastor found St. Joseph waiting for him inside the sacristy door one morning. The organist encountered dead mice on her keyboard. Scanty underwear (well, by 1940 standards) showed up on convent clotheslines. St. Teresa appeared on the altar of the Lutheran church. Democratic posters blocked the windows of the Republican ward office and vice versa. Sister Superior wrote obscene notes to the pastor and vice versa. Hearses pulled up at parties. Singing telegrams came in the middle of the night. Christmas cards arrived from the king, the pope, and the president. The oddest people sent each other valentines.

The Gray Ghost was on the loose.

Mostly, the Gray Ghost was four people: Terry, Tony McCarthy, Ed O'Connor, and Julie Quinn. At that time a tiny, grim-faced redhead, she was the worst of the lot because she egged the others on. I was left out; Julie correctly decided I was a coward.

She was the driving force; Terry the imagination. I can still see him, his pinched little face, framed by wiry, black hair, his darting leprechaun eyes, his wickedly grinning mobile mouth. The Gray Ghost's raids were the high point of Terry's life. I was useful, I guess, because I was the appreciative audience he could share it with afterward.

It went on for three years; they were not greedy; a raid every couple of months, carefully planned and daringly executed. Many of their victims were not amused. I guess there was a touch of cruelty about some of what they did. Most of us thought that they made up for it by their flair, their wit, and their imagination. They danced lightly through the neighborhood, dangerously close to the flame, perhaps, but at least they danced.

The police must have found a pattern. I suspect that some of the neighborhood cops knew from the grapevine who was involved. They laid off, perhaps figuring that there were worse criminals on the loose. Certainly the Protestant church raids did not offend the police one bit.

One of the congregations of what we now call our separated brothers had a revival tent on Division Street in the summertime, with prayers, preaching, conversion, and tongue-speaking going on every night. We used to hang around in the back some of the time because it seemed great entertainment, little realizing that we would see the same kinds of goings-on in Catholicism in twenty years. One hot, sticky evening with the acrid smell of the stockyards riding strong on the south wind, Terry decided to "get converted." At the personal testimony time of the prayer meeting, he rushed down the aisle, and in a thick Irish brogue announced to all that he had been a terrible sinner and had lived a life of drunkenness, lechery, blasphemy, and idolatry. Our separated brothers and sisters were so delighted that it never occurred to them that this fifteen-year-old hadn't had enough time for all the sinfulness he confessed, unless he had started out at two and a half. Terry then led them through a session of hymn singing, shouting out in his rich off-key Irish tenor voice their favorite songs with enough caricature to send us into peals of laughter, but not enough to make them anything more than slightly uneasy.

At the end of the service, after the preacher gave thanks for the conversion of this "papist sinner," Terry grabbed the microphone one final time, shouted to the multitude, "God damn you to hell, all you Protestant bastards. Long live the pope!" and ran full speed for the door of the tent and the safety of the summer night. In the back, we all scattered with equal speed. Our separated friends followed vigorously, but they were not nearly fast enough. After that, there was hardly a minister in the neighborhood who didn't have a sincere questioner or a loud heckler or several off-key singers in his congregation. Apparently, the ministry didn't communicate with each other because none of them was prepared to give chase when Terry and the gang took to their heels.

It was this unecumenical activity which finally brought the career of the Gray Ghost to an end. There was some very important function at the local Missouri Synod Lutheran congregation. Terry and Julie got a chorus of thirty papists to stand across the street singing hymns to the Blessed Mother all evening long. The police were called, but in 1942, what Irish cop was going to put kids in jail for praising the Blessed Mother?

The Lutheran pastor went to see the monsignor in solemn high procession, an unheard-of event, and the monsignor, who knew nothing of the exploits of the Gray Ghost, gave the young curate strict instructions to "stop that blasphemy." The young curate knew all about the band of the Gray Ghost, but had minded his own business. Now, he laid down the law.

Though Julie wanted to go on, soon afterward, she decided that it was time to be a dignified young woman instead of a tomboy. Terry was not a presentable boyfriend she could bring to school affairs. She was now at the stage of adolescence (junior year) when she was three or four years older than her male contemporaries in poise, sophistication, and interests. There never had been anything "romantic" between her and Terry as far as we know, so it was not a "breakup," but the passing of a phase in life.

Now, Julie was a tall, strikingly beautiful girl with long red hair and flashing green eyes. She and the others were on their way to adulthood. Terry was still a kid, hanging around the pool hall, the softball field, the basketball courts. They worried about dances, parties, proms; he worried about getting a couple of bottles of beer. He found a group of older guys who were interested in the same kind of thing and settled down to the life of the permanent adolescent, which was possible in those days before you went into the service. He managed to make it through high school, though only barely. The war came to an end. While Tony and Ed and Julie went off to college and I to the major seminary, Terry started to work for the city like his father before him, caught in a swamp of failure before he had a chance at anything else in life. Terry's family were slovenly shanty Irish; his father, a huge, fat, brawling character, worked for the sanitation department and was drunk every night of the week. His mother, from whom Terry inherited his physique, was a shrewish, wispy little woman who sighed in every second sentence. There were vague, slatternly grandparents, aunts, and four younger sisters hanging around the back of their house. In grammar school, kids don't notice those sorts of things, but in high school they got finely tuned into social-class distinctions. We knew that Terry didn't quite belong and never would. The Gray Ghost exploits were the peak of his career. He drank more and more and drifted out of our lives. A soul in purgatory.

He was in church every Sunday, dressed uncomfortably in the suit and tie his mother made him wear, though sneaking out early for the cigarette which he desperately needed. He played softball and bowled in the parish league and helped the young priest at all the carnivals. He even worked at night as a janitor when Mr. King, our perennial parish janitor (they had not yet been promoted to engineers) was on vacation. Being part of the church was, I guess, some sort of compensation for being excluded from the crowd of his old friends. "He'll die young," my mother predicted. He usually came by our house when I was home on vacations. I was something of an outcast. Julie never liked me much and was abusively angry that day on the beach at Twin Lakes when I foolishly suggested that Terry belonged in the seminary. In those days in our neighborhood, if Julie wrote you off, you were written off.

One summer night Terry and I were sitting on our back lawn having a long, aimless conversation (we lived on the corner, so the back lawn was an ideal gathering place). I remember it quite well because it was the strange, haunted week when both the old monsignor and the young priest died within two days of one another.

"Terry, you should go to college."

"Ah, they'd never let a dumbbell in, besides what's the point, I'll get my union card next year and I'll make good money."

"You're not dumb. You just didn't study at Philip's" (St. Philip the Servite High School, now defunct).

"It's too late." He chewed nervously on his cigarette. "If I had thought two years ago that we weren't going to have another depression right away, I might have given it a whirl.

With some of the mutts that are getting higher learning, though, sure, someone has to do the plumbing," and he went into the Irish brogue to which he always fled when he was uneasy.

My mother had long ago foretold that "Terry Dunn will have a nervous breakdown someday." He had always been "high-strung," but you didn't notice that sort of thing when you're a kid. Now, the nervous movements of hands and feet, the chain-smoking, and the puffing of his face from too much beer told you there was something a little different about Terry.

"The world is changing, Terry. There isn't going to be another depression and everyone is going to go to college. You should give it a try, even in night school."

He was silent in the warm darkness. "You worried about me trying to soak up all the beer on the west side?"

"I'm worried about your talent going to waste!"

Again a long silence in the patient night. "I guess you're right. Maybe the Gray Ghost ought to go to Mayslake this weekend and get his life squared away." He had gone to the retreat house every year since he was sixteen. After each retreat, he went on the wagon for a while. In those days, Mayslake offered a brisk, locker-room masculine Christianity. "That's a heck of a good idea," I said, though I had seen this therapy fail before. There was yet another silence in the night, then an embarrassed, "You're a great pal to worry about me." I'd swear that there was a sob in the Gray Ghost's voice.

Terry came home from that weekend and announced that he was going to be a priest. He joined the Franciscans and was off to their college within a month. I knew the strains of life in the seminaries in those days and wondered why the Franciscans had not done any checking on Terry's psychological background. At that time a lot of us didn't believe in psychology.

He lasted longer than I thought he would—eighteen months—and then he came home with a bad ulcer, trailing behind him rumors of a "nervous breakdown," just as my mother had predicted. He kept away from me in our January vacation. By summertime, he was back working for the city and seriously pursuing his campaign to dispose of all the beer on the west side. I didn't hang around the ball field much that summer, mostly because I didn't want to embarrass him. I was not far enough in life to smell doom. At twenty-two, Terry already had the stench of it.

Then, he went to Mayslake again, took the pledge, and tried once again to get "squared away." He enrolled full-time at Loyola, worked an evening-watchman job for the city, gave up drinking and smoking, lost weight, kept his hair cut, and acted like a bright young man in a hurry. I saw him briefly during our January vacation; the light was back in his eye. He looked better than he had since the sophomore summer at Twin Lakes and was getting *A*'s in all his courses. He was already talking about law school and a career in politics. His fingers were reaching eagerly for his passport to suburbia. The word was out in the neighborhood that Terry Dunn had finally "straightened himself out." Even my mother admitted that he had really "pulled himself together." He went to double-semester summer school so that he could make it into law school a year from September. I barely saw him at all that summer. He was dating Julie Quinn, much to everyone's amazement and to the anguished dismay of Dr. Quinn and his wife. The Quinns hated to see the daughter of the neighborhood's richest family waste herself on an alcoholic shanty Irishman. The neighborhood said they were great for each other. They drove by one night in her white convertible when I was walking home from church. In those days, even college types rode the bus on dates, unless they were well off. "The Gray Ghost rides again," he shouted. We talked for a few moments, Julie impatient and not liking me any more than she ever did.

They were engaged at Christmas, the wedding was scheduled for June. He had a law-school scholarship and a job.

She was going to teach school at St. Ursula's. My mother thought they were both crazy.

I was invited to the wedding. I half suspected that Terry would turn up on the doorstep one night with cold feet. Better, I thought, for him to take the initiative.

It was Julie who came. Ten days before the wedding, I was in the house alone, reading Joseph Conrad; the doorbell rang, and to my dismay, the white convertible was in the front and the redhead at the door. She was cool and elegant in a white dress with a thin red belt at her waist, tall and slender on her high heels.

"Can I come in and talk?" she asked shyly, then groping for confidence. "The one night I hoped to find you on your damn throne in the yard, you have to be inside."

"Beautiful women can always come in," I said gallantly.

Her green eyes flashed at me. "You've changed."

I didn't offer her anything to drink, mostly because I forgot to.

"I have to talk to someone."

"Cold feet?"

"I'm scared silly. I love him so much and yet . . ." Tears began to pour out of those green lakes. She fumbled for a handkerchief.

"Julie, it's great to see the band of the Gray Ghost together again."

The impish grin from the old days came back. "We're really so good together. I steady him down and he makes me laugh. He's such a great person . . . of course, I don't have to tell you that, so kind and gentle and . . . and . . ." Now she was sobbing. For an errant moment, I thought it would be very nice to have such a woman sobbing for me. I made a big leap, much more than I would do in later days in the rectory.

"You're not sure that saving a man is a good enough reason for marrying him." She fought the sobs.

"Is that what the neighborhood thinks? My mother says

73

that's what I'm doing . . . I don't know . . . whether . . . What do you think?"

I chose my words as carefully as I could. "I haven't heard anyone say that. I'm not sure you're the martyr type, Julie. He is a reformed alcoholic; that's a big risk."

She flushed with anger. "You call yourself a friend?"

"I'm simply stating the facts. You're taking a bigger risk than if he didn't have his record. If you win, you win big . . . if not . . . anyhow, you wanted to know what I think."

"I'm sorry. You're right. I know it's a big gamble. That crude, vulgar family of his . . ."

"Shanty Irish," I said.

"If only I could know the future. I care about him. I love him. I want to be with him forever. I'm frightened. I don't want to hurt him."

"And hurt yourself in the process."

"I don't care about me."

"Sure you care about you. What happens in church next week might ruin your life."

"I don't want people to say that I'm a spoiled, selfish brat."

"Better to say that than to say five years from now that you were a blind fool."

The tears stopped. She was cool and composed. Those shrewd green eyes glinted at me. "Are you telling me not to marry him?"

I felt very tired. "No, Julie."

"The argument for him . . ." She leaned forward intently from the edge of her chair, hoping for some sign from heaven.

"He loves you. You've given him a new hope in life. He's been on the wagon for almost two years. You're happy whenever you're with him. And cold feet come before every marriage."

Our old living room lit up in the radiance of her smile.

She stood up. "Thanks, you've been a darling. See you at the wedding." As she left in a swirl of white dress, she gave me a hasty kiss on the cheek. Lucky man, Terry Dunn, I thought.

At eleven, a week from the following Saturday, I was in the old basement church with a thousand other people, the altar awash in roses, the sanctuary filled with clergy for the solemn high nuptial Mass of Julie Anne Quinn and Terrance Michael Dunn. The twelve men in the wedding party looked uncomfortable in their stiff summer formals. The ladies of honor were awkward, if lovely, in their tight rose dresses, chosen, I'm sure, to match Julie's hair. All of us were eagerly awaiting the march of the lovely bride down the red-carpeted aisle.

Only she never came.

Terry went on a two-week binge, did not graduate from college, never tried law school, and went back to work for the city. He soaked up all the beer on the west side and began to work on the north-side supply. He was a chronic alcoholic by the time of my first Mass, which he was not able to attend because he was in the hospital drying out.

The Quinns moved out of the neighborhood in disgrace and bought a home in Lake Forest. And until that day at the Yacht Club, I never saw Julie again.

Terry was dead at thirty of a liver ailment, they said. I didn't have a car (we couldn't own one for five years after ordination in those days). I made it to the wake on public transportation the final night. I knew I would not be able to get from Beverly to the west side for the requiem mass the next morning.

His mother, now white-haired and frail, gripped my hand tightly when I offered my sympathies. I didn't recognize the Gray Ghost in the casket; he looked as though he were sixty years old.

"It was that redheaded bitch who did it to him," she screeched at the top of her voice, causing everyone in the funeral home to jump with dismay.

While a cold November rain fell on the tiny knot of mourners, the Gray Ghost was laid to rest in Mt. Carmel Cemetery the next day. None of his band were at the grave side.

I stirred out of my reverie. A long way from Mayfield and Potomac to Port Dickson. Did Julie recognize me after all these years? Probably not. Even if she did, would she want to talk to me? Probably not.

Derek, Roberta's husband, came back with the children. The sun was sinking toward Sumatra. The expatriates at the swimming pool were clinging to the last splendid hours of a Port Dickson weekend.

"A bite to eat?" asked Derek.

I made a decision. "Give me a couple of minutes. I want to make peace with someone." Julie was momentarily alone. I picked my way through swarms of dashing, shouting kids and stood above her. She did not look up from the book she was reading. While I watched and waited, wondering what I could possibly say, she sipped from a half-empty gin and tonic glass.

Roberta had understated it: Julie was not merely handsome; she was beautiful—body still firm beneath the form-fitting green swimsuit, legs still trim, red hair still bright, shoulders still thrown back in defiance. Time had touched her gently.

Roberta had said she was happily married. Durable beauty and a happy marriage—not everything in life surely, but more than enough. There were, I felt sure, no demons to be exorcised, no guilts to be healed. Why bother her?

Maybe because I was a priest.

"Hi," I said creatively.

"I hoped you wouldn't recognize me." She lifted her head; the green eyes were filled with tears. "Have you finally forgiven me?"

What can one say except benediction? "Nothing to forgive, lovely lady. You did the right thing. It never would have worked."

"I loved him," she choked. "I really did love him, please believe that. I was afraid. I lost my nerve. My family kept telling me that he was incurable. I finally believed them."

I listened.

"My life has been happy. I purchased my happiness at the cost of his suffering. I've never been able to forget that."

I repeated my previous words, not sure myself how true they were. "It never would have worked."

How much of a gamble can you demand of a young woman? How much of a long shot can love endorse?

Her neatly carved face twisted with anguish in the golden rays of the setting sun. "How do you know? How can I know? How can anyone ever know?"

"You haven't forgiven yourself then?"

"I have no right to. I killed him."

Maybe. Maybe not. The Founder had said let the dead bury their dead. I was a priest for the living.

The sun eased down into the Straits of Malacca. I wished the Gray Ghost was there at Port Dickson to bring light and laughter into her haunted face.

I sat down next to her, a priest about to hear a perhaps unnecessary confession and give long-overdue absolution.

❧ Lisa ❧

Catch a falling star
Put it in your pocket
Save it for a rainy day
Catch a falling star
Put it in your pocket
Never let it fade away

There were mixed emotions in the neighborhood at the news that Lisa was coming home for Christmas. "Yeah," said Blackie Ryan, who had gone to school with her and dated her occasionally, "a mixture of envy and resentment. The neighborhood doesn't need a star at Christmas time."

Blackie, a cherubic little man with kindly eyes blinking behind thick glasses and a "Father Brown" manner which is not altogether accidental, was being imprecise. In fact, most of the people in the neighborhood couldn't have cared one way or another. Way behind on their Christmas shopping and uninterested in stars anyway, they had only the dimmest idea who Lisa Malone was or that she had once lived in the neighborhood. Some of the quiet people were kind of happy that our own celebrity would be home again. The rest of us, the self-anointed arbiters of the taste and the keepers of the conscience of the parish (people like my mother), were outraged.

Either Lisa would come home as a movie and TV

superstar and would be denounced as "putting on airs" or she would reappear as the same old Lisa and be condemned for trying once more to win our affection and respect, something that we would never give her.

"She has three strikes already," Blackie went on dourly. "She had the effrontery to pursue a career, the shamelessness to choose a career in Hollywood, and worst of all, the unforgivable audacity to be an enormous success. The woman is intolerable, there is nothing else to be said about it."

There were those who would have said that the neighborhood was none of Blackie's business, since he had been ordained and assigned to a working-class neighborhood in Jefferson Park ("That's the end of him," the Ryan-haters in the neighborhood said with a sigh of relief, premature as it turned out). In any event, his assessment was correct: our shooting star blazed a dazzling trail across the Christmas sky over the neighborhood, flicking out sparks of light which touched a lot of us, and then streaked away for Los Angeles, her brightness undimmed but some of the luster of her innocence forever lost.

It might have been better, all things considered, if she had descended on the neighborhood with a limo, a chauffeur, a maid, a mink coat, two French poodles, a press agent, and several trunks full of clothes. Even my mother would have been impressed, although offended. Lisa elected to return as the same old Lisa, riding the Rock Island (still called that even if it is owned by the RTA) in brown slacks, sweater, scarf, and beige cloth coat, wearing no makeup and carrying her own garment bag, a pretty young woman returning for Christmas, perhaps from graduate school. We met at the end of the car as we prepared to exit at the Ninety-first Street Station.

"You can't hide from me behind those horn-rim glasses, George." A brush of lips against my cheek. "Not married, I see. Wouldn't be working on Saturday if you were. Poor Lou Anne. You look very proper and conservative and successful. And nice." Second quick kiss.

Somehow, while I was recapturing my breathing mechanisms, her garment bag was transferred to my custody. You've seen her on TV, of course, so I don't need to go into many of the details of what took my breath away. Lisa looked like a young woman in an ad for the Irish Tourist Board, maybe a little bit too voluptuous for the Church-sponsored tours, but perfect for attracting young American men to Irish universities: short ebony hair, skim-milk skin (she hated suntan), dancing hazel eyes, a glowing impish smile which lighted a delicately sculpted face, and a figure which for all its obvious appeal also hinted at fragility that needed to be protected. "Chaste Irish Catholic eroticism," said one of the reviews of her first TV special ("Lisa!") earlier that year. "Sugarcoated sexuality," sneered another.

Those of us who knew her would not have argued with either description, but we would have rejected any suggestion that her screen image was different from her private image. She could not pretend even if she wanted to. She stole her first big feature film, *A Time Without Tears,* from the leads simply by being Lisa for the audience—funny, cute, energetic, and incorrigibly if subtly graceful. In the bedroom scene, without most of her clothes (to the deep offense of my mother and her friends, although Lisa was overdressed by the standards of many films), Lisa, as the ingenious if innocent virgin, blended grace and comedy into an irresistible combination.

"Shameful," clucked the neighborhood.

"Lisa!" exclaimed those of us who knew her.

So to be kissed—twice—by such a person on a snowy Saturday early afternoon in December was an experience not lightly to be dismissed. Twice.

"Lou Anne was tired of waiting. And I work for Arthur Anderson, not my father. But I am an accountant and I still live at home. So, unlike you, I've only partly broken with the neighborhood."

"I haven't broken with the neighborhood." She accepted my hand for help down the steps of the train. "Why would I want to do that? I've gone away for my education and career. This is still home and always will be. Why not?"

Indeed, the same old Lisa, blithely oblivious to the more mean and nasty human emotions. She was not coming home for this Christmas of 1970 either to impress us or to win our affections. She was coming home because it was home and because it was Christmas.

"I suppose you must find Los Angeles's Beverly Hills much more interesting than Chicago's?" I held her arm tightly, lest she slip on the ice of the station platform. Large flakes of snow were drifting lazily across the little park, touching the black hair which escaped from her scarf.

"Oh, I don't know, there's a lot of cougars in those canyons and I don't mean Mercury Cougars either. Mary Kate Ryan Murphy said she'd meet me"—the merry laugh which charmed her film and TV audiences—"as if I didn't know where the Ryan clan lives." She glanced around the station.

A small girl child appeared; she was perhaps ten, with a blond ponytail, piquant face, and vast blue eyes.

"Good afternoon, Miss Malone," she recited from memory as if repeating an elocution-class exercise. "I'm Caitlin Murphy and my mother said that I should meet you and that she had patients till three today because all the sick people are sicker at Christmas and that you're welcome home and that . . ." She sniggered as breath and memory failed her.

"That you should lead me home." She kissed the child on the forehead. "I remember you when you were two years old, Caitlin. My, you're so grown up. You know George? He's big because he played football, but he's nice. He kind of carries my garment bag and fights off cougars, middle-western ones that is. Can he walk home with us?"

Caitlin considered me dubiously and then sniggered again. "Okay, I guess."

Lisa took Caitlin's little mittened hand and Caitlin took mine. We walked the two blocks to the Murphys' house (Joe Murphy, Mary Kate Ryan's husband, is a psychiatrist, too) singing that Santa Claus was coming to town and praising

Rudolph the Red-Nosed Reindeer.

"My mommy says your best carol is 'O Holy Night.'"

"All *right,* Caitlin." Hands on her hips in mock exasperation, with the snow falling harder and darkness descending rapidly on the tree-shrouded houses with Christmas lights already shining in the windows, a woman hailed recently as the hottest young actress in Hollywood, sang Adolphe Adam's "Cantique de Noël" for a ten-year-old worshiper and a twenty-eight-year-old cougar fighter. At that magic moment the latter would have quite willingly taken on a pride of saber-toothed tigers for her.

"I *certainly* hope that nonsense isn't starting again," my mother commented fifteen minutes later when I arrived home, such is the speed at which scandalous news travels in our neighborhood. I had long ago learned simply to not reply to such comments.

When pressed with the accusation that I had once dated Lisa Malone, my mother would smugly reply, "I put a stop to that nonsense in a hurry." Lou Anne Sprague's father is my father's partner, and on the day she was born, my mother began to make the plans for our wedding. It was possible that I might marry someone else, but unthinkable that it be "Mary Malone's affected little brat."

My mother is very good at taking credit for whatever happens. I did come home from Notre Dame to date Lisa occasionally in her senior year (I'm two years older) and we went out often both in the neighborhood and at Grand Beach the summer after she graduated. (Blackie was bound for the seminary by then.) No one ended it, however; Lisa and I simply drifted in different directions. I was a bookish, shy accountant-in-the-making, with musical tastes which ran to the classical and the serious, and she was a comic-opera comet already exploding toward her place in the starry firmament.

I noticed her for the first time when I was in fourth grade and she in second grade. She sang the "Ave Maria" for the May Crowning that year ("No second-grader has ever sung at the May Crowning before," the other mothers complained bitterly). She seemed to me then to be an incredibly pretty little girl with a sweet smile and a lovely voice. I fell in love with her on the spot. Remove the word *little* from the last two sentences and I don't suppose much has changed.

It occurred to me as I went up to my room and began to read a computer magazine (there were only a few in 1970) that she must have known that I did not marry Lou Anne. I was sure that she and Blackie Ryan kept in touch with each other. Indeed, there were vague hints among the Ryans that he had helped her with a drug problem four or five years before. The headlines had said, CHICAGO STARLET IN DRUG AND SEX BUST. It turned out that she hadn't been involved in the sex and that there were no drug charges filed against her. "Where there's smoke, there's fire," my mother insisted.

Blackie had flown to Los Angeles during his summer vacation, and one had the impression that the Ryans all heaved a sigh of relief upon his return, not for Blackie, but for Lisa.

So why was she pretending to have only just discovered my bachelorhood?

I thought as I went to sleep the night she sang for me and Caitlin in the snow on Glenwood Drive, that our little scene would make a great setting for her next special. It would be pleasant, I admitted in my last conscious moment, to have a daughter like Caitlin.

From second grade on, Lisa had a circle of admirers and friends who were entranced by her enthusiasm and charm. When her mother pulled her out of St. Praxides (after a big fight with Sister Superior) and sent her to a private academy ("A talented child like my Lisa needs special training") she continued to be friends with the others kids in the parish. Finally, after two years of high school, she persuaded her father, a defense attorney who worked mostly for the Outfit and left the rearing of the children to his much younger wife, that she belonged in a Catholic school. She was an instant hit at Mother Macauley, carrying off leads in the school play and soloing in the choir's annual Christmas record both the years she was there ("O Holy Night" both times, of course). Her circle of worshipers expanded dramatically, as did the circle of resentment.

Christmas was Lisa's special time above all others. She poured her considerable energy and organizing skills (as evidenced by her recent success as a producer) into a round of parties, concerts, benefits, and sessions of strolling carolers. Was the temperature below zero? Dress warmly; there's only one Christmas every year. Was there a foot of snow? All the more fun to mix caroling with snowball fights. And heaven help you when Lisa decided that your face required washing.

There were many of us boys, of course, who could hardly wait to be dragged into a snowbank by Lisa.

None of us who adored Lisa expected her success—two platinum records and an Academy Award nomination before she was twenty-six. But neither were we surprised by Lisa on the screen. She was the way she'd always been. Her acting skills were more polished, her voice in much better control (the voice teachers Mrs. Malone hired turned out to be inept), her humor a little more deft. Otherwise it was an act we'd all seen before.

Her voice, as you know, is "sweet" rather than powerful, and limited in its range. She doesn't do much rock and only the lightest of light opera. ("Bridge over Troubled Water" and "Raindrops Keep Falling on My Head" were her favorites that year. That was before her annual Christmas Special became almost as much a part of Christmas in America as the wise men.)

One critic suggested she was born in the wrong era: Lisa Malone, he said, was designed to sing Victor Herbert. At a time of Altamont and Woodstock, she sang as though the Beatles didn't exist. "Nonrelevant music," sniffed *Time*. "A Singer for Escapists," said *Rolling Stone* contemptuously. "A Kathryn Grayson or an Ann Blyth for her generation," *The New York Times* said, perhaps more accurately.

There was no ideology in her music, not because she lacked political concerns ("Why should anyone care what I think about politics?" she asked one interviewer) but because, as always, she did what she could do and did not attempt anything else. She admitted that she hated the Vietnam War but that did not prevent her from going to Vietnam one Christmas with Bob Hope.

In Vietnam I had not heard about her success in her first appearance at Las Vegas and hence could not believe it was the same Lisa Malone. Still, I pulled all kinds of strings to get to the Bob Hope show, but was so far back I couldn't tell whether it was our Lisa or not until she started to sing.

I don't suppose I could have talked to her that night even if I tried, but I didn't try.

An attractive, talented young woman from our own neighborhood, ideologically inoffensive, who managed in her interviews to sound intelligent, pleasant and even-tempered; why did we resent her instead of celebrating her?

Those who come from neighborhoods like ours or small towns will understand why. "She could win the Oscar, the Emmy, the Tony, and the Nobel Prize to boot," Blackie Ryan observed, his eyes blinking rapidly. "And it wouldn't help. She's still May Malone's daughter. That mean's she a reject by definition."

In communities like ours, some people are always "in" by definition, no matter what they do. The Ryan clan is loud, contentious, attractive, and dissident. Kate Collins Ryan (Ed's first wife and Blackie and Mary Kate's mother) was a radical always and at one time a communist. After she died, Ed married a much younger woman (selected, it was said, by Kate on her deathbed) and set about raising a second family. The Ryans collect strays and rejects, like Lisa, and me (if I'd let them), and defy the neighborhood arbiters of taste. Half the people in the parish bitterly resent them. Yet no one would dream of suggesting that they are outsiders. If you are a Ryan, you can do nothing wrong.

If you are May Malone's daughter, you can do nothing

worthwhile, and TV specials, platinum records, even critical kudos are irrelevant.

As any community does for its rejects, we fashioned brief descriptions of her which were applied from her sixth birthday to her twenty-sixth—"affected" (or "stuck up"), "spoiled," and "her mother pushes her too much." In 1970 the only change brought on by her success was to put "push" in the past tense. Once a community said, "Is this not the carpenter's son? How come he's working miracles?" We said, "Is this not May Malone's daughter? What difference does it make if she has her own TV special?"

May was, you see, a very pushy woman. There was nothing wrong with being a social climber in our neighborhood. In those days women whose children were in school often had little else to do. There were, however, unwritten but very important rules. May violated them left and right. She joined the Saddle and Cycle Club rather than the Beverly Country Club. She aspired to associate with Lake Forest elites. She went to polo matches in Oak Brook. She dressed her daughter in "daring" dresses (fashions of the year after next), intruded her in theatricals and weddings where she wasn't wanted, arranged her debut at the Passavant Cotillion instead of the Presentation Ball, tried to send her to Bryn Mawr instead of St. Mary's of Notre Dame, made a nuisance out of herself jabbering about Lisa's dates with South Shore and North Shore boys, and didn't show proper respect for her betters (women like my mother and Lucinda Sprague and Harriet Finch, none of whom would be forced to admit, as was May, that their father had been a "saloon keeper").

In 1970 they would add that "poor" May got what she deserved. She did not expect that Lisa would break the deadlock of St. Mary's versus Bryn Mawr by opting for UCLA and Hollywood. Nor did she expect that as a sophomore Lisa would appear in very minimal attire in a bit part (no more than thirty delicious seconds) as a young singer in the undistinguished spy thriller *Bloodnet*.

A week after he saw the film, her father had his third and last heart attack. Everyone in the neighborhood (except his cardiologist) blamed the attack on *Bloodnet,* including, it is to be feared, May Malone. At the wake Lisa was treated as though she were a leper even by her own family. Her mother went off to live with Lisa's older brother, a hotshot surgeon in Connecticut ten years older than Lisa, and neither mother nor daughter ever returned to the neighborhood. In the interviews Lisa says that she visits her mother whenever she is in New York and that they are "good friends."

I have a tape of the film; while Lisa's clothes may leave something to be desired, she was anything but lascivious. Truth to tell, she could not be lascivious if she wanted to. Even if she were stark naked, she'd still represent chaste Irish Catholic eroticism, which, mind you, is not necessarily bad.

So why come back to the neighborhood for Christmas after all that? Why come back to a place where you have only a thin network of friends and a highly organized public opinion against you?

The answer reveals the final secret about Lisa and the one which tarnished her innocence during the 1970 visit: immune to resentment and envy herself, she hardly noticed the vices in others. She could not help but realize that some people in the neighborhood didn't like her. Yet even at her father's funeral she was utterly unaware of the smug satisfaction of those who had always detested her. She came home at Christmas in 1970 not for vindication, not for acceptance, not to impress, but because she thought, poor gentle girl, that the neighborhood was home, a place where she loved and was loved.

She swept down on the community like a playful winter storm. On Sunday after the 11:15 Mass, she shook hands and hugged old friends in back of church like she was the pastor or a candidate for public office. She even shook hands with and hugged the pastor. That morning she agreed to sing at the parish Christmas dance, the country club

Christmas dance, the High Club dance, the YCS program at the County infirmary, the High Club Christmas play, the grammar school Christmas pageant, and the Mother Macauley Christmas festival.

Everyone wanted her to sing "I Think I Love You" (which the Partridge Family was doing at the time), "White Christmas," and "O Holy Night." Although my mother and her friends complained that it was all a public relations gimmick, there was no PR person present, and except for a note in Kup's column in the *Sun Times,* no press notice of her visit.

Lisa was having the time of her life, not enjoying a happy girlhood she never had, but rather reenacting a girlhood whose happiness was not tainted by her mother's silliness or her neighbors' resentment. The neighborhood loved it. As John O'Connor had remarked in his column in *The New York Times,* "Even if you are determined to resist Lisa Malone, her laughter and her innocent beauty force you to smile." A lot of us smiled the week before Christmas of 1970.

Much of this was reported to me secondhand and with considerable disapproval. I didn't follow Lisa around. I was, however, constrained to be her date for the country-club Christmas dance. Mary Kate Murphy complained to me that she had run out of residents from Little Company of Mary Hospital and would I please take Lisa as a personal favor.

Run out of dates for someone who had been named by *Esquire* as one of the fifteen most beautiful women in America? I went along with the game, however.

Her wardrobe did indeed seem to be limited to the single garment bag: a wine-colored suit, a white knit minidress with a red belt, and a white formal also with red trim, which she wore to the country-club dance. The last-named garment was modest enough to satisfy the morals of the most finicky mother superior. Not that it mattered: Lisa's figure was (and is) so attractive that she is erotic in almost anything. Especially to a lonely twenty-eight-year-old bachelor.

Mary Kate insisted that I dig my tux out of mothballs and wear my contact lenses.

Remember what kind of a year 1970 was. The sixties were over but there was still plenty of trouble. It was the year after Altamont, the year after Woodstock, the "incursion" into Cambodia, the Kent State and Jackson State shootings, the "interim" in which college kids were supposed to work for "peace" candidates (and mostly played basketball), the revelation of the My Lai massacre, the collapse of Biafra, the murder of the Black Panthers in Chicago, the Bobby Seale trial in New Haven, and airline hijackings almost every other week. We all needed a little light and a little laughter. And our own local Tinker Bell returning from the land of the stars showered us with both.

Her first words when I picked her up, radiant and glowing, at Mary Kate's, were that the pastor had invited her to sing "O Holy Night" at the midnight Mass, "The first time I've sung in church since I left . . . Mind you, I go to church, so don't look so shocked."

I pleaded that I was dazzled, not shocked. Then, since it made her so happy, I added my congratulations on the midnight Mass song, something which in the past had always been reserved for adults.

She was an adult, too, but it was hard to admit. She was still Lisa, our luminous teenage package of concentrated womanly energy.

"I never dated a movie star before," I said in self-defense.

"I'm just Lisa." She smiled affectionately. She then proved it for the rest of the evening by needling me, gently but tellingly, about being a conservative, stuffy accountant. I responded with the defense that I was not a conservative and that's why I didn't work for my father, who believed that computers would never be important in our profession.

She listened carefully to my explanations about the future of personal computers and nodded intelligently. I had no idea whether she understood me, but she was so gorgeous that I didn't much care.

I also realized that she was sexually available to me. Nothing so crude or lewd as a proposition; no one else on the glittering dance floor would have noticed. We were not even dancing all that close. The body I held in my arms as we danced was subtly submissive, inviting me to accept it, willing to yield itself completely to me, offering itself as a gift with no strings, other than Christmas ribbons, attached.

One of the fifteen most beautiful women in America in red and white wrapping as a Christmas present for you, George the bean counter. Are you going to accept the gift package? What are you going to do?

Her sparkling hazel eyes were amused by my mask, as she saw it, of the precise and dusty bean counter. She thought she saw something beneath the mask that she wanted, lightly, playfully, but definitely.

I love you, George the bean counter. Please love me in return.

All without a word being said. It's what happens when you find yourself dancing with an accomplished actress, more accomplished than her directors and critics realized then, in a white Christmas evening dress.

Lisa knew her target. She realized that she was in no danger of a one-night stand or anything of that sort. The invitation, however, contained no restrictions or limitations. It was a gift, pure and simple.

I was flattered and terrified and determined to run away as soon as I could escape from the club. How else would a sensible bean counter react?

That night as I wrestled with fantasies and tried to sleep, I wondered if she had always danced with me that way when we were kids and I had never noticed. I also realized that she had returned to the neighborhood with an ulterior motive after all. Me. Doubtless it was a conspiracy set up by Blackie and Mary Kate. George the stray would be ministered to whether he wanted such attention or not.

I avoided her until midnight Mass. By then the luster of the shooting star had been snuffed out temporarily.

Our pastor at the time was an old-line Catholic liberal; he hated Nixon, denounced racism, and invited Dan Berrigan to speak in the parish hall. But he was pathologically afraid of complaints from parishioners. An anonymous letter or two, a few phone calls, a suggestion that "people" were criticizing him, was enough to cause him to make a quick and arbitrary and undiscussable decision.

Harriet Finch, the chairman of the local Christian Family Movement group, called him the day before Christmas Eve to report that there was "talk all over the parish" about Lisa. "What's the point in keeping our kiddies away from R-rated movies and restricting their TV programs when you permit a woman who is not much better than a harlot to sing at midnight Mass? People are saying that they don't see why they should contribute to the Christmas collection when there is such hypocrisy in the Church."

That was that. A call went to the Murphy house five minutes later. Lisa was not home. Joe Murphy was told that "it has been decided" that there would be no soloists at midnight Mass, the implication of the language being that the choir director or the curate in charge of the liturgy or maybe even the liturgy committee had made the decision. Joe, who is quiet man compared to his in-laws, said that it was a very regrettable decision and hung up.

Worse was yet to come. Someone, not my mother but probably my former fiancée Lou Anne Sprague O'Neill, cornered Lisa at the Rock Island Station on the morning of Christmas Eve and chortled about the cancellation of "O Holy Night."

"You're an evil woman," she was told. "You act in dirty films, you wear filthy clothes. You flaunt your vulgar body. You lead a scandalous life. You sing obscene songs. You're a drug addict. You killed your own father. How dare you come back here and shock our innocent children? Thank God the monsignor has finally come to his senses and

91

thrown you out of the midnight Mass. No one here ever liked you. You were always a spoiled, stuck-up brat."

"Stuck-up" was the kind of phrase Lou Anne would use.

I learned all of this from Blackie, who called me before confessions (there were still a lot on Christmas Eve in those days).

"Bitches!" I exploded.

"She-cougars," he replied. "The males of the species, however, do not disagree."

There was a dig at me in the cougar crack. What, I asked myself after the conversation, could I possibly do to heal the hurt, to wipe away the tears, to restore the innocence.

Nothing, I replied to myself. Not a darn thing.

No shooting star this Christmas.

Still, she at midnight Mass. I saw her walking down the aisle to Communion in beige coat and wine suit with a red and green Christmas scarf, as I was returning from the altar rail, the hurt only in her eyes.

Midnight Mass is the most spectacular of our Catholic services: lighted candles, poinsettias and evergreens, carols, bells ringing, feet crunching on snow perhaps on a crisp starry night, young people home from college, excited chatter and laughter as everyone wished each other "Merry Christmas." Through the years St. Prax's has learned how to do midnight Mass with style and taste and authentic Christmas joy.

For me that night there was no joy.

I slipped out of my pew and waited in the back of church because I was sure she would leave before the end.

"Merry Christmas, Lisa." I shook hands with her realizing that there was nothing I could say that would help.

"And to you, George." She shook my hand firmly in return. Consummate actress that she was, she exorcised the hurt from her eyes.

"Where's the Ryan and Murphy clan?" I was reduced to making small talk.

"Father Blackie is going to say Mass at his dad's this

afternoon. A few people are coming over. I'm sure he would want you to join us."

"I'll be there." Christmas was beginning to look merry again. The pastor's Christmas collection would be dangerously lower this year. The Ryans were the most generous contributors in the parish. Moreover, Ed Ryan and Mary Kate and Joe and Packy and Tim and Nancy and their spouses would all make it clear to the pastor over the next two weeks why they were not throwing envelopes into the collection.

There must have been fifty people in Ed Ryan's house when I arrived. Ed and Helen and Chantal, the oldest child of the second family, greeted us at the door, the gentry admitting the rest of the village.

Blackie was fumbling around at the temporary altar next to his late mother's grand piano. Eileen, who is a lawyer married to Red Kane, the columnist, and is the official family musician, was thumbing through sheet music.

Caitlin materialized next to me. "Know what, George? Chantal Ryan is my aunt and she's only a year older than I am."

"No!"

"Yes!" Giggle. "Do you love Lisa?" Another conspirator.

"Everyone does, Caitlin."

Lisa stood at the far corner of the room in her white knit minidress, fighting back the tears. By the time Blackie had himself organized, there must have been two hundred people crowded into the house, including the two curates, a half dozen of the nuns, and with her usual ability to adjust to the inevitable, my mother.

"Now let's see," Eileen said in her best courtroom voice. "We should keep the carols simple. 'Adeste' . . . slowly please . . . at the beginning. 'The First Noël' at the offertory. 'Silent Night' at the end. And . . . hmm . . ." A small smile. "How about 'O Holy Night' at Communion? Could you lead us in that Lisa, dear?"

The poor child could only nod.

Blackie never fumbles and bumbles when he preaches. "Today is the feast of light. We celebrate the return of the sun. The coming of the Son of God, the light of the world which the darkness can never put out. We also rejoice that in his love we, too, have our own light to shine on the lives of others, each in our own way, light essential, light indispensable, light glorious. In the power of God's love and in the power of our own love for one another, our light, too, will never be put out. We celebrate especially the light of those to whom God has given extraordinary gifts for bringing light and laughter and love to others. We promise that we will cheerfully cooperate in God's efforts to see that their special light is never put out."

So there. Lisa surrendered finally to tears. Caitlin, standing next to her, held her hand in mute adoration.

At Communion time she sang "Cantique de Noël" like she had never sung it before:

> *O Holy Night, the stars are brightly shining;*
> *It is the night of the dear Savior's birth.*
> *Long lay the world in sin and error pining,*
> *Till He appeared and the soul felt his worth.*
> *A thrill of hope, the weary world rejoices,*
> *For yonder beams a new and glorious morn.*
> *Fall on your knees, O hear the angel voices*
> *O night divine, O night when Christ was born*
> *O night divine, O night divine!*
>
> *Led by the light of faith serenely beaming,*
> *With glowing hearts by His cradle we stand;*
> *And led by light of stars so sweetly gleaming,*
> *Here come the wise men, from the orient land.*
> *The King of Kings thus lay in lowly manger,*
> *In all our trials born to be our friend.*
> *He knows our needs; to our weakness, no stranger.*
> *Behold your king! Before Him lowly bend.*
> *Behold your king! Your king, before Him bend.*

Need I say that there was hardly a dry eye in the room? Even Blackie had to polish off his thick lenses. Fortunately, I was wearing my contacts still.

I didn't have a chance to talk to her after Mass because there were so many people wishing her well (my tearful mother, of course, among them). I did hear Lisa remark to Red Kane that there were a lot of cougars in the canyons of Los Angeles. I don't know whether I was supposed to hear that. Probably.

I am, as you have doubtless noted, a cautious, careful man. An assiduous, if computerized, bean counter. I did not reach a decision till New Year's Day, almost a week after our shooting star went away.

The decision was obvious. There was no room for George the bean counter in the life of a woman like Lisa. That, sadly, was that.

So, on Twelfth Night, I called Blackie from O'Hare to tell him I was flying to Los Angeles.

"I want to see," I told him ruefully, "what can be done about reducing the cougar population in those canyons."

❧ Cindasoo ❧

"P.O./3d C. S. McLeod of the Yewnited States Coast Guard, Michigan City Station, suh. I'm a-searchin' for two bodies. Have you noticed any unusual bodies on the beach, suh?" The voice was exhausted, the body was short, the green eyes were weary, the face was pinched and red, the navy blue jacket and jeans were soaking wet.

I was about to tell the waterlogged kid on the doorstep that I didn't want to buy any magazine subscriptions when the phone rang. It was my mother, wondering whether I had finished my term paper—left over from summer school and required for graduation next summer.

"The coast guard is here looking for bodies," I said, trying not to sound too groggy. "I'll call you back."

"Your mammy?" A green eye considered me with more shrewdness than seemed appropriate.

"You know what mothers are like." I shrugged.

"Shunuff." The kid, dripping wet, edged into the kitchen of our beach house, a businesslike walkie-talkie bulging out of a blue jacket pocket.

I made one more effort to clear my head from the effects of the previous night's six-packs and said, "Bodies?"

"Yassuh," responded the kid forlornly. "I've been a-ramackin' the whole beach since five o'clock this morning. But I can't find none nowheres."

"Smack dab out of bodies?" I said, showing off the course in American dialects from last year (and an *A* at that).

The thin shoulders straightened up, like an undersized line backer bracing for a blitz.

"I've been instructed to interview civilian residents to ask if they have observed any bodies." The high-pitched voice was pure redneck; the short, cropped auburn hair was dripping water, as were the navy blue jeans and jacket, on our kitchen floor.

"I'll make you some coffee," I said. "No, I haven't seen any bodies. How do you folks expect to find bodies with twelve-foot waves wiping out the beach and rain pouring down for three straight days? It'll just be a chance if you uns find any bodies."

"I know all about the rain, suh," said the weary redneck voice, in perfectly grammatical Standard English. "Do you mind if I sit down?"

I gestured toward the kitchen table and then made a remarkable discovery as the redneck coast guard sank into a chair by the table. Maybe it was something about the set of the thin, tired shoulders. Anyhow, I tightened the belt on my blue terrycloth robe. The coast guardsman was a coast guardswoman. Or maybe I should say coast guardperson.

"What's this about bodies?" I asked, putting the teakettle on to boil. Whatever gender, the best I could do for the Department of Transportation on a gray rainy day in late September was instant coffee.

"A civilian craft ran out of fuel just before the gale blew up three days ago, suh." The green eyes watched the teakettle hungrily. "There were five people aboard. Three stayed with it and two elected to swim for shore. The three came aground in the craft the day before yesterday. No trace of the other two."

I found some donuts in the icebox. One of them disappeared as soon as I put it on the table. "Craft, fuel, elect, civilian"—they'd taught this teenage redneck waif to use coast-guard talk. I wondered if she'd ever seen a body when Lake Michigan finished with it.

"You certainly don't figure to find any bodies in waves like those?" I gestured at the ugly white walls sweeping in at the front of our dune.

Now, as my mammy, Dr. Mary Kate Ryan Murphy, the distinguished psychiatrist, would note, I am at that age in life when anyone of similar age and with a certified set of female reproductive organs excites libidinal interest. So I was libidinally interested in C. S. McLeod, P.O./3d, Yewnited States Coast Guard. Mild libidinal interest. Like wondering what she'd look like if she was not wearing her vast jacket.

She compressed her thin lips. "May I call my base, suh?" she asked.

"Yas'am," I agreed. I'm an anthropologist, not a linguist, but placing redneck talk is a kind of a hobby. "Southwestern West Virginia, isn't it, way up in the hills?"

I was rewarded with a faint, crinkly smile for my efforts.

"Stinkin' Creek, suh," she returned to Appalachian English. "Brown's Holler, tell the truth. Ah joined the coast guard to get shet of the mountains and see the world out yonder."

"Is Michigan City, Indiana, any better than Stinking Creek, West Virginia?"

"Yassuh." She removed her walkie-talkie. "Not much, though . . . Mobile one to base, mobile one to base. Can you read me, base? Over." She turned away from me, her neck actually turning red.

Reevaluated from the perspective that she was a coast guardswoman, C. S. McLeod could be rated cute, even pretty, possibly beautiful, but that would be going too far before I had more data.

Base didn't read her until she had fiddled expertly with the machine. Then base came through loud and clear. "That you, mountain flower? Where the hell you been? Over." That voice was pure New Orleans black.

"Roger, base, this is mobile one. I have been interviewing a civilian resident in a home on the beach, the first civilian I've found this morning."

I put the coffee in front of her. Again the wry, crinkly smile. Definitely kind of cute. Arguably gorgeous. Short even for a woman, but not too short. Take off the jacket, kid.

"He reports seeing no bodies."

"Roger, Cindasoo. Call the CO in Cleveland on the phone; he'll give you more instructions. Over and out, mountain flower. Stay dry."

She sighed and put down the walkie-talkie. "May I use your phone, suh?"

Somehow another donut vanished. She was gratefully sipping the coffee. I nodded my head.

She called collect and asked for the CO. "McLeod here, suh. I have been patrolling the beach since five. Yes, suh, I am very wet. I have found one civilian resident who I am interviewing . . . yes, suh, a young man about twenty, football-type ape with red hair. Just out of bed, good-looking in a shanty Irish sort of way . . . suffering from a hangover. . . ." She flashed the damn crinkly grin again. "No, suh, not my type at all. My mammy done warned me about you Irish papists. Said you were no-'count and shiftless." The lips tightened. "Yes suh, yes suh . . . Suh, do you want me to continue the patrol to New Buffalo? Yes suh . . . I was afraid so . . . yes suh, shunuf, I'll try to stay dry." She hung up with another sigh, kind of like the one patented by my uncle, Blackie Ryan the priest.

"Pete Murphy is the name which goes with the shanty Irish hangover," I said, putting the final donut in her open mouth.

"And James McCarthy is the name of that damn male chauvinist hound dog who is my boss," she mumbled through the donut. "All you Irish are alike."

I said something nasty about how a teenage punk coast guard rating from out of the hills couldn't hide the fact that her ancestors were Irish, too, an' they probably came over after Culloden Moor an' left the true Church.

She replied, unzipping her jacket, that her 'uns had been in Stinkin' Creek thirty years 'fore that Dan'l Boone fella came over the hills. They were shunuf Americans, not biggety 'mgrants.

I complimented her on her study of the drinking subculture of the Irish papists but asserted that we hadn't invented moonshine.

Underneath the jacket, as best as one could observe through a heavy navy blue sweatshirt, she was more than presentable. I exercised the horny male's right to fantasize about helping her out of the sweatshirt.

She countered in kind that if you have to live with hound dogs you study their moods. I remarked that Michigan City must seem like paradise compared to the mountains where they had sure enough hound dogs. She said, her green eyes shooting fire, that the real hound dogs were better than the human kind, grinned her crinkly grin, which was kind of growing on me, and put out her mug for more coffee.

"Why the rush to find those bodies, Cindasoo McLeod?" I asked, deciding that they were nice young breasts and that she probably could be considered beautiful. "If they wash in at all, it will be after the storm stops."

She was serious again. "Have you seen anyone on the beach at four o'clock in the morning, Mr. Murphy, suh?" The title was not ironic. They sure enough trained her to be polite.

"Dead or alive?" I asked, intrigued.

"Alive." Her eyes were now fixed on my face.

Oh, my God, a redneck girl detective. "Sorry, Cindasoo

McLeod, girl detective, ma'am, but I'm usually sleeping off my hangovers at four o'clock in the morning. What night?"

"Monday night. The woman in the house with the blue gazebo was interviewed yesterday by one of our personnel. She 'lowed that she woke up precisely at four o'clock and thinks she saw two subjects on the beach."

So that was what she had to ask the CO about. "And they fit the description of the people who didn't make it to shore?"

She nodded. "Do you know a varmint from Long Beach named Harold O'Connell?"

"Was Harry the one who drowned?" I asked, embarrassed at being out of touch with the news. "I've been doing a term paper. . . ."

"Keepin' yah poah mammy happy? . . . Would you recognize this varmint if you saw him on the beach at four o'clock in the morning?"

She was boring in like a truck. This Cindasoo McLeod, girl detective, was something else. She'd checked me out, too, the little imp. And decided that she could play her cute li'l redneck game for all it was worth.

I found another box of donuts. "Okay, mountain flower, let's have the whole story from the beginning. The CO told you it was all right to fill me in. Play it straight and I'll help."

The eyes narrowed and the sweet little face peered at me for a moment of raw shrewdness. I guess I passed the test, though I'd hate to have been a varmint up in the hills that she was going after with a squirrel gun.

She shrugged her thin shoulders. "My name is not 'mountain flower,' despite what that black trash J. G. calls me. This ridge runner Harry O'Connell is in slathers of trouble with his father-in-law. He done red off from the family brokerage firm with a whole heap of money—more than a half million dollars in negotiable securities. He also done committed adultery many times with a nurse he met

101

at the hospital when his last littleun was born. His father-in-law done told the U.S. attorney's office in Chicago. They were going to drop in 'n' talk a mite with Mr. O'Connell on Monday morning. Then he hears the powerful bad news that Mr. O'Connell and this here scarce-hipped nurse drowned on Sunday afternoon. Name a Moira Walsh. Typical no-'count Irish papists." She grinned at me. "No one done found the securities neither."

"So the guess is that they are on their way to South America?" I said wisely, and then as an afterthought, "And I'm infinitely more virtuous than Harry."

She ignored my defense and returned to SE, excepting she always pronounced "United" as "Yewnited"—the correct way I suppose she would have argued. "The United States attorney's office was very anxious about our finding the bodies. When one of our personnel interviewed Mrs. Blue Gazebo yesterday, Commander McCarthy, using his native wit, thought that maybe the good old Northern District of Illinois was sure enough not telling us everything it ought to. So they allowed finally as how death by drowning was mighty convenient for Mr. O'Connell and Ms. Walsh. So this refugee from the hills and the hollers is likely to catch her death of cold unless, please suh, you give me some more coffee."

I was beginning to think it might be a good idea to fall hopelessly in love with her. For her part, less romantically but more realistically, Cindasoo McLeod was trying to make up her mind whether she liked me. She wasn't much to look at, a little tad all bundled up in her sweatshirt and jacket again, but I wanted her to like me. Anyhow, I gave her the coffee. She eyed me speculatively. I thought maybe I passed another test.

"Why would they hang around the beach, Cindasoo McLeod? Why not head for South America right away? Should not the Northern District have the feds watching airports instead of wilted mountain flowers slogging through the sand?" Okay, I was walking on thin ice. She didn't seem to mind. Hell, the race keeps going because people our age size each other up. I wished she'd take off her jacket so I could do some more sizing. I sat down across the table from her.

"It's the wilted mountain flower's own fault. I observed to Commander McCarthy that if I were running away with a half-million dollars, I would lie low for a long time before heading for an airport, even if I had staged a drowning. So I would go to ground, uh, take refuge quite near the place where I landed on the beach, and stay there until . . ."

"A snowstorm covered my tracks."

"Uh-huh. Anyhow, the commander, whose father was one of your corrupt Chicago cops, said I was in the wrong branch of government service, that I had a mind like a corrupt cop, and would I like to patrol the beach and interview residents to establish my theory? He then arranged for it to rain for three days. . . ."

"Why did you leave West Virginia and join the coast guard, Cindasoo McLeod?" I asked, wondering what she thought about sitting at a kitchen table with a man who was twice her height and weight (well, almost), wearing only a battered blue terrycloth robe.

"Personal questions are irrelevant to my patrol responsibilities, Mr. Murphy," she said primly. Then, relenting, she added, "The coast guard guarantees to keep you away from mountains after you're out of junior college. Now I must continue my patrol. Thank you for the refreshment."

She stood up, hunched her shoulders like she was going out on a raccoon hunt, and eased toward the kitchen door. I'd scared her. Damn.

"Can I come help? I've always wanted to be a detective." Lame, but the best I could do on the spur of the moment.

"You're not authorized government personnel, Mr. Murphy, suh. If you saw Harry O'Connell anytime since Monday night and could tell me . . ."

"Cindasoo, I feel sorry for anyone who married into the

Haggerty clan, but I never did like Harry much, and I don't approve of larceny. If I'd seen him, I'd tell you. . . ."

She looked up at me, again the shrewd mountain animal, nodded her head as though I had convinced her, and walked out into the sheets of rain. She winced when the first deluge of water hit her. "Thank you very much for the coffee and donuts, Mr. Murphy. The commandant of the coast guard thanks you, so does the secretary of transportation, and so does the president . . . only"—and she actually smiled very pleasantly at me—"don't try to deduct the expenses from your income tax."

So I 'lowed to myself that I was in a whole heap of trouble, cogitatin' 'bout fallin' in love with a female varmint from the hollers when I should have been doin' up my term paper.

Then I 'lowed as how my poah ole mammy would dote on Cindasoo and would never forgive me for not hog-tying her if she found I had the chance.

One thirty I finished exactly two paragraphs about the Irish traveling folk (or Irish Gypsies, if you want to call them that, though they're not really Gypsies) in America.

I gave it up, made two large hamburgers with everything and a thermos of hot coffee, and walked down the slippery stairs to the beach. I noticed that the storm winds (in excess of forty knots, according to KWO from Sears Tower) had knocked over the totem pole at the house next door. It hung drunkenly over two nymphs and fauns in the rock garden, as though it were going to fall against the door on my nutty neighbor's terrace level.

Down on the shore the ugly white walls were still sweeping in. It was a nice, soggy beach to walk on, with the sand squishing under your feet, if you didn't mind twenty-seven knots of wind blowing straight down the lake from the Soo.

I found Cindasoo a half mile down the beach in the New Buffalo direction, a lonely little figure huddling against a battered old boat house, shivering with the cold and looking all plumb tuckered out. She refused neither hamburger nor coffee.

"Nice of you to shuckle out and bring me vittels."

I pointed out that if you huddled under the overhang of the boat house, you only got half the rain you'd get out on the beach.

"How long you out here?" I asked over the howl of the wind.

"Twelve-hour duty. Me and my big redneck mouth."

"You don't really expect to find them out here, do you, Miz Cindasoo?" I asked in my best corn-pone accent, digging into the second half of my hamburger.

"Look, Pete Murphy, boy anthropologist"—the little bitch had guessed that—"don't patronize me, or I'll go after you with my varmint gun."

Again she started out being angry and turned friendly. I was getting kind of worried.

"Anyway, I figure it has to be somewhere between the crick and New Buffalo. No way you can cross the crick when the waves are rolling in. If they walk down toward New Buffalo, they'd run into the permanent residents. That gives them about a mile and a half of beach. . . ." She continued to munch efficiently on her hamburger. Small girl with a big appetite. And, I filed it away for future reference, a very neat little rear end.

"If they have the kind of criminal minds that you have and are smart enough to think that way . . . Harry O'Connell is no prize when it comes to brains."

"The woman is. Woulda worked, too, 'ceptin for Mrs. Blue Gazebo."

"How do you see the case, Cindasoo McLeod, girl detective?"

"Well." She dragged the introductory word out and once again paid no attention to my sarcasm. The attractive little petty officer was perfectly prepared to accept the label of detective. "I been figurin'. If I was goin' to disappear round hyar, and if I knew this crazy lake, I'd think, Cindasoo, what if the sky clabbers up and the waves turn right smart? I'd take a gander at the beach and not want to climb over that pesky groin in front of you'un's pump house."

"So if you were planning to disappear somewhere near the blue gazebo, you'd have to come ashore between the pump house and the crik . . . uh, creek."

"Yassuh, twixt the pump house and the crik . . . lessen you get plumb knocked in by them powerful wave things."

She drew a diagram on the sand. "So happenchance that you'd be hiding in one of these eight houses 'twixt the crik, hyar, and the pump house, hyar."

"That narrows the search, doesn't it? Only eight houses where they might be, ifin your theory is right, Cindasoo, girl detective."

"Six. Ah cased your house this morning. And we can eliminate Mrs. Blue Gazebo." She rubbed out the diagram with the impatient toe of an absurdly tiny coast-guard sneaker.

"*Cased* is not Appalachian English."

"Is now." She smiled at me and my heart stopped stone dead.

"Let's go case the other six houses."

"Ah cain't do that. Ah don't have no federal warrant."

"Can't you watch a civilian poke his shanty Irish nose around?"

"Ah suppose so . . . would you really, Mr. Peter Murphy, suh?"

"For that smile, Cindasoo McLeod, I'd do almost anything."

So we climbed over the groin and up the side of the dune, and worked our way through the gardens and the poolsides and the patios on our part of the beach, a-peekin' an' a-pookin' and a-prowlin'. Have you ever prowled a summer resort in early autumn? It'll give you an idea of what earth might be like the day after the end of the world.

We didn't find nothin'. So drippin' wet, we stood on a concrete seawall and surveyed the angry lake.

"Ah'm just about ready to holler calf rope." Cindasoo sighed. "I'm plumb tuckered out."

"Climbing up all them stairs like a jackrabbit would tucker anyone out."

She had led the way on our a-pokin' and a-prowlin' like a forest creature bounding through the mountains, a slender, fragile li'l varmint whose energy and charm would break your heart. Mine anyway.

"Peter Murphy, suh, the pump house!"

"You don't think they could be hiding there?"

She charged down the dune to the pump house without bothering to answer. I traipsed along after her and arrived a good half minute after she had thrown open the door and bounced inside.

Thank God the place was empty, save for a powerful lot of spiders.

I took firm possession of her attractive little shoulders and held her against the slimy and rusty green wall of the dim old pump house.

"Cindasoo McLeod, don't you dare take a chance like that again, lessen I have to put you over my knee and spank that gorgeous rear end of yours."

"Varmint." She sighed as I kissed her.

I could tell Cindasoo hadn't been kissed very often before. She was startled but not exactly offended.

"What for did you do that for?"

"My mammy, who is a psychiatrist, says that it's natural for young men and women to kiss one another."

The good doctor had never quite said that; she never needed to.

"Ya mammy is a shunuf head shrinker?" Her green eyes opened wide.

"Uh-huh. So's my pappy." I touched the side of her face. "And my uncle is a pure quill Catholic priest."

"Does he have horns?"

I realized that much of her redneck act was just that: an act. Half fun and full earnest, as Grandpa Ned would say.

Partly a defense and partly a put-on. Grandpa Ned would like Cindasoo.

I kissed her again. She pushed me away, but not decisively.

"Go 'long with you. I'm a decent acorn calf. You got no call to try to hornswoggle me; you're nothing but a sky-gogglin' side-hill slicker, a bodacious fuddle-britches."

I laughed. She didn't.

"Get out of here, ya hear?"

I had scared her. Shame on me. Shanty Irish bumbler. Still, she was close to laughing.

"Sure enough, mountain flower." I walked back into the wind, which seemed to have picked up while I was kissing Cindasoo. I thought that somehow it was friendly wind, thoroughly approving of my romantic advances. "But at five o'clock—'scuse me, ma'am, seventeen hundred hours, —I'm going to be on our sundeck with something in the way of supper. If you show up, I might just note another tax deduction."

Cindasoo McLeod, girl detective, looked at me coldly, almost said something rude, turned her face away, and mumbled, "Can't tell what someone might do at five o'clock if they're hungry enough." She laughed, first time I'd heard it, a kind of bell-like sound in the middle of the woods.

"The coast guard," I said, "should not be searching for anything but dead bodies. You sure you don't want company?" I shouted to be heard above the banshee wind as she walked away.

She turned back and shook her head decisively. "I'm jes' moseyin' round to the beach lookin'. That doesn't need help. You go back and finish your term paper so your poah old mammy won't have to worry about you."

She must have guessed that, too. Sherlock Holmes at Grand Beach. And I still wondered what she looked like under that sweatshirt.

Anyhow, at five o'clock—oops, seventeen hundred hours

—Cindasoo Lou McLeod (her full, sure-enough name, and her mammy made corn pone and moonshine up the hollers and I didn't believe any of it anymore) and I were sitting on my family's sundeck overlooking the seawall which keeps the lake away from the dunes, eating steak and sipping some of my poah father's best 1961 burgundy. The clouds had finally blown off and the sun sinking toward Chicago turned our lake into a surging mass of expensive diamonds. Cindasoo ate the steak and guzzled the wine like both were going out of style.

"You shunuf put the little pot in the big pot for me, Mr. Murphy, suh." She glanced at the vintage year on the almost empty wine bottle, of which she had consumed at least her full share. "Your pa sure must have a powerful heap of money."

I said it was better than the mountain dew her father made at the still back by the outhouse. She grinned crookedly and 'lowed as how it shunuf was.

Well, it was getting to be pleasant, what with the blue sky and the burgundy making me feel warm, and Cindasoo squinting up at the sun. She talked a lot about the hills. I could see why she liked them and why she wanted to leave. Then the grin faded and I had the girl detective on my hands again.

"Six houses"—she ticked them off on her tiny fingers—"two with concrete seawalls that would be hard to climb, one with that high-headed ole totem pole, 'nother one with an empty prefabricated storage hut by the side of the pool—"

"'Nother one with a shanty Irish football player."

She held my jaw steady with her right hand and kissed me. Her lips tasted of steak sauce and burgundy.

"Who kisses putty good for a papist."

I realized I was being pursued by a shrewd hunter with a varmint gun. No, not pursued, hog-tied, 'fore I knew what had happened.

"You're tryin' to seduce me, bodacious Cindasoo."

109

"Tell me, Peter Murphy, suh"—she changed the subject abruptly—"about that weird old house next door to yours," she said thoughtfully, eyeing the tilted totem pole, the rock garden, the nymphs, fauns, and elves, and the ugly rusty seawall. "We didn' find anythin' there either, but it sure is a passin' strange place."

"It belongs to a crazy lady who is never around. There are all kinds of work persons who come in periodically and do things like trimming the hedges, painting the nymphs, and straightening out the totem pole."

"Could anyone be hidin' in that house?"

I swear she was sniffing the air like a hound dog.

"Not likely," I said. "She pays the town marshal to look around inside every night. I saw him go in last night."

"Hmm . . . well, it was a nice idea. Give me some more of that dew; it shunuff makes the cold go away. . . ."

So I poured out the last few ounces of the wine. Our eyes must have locked on the door at the terrace level of the nutty rock garden at the same moment.

"What's . . ." asked Cindasoo.

"It's supposed to be an apartment she built there for her husband. A couple of rooms in the side of the hill with beads and cushions. At least that's the beach legend. . . ."

It was crazy, but we went up to have a look. I didn't even argue. We crawled over the old retaining wall, crept across my neighbor's smoothly cut lawn, and got to the edge of the roof of the apartment. Cindasoo had her ear to the ground.

"Don' hyar nothin'," she said, now completely the mountain huntress. "Let's go have a closer look-see. . . ."

I helped her down the face of the retaining wall and jumped down next to her. We were right in front of the door, which was a sure enough damn fool place to be.

The door swung open suddenly. There was a woman, blond and hard-faced, dressed in jeans and a white sweater, pointing a gun at us. Harry O'Connell was cowering behind her, a gun in his hand, too. I wondered, almost as an abstract speculation, whether they knew how to shoot and whether they were going to add murder to larceny and adultery.

Cindasoo Lou McLeod did more than speculate. She dived at the woman, hitting her in the stomach with her auburn head, shoving the gun away with her left hand. The gun went off, a bullet whistling a safe distance above my head.

Harry ran over me like a semitrailer, a briefcase in his hand. I never did like the lout. Remembering that I was a strong-side safety, I grabbed an ankle with one hand and tripped him up. I would have had him, but out of the corner of my eye I saw a gun barrel come down on Cindasoo's head. I let him go and jumped the woman, who was pulling the gun back to strike again.

She was, let me tell you, a biting, scratching tiger, a real cave woman. Finally, All-American honorable mention that I was, I managed just barely to wrestle the gun out of her hands. She took off after Harry, who was scrambling up the hill.

I carried Cindasoo into the stuffy cave. It did have beads and pillows just like we had believed when we were growing up. Cindasoo's hair was bloody, but she seemed to be breathing all right.

I pulled her walkie-talkie out of the jacket. "Mobile one to base, mobile one to base. This is Pete Murphy. I hope you folks are listening. They're heading for the highway. They're carrying a briefcase with a half-million dollars of negotiable securities. Get a doctor here; they've knocked Cindasoo out."

"Base to mobile one." The slob sounded remarkably cool. "Can you identify the subjects for us, Mr. Murphy? We will notify appropriate police personnel."

"To hell with police personnel . . . get medical personnel here. Didn't you hear me say they hurt Cindasoo?"

I turned the damned thing off. Cindasoo was stirring.

I still hadn't solved the mystery of what she looked like with her jacket off, but she felt very nice and soft in my arms. She opened her eyes, focused on me, then looked frightened. Firmly and insistently she pushed me away. Well, I told myself, you've been given the brush-off before.

An hour later we were standing on Lake View Avenue behind our house. Everyone was there—the state police, the county police, the township police, and the village marshal. All of them with their red and blue lights whirling. The fugitives had been "apprehended" in the woods, we were told. There was also a battered blue government motor-pool car with a very handsome black J.G., his coast-guard academy class ring on one hand and a wedding band on the other. Cindasoo Lou McLeod, girl detective, looking woebegone and confused, leaned against the hood of the car.

"You are in real trouble, McLeod." He seemed 'bout ready to cry. Everyone liked my Cindasoo. "You were not authorized to take subjects into custody. You should have radioed base before you attempted to apprehend them."

She shook her head, still dazed. "No, suh, I mean yes, suh, I mean, suh, the information was that they were armed and the woman might be dangerous. I was afraid that they might have radio equipment with which to monitor our calls. If you inspect the apartment, suh, you'll see I was correct in my surmise. I did not feel justified in risking Mr. Murphy's life, suh, by attempting communication."

He sighed with relief. None of it was true and he knew that, but now he could write a report. He patted her arm. "Okay, mountain flower, I guess we can stand to have a heroine, though we'd sure as hell hate to have anything happen to you. We need a redneck around here to beat up on." He flashed even white teeth at the two of us.

I wasn't going to be the one to ask why she couldn't make a telephone call. Or why she endangered my life by trying to peek into the apartment. I was in love, you see, and I figured by the time the CO got around to thinking of those questions, either he'd be content with a real live redneck heroine or Cindasoo would have an answer for him.

Besides, if our friends had seen us looking at the rock garden from the seawall and were ready for us, they might never have let us back into my house to make the call.

So who wanted to argue?

The next week I was sitting on the beach late in the afternoon correcting typos on my term paper (which the professor had told me rated another *A-plus*, much to my poah ole mammy's delight) and soaking up the eighty-plus Indian-summer sun. You'd almost forget that there had ever been a storm. A light, peaceful haze hung over the mirror-smooth lake, the smell of burning leaves in the air.

A girl in a green string bikini with a shirttail type thing over it was walking down the beach. I tried not to stare. She sat down beside me. I wondered how come I was so lucky. But honest, only when she began to talk did I realize it was Cindasoo McLeod, girl detective.

"You won't believe it"—she sighed, no redneck accent now—"but it was a waste of time. Mr. Harold O'Connell's wife and father-in-law are disposed to be forgiving, especially since they have both him and the money back. I guess he found out that there was more to Nurse Walsh than sex when they were locked up in that horrid cave. So unless you and I want to make a fuss about assault with a deadly weapon, the whole thing is dropped."

"They might have killed you, Cindasoo," I said protectively. My question about what the real Cindasoo looked like was now answered. The lines were much more than satisfactory, better than I had hoped; for to tell you the truth about my dirty imagination, it wasn't her green eyes I was looking at anymore.

She was embarrassed by my inspection, but no way did she turn or blush. "I know what it's like to want to run away," she said simply, "but it's up to you, Peter Murphy. If you want to press charges, you are perfectly within your rights."

"What made you think it might be that house?"

"That bodacious ole tot'm pole. I sez to myself, Cindasoo, suppose you're thinking 'forehand that you'd be out on that wicked lake and are looking for a sign that you've come to the right beach late at night; what you goin' to be searchin' for? And I sez back, Cindasoo, happen you remember about that ole pole and the cave house under it. And then I'd say, Cindasoo, why not hide for a few days in that ole cave, 'specially since that gollywhooper of a pole will tell you whar it is, in the stone dead a-night."

"So you dressed up all fancy in that expensive swimming thing just to come to tell me I ought to give people another chance and to explain how you solved the mystery?"

She drew a very long breath, a movement which made my eyes pop and my heart leap. Again the mountain-hollow shrewdness in her face. "No, Peter Murphy, suh. I got all gussied up in this wicked thing to see if you'd give me another chance. I lost my nerve the first time. . . ."

It was a pretty amateurish kind of kiss, both of us being scared stiff, but she felt even nicer in my arms this time. We both knew we were crossing an important line in our lives.

I'd held young women in my arms before. But none whose little heart pounded so fiercely against her ribs till I soothed it into serenity. And none whose offering of her whole self was so filled with trust.

The kind of trust which hog-ties you with respect and reverence.

"My mammy done warned me," I lied, "about green-eyed mountain critters that hog-tie you with trust."

She just giggled and snuggled closer.

"I think we're in love, Cindasoo."

"Shunuff," we said together.

~Peggy~

"We can't permit outsiders to be buried from St. Finian's. The priests would have to spend all their time at wakes and funerals."

The handsome young priest's gray eyes were expressionless, his voice cold, his thin lips implacable under a trim mustache. At first Peggy was glad that the priest who came to the rectory office was young. Perhaps he would say something which would free her from numbness and permit her sentence of suffering and grief to begin. Now he sounded like the old monsignor in the parish where her mother grew up who would not permit a priest friend to say her uncle's funeral when he was killed in the Second World War.

"This is our parish, Father," she said, struggling to climb out of the pit of numbness and to sound like the rational adult and the dedicated Catholic she was. "Our children went to school here, they were married in the church, Dick was on the parish council, I was president   the Altar Guild, we chaperoned High Club dances. . . ."

Dick loved the High Club as much as the kids. It was impossible to link the cold body next to her in bed that morning with the gregarious idol of several generations of sophomore girls.

Father Reid smoothed his mustache with tender affection. "You don't live here anymore." Dressed in a brown and white sport shirt and brown slacks, both fitting him perfectly, the priest looked a bit like a broad-shouldered, big-handed Richard Gere. He spoke in short, terse sentences, none of which had hinted at sympathy. "The Cathedral is your parish. Your husband should be buried from there."

"Can we see the pastor?" Rick, her second child and first son, a bantam-weight lawyer, even more of a brown-haired freckle-faced street fighter than his father, spoke for the first time, probably to cut off his wife Deirdre.

"The pastor is away. I'm the administrator."

"How old are you, Father?" Deirdre, small and fiery like her husband, had been uncertain about the Walshes at first. It had taken Peggy a long time to win her over. Now her loyalty to Peggy was more intense than that of her own daughters and they were fiercely loyal women.

"Thirty. What does that have to do with it, Mrs. . . . . er—"

"Walsh." Rick was on his feet, jabbing his finger at the young priest as though he were a criminal on the witness stand. "If you had bothered to listen, Father, you would have remembered that she is my wife and our name is Walsh. Her point is that we are the same age and that I have had to work for every bit of income and prestige I have. You've been handed it all on a platter. You mean nothing—"

"Rick," Peggy pleaded. He and his father had always battled, often—especially since Rick had married and graduated from law school and there was nothing serious to fight about—for the pure love of battle. Now Rick's love and grief were coming out the only way they could. If only I could grieve, too, she thought. Any emotion would be better than this awful emptiness.

"Leave him to me, Mom." He balled his hands into fierce little knots. Deirdre's were already white from the pressure of squeezed fingers. "A lot of my father's money is in that new church, Father, and a lot of his life went into this parish. His funeral Mass—"

"Eucharist of the Resurrection." Deirdre's propensity to interrupt was uncontrollable. Somehow Rick seemed to like it.

"Right, Mass of the Resurrection will be from St. Finian's, if I have to go to the cardinal himself. Do you understand?"

If Father Reid understood, it did not show in his expressionless eyes. "The Cathedral is his parish. The funeral Mass will be there."

I don't care where it is, Peggy thought. What difference does it make? He was never sick a day in our thirty-two years of marriage. Now he's dead and I don't care whether I live or die.

"You want to bet?" Rick's eyes glowed with the joy of combat.

"You'll lose," Deirdre told Father Reid, her tiny, pixie face hard with anger.

I always tried to moderate Dick's fire, Peggy reflected. She's so different. Why does she egg Rick on?

As they left the rectory, she realized that Rick was not his father and that Deirdre probably knew what she was doing. Theirs was a happy if turbulent marriage. Briefly she envied Deirdre because she still had a husband. Then she dismissed such feelings as absurd. If only she could really cry instead of sniffling into a tissue.

She felt proud of her children for their loyalty and courage. Slim, erect kids, pale skin, snapping blue eyes, brown hair, bristling Irish wit, the four of them looked like they had been stamped out of the same mold; yet each was different: Ellen, the oldest, a radical, Rick a fighter, Nora an imp, and Brendan, the youngest, still at Notre Dame, a dreamy mystic. Perhaps, she sometimes thought, a priest.

As they entered Rick's Volvo she glanced around the St. Finian's schoolyard. Four June Sundays in twelve years they had stood in that yard as their children, maroon and white ribbons blowing in the breeze, squinted against the sun and the flashing camera bulbs. The Walsh kids were so important, bright, athletic, articulate, often troublemakers, too, that it would have been impossible in those days to imagine a time when St. Finian's would not remember them.

Time passes so quickly. Now it would drag. Thirty more years on the average, she had read aloud from the paper to Dick just the other day. Thirty years of loneliness.

How soon could she begin to mourn? Would she fall apart like so many widows did in the year assigned to mourning? And then emerge from grief, silly and a little like an overaged adolescent? She had worried about that before, as an abstract possibility, not something she would have to face so soon.

Somehow it was decided that Deirdre (never, but never, to be called "Dee Dee") and Rick would stay with her while she bought a mourning dress, made arrangements with the undertaker, and had her hair done. Ellen and her husband Steve would return to St. Finian's after Rick made his phone call to the Cathedral, whose rector, Monsignor Ryan, had the cardinal's ear.

"They're less likely to gloat," Deirdre remarked philosophically. "More conservative, too."

She and Dick had not done too badly with their children: Ellen, who had matured during the Vietnam War, had lived with Steven for a year before they were married and had used drugs. Now she and her husband were determined Catholics, possibly more conservative in their plans for raising their three children than her parents had been. Three marriages, all to Irish Catholics, six grandchildren, and one, maybe even two more on the way. What a pity Dick would not be around to enjoy their teen years as he enjoyed the adolescence of his own.

"It will be more fun," he had joked, "because I won't have any responsibility at all."

"Not that you took all that much with your own," she had sniffed. "They were your children till they got into trouble, then they became mine."

He had laughed, as he always did when she scored a point, and swept her into his arms.

They had their share of troubles, though their relationship had not been as volatile at its worst as Rick and Deirdre's was at its best. It was hard for either of them to stay angry for very long. Neither had much control of their sense of the absurd or their propensity to succumb to laughter at the height of a quarrel.

The days of laughter are over, she thought as she escaped the purgatory of the hair dryer. Now begin the days of grief.

The thought of purgatory caught her up short. She had yet to pray for Dick. No prayer, no tears. Dear God, have I lost my faith as well as my husband?

Rick won his argument, as she was sure he would. The Mass of the Resurrection would be offered at St. Finian's. Father Reid would say the Mass and preach and lead the service at Crawford's Funeral Home, near the church. "It's for the best, Ricky," Ellen insisted. "He does represent the parish, and how can we choose among all our priest friends?"

Rick looked like he wanted to argue, as he almost always did. Then he glanced at his mother and said ruefully, "Thank heavens there's one mature kid in the Walsh clan, huh, Mom?"

"Last one they thought would make it." Ellen grinned back. They all laughed.

"You'll laugh at your own wake," Peggy had often said to Dick.

His wake, like her own widowhood, had never been

anything more than a joke. Now it was real. And, yes, the Walshes would laugh. Tears would come later.

Most of the bad times stopped when Dick gave up drinking. "Not quite an AA yet, but it wouldn't take long," he said after he had piled up their Olds coming out of the country-club parking lot. "We have to learn from everything that happens to us"—crooked grin and a precinct captain's wink—"especially the disasters."

Death was a disaster. What did he learn from that? What did she learn? That she could be calm in the face of tragedy? Call the emergency number, call the Cathedral rectory, call your oldest, do all the right and reasonable things, even though you knew the man whom you adored more every day had died in his sleep next to you?

Wonderful learning experience.

Rick probably didn't even realize that he was driving the Volvo by their old home. Deirdre's quick intake of breath indicated she knew. Peggy touched her hand reassuringly. I won't break down now. Would that I could.

Something had died the day they moved out of that house; a quarter century it had been home. They both agreed that sentimentality shouldn't keep them in a place which was too big after Nora and Ed married. Besides, they both had always planned to move back downtown. Just the same, they cried the day the deal was signed.

Their new life in the city had lasted only two years, just long enough for her to begin to like it. Now there was an empty apartment and an empty life. What will I do when the worst of the grieving is over?

The first few moments at the wake were the worst. She stood mute at the side of the wooden casket—Dick's specific instructions—assaulted by the terrible sweet smell of memorial flowers. She did not recognize the stranger in the casket. Those purple lips were not the ones which had kissed her when they necked and petted shamelessly on their first date. That was not the body of the man with whom she had mated, at first awkwardly and without pleasure and then with graceful passion through the years. Her husband was somewhere else. Taken from her, perhaps forever.

"A real Irish wake," Brendan said as the long line of mourners filed past the first night. "Dad would love it. He always said the wakes were happier than the weddings."

"And with good reason." She giggled despite the terrible pain beneath the numbness. I'm laughing at your wake, darling, the way you wanted me to.

"Terrible people, the Irish," Brendan continued like he was a wise old man instead of a heartbroken twenty-year-old. "Did you know that they used to screw in the fields while the wake was in progress? That's why the Church in Ireland finally banned them."

"Brendan," she said in the tone of mild reproof she used when anyone in the family used improper language.

"It meant something important." He shrugged his thin shoulders. "It meant"—his voice choked—"fuck you, death."

The young man slipped away from the line, so quietly no one noticed. To break down in the men's room. He can mourn and I cannot. It will come, it will come, and I will think that it will never end.

Fuck you, death.

That night she dreamed that it was all a nightmare and woke up sure that she could touch Dick's hand next to her. When she felt nothing but an empty bed, the pain became worse. She thought she would lose her mind for a few moments of wild delirium. Then, sanely and reasonably, she went to the bathroom and took a pill the doctor had given her. She must have a few hours' sleep to be ready for the second night of the wake.

That was the night the priests came; she thought, Have we known so many of them in our marriage? Jesuits from Loyola, Holy Cross men from Notre Dame, the priests who had served at St. Finian's, the priests who were important to the kids, the pastor of the parish in which Nora and Ed lived, even Monsignor Ryan from the Cathedral, a funny-looking, confused little priest with lovely blue eyes and the kindest smile she had ever seen.

Joe Stack, who went to grammar school with her and on whom she had a crush before he went to the seminary, came with his wife, an angry, hateful ex-nun who hardly seemed able to contain her joy at Peggy's bereavement.

Joe looked haunted and old. He had not been happy as a priest; they had said it was his mother who had the vocation, not Joe. He did not seem any happier now. Peggy shivered slightly. No matter how bad your predicament might be, someone else's was always worse.

She wondered where Father Reid was. The new wake services were beautiful. Nora had brought her guitar and rounded up her friends from the days of the teen choir to sing the psalm. When the Walshes were not laughing, they were singing. "Mrs. Walsh," her children's friends used to say, "is really excellent on the piano, she can play, like *everything*!"

Mary Anne and Jim Foley, her kid sister (a year younger) and her husband, stood next to the family. We had so much fun when we doubled-dated in high school. How does it slip away so quickly? I was a kid, then a wife, then a mother, then a grandmother, now a widow. I don't feel any older than when I was a kid. That was only yesterday.

"Father Reid's here." Mary Anne touched her hand.

The young priest was strikingly handsome in a clerical suit which had to have been tailor-made to fit so well. He cut to the head of the line, so swiftly that no one seemed to have noticed he was in the room.

"At least he wore his Roman collar," Rick said in a stage whisper.

Nora, energetic as always, bounced up to the priest, prayer card in one hand, guitar already in the other. One of those preceremony conferences with the priest in which the new clergy received their marching orders from the new laity.

Father Reid, expressionless, impassive, raised a massive hand to decline the card, knelt at the casket, and began the "Our Father" in a resonant baritone voice. The hubbub of the funeral parlor declined gradually as mourners began to realize that prayers were being said.

"A decade of the fucking Rosary," Rick protested.

"Shush," his mother replied in a tone which the kids knew meant they had better behave.

After the final "Eternal rest grant unto him, O Lord, and let perpetual light shine upon him," Father Reid shook hands solemnly with each member of the family, speaking not a word of sympathy to any of them, indeed not a word of any sort. Then, as quickly as he had come, his broad shoulders went through the doorway and out into the air of the early spring suburban night.

"Bastard," Nora exploded through her tears.

They were all crying, even the spouses. Why was she the only one without tears?

"He's like a lot of the young ones we're getting," Ed said as he held Nora tightly against his massive chest. "All they care about is the status that goes with the office. People don't matter to them anymore."

Ed and Nora always spoke about the Church as though they were running it. "A lot of the young ones *we're* getting." If ever the Church permitted a husband and wife to exercise a joint priesthood, those two kids would be at the head of the list of applicants.

"We must pray for the poor man," Peggy said tersely, signaling them that there would be no more discussion of Father Reid.

Ellen, as always, had to have a final jab. "He has a sociopath's eyes."

Before she could reply to Ellen's last word with a last word of her own, Peggy noticed that the murmur of noise at the entrance of the funeral home had suddenly grown louder and more cheerful. A short, white-haired priest, with

123

a wide chest, thick glasses, red face, and penetrating voice had appeared and was already working the wake the way Mayor Daley did when he was alive.

"Mugsy Branigan!" exclaimed Ellen.

"All the way from Florida." Nora's tears were turning into laughter.

"He gave up a day at golf to come." A wide grin split Rick's face.

"But not a chance to talk about our football team," Brendan enthused. "The greatest Notre Dame fan in all the world."

The crowd of mourners fell away and Monsignor Mugsy, step firm as always, walked toward her with open arms, like she was an empress and he was the papal nuncio.

"Greetings and salutations." The words he had spoken as she tripped coming up the steps on her wedding day.

"Monsignor Mugsy." They gripped each other's hands; somehow it didn't seem right to hug a ninety-one-year-old Monsignor.

Martin J. "Mugsy" Branigan, the oldest priest in the archdiocese, perpetual member of Butterfield Country Club, sometime (long ago) shortstop for the Chicago White Sox, longtime superintendent of Catholic schools, longer-time pastor of St. Ursula's, and longest-time-of-all incorrigible Notre Dame fan.

"I'm so sorry, Margaret"—he stood at the casket—"so very, very sorry." For a moment the mask of geniality slipped and Monsignor Mugsy was an old man who had come a long way on an airplane to pay tribute to a man he had baptized. He was tired, sad, frail, but still didn't seem ninety-one.

Then, the concession having been made to death, he turned to the children and the two solemn-faced grandchildren. "These galoots of yours have grown up, Margaret, not bad-looking kids. This guy, I hear he's a great tennis player at Notre Dame."

"Chess, Monsignor!" Brendan knew that in the game with Mugsy you did not defend yourself. Rather, you attacked.

"Only the Russians make money on that . . . did I baptize all of them, Margaret?"

"Yes, Monsignor."

"Well, it seems to have worked pretty well, more than I can say for some of my other baptisms. This one." He pointed an accusing finger at Rick. "The exorcism part never took on him."

"I'll give you nine strokes and beat you at Butterfield any day next summer."

"Twelve," Mugsy retorted. "Two for each decade of age I give away."

He had a joke, a wisecrack, an accurate jab of wit for each of them—someone had surely prepared him beforehand—and moved on to the rest of the precinct, leaving a trail of laughter and love behind him without having to say anything more in sympathy except one sincere "I'm sorry."

It was not fair, she told herself as she fell asleep in the strange bed in Ellen's guest bedroom that night, to compare poor Father Reid with Monsignor Mugsy. Few priests would win in a comparison with the old man. Yet neither of them had said anything particularly religious. One had made them all angry and the other had made them all laugh.

"Mugsy doesn't wear his piety on his sleeve." Dick had defended him once against a woman who complained about the Notre Dame football player in the stained-glass window at St. Ursula's. "But he's a hell of a good priest."

"My husband, however," Peggy had observed promptly, "does wear *his* piety on his sleeve. Prays at least once a year."

More laughter; so much laughter, now almost over, only a few traces like the last snowdrifts of winter melting in the pitiless March sun. Laughter yielding to tears. Her own tears had yet to begin. She was still hiding her grief under the blanket of compulsive Irish female bravery. One more day and she could collapse. What would happen then?

Poor Father Reid. How could one so young be so stuffy and conservative?

After the homily the next morning, she was not sure that *conservative* was the right word.

She had resolved that she would walk down the green-carpeted aisle of St. Finian's with a steady step. She would not be one of those widows who had virtually to be carried to the front pew by her children. Her courage had sustained her thus far; she would endure the final day.

An Irishwoman to the end, she told herself with a bitter smile.

She had almost been undone at the funeral parlor when she overheard a woman remark, not totally devoid of cattiness, that she was an "attractive widow." She did not want to be attractive; she'd paid a high enough price already in her life because of other women's envy of her good looks; she did not want to be widow; and most especially she did not want to be the object of a mixture of pity and contempt, an attractive widow.

Tears were dangerously close as she left Crawford's, tears which would be the prelude to collapse, and they were tears of anger, not of grief.

Poor woman meant no harm.

No, that wasn't true; she did mean harm.

St. Finian's, with all its memories of First Communions, confirmations, graduations, weddings, midnight Masses, always with Dick at her side, muttering an irreverent joke to which she would reply in kind despite herself, was like a brutal slap on the face. The taste of bile surged into her mouth, worse than the couple of hangovers which had occurred in her abstemious life. I am going to be sick, she thought as she walked from the vestibule into the elegant, modern church.

Yet she made it down the aisle, with firm step, upright head, dry eyes. She stumbled only at the last minute when she slipped into the pew, Rick on one side of her, Brendan on the other. So many friends in church. The sanctuary filled with priests. All the accoutrements of Irish grief for the brave Irish queen whose only goal now was to postpone collapse.

The Eucharist of the Resurrection, as the transformed Requiem Mass must now be called, is resolutely hopeful; white vestments, hymns of muted joy, ritual movements hinting at eternity. She yearned for the black and purple of the burial Masses for her parents. She did not want to hope. She had not hoped since she found the cold body next to her in bed. There were no grounds for hope. She would never hope again.

Irish she might be in her repression of public grief, but Catholic she was not in her repression of private hope.

Not a bad epigram. After all, she had gone back to college after her children were raised.

Father Reid sang with a rich baritone voice, hitting the notes perfectly, better than most priests. The Gospel was from St. John. The Lazarus story. Read at her father's Mass and her mother's, too. "I am the resurrection and the life."

Hope challenging me even when I don't want it.

"Where is Lazarus among us today?" he began the homily. Nice delivery, good technique. Her speech teacher at the Mundelein College weekend program would approve. "Look around you, my friends, where is the man Jesus raised from the dead? He is dead. Jesus is dead. Richard Walsh is dead. We will all someday be dead. Did Lazarus rise from the dead? Have you ever seen him? Did Jesus rise from the dead? When is the last time you saw Him?

"Death is the end of all we know. Life is a temporary interlude between two oblivions. We mark an end here today, the end of the Richard Walsh that we knew. All about which we can be certain is this body which we will soon place in the tomb at Queen of Heaven Cemetery. His life is over. Our lives will be over soon. The lives of everyone who has gone before us are ended. Including Lazarus. Including Jesus.

"Thomas Merton says, 'That widow's son, after the marvel of his miracle/he did not rise for long, and sleeps forever.'

"Is there anything else besides sleep forever after death? Any pie in the sky when we die? The answer is that we do not know. We must not deceive ourselves about this. There is no solid reason to believe that life is strong enough to survive death. If we live with the self-centered hope of personal survival, then we will not accept our social responsibilities in this life. We will flee from the challenges of this world to naive daydreams about the next world. We must dedicate ourselves today not to any foolish hopes of seeing Richard Walsh again, but rather to living as Jesus did and dying for the cause of justice and peace as Jesus died. There is no other way to give meaning to our brief interlude of life."

She stopped listening. No, he wasn't exactly a conservative.

She did not want hope. Neither, however, did she want her Church to tell her that there was no reason to hope.

"Death is stronger than life," he was concluding. "That is the only thing we can know with certainty as we say our last farewell to Richard Walsh. In the name of the Father and of the Son and of the Holy Spirit. Amen."

The congregation behind her stirred restlessly. Catholics didn't listen to homilies. Someone had said that a priest could announce that a hundred virgins would be sacrificed to Moloch next Saturday at dawn and there would be no reaction from the people in church. However, the congregation seemed to sense that there was something not quite right about this homily.

Still, pious old women, like herself in a few years, would

swarm up to the handsome young priest and congratulate him on his wonderful eulogy.

In the sanctuary, the other priests seemed untroubled.

"They're used to shit like that," Rick whispered. "Nothing a priest does surprises other priests anymore."

She did not tell him to shush. They all should be angry, she supposed, but they were too tired.

She sank into a passive lethargy, a protective coat sealed by numbness, through the rest of the Mass, the ride to Queen of Heaven, and the procession into the chapel; there were no graveside ceremonies in Catholic cemeteries anymore. They interfered with the work schedule of the gravediggers.

"Merton ends the poem," Ellen's husband Steve murmured to Peggy, "'And learn the endless heaven/promised to all the widow church's risen children.'"

She nodded, not knowing just then who Merton was or what poem Steve was quoting. The Church is a widow like me? Maybe someday I'll find consolation in that.

The mourners gathered around the casket in the chapel and waited patiently for Father Reid. Old Mr. Crawford, the undertaker, who had buried both her parents, finally stumbled up to her. "Father Reid said that one of the other priests"—he nervously fingered the rim of his formal hat—"could say the final prayers."

Awkwardly she took the prayer card from his hand. Her head whirled, her stomach churned, she was about to float away into peaceful oblivion.

"Monsignor Branigan," she said in a loud, clear, controlled voice. "Would you say the prayers for us, please?"

"I'll be honored, Margaret." He waved off the card. "When your eyes are as bad as mine, you memorize the prayers."

More laughter. Mugsy laughter. Dear God, Mugsy, you bring laughter everywhere.

With laughter comes hope. I will not hope.

But it's hard to resist it.

The final act was what Brendan called the "afterwake," a sumptuous buffet lunch in a wood-paneled restaurant dining room at the Oak Brook Mall. On Saturday someone's wedding banquet would be in the same room. Death and sex. Maybe Father Reid was right. Maybe there was nothing else in the universe. He didn't mention sex, of course. Too much hope in that perhaps.

"Mother," Ellen whispered in her ear. "Should you ask one of the priests to say grace before we begin to eat?"

"Monsignor Branigan," she said automatically, "will you lead us in prayer?"

The old priest stepped up to the microphone at the center of the head table. "I don't know about leading in prayer, Margaret. When I was a young priest only Protestants did that. But I will say grace. . . ."

More laughter.

"Not that there's anything wrong with Protestants."

Yet more laughter.

"Some of the best football players at Notre Dame are Protestants."

Applause.

"Not Irish either. To say the least."

Louder applause.

The old priest paused, groping for a word, perhaps for an idea. "This isn't a very good day. I baptized Dick Walsh, I married him, I buried his mother and father. I baptized these wonderful kids of his. I wonder why God gives me forty years more than he gave Dick. It doesn't seem fair. . . ."

The dining room filled up with silence, like a balloon filling with air. It was a different line for Monsignor Mugsy.

"He was one of the finest men I have ever known. A great football player at Notre Dame; and his kid, this big galoot Brendan here, is on their tennis team. They had a better record than the football team this year. . . ."

Uneasy laughter now. Was the old man wandering?

"There's always next year for football teams. Always next

year for us. Even after we're gone." Behind the thick glasses, Mugsy's blue eyes were watering. "I don't know. We heard a lot of talk at Mass about life and death. Well, I've had more of life than any of you, more than a lot of you put together. If I've learned one thing in these ninety-odd years, and it's the only thing that matters, it is that life is too important ever to be anything but life. Well . . ." His train of thought seemed to leave him. It didn't matter. "Bless us, O Lord, and these . . ."

To a person, the Walsh clan rose with a standing ovation. The rest of the dining room joined them at once. Tears pouring down her face, Peggy Walsh embraced the weeping old priest. The two of them sobbed in each other's arms.

Now there would be grief, mourning, agony. Beyond that she could see life continuing to be life. She would be all right.

❧ Paula ❧

"Good morning, Sister." Ms. Walsh smiled her sweetest Women's Altar Guild president smile, trying perhaps to match the brightness of the potted bronze mum on her desk. "Lovely day, isn't it?"

Paula needed all the emotional restraint acquired in the novitiate and all the intellectual discipline learned in law school to control her response. "Are there any messages for me?" she asked, her voice even, neutral, professional.

Someone should tell the woman that, widow or not, she should not display potted plants, with their funeral-home smell, on the reception desk of a serious law firm; probably none of the men in the firm would have the courage to do so.

Peggy Walsh, too vain to wear her glasses until she was forced to read, fumbled nervously with them, slipped the temples through her carefully coiffed silver hair, and searched anxiously among the disorderly stacks of paper on her desk. "I think there were two calls, Sister." Her elegant fingers, an expensive ring on each hand, trembled as she shuffled the papers. "And one last night after you left the office."

Dear God, give me patience, Paula pleaded. And protect me from becoming a dithering old woman at fifty-two.

"Here we are, Sister." Fingers still trembling, she handed over to Paula three pink message sheets, lost treasures rediscovered; her delicately made-up face beamed as it must have when she placed the crown on the Blessed Mother in eighth grade.

"Thank you, Ms. Walsh." Paula glanced at the notes: all calls from women, three more cases, either discrimination or sexual harassment. Would the oppression never end? "Incidentally, I thought I was to be Ms. Flynn or merely Paula during work hours? I'm not ashamed of being a nun, as you know, and certainly not ashamed of my vocation to defend the rights of women in court. But it is improper for me to be treated differently from any other woman lawyer our firm might employ."

I hope I don't sound patronizing, she thought.

Peggy Walsh blushed, a show of embarrassment she had doubtless learned as an adored and pampered little girl. "I'm sorry, Sis . . . Miss Flynn. Old habits die slowly. . . ."

"Ms. Flynn." Paula walked briskly away from the reception desk and down the thick beige carpet—appropriate for a highly priced bordello, she had once complained at a partners' meeting—to her own deliberately spartan office.

Women like Walsh were victims, she thought as she lit her first cigarette of the morning, not all that different from those for whom she pleaded in the courtroom. But the Walshes of the world didn't know they were victims. That made them part of the problem. Peggy Walsh's attractive, late-middle-aged face and trim, well-preserved body, encased in closely fitting designer dresses, confirmed every male lawyer in the firm in his figure-ogling chauvinism. Widow as sex object. Jim Foley merchandising his lovely and now available sister-in-law at the reception desk as surely as though he were auctioning her on a slave block.

All right, the poor woman's husband had died suddenly, she had never worked a day in her life, she had married too young to finish college, she was confused and frightened in her first "job." I sympathize with her grief, Paula told herself, but I resent the false consciousness which makes her a willing participant in her own objectification. She doesn't need the money. She is taking it from some poor black or Hispanic woman who does need it and could record telephone messages efficiently and accurately.

One of her rings could feed a third-world family for a month.

Paula punched the number on the first message slip. She pulled her weight in the firm, a small but very prestigious partnership specializing in litigation. Some of her work was pro bono, but the courts were now making awards for sexual harassment and job discrimination, which turned such cases into a profitable legal specialty. There was not the slightest suggestion of favors for the big, solid nun—"no nonsense from her closely cut hair to her flat-heeled shoes," the *Sun Times* feature writer had gushed—who worked hard for everything she received. There was a different standard, however, for the fragile, beautiful little widow.

She was definitely part of the problem.

"The number you have called, nine-five-three, two-nine-six-seven, is not in service," a computerized voice screeched in her ear. "Nine-five-three, two-nine-six-seven is not in service."

I must be patient, she told herself as she ground her cigarette into an ashtray. The woman is a victim even if she doesn't realize it. So is the woman who tried to call me this morning and will never receive my return call. What if she loses her nerve because she thinks I have rejected her?

"Ms. Walsh," she said softly in the phone. "The message for me from Ms. Brand. Are you sure you wrote down the number correctly? Was it really nine-five-three, two-nine-six-seven?"

"I think so." The receptionist sounded close to tears, her reaction to the discovery of every new mistake. "I wrote it down somewhere before I put it on the message sheet. . . . Yes, here it is. Mrs. Marian Brand, nine-five-three, two-nine-six-seven."

"The phone company tells me that number is out of service." She kept her voice clinical and nonjudgmental, the way she had learned to administer reprimands in a summer workshop on sensitivity training in the early seventies.

"I'm sorry, Sister." Peggy Walsh, like a high-school sophomore who had broken a vase in the chapel sacristy, was preparing to dissolve into hysterical tears.

Paula pressed her finger on the phone button, cutting her line to the reception desk, lit another cigarette, and savagely punched the second number. The woman who answered asked several questions for a "friend" who had been the victim of sexual harassment. Paula accepted the fiction just as in years gone by she would have listened to a troubled teenager who asked questions for a friend who thought she was pregnant.

She glanced at the next message. God Almighty, a call from Lilian Majewski at the U.S. attorney's office, five o'clock yesterday afternoon! Urgent! I was still here.

Frantically she punched Lil's number. Too late. She was in court. An opportunity lost for a plea bargain which would save a bright black woman from a term in prison on a federal narcotics charge.

"Ms. Walsh," she snapped into the phone. "I was here when Ms. Majewski from the U.S. attorney's office called. Why didn't you give me the message?"

"I don't remember. . . ." A voice rent with terror. "I think I rang your office." Like a little kid trying to find an excuse for a shattered cream pitcher. "You didn't answer."

"I told you I was stepping into Mr. Foley's office and that I was expecting Ms. Majewski's call."

"I don't remember. I'm terribly sorry, Sister, I guess I'm confused. . . ."

"There is a black woman about the age of your younger daughter who will go to prison because of your confusion."

She cut the line and strode down the corridor to Foley's office, reflecting that the corridor would be more appropriate for a luxury hotel.

"Jim, I am moved by the pain in her eyes. I feel terribly sorry for her. But this simply cannot go on."

She told him about the two phone messages.

"She and Dick were so much in love." He drummed his pen on the blotter thoughtfully, as he always did when faced with an unpleasant decision. "Their romance lasted from their first date for thirty-four years till the day he died."

"She's your wife's sister. I don't want to have to bring it up at a meeting, Jim." Somehow women and especially women religious still had to draw the firm line, as in the old days in the parish when pastors turned soft on undisciplined children. "One woman will go to jail. Another may never bring her case to court. It's too high a price to pay."

"You can still work out a plea bargain with Lil." His pale brown eyes turned away from her. "It's not settled yet. . . ."

"That remains to be seen. My point is that we can't continue to take such chances."

"I suppose you're right." He ran his hand through his sparse hair. "I'll talk to her. Let her down easily. You don't mind if she finishes up the week, do you?"

"That's on your conscience," Paula said firmly. "I won't raise the problem at the partners' meeting until next week."

"Thanks, Paula." He folded his hands and stared at them glumly. "I appreciate that."

If you really wanted to raffle off your wife's useless sister, you should have stuck to your guns, Paula thought. You're too weak even to do that. Why do the great male trial lawyers become wimps when they deal with women?

"She wears a mink coat to work, Jim. A receptionist in a coat that even the women partners could not afford."

He nodded, not looking up from his hands. "I asked her about it. She says it's the only decent winter coat she owns.

136

She was going to buy a new cloth coat with her next paycheck."

Such a statement was too absurd to merit a reply.

"She graduated summa cum laude from high school," he continued, the softness of his lean face hinting at nostalgic adolescent fantasies.

"And was doubtless sodality prefect, too, Jim, but that was forty years ago and irrelevant to a gatekeeper position in our firm. We can't deprive some smart young black woman of employment because Ms. Walsh was once a sodality prefect."

"She went back to college after the kids were raised to get her degree."

"It was not in professional competence at a law-office telephone. . . . Jim, I repeat that I feel sorry for her, but that phone is a critical gate and she's an inept gatekeeper."

As she had said during her interview on Channel 5, why must I devote so much of my ministry at this firm to challenging the flabby conscience of my self-described liberal male partners?

"Some of our clients"—he wouldn't look at her as he made his final, frivolous plea—"say that her smile out there brightens their day."

"Men clients?"

"As a matter of fact . . ."

"There's nothing behind that smile, Jim. You know that as well as I do."

"Well . . . maybe. Warmth, I suppose . . . "

"We are not"—she rose decisively from her chair—"in the warmth business. We practice the law in these offices."

"You're right, of course." He sighed wearily. Jim Foley could be forced to follow his conscience but never gracefully, like the adolescent boys who used to perform in her high-school plays but were too interested in flirting with the girls to learn their lines.

With considerable difficulty she persuaded Lil to reopen

the plea-bargain negotiations. Then, at the end of the day, she rode down on the elevator with Ms. Walsh. The receptionist carried her potted mum, wilting as was her frivolous and empty existence. Paula noticed that the woman's mink coat had seen better days and felt a pang of sympathy for her. Despite a lifetime of effort to please men with her pretty face and a nice figure and instant submissiveness, Margaret Jane Walsh would return to an empty and lonely apartment, alienated from her own womanliness. Paula, on the other hand, would go back to warmth and support, a nutritious meal and a bottle of good wine, with her sisters in the commune, an authentic community of the sort the religious life had promised in the past but never achieved. Perhaps it was not too late to touch the sleeping consciousness of Margaret Walsh.

"It must be difficult for you to adjust to the idea of a sister working as a lawyer," she said in her woman-to-woman voice.

"You do a lot of good helping those poor girls." Peggy's greenish blue eyes looked up at her, apparently surprised at the offer of friendship. "I think that's wonderful."

She sounded like a high-school senior twenty-five years ago who was about to say that she thought she had a religious vocation.

"The religious life has changed a lot since you were in high school."

"I've often wondered what happened to Sister Mary Inez." Peggy shifted the mum from her right to her left hand. "She taught me in seventh grade."

"I believe she's living in our golden years center." They stepped out of the elevator into the white marble lobby. "The poor woman lives in the past."

Peggy nodded thoughtfully. "She seemed very unhappy even then. I remember once we were supposed to serve at a mothers'-club tea. I wore an apricot dress with white trim. My mother thought it was very nice. Sister lost her temper.

She said I was putting on airs and couldn't help at the tea. I went home in tears. Mom said Sister hated me because I was pretty."

"That wouldn't happen anymore." Paula adjusted the shoulder strap on her heavy cloth briefcase. She always felt embarrassed when someone told her about what a foolish woman had done a long time ago. "We must sympathize with poor women like Sister Inez. They lived under terribly oppressive conditions."

"I'm sure." Peggy seemed hardly to have heard her. Like Jim Foley earlier in the day, she was lost in memories from the past. "I'll never forget the hard, angry light in her eyes as she ridiculed my dress."

"Poor woman," Paula repeated, wishing she hadn't started the conversation and looking for an excuse to escape. Was there not, after all, a statute of limitations on offenses committed by frustrated and exploited women long ago?

Peggy turned toward her thoughtfully and considered her the way she would stare at a creature in the primate house at Brookfield Zoo.

"I'm afraid I have to run. . . ." Paula tried to escape the woman's searing eyes.

Another elevator opened and disgorged a swarm of men, automatons rushing blindly for their commuter trains; Peggy whispered something softly.

"I'm afraid I didn't hear you, Ms. Walsh." Wishing she had a cigarette, Paula leaned closer.

Peggy's brow knotted in a frown as though she were trying to work out the final word in a crossword puzzle.

"Your eyes, Sister, are just like hers."

⚜ Deirdre ⚜

She would not have been so angry, if his mildly lecherous flattery had not slipped underneath her armor of grief and self-pity and wounded her with a stab of pleasure. Delight, guilt, remorse, fury—she was conscious of the shameful infection as it coursed through her soul.

Fury more at herself than at him.

"What's so amusing?" A light question as she walked across the waiting room of the law firm to her desk, trying to hide her embarrassment at his frank assessment. I must not lose my cool. Be self-possessed, aloof, but courteous.

At first he never smiled when he came into the firm. It took her two weeks to persuade him to move his lips a little—part of her job, she felt, was to bring a bit of brightness and cheer to the clients. She had learned the skills of a darting shaft of sunlight slowly at first; she did not often feel like she could be sunlight for anyone. Now she was a competent professional receptionist, she could make almost anyone smile. Not very sophisticated or complex competence, but a beginning.

Dan Carlin, lean, silver-haired, saturnine, somber, was a

140

special challenge. He did not have much to smile about, poor man. After two weeks she managed to extract a faint movement of lips from him. "Good morning, Mrs. Walsh. Do you think the Bears will win next Sunday?"

"Good morning, Mr. Carlin. Have I been wrong yet?"

Then the twitch of lips. "Infallible, except for Miami."

"I don't claim expertise on Monday-night games."

Then another slight twist of lips. Twice in one morning. I'm making progress.

Now he's staring at me like he wants to chain me with his eyes and smiling like a father watching a two-year-old daughter totter across the room. I'm scared and flustered. Have I overdone it? Does he think I'm flirting?

"Since you ask, you're amusing."

Carefully she placed the stack of computer output on the desk—half of her time now was devoted to an unofficial role as the firm's business manager—and turned to face him.

"Oh?"

"Very amusing." His appraisal seemed respectful, gentle, considerate—like that of an elderly priest for a daffy teenage girl. How could a wife walk out on a man like that after twenty-five years?

Flushed with a warmth she had not felt for a long time, she sensed her defenses slipping away; she liked being appraised by him. "In what respect, Mr. Carlin?"

"Well, to begin with, Peggy"—he spoke softly, slowly, considering every word carefully—"you're very generous with yourself."

"What does that mean?" She reached for her grief, shock, and anger—the thick, familiar cloak of protection under which she had huddled for more than a year. It eluded her. I'm naked like in a nightmare, a very nice nightmare. I don't want this to be happening, but I can't stop it.

"It means"—he considered his slender strong fingers, the hands of an All-American (honorable mention) basketball player thirty years ago, before he turned to the Mercantile Exchange and made his money—"that your compassion for others despite your own grief is enough to make a person want to cry."

Oh, dear God, he's going to proposition me. And it won't be ugly or disgusting like the others. I went too far. He does think I was flirting.

Was I?

"It's an epidemic, Peggy," Nick Barry had said to her. "Women her age realize they are getting old and think they have little to show for their life. The husband is an important person in the big world, sometime president of the Merc, and they're no one, not in their own little world, now that the children are all raised. They need somebody to blame; the husband is a perfect target because he is the closest target. Even if, like Danny, he has encouraged her to develop her own talents. So they walk out because they want to live 'a life of their own.'"

I never felt that way, she had thought. I didn't want a life of my own. I have one because God took my man away. I live by myself in a cold inhuman skyscraper and shiver and cry myself to sleep every night.

At least she didn't complain about it aloud; she'd learned through the months that no one liked a widow's rage or self-pity. The cold doesn't leave you, but you pretend that it does so you won't be a bore.

When Sister Paula had tried to fire her without consulting the other members of the firm, she had stood her ground firmly but without anger or self-pity. She felt certain she would lose. Sister Paula was a partner, she a receptionist. Somehow she had won. Poor Sister stormed out of the office shouting words a nun should never use.

"That's very kind," she stammered in response to his praise. "Grief ought to be absorbed inside instead of being imposed on others."

That's right, take refuge in platitudes when you should

pick up your stack of computer paper and retreat, with calm dignity, somewhere else, anywhere else.

"And you're so wonderfully lovely, too." It was his turn to stammer; he was losing his cool as his emotions raced ahead of his words. *Poor man. I* have *led him on. I didn't mean to. At least I think I didn't.*

Their firm did not handle divorce cases. Nick Barry, who had played basketball with him long ago, was rearranging Dan Carlin's estate planning now that the divorce and annulment were out of the way, a process which she thought was being deliberately prolonged so Nick could keep an eye on his anguished and confused friend.

"You must have swallowed the blarney stone when you were in Ireland." *I could escape the anguish that's coming if only he didn't look so happy. He's going to speak words that we will both regret for a long time.*

"So when you caught me looking amused"—he strove to be smooth, casual, relaxed, and was not quite successful— "I was pondering the very pleasant subject of how . . . how elegant you would look with a lot less clothes on. . . ."

She was swept up in a wave of shame, sweet, languid, enervating delicious shame. And the first distant hint of sexual arousal, as her body strove to remember long-unused reactions. She realized how useless her armor had become. Her firm resolution to avoid sexual involvement for the rest of her life disappeared. "Grandmothers don't date," she had firmly told her daughters. "Why can't I take a vow to be a consecrated widow?" she had demanded of the priest at the Cathedral.

The young man merely laughed. "You're not the type, Peggy. Not the type at all."

He's been stripping me in his imagination was her first thought. *And I'm delighted that he likes me* was her second thought. *Dear God in heaven, where is my anger? I am too old and I've suffered too much to be inspected this way.*

"Do you think that is an appropriate comment, Mr. Carlin?" Her voice was shaky and her hands trembled as she snatched up the computer output and hugged it protectively to her breasts.

He had blurted out his praise of her sexual appeal; already a grimace of regret twisted his face. "I'm sorry if I've been offensive. I didn't mean to—"

"Do you think it proper to strip women mentally in a law office?" She had found her anger at last.

"Only breathtaking ones"—he tried to grin—"and only with the greatest admiration and respect."

"So you turn only some of us into sex objects?"

Thank God for feminist rhetoric.

"I don't think you're a sex object, Peggy." He was staring at his fingers again. "And I didn't mean to be offensive. It sort of slipped out."

"It's called sexual harassment." She spat out the words; now that she had controlled her pernicious self-satisfaction, she was truly furious. "Do you think a man of your age should be looking at a woman like . . . like she was so much meat on hoof?"

Dear God, I sound like Sister Paula.

"Am I a dirty old man, Peggy?"

He looked so sad that she thought her heart would break for him. Poor dear, lost man.

"You sound like one."

"I don't consider you meat on hoof; men admire women like you, Peggy." He twisted his hands miserably. "If I didn't desire you, I'd be old and dead. My imagination isn't dead quite yet."

She almost said that she wished she was fat and ugly. But she held back the words. First of all, they weren't true. Why then would she be working out for an hour every day? Secondly, there was enough Irish superstition in her to consider the possibility that as punishment God would grant that wish.

"I believe the old name for that, Mr. Carlin, is lust. And the new name is objectification. Under either name I find it repellent."

He smiled sadly, touching her wildly erratic heart. "Neither seem to be accurate names for what I feel, but please forgive me anyway."

"All right," she said grudgingly, trying to think of an excuse for running. Then to make sure that he did not think she was weakening: "I trust there will be no more propositions in this office."

"Was I propositioning you?" He gazed out the window at the Merchandise Mart across the street. "I don't think I was. Well, maybe I was at that. Not a bad idea, actually . . . Could I make peace"—his eyes returned to her, hurt, contrite, and still fascinated, even resolute—"at dinner tonight?"

"Certainly not." She fled down the corridor to the women's room, where she could sob in relative privacy. And be secure from the possibility of changing her mind.

Why could not God arrange it so that desire dries up after we've raised our children? Why does he burden us with these gross emotions?

Superstitiously she considered that possibility. Might God punish her by depriving her of all passion? And all power to excite passion in men?

Not likely. So she didn't have to worry about her request being granted. Hence she did not formally withdraw it.

And why doesn't he make men less crude in their approach to affection? Madame, may I take off your clothes and ogle and make sport of you? Only an hour or two of my precious time? Tonight please. At your apartment. Wear lace.

Ugh!

The response in the back of her brain which had almost exploded as an instinctive reply, though of course she could never say it, was, "I would love to be standing here with 'a lot less clothes on' and be admired by your appreciative and kindly eyes. Thank you for the wonderful compliment. But this is not the place to talk about such a possibility, is it? Supper? Well, in a public place where I might be reasonably safe"—a mildly provocative smile—"yes, I would enjoy that." Sophisticated, unthreatened, grateful. The kind of reply of which she might have been capable if she had become a slightly different person long ago—a poised and experienced woman of the world.

Classy, responsive, but still noncommittal.

It would drive the poor dear man mad with longing, which is just what he doesn't need now. And I don't need it either.

Still, I almost said it. And I would have turned a corner down a new street that I've never walked before. Irrevocably turned that corner.

I will never do that. Never.

It is so cold. Ought we not store up all the precious moments of warmth that we can give and receive? If the universe is cold, and I often think it is these days, then what harm can the warmth do? And if the universe is a blast furnace of love, as that poor young priest says it is, then our warmth would merge with it . . .

Well, that's neither here nor there. I turned down a proposition and there'll be no more from Dan Carlin. I am indeed a virtuous widow. I humiliated him. Rid myself permanently of him.

She dried her eyes, redid her makeup, drew a deep breath, and prepared to return to her desk. I'm glad, she thought, that I'm having lunch with Deirdre. I won't tell her what happened of course, but she's always fun.

That turbulent daughter-in-law of mine who is my only confidante.

Did he say "elegant"? No, of course not. That was my imagination. No one thinks I'm elegant, fully dressed or not.

Still impressed with her own virtue, she did not peek into the mirror to consider the possibility that a man might rate her as "elegant."

He was not in the waiting room. Either in Nick's office or gone. I hope I don't have to face him again today.

As she pored over the computer sheets and answered an occasional phone call—with her brightest and happiest voice—she confessed contritely to herself that she had hurt the poor man badly. He had not meant to be insulting or chauvinist. He had stumbled into saying the wrong thing. Or at least saying the right thing the wrong way. Her anger had been directed at herself for permitting her head to be turned by a few smutty words. So she had punished him. *Well,* that was his own fault for saying what he did. And she could not apologize without making matters worse. That was that.

She left for lunch with Deirdre promptly at twelve, muttering a prayer of gratitude that she had escaped before he emerged from Nick's office.

Deirdre was already at the table. She watched her mother-in-law cross the dining room, with the pug nose in her pert, mobile little face turned up even higher than normal.

Why is everyone critically appraising me today?

"Wow!" Deirdre kissed her. "The heads are really swiveling today when Peggy Walsh walks in!"

"Deirdre!" she said reprovingly.

"What happened to make you look so satisfied with yourself? Some rich, handsome geek proposition you?"

"I really don't think that's an appropriate comment," she said stiffly, knowing that whatever the contentious little brown-haired, brown-eyed child's virtues were, they did not include restraint in her spontaneous remarks.

"Come on, Mom, you've always been a classy broad. And now that you're working out and looking radiant like you do today, you leave a trail of sexual allure wherever you walk. Like a mare in heat. All the men and half the women in this place turned to watch you. And it's not just that blue knit dress, though it helps. Not bad for an old gal. Not at all."

"I'm not a sex object, Deirdre." She focused her attention

on the menu. I was offered a little warmth today and instead I chose the cold. I listened to words and missed the meaning. I was asked for a slice of bread and I gave a stone. I chose the old pain rather than run a new risk. Not that much of a risk either. Not really. Foolish old bitch. Slammed the door shut on the poor man. Permanently.

"Hell you're not."

"That part of my life is over, dear. I don't want to discuss it."

"If God wanted to pull you out of the sex game"— Deirdre raised her hands like a street peddler negotiating over two pounds of apples—"He wouldn't have given you such pretty boobs." She rolled her eyes appreciatively. "To say nothing of the rest of you."

Deirdre and Rick had become religious as the result of some program in their parish. The young woman's approach to the God she had discovered or rediscovered was unique, to say the least. Her God seemed to have sex on the mind a lot of the time, if not all the time. (An observation which, when repeated with protest, had caused the young priest at the Cathedral considerable amusement.)

"Deirdre! *Please!* That's altogether too personal!"

"Come on, Mom." It was practically impossible to offend the girl. "You want me to say you don't have a cute figure? What's the matter with your generation anyway? We're made with bodies, right? And hormones? Don't tell me that you don't have any. Why fight it? If you don't like the way you're put together, complain to God, not that it will do you any good. Personally, I'm glad He gave me a body. I'd be even gladder if mine was as outstanding as yours—and you not taking care of it much until now—but I'll make do with what I have."

"I don't think we should talk about such things." Dear God, can I possibly be that much of a prig—not that it's going to stop her. Or even slow her down.

"I should be so lucky when I'm an old dame." A tiny

hand reached across the table and squeezed Peggy's. "No bullshit, Mom; you're a threat to traffic these days. You must drive all those male lawyers and clients out of their frigging minds. Send them up the walls of their offices with great fantasies. The old biological imperative or whatever. What's Peggy like with her clothes off? Is she any good in bed? Wouldn't it be fun to find out?"

"Deirdre!"

"Nothing wrong with thinking it"—the wise old child winked, utterly untroubled by her mother-in-law's dismay —"so long as they don't mess around."

"Most women my age—"

"You're not"—Deirdre waved her hand—"most women your age. Hey, you don't have to do anything with it; that's up to you. But, face it, you're a knockout and you're going to attract men. Nothing bad about that."

"I didn't use to be—"

"You are now." She jabbed her index finger at Peggy. "And don't try to pretend you're not. Men daydream about you in bed with them, even younger men. Real young men, my age." She beamed mischievously. "Can't blame them. Luscious old broad. If I were a man"—she considered her mother-in-law critically—"I think I'd want you in my bed."

Sometimes Peggy suspected that her daughter-in-law's apparently spontaneous outbursts were carefully prepared homilies.

"Thanks, darling." Her face was on fire. "That's a very kind, if rather, uh, clinical compliment."

"Clinical, shit. That's the way men think, God bless 'em for it, should you ask me, which I know you didn't. If things had to wait till we got around to being stirred up, it would take a hell of a long time and then where would we be? A lot less fun and games, let me tell you. But like I say, I should be so lucky when I'm an old dame. The thing is"—good little terrier that she was, Deirdre never let a bone out of her mouth—"it's not just working out, though that starts the

149

juices flowing again, it's that you're beginning to let yourself be happy. That makes you devastating."

"You mean shedding ten pounds."

They laughed together and relaxed.

"So I'm proud of you."

"The loss never goes away and maybe the grief doesn't either, but you have to be happy for others and for yourself."

"That's what life's about."

"I knew that all along. It took time to work it out."

"Classy old dame." A touch of fingers this time. "Naw, that's not the right word. Let me see, graceful? Well, yeah, but not quite right. I got it! Elegant! Today, Mom, you look elegant. And sexy as hell."

"Thank you, dear . . . now tell me how are my son and grandchildren."

"Yeah, they're great as always. The guy improves with time, you know? Great raw material. Needs a little polish now and then. Fact is we had a big fight last night. His fault this time, so help me, a hundred percent . . . well, maybe sixty-five. Don't look nervous, Mom, it'll be fine tonight, better than ever."

"I do admire how you two handle conflict," she said, perhaps too primly.

"Handle, shit . . . yeah, we'd like to order. I'll have the spinach salad and my sister here will do the fruit, with cottage cheese, of course. Decaf for her and iced tea for me. What was I saying, oh yeah, fighting with the guy. Look, the way I figure it, God has really done a nifty thing with us. I mean, He could have made us so that we only get one chance, know what I mean?"

"I'm afraid not." Her heart was beating rapidly because she knew that the little imp child was about to say something very important, perhaps decisive for the rest of her life. And, truth to tell, she did know very well what Deirdre meant.

"Well, like if the guy and I fight, which we do a couple times a week, what happens? The next day or that night when we're going to bed, we kiss and make up, well, usually a little more than kiss, know what I mean? It's not like, one chance, and if you blow it, that's that. I mean, you know, we take second chances for granted. You blow something, like I do all the time, so there's another chance real soon. Next week at the latest. It doesn't have to be like that. Pretty clever of God to give us second chances, you know? Nothing ever lost till it's really lost."

"Pure grace."

"Right." She grinned crookedly. "Well, sometimes not all that pure, but still grace."

The temperature had slipped below the zero mark while she and Deirdre were eating. The wind was howling down off the lake and down Madison Street as she returned to the office on LaSalle Street from Fields. Three blocks each way, six blocks altogether, three-quarters of a mile. If she should walk home, that would be another mile. More virtue.

But it was so cold.

Back in her office she sat at her desk, still shivering. A blast furnace of love—that's what the young priest at the Cathedral had said. How could a God who was a blast furnace of love expel her into the cold?

She considered the appointment book but did not open it.

To be angry at God, the priest had replied, is to acknowledge his power and his love.

The cold was better than the warmth, less risky.

Windchill factor forty below at least.

She had felt that windchill for more than a year. Now she was being lured deviously back toward the risk of the furnace.

No. I will not be tricked again. I will stay in the cold.

Can I get away with that?

Absently she opened the appointment calendar to Nick Barry's appointments for the coming week. An apology?

The door she had slammed shut might still be ajar. Possibly? Maybe? Nonsense, of course it was. Next week at the latest? She smiled complacently to and at herself. How clever of the blast-furnace God to give us tough, loving little daughters-in-law like Deirdre.

And second chances.

❧ Andrea ❧

T he first time I saw her—I remember the date
well, July 22, 1946—in the railroad station cafe in Tucson, I
thought she was a ghost.

Hoagy Carmichael was singing "Old Buttermilk Sky" on
a wheezy jukebox.

"She's dead." It was a fleeting impression, recorded in a
brain dazed by habitual depression, a lifetime of bizarre
romantic fantasy, months of terrifying nightmares, and a
night-long drive across the desert: milk-white skin, pale
blue eyes, slender ethereal body, slipping past the chairs and
the tables, with a heavy cardboard piece of luggage in one
hand. She approached the counter and sat down across
from me so quietly that no one seemed to notice her. She
had to order her coffee twice before the waitress was aware
that she was sitting at the counter.

She looks like she's from beyond the grave, I thought, and
then tried again to dismiss the impression.

She was too young and too pretty to be a ghost, I told
myself. Ghosts don't have dark red hair shaped like a crisp
halo around their high, intelligent foreheads. They don't

153

have gracefully swelling breasts and they don't move lithe young bodies with unself-conscious grace.

Why not? my gloomy imagination wondered.

She laid a dime on the sloppy counter next to the coffee cup which had been slapped down in front of her with such vigor that some of the dismal liquid spilled into the saucer.

Why can't ghosts be gorgeous? I asked myself, not quite ready to give up my grotesque fantasy. I was driving from San Diego to Chicago in one last romantic binge before I settled down to college and law school and River Forest affluence. What would be more appropriate than to meet a pretty ghost on the first leg of the trip?

From the perspective of four decades I can understand why someone would think I was asking for trouble.

"It's fifteen cents." The slovenly waitress wiped the counter indifferently with a dirty towel.

It was already hot in the station. My guidebook said that in summer the usual thirty-degree variation in Tucson temperatures continued—between eighty and a hundred and ten. And during the monsoon, it added helpfully, humidity added to the discomfort caused by the heat. Monsoons, I thought, happened in India. And whoever heard of a humid desert?

I had a lot to learn about this country I was exploring for the first and probably the last time.

The young woman reached into her worn purse and almost furtively searched for another coin. She withdrew a second dime, one of the tarnished "war dimes," and laid it next to the first. The waitress scooped them both up and replaced them with a nickel.

An elegant hand reached out to reclaim the nickel and then, it seemed to me shamefully, retreated, leaving the tip for the waitress, who would certainly not be grateful.

Sexual desire, which had deserted me somewhere between Hollandia and Okinawa Jima, made a faint, furtive, and very tentative reappearance. She was dead tired, lonely, a little frightened, and broke.

I had ten crisp hundred-dollar bills in my wallet and a checkbook which could duplicate that many times over. Perhaps I could help.

Her brown skirt and white blouse were wrinkled—all night in coach—and shabby. The leather on her low-heeled shoes was cracked. Her hair was rumpled. Yet she drank the coffee, black the way it should be, with natural elegance. And she was young, painfully, desperately young; certainly not twenty yet, which from the heights of my almost twenty-four made her virtually a child.

With a child's innocence softening the lines of weariness on her gently curving face. And a hint of pain which no child ought to have suffered.

Four decades later I can still feel the sting of need which accompanied my sentiments of tenderness.

Then I saw the thin gold wedding band, little more than Woolworth jewelry. To my shame it must be confessed that the recognition had no impact on my sexual longing.

"Your husband in the service?"

Startled, she glanced around, uncertain that I was speaking to her.

"He was on the *Indianapolis*."

A sentence of death. No wonder the terrible pain in her soft blue eyes.

"I'm sorry."

She nodded, accepting my sympathy. "I hope he died on the ship before the sharks got to them."

"What did he do?" Navy talk to cover the awkwardness and the sorrow. Somehow my intentions became, if not completely honorable, at least more respectable than they had been.

"Radar." She reached into her purse. "He said that electronics training would guarantee a job after the war. Even better than civil service." She opened a cheap wallet to show me his picture. A towhead in high-school graduation pose. "He was only nineteen."

"Classmate?"

"Year ahead. I was a junior when I married him."

Just barely legal age. In some states. Probably had not graduated from high school.

"I'm sorry." What else could I say?

"What kind of plane did you fly?"

It was my turn to be startled. How did she know that I was a pilot?

"F6F."

"Hellcat. What ship?"

"Enterprise."

She raised an auburn eyebrow. The Big E was a legend. "Lieutenant?"

I spread my hands in fake humility. "Gold oak-leaf type."

She smiled and Tucson disappeared for a couple of moments. "Impressive."

"Survival."

I wanted to tell her everything. She would understand. I hated the killing and the dying. I missed my friends who had crashed into the Pacific—Saipan, Leyte, Yap, all those other places which had even now blurred in my memory. But I also missed the roar of engines, the surge of power as my Grumman lifted off the deck, the sky dark with our fleets of planes, the excitement of battle, the triumph of return, the fierce yank of the arresting gear as I touched down on the deck, then the horror of counting noses. . . .

"A trip across the country before you settle down?"

"And begin to grow old." Did she read minds?

"Real old-timer." She smiled again; her teeth were fine and even, like her delicate facial bones. She was a natural beauty, needing neither makeup nor expensive clothes to strike at your heart.

"The war made us all grow up too soon." I pushed aside my plate of soggy pancakes. "I wish . . . I don't know what I wish."

"I wish," she said, and finished her coffee, "I had my husband back."

"Let me buy you a real breakfast." I stood up from the counter and walked around to her other side.

"That isn't necessary." She clutched her purse. "I'm not hungry."

I picked up her suitcase. Heavy, probably all her worldly goods. "Yes you are. I don't have any . . . well, bad ideas."

She considered me very carefully, her eyes probing at my soul like a doctor's exploring scalpel. "You do too, Commander, but you won't act on them, will you?"

"Not at the breakfast table."

"Nor with an enlisted man's widow. All right, sir." Yet another smile. "I'll admit I'm starved."

Four times she had read my mind. I thought it odd, but not frightening, much less dangerous. Only later would I try to fit it into the whole strange picture of Andrea King, if that really was her name.

We walked up Sixth Street and turned into Congress. Tucson was not much more than a small town in those days, thirty thousand people according to an old almanac I checked while I was thinking about this story. East of the railway there were blocks of adobe homes, slums for Mexicans. In the other direction stretched neat lines of bungalows with withered grass lawns—home designs transplanted from New England or the Middle West. Why would anyone want to live in this furnace? I wondered. Humid furnace at that. As I drove in at sunrise on Highway 86 I passed the sleepy red-brick University of Arizona. It would be on the bottom of my list.

Yet the desert mountains all around—the Catalinas looming to the north, the lofty Santa Rita's on the south, the Tanque Verdes to the east, and the Tucson mountains to the west—held my attention: barren desert mountains, not a bit like Fuji. But American mountains, thank God. And hence dear to a man who had decided after Yap that he would never live to see America again.

The hotel was better than the railroad station. The tables were clean, the service friendly and polite, and a primitive form of air-conditioning was huffing away.

"This town will never amount to much." I held the chair for her.

"Until they put air-conditioning in every home."

"That will never happen."

"How can people live in brick homes in this weather?" I sat next to her and picked up the menu.

"Did you notice the homes with the walls all around them? I suppose that's the Spanish emphasis on privacy."

"You wouldn't have to wear much behind those walls."

"I bet they do."

She ordered orange juice, bacon and eggs, pancakes, and coffee and demolished the meal with quiet efficiency.

"Not hungry, huh?"

"Very hungry, Commander."

"Jerry. You're?"

"Andrea. Andrea King. Where are you going next?"

"Down to Colossal Cave and over to Tombstone, then up to Phoenix, probably by way of the Superstition Mountains."

"What are those?"

"Where the Lost Dutchman Mine is supposed to be. I'm curious."

"Yes. I know. Is that any relation to the *Flying Dutchman*?"

"Who's he?"

"An opera about a sea captain who is doomed to roam the world forever without ever finding port."

"I don't know much about opera."

But she did. And she hadn't graduated from high school.

"Where are you going?" I asked.

"Phoenix. I know someone who thinks she can find me a job. Waiting on tables in one of the winter resorts. They call it the Arizona Biltmore."

"Can I give you a ride?"

158

"I don't think . . ." She considered me again, even more cautiously, over a fork of syrup-drenched pancake. "That would be very nice. I don't have much money."

I was not a total innocent. She should have insurance and a pension. But the navy department was slow. She'd run out of the money she'd saved from John's family allowance, which was sent routinely while he was still alive.

I didn't pry. It was none of my business why she had left San Diego or why she hadn't been able to hold a job there. And the questions I asked about her background were gently deflected. She was from "the east"; she didn't have any family; she didn't know what she would do with her life. Probably try to finish school when she had saved some more money. No, of course, she didn't mind if we detoured to the Cave and Tombstone before driving up to Phoenix. The job, she had been told, was waiting for her whenever she came.

A thin but not improbable story. I was not inclined to question it. An hour before I was an ex-naval officer struggling with depression and wondering what point there could be in the rest of my life. Now I had a beautiful young woman to protect and care for.

At almost twenty-four that is enough. Even if the young woman is smarter than she has any right to be.

And even if there is something just a little strange, almost uncanny about her.

That's the right word. Uncanny. Andrea King was not quite of this world. In the back of my head even then I think I knew that. I did not want to pay any attention to what I knew.

I glanced at the *Arizona Star* on the newsstand in the hotel lobby. SEVENTY-SIX DIE IN JERUSALEM HOTEL BLAST! I bought the paper. Zionist terrorists had blown up the King David Hotel. I no longer asked when the killing would finally stop. I knew it would never stop.

"Why did they give you the Navy Cross?" she asked as we

walked into the thick soggy curtain of heat on Congress Street.

"Philippine Sea. I saved some TBFs that were in trouble. Zeros."

"Does that help?"

"Some American women are not widows—if the TBF men made it through the rest of the war. Some Japanese women are."

Immediately I regretted the harshness of my reply. It did not, however, seem to bother her.

"We didn't start the war."

We turned down Stone, almost as though she knew where my 1939 Chevy ($799 FOB Detroit) was parked.

"How did you know I got the Navy Cross?"

"I guess," she said, tilting her head to glance at me ruefully, "that I'm a pretty good guesser."

She stopped next to the battered blue car before I did.

"Damn good guesser."

"Only car on the street." She laughed for the first time, a pure, open laugh which hinted that long ago she might have been the life of the sophomore hops at her high school.

A long, long time ago.

"Yeah, but you knew the street."

She laughed again and waited till I opened the door for her. "Thank you."

Nuns, I thought. Catholic high school. I bet they expelled her when they found out she was married. Pregnant? Lost a child?

I rolled down the window of the Chevy and turned to the sports section. The Cubs had lost again. A long way down from the World Series last year. Then the comics. Terry and the Pirates. Smilin' Jack, Dick Tracy.

I looked up. Andrea was smiling at me, a mother watching a funny little baby. Navy Cross and Smilin' Jack. I suppose it was funny.

Her smile quickly faded. "I had a miscarriage after John

sailed. I don't know whether my letter ever caught up with him. I hope it didn't."

"I'm sorry."

She nodded again.

"God provides, Andrea," I said weakly.

"It's not God I'm worried about."

We took the Benson road out of Tucson, across the harsh, brown desert.

"My guidebook says that this was all cattle country till the end of the last century. Tombstone folded up because the silver mines flooded and the ranch land dried up."

She nodded, a favorite gesture, conveying appropriately different reactions. God, she was lovely. I was glad that she would be with me for the day.

"Did you work in San Diego?"

She'd been a waitress at the Del Coronado Hotel after it reopened. She was not very good at it. Couldn't concentrate. Too many memories. Too much navy. She thought she should start over somewhere else. They had been very nice to her, but she couldn't exist forever on pity.

"I used to drink there occasionally. I'm sure I would have remembered you."

"After how many drinks?" Her laugh, I decided, was pure magic.

"Touché. But you are the kind I would remember, even drunk."

"If we're going to exchange compliments, Commander, I think I would remember you, too."

Young and innocent, but somehow experienced and wise. I thought I might just be falling in love with Andrea King.

And I would have remembered her if I had seen her at the Coronado.

So I didn't say much on the road to Tombstone. Just short of Benson, U.S. 80 branches off from Arizona 86 and heads due south. We slowed down to twenty-five miles an hour on the outskirts of St. David.

"Mormon town." I glanced over at her. She seemed far, far away from southern Arizona.

"Tell me about Tombstone." She shivered. "It's a frightening name."

I told her about the Earps and the Clantons, and the McClurys and the gunfight in 1881, all memorized from my guidebook.

"How terrible."

Tombstone was even less impressive then than it is now. Wyatt Earp had yet to become a TV hero, and the old town had yet to discover it could squeeze a few extra dollars a year from tourism. I pulled up in front of the Post Office Café on the main street.

"Want another cup of coffee?"

She was staring out the window, seeing neither the Post Office Café, nor 1946 Tombstone.

"Andrea?" I said gently, touching her arm, the first of what I was beginning to hope would be many touches.

"I'm sorry . . . what did you say?"

"Do you want a cup of coffee before we do the OK Corral?"

"No . . . Commander . . . uh, Jerry . . . do you mind if I stay in the car? I'm afraid of this place."

She huddled against the door; her body was tense, her face tight with fear.

"It's just an old western ghost town." I took her hand.

"Please."

"Of course."

The OK Corral was a disappointment—just a yard next to a house. Reality so much more bland than story. But I explored Tombstone with a singing heart. A new challenge had entered my life to replace war, just as war had replaced flight training and chemistry and basketball. Pretty, haunted young women were, I told myself, the best excitement yet.

She was still crouched against the door, now reading a

book. *All the King's Men.*

"Good book?"

"Very. About politics and corruption. I'm sorry if I disappointed you."

"The sights on this tour are an option. We'll get you to Phoenix 'fore sundown, ma'am."

"Silly."

She was still terrified.

Colossal Cave did not help any. If anything, the entrance frightened her more than the streets of Tombstone.

"I can't go in there. I'd die."

She sounded like she meant it.

"You don't mind waiting?"

"Of course not."

The cave was dark and slimy and disappointing.

"Not very scary at all," I said as I climbed back into the car.

"I would have died," she repeated as she closed the book and laid it next to her—and between us—on the front seat. "I'm sorry."

"Don't be. It's nice to have someone waiting."

She didn't smile or nod. Still scared.

She did get out of the car at the old St. Xavier Mission— the "white dove of the desert"—and walked into the church with me. She fell on her knees in the back of the dark nave and prayed fervently—like someone pursued by demons, I thought. Outside, she pleaded to be excused from visiting the tiny cemetery next to the church and scurried back into the steaming car.

"What frightens you?" I tried to keep my voice soft and reassuring as I started the old Chevy.

"Everything."

I didn't pursue the matter.

As we drove away from the mission, she grabbed my arm—first time and I hoped not the last. "Those clouds over the mountains!"

Great black clouds were piling up behind the Catalinas; huge, ugly, threatening thunderheads building up strength for a mad rush down the side of the mountains and the foothills and a slashing attack on Tucson.

"I'd hate to have to fly through them. But they're only thunderstorms. Typical late-afternoon phenomenon here."

Her fingers dug into my arm. "Please . . ."

I pulled over to the side of the road and turned off the ignition. "Please what, Andrea?"

She turned her head and looked at me sorrowfully, tears forming in her eyes. "Please . . . do we have to drive through them?"

"Not if you don't want to."

"Leave me at the bus station. I'll go to Phoenix tomorrow."

"Do you really think I would do that?"

Her stiletto eyes considered my soul again. "No."

"There's a wonderful old resort on the edge of the city, called the Arizona Inn. We could swim and have a decent meal . . . I forgot about lunch, didn't I? . . . separate rooms, Andrea King, different wings of the Inn."

"I trust you. . . ." She hesitated. "I'm not proud enough to say no to a place where I can take a shower."

"I'm thoroughly trustworthy." I patted her arm and started the car.

"Not thoroughly, but sufficiently." She laughed through her tears. "I'm sorry that I'm being a nuisance."

"I'm not."

Later when the storm had swept through Tucson, leaving big puddles on the street outside the Arizona Inn, I walked into the swimming pool area, a copy of the *Tucson Citizen* under my arm. Had to read the evening comics, too.

Andrea King was already in the pool. She was neither a strong nor a skillful swimmer, but she cut through the water with the grace that characterized everything she did.

I sat down on a deck chair and opened the paper, waiting

164

eagerly for her to climb out of the pool. In a swimsuit, she would be sumptuous.

And she was even more than that. Her rich, full womanly body, encased in a white, corsetlike strapless suit, demanded to be embraced and loved.

A demand that I resisted with the mental note that my long vacation from sexual feelings was certainly over.

"You take my breath away," I admitted as she spread out a towel and sat on the tiles next to my chair. The loudspeaker played "Tenderly," then "How Are Things in Gloccomora"—just for us.

"A cliché, Commander, but thank you anyway . . . this is a lovely place. So few people. Summer, I suppose. That man looked like he thought you were crazy when you insisted on separate wings."

"Maybe I am."

"Not really." She shook water out of her hair. "Reading comics?"

"Almost illiterate."

"You are *not*."

She leaned forward, arms around her legs, tops of her wondrous breasts pushed against the swimsuit.

"I want to live, Commander."

"I should hope so." I touched her shoulder, still wet from the pool. Her fingers took possession of mine, not so much to fend them off as to hold them.

"If I were better educated, I could say it more clearly . . . now don't tell me I'm smart. I know that. But I'm still uneducated. . . . I wanted to die. I still want to die most of the time. But inside me there's something stronger that tells me I want to live, something as powerful as the ocean or the sky."

"Will to live."

"I suppose. I've thought about killing myself." Her hand relinquished mine and her fists knotted fiercely. "I've given up so often. John . . . the baby. But I can't and I won't and

165

it's almost not up to me. . . . Do I make any sense?"

"Yes."

What would have happened if I had taken her into my arms then? I'll never know. Not that it matters.

"I won't give up. I won't quit."

"I know that."

"And you're thinking about how much fun it would be to take off my swimsuit."

"I am *not*!" I felt my face flame, because of course I was.

"Yes you are, and that's all right, too. Except that wet suits are not so easy to remove. Now do your swimming and cool off."

So in the fading daylight, while she finished Robert Penn Warren's book (which she had started in Tombstone), I struggled through a half mile and wondered who she was.

And why, despite living in San Diego for a couple of years, her skin was so pale.

At supper she wore a sleeveless white dress, matching white shoes, nylons, and a tiny gold cross at her neck. There was, I suspected, an iron buried in her cardboard luggage.

The wedding band was still on her finger.

We ate steak and pan-fried potatoes and drank red wine and laughed like two people who were falling in love ought to laugh. I have no recollection of what we said, so it could not have been of any moment. She was, I thought, a charming dinner companion. I had about made up my mind—after fifteen hours—that she was the woman for me.

In her white dress, she seemed innocent, virginal. Innocent she might be, but virginal, of course she was not. She had slept with a husband, conceived and carried for a time a child, suffered twin losses. And was afraid of demons I did not understand.

I do remember the conversation over our chocolate ice-cream sundaes.

"I think, Andrea King, that God sent me to take care of you."

The big spoonful of chocolate-drenched ice cream stopped in midflight and then returned to its goblet.

"Don't say that."

"Why not?" I tried to laugh it off. "I think it's true."

"It is not true." Her lips, normally generous, narrowed into a thin hard line. "I don't want to hear it ever again."

"I'm sorry if I made you angry."

"It is *not* true." Hands pressed together on her lap, she pushed her chair back from the table. "God did *not* send you."

Unaccountably she was furious.

"If you say so . . ."

"Maybe"—the steam seemed to hiss out of her anger—"I'm the one who was sent."

"I'll gladly agree to that." I reached for one of the hands.

"And maybe . . ." She pulled the hand away. "God shouldn't be blamed for that."

There was an awkward pause. She was still angry but beginning to regret her outburst. I was baffled.

"Don't let your ice cream melt."

She laughed happily. "You're wonderful, Commander."

"When you smile at me that way, I think so, too."

"Irish." She dug into the sundae with renewed vigor. "You're incorrigibly Irish."

"You deserve the best, Andy King, if that's your real name, which I doubt."

"The best?"

"Clothes, homes, food, drink." I filled her wineglass again. "Cars, jewelry, children, lovers, everything."

"Why?"

"As a setting for your beauty."

"That only earns you something if you're willing to sell yourself. I'm not."

"I don't mean economically." The drink, as my mother

167

would say, had loosened my tongue. "I mean artistically."

"If I were better educated . . ."

"You would agree with me completely."

We laughed together and the world seemed right in a way it hadn't since St. Mark's won the West Suburban grammar-school basketball championship ten years before.

After dinner we sat alone on the terrace, in the still, dark night, and sipped coffee—still black—and Napoleon special reserve brandy. I was happily in love and she was preoccupied.

"We both need sleep. Neither of us had much last night."

"How did you know that?"

"You drove all night, didn't you? Besides, you're so old, you should get your sleep."

I hadn't told her that I drove all night. But it didn't matter.

"I'll walk with you to your room in the other wing."

"That will be nice."

It took us some time and much tipsy laughter to find the right corridor.

At the door of her room, in the dimly lit and suggestive pastel hallway, I kissed her forehead. She lowered her eyes. "Good night, Commander, and thank you."

"Thank you," I said, and departed, full steam astern, if you please.

If I had invited myself into her room and into her bed, she would not, I thought on that stern run, have resisted. But we had a whole lifetime ahead of us. Why should I rush her?

I was, after all, trustworthy, if not completely trustworthy.

Only as I was falling into a happy, if slightly inebriated sleep, did I wonder who she thought had sent her into my life. If not God, then who else?

She was quiet and reserved at breakfast the next morning. I wondered if I had offended her the night before. Perhaps she had expected me to make love to her. She was, after all, sexually experienced, probably much more than I. I had treated her like a seventeen-year-old virgin on a prom date. Perhaps she was disappointed and frustrated.

She had given no sign that she wanted me in bed with her, had she?

How would I know what the signs were like?

And pushed by the demons of curiosity which had almost landed me in naval intelligence instead of in the cockpit of an F6F, I made my cursed phone call after breakfast to the manager of the Del Coronado.

"No, Commander, we have not employed a woman named Andrea King since we reopened. No Andreas and no Kings. Not at all, Commander, glad to help."

Right.

I gave the cashier one of my hundred-dollar bills and waited for the change.

"Very lovely young woman, sir." He had a leathery cowpoke's face. "Terribly pale, isn't she?"

"Pigmentation," I murmured.

"When she talks and smiles, you don't notice, but before that you wonder if she's stepped out of a coffin."

I checked the remaining bills. Nine of them all right. "Doctor says she has very sensitive skin. Should stay out of the sun."

Already lying to protect her. Andy King, or whoever she might be, was lonely and alone. She needed my protection. Everything else would take care of itself.

I noted that her blouse was clean and her skirt neatly pressed. There was certainly an iron in the luggage I had hefted into the backseat of the Chevy.

She was not wearing her thin wedding band. What did that mean?

I was not sure I wanted to think about that subject.

"Where are your Superstition Mountains?" she asked as I reached for the ignition of the Chevy.

169

"Between Florence and Phoenix. I'll drive you to Phoenix first."

She hesitated, closed her eyes, and murmured, "Why do they have such a strange name?"

"Maybe because they look so strange; there's lots of legends about ghosts and Apache thunder gods." I picked up the guidebook next to me and opened to the page where there was a picture of the Superstition range—stern, foreboding volcanic tuffa which seemed to warn you to stay away. "They are a bit intimidating, aren't they?"

She opened her eyes, looked at them, and shuddered. "How terrible."

"Just dactite rock."

She crossed her arms in front of her breasts, huddling from the cold which the mountains seemed to radiate for her. "That's where your Dutchman is?"

"And your Dutchman wanders around on a ship, wandering around singing melancholy Dutch songs!" I touched her arm in cautious reassurance. "Weird people, the Germans!"

Her face relaxed in that wonderful smile, as though I had pushed a button. "Aren't we Irish terrible bigots?"

I gulped and leaned back against a seat. "Has anyone ever told you about your smile?"

"No." She was watching me suspiciously. "What's wrong with it?"

"It turns out all the other lights."

"The Irish are terrible indeed." And she smiled again. I was captured. Years of celibacy, partly voluntary, partly involuntary, vanished in the mists. I wanted her.

"Tell me more about your Dutchman." She turned, embarrassed by my desires, which she seemed to absorb like everything else I thought or felt. Embarrassed but not frightened or repelled.

So I told her about the pre-Christian Indian mines, and Coronado, and the early Spanish mines, and Peralta's

Sombrero Mine in the shadow of Weaver's Needle, and the Apache massacre, and the survival of one Mexican woman who for a time was "married" to Jacob Walz—the Dutchman. Then I added the more recent parts of the story: Walz's murder of his Mexican workers and eventually of his friend Miez, the earthquake which closed the door of the mine, the floods which the thunder gods sent, rumors of Apache warriors still guarding the approaches to Weaver's Needle, the death of Walz and his legacy of a map to Clara Thomas, a Negro who was an ice-cream-shop proprietor, the search for the mine by Thomas and her friends the Petrasch brothers, the discovery of bodies with arrows in the back, the death of a woman doctor just before the war.

"And you want to find that treasure!" She regarded me with a mixture of terror and disbelief. "How could you?"

"Not really." I removed the guidebook gently from her hand and closed it. "I don't need the money or want it. But since I was a kid and read *Treasure Island,* I've been fascinated by buried treasure." I shrugged indifferently, not exactly having an explanation myself. "It's a great American legend, like Wyatt Earp. And I'm on a great American tour."

"I'll go with you," she said decisively. "I think it's horrible and I'll be scared every moment. But I can't let you go up into that terrible place"—she gestured toward the guidebook—"by yourself. You might get hurt."

"And what would you do then?"

"Well . . ." She actually grinned. "I could drive for help."

"Can you drive?"

"No . . . but please let me come. I promise not to smile too much."

And she smiled again and I couldn't say no. I touched her red hair, glinting in the morning sunlight, and said, "Delighted to have you."

It sounds like the beginning of a romantic adventure story, which is just what I was looking for at that troubled time in my life. But even then it did not quite ring true. I

171

had not forgotten the manager of the Del Coronado. And I had not shaken my strong instinct that this pale, pretty young woman was not quite alive, not the way the cashier at the Arizona Inn and I were alive. She was some sort of in-between creature, a red-haired Irish Flying Dutchman. Or Lost Dutchman. Or lost Irishwoman. Or whatever. Wandering for a time between life and death and seeking my help, even though she knew that I could not help.

It's been forty years, yet I don't think I embellish my memory of that feeling. Why did I not drive her to Phoenix and get rid of her?

Because she was young and beautiful and she needed help and because I was young and I wanted her?

I suppose so. And also because I didn't seem to have much choice. We were both fated, I thought as I drove down Elm Street toward First Avenue and the road to Globe, and that was that.

"Would you mind if we took the roundabout way and saw some mountains and copper mines?"

She hardly seemed to have heard me. "You're the tour guide."

So we lurched across the desert under the scorching sun, sometimes in clouds of dust so thick they reminded me of the morning fog over the Sea of Japan.

In those days, U.S. 89 was paved all the way from Tucson to Phoenix, and Arizona 77 was blacktopped from Oracle Junction to the San Manuel Mines behind the Santa Catalina Mountains. But the rest of the picturesque trip through the Dripping Springs Mountains up to Superior and U.S. 60 was on a "macadamized" road—an uneven mixture of treated gravel and dirt (the sort of highway in which my children resolutely refuse to believe).

The Sonora Desert is a weird place—saguros (giant cactuses with arms raised to heaven in prayer), octilos (trees which produce leaves only after rain, but after every rain), palo verdes (trees with their chlorophyll in the bark), rattlers, sidewinders, scorpions, Gila monsters, tarantulas, an occasional herd of mountain sheep, and once in a great while (so my guidebook said) a solitary mountain lion.

Andrea's moods changed as dramatically as did the scenery. In the barren desert north of Tucson she frowned with disapproval and informed me that she thought the bojimba tree with its skinny finger reaching skyward was "insane."

"Take that up with God. He made it."

"You don't believe in God."

I didn't remember that I had told her about my loss of faith on the carrier. "You do?"

"I wish I didn't."

But in the mountains she twisted in every direction to marvel at the spiral peaks, the occasional Mormon irrigated farm ("like a beautiful green carpet!"), and the indifferent cattle grazing near a wash which provided enough moisture for grass and a stand of cottonwood or oak ("aren't they cute?").

I played the tour-guide role, explaining the formation of the mountains, the history of the Mormons, the reasons that the desert and the grass country often existed side by side, the terrible conflicts between the Wobblies (Industrial Workers of the World) and the copper-mining companies.

"You know everything." It was a statement of fact, neither criticism, nor compliment.

"You know more about literature and music."

"Much good that does."

At the lookout point above the vast Ray Mine between Hayden and Superior we stared in silence at the rusty, tarnished, man-made grand canyon, stretching for miles in either direction.

"Strange but beautiful," she said. "And scary too."

Still a child on a tour, curiosity and wonder not yet dead.

I put my arm around her and led her unprotestingly back to the car.

"People died here." She shuddered.

"It has always been violent. The unions haven't won yet. The Mine, Mill, and Smelter Union is communist. I can't blame them for being radical—"

"Hold me, please." She pressed against me, trembling violently.

Normally I would have relished the opportunity to embrace an attractive young woman. But there was too much terror in that slim frame for me to permit any erotic feelings. Well, perhaps there were a few.

"What should I do?"

"Get me out of here. Quickly."

So I led her to the car and chugged up the mountains, across the sweeping curves and down toward Superior, driving slowly not only because of the dirt road, but because, inexperienced mountain driver that I was, I was scared stiff of the steep canyons that yawned only a few feet off the road.

She clung to my arm until we were safely through Superior and back on the paved road. Then she revived completely as we drove up U.S. 60 through the burnished peaks of Queen Creek Canyon.

"This is the most beautiful place I've ever been!" she exclaimed.

"Please sit still. I'm not used to driving on mountains."

"Yes sir, Commander, sir."

"And stop laughing at me."

"How do you know I'm laughing when you don't even take your eyes off the road to look at me?"

"Shut up."

"Yes, Commander."

Without any exchange of affection, we spent the night (in separate rooms) in the red-brick Pioneer Hotel in Globe; like the rest of the town, the Pioneer was not quite frontier, but not quite postwar either—a somewhat careworn place which had known better days and did not expect to see their like again.

(Mining towns always look poor, even when they are prospering. I saw Globe on TV during a recent strike. I was struck by how little the feeling of poverty had changed.)

Despite the musty, acrid smell of the room, and the hard mattress, I fell quickly to sleep, exhausted by my struggle with the mountain roads. Sometime during the night, a few hours later perhaps, the dreams came again—thousands of men screaming as their battleship rolled over and died, then my own comrades who had perished because of my orders and my mistakes.

I woke up, drenched in sweat, although the temperature had fallen and it was cool in my room.

Terrified and hungry—for a woman, not food. I knew, or thought I knew, that she was waiting for me. I clenched my fists and said no. I may have lost my Irish Catholic faith, but I had not lost the accompanying morality.

Or inhibition.

After a silent and soggy breakfast, we walked, at my suggestion, along Broad Street—a two-story, brick Masonic temple stood across the street from the hotel, a depressing department store next to it, an old Southern Pacific station farther down.

"I could put you on the train to Phoenix . . . "

"Of course not," she snapped. She didn't seem to have slept much either.

She was wearing the white blouse (doubtless laundered overnight) and white tennis shorts. She had, as I noted before, beautiful legs, and, with an extra button on the blouse open, wondrous breasts.

"I should put on slacks before we leave?"

"Might be a good idea. Rattlesnakes."

"On this tour?"

"Can't promise them, but we'll try."

A long period of silence as we stared thoughtfully at the SP station. I tried to break it.

"It would be horrible to live in a place like this, wouldn't it?"

"Do you really think so?"

Across from the station, at the top of high steps, was a squat Romanesque church—Our Lady of the Angels.

"Can we go in?" She nodded toward the church.

"Why not?"

A priest was finishing Mass, polishing the chalice after Communion. There were twenty or thirty people scattered in the pews. The inside was modest but tasteful. Some of the names in the stained-glass windows suggested a Czech past, but the priest's Latin did not hide his Irish brogue.

I stood at the back while she kneeled in one of the pews and bowed her head in what seemed to be fervent prayer.

"Were your prayers heard?" I asked as we walked back down the steps.

"No."

That was that.

The old priest was standing on the street corner in front of the tiny white rectory next to the church. He saw us and strolled over.

"Sure, if I knew we were going to be after having visitors, wouldn't I have started a few minutes later so you could have received Communion?"

"Would you have?" I said, playing the rules of answering a question by asking one.

"Would I not?"

He chatted pleasantly for a few minutes, asking where we were from and where we were going and, clearly convinced that we were on a honeymoon, cheerfully wishing us a lifetime of blessings.

Andy hung back from the conversation, apparently afraid of the kindly old man.

"Why didn't you talk to the poor man?" I asked as we walked back to the hotel.

"Why should he talk to someone who is already damned?"

"If I believed in God, I know he wouldn't damn you."

"I wish I could escape from believing in Him."

"The friars taught us in high school that no one is damned till the end of their life. You're still alive. So you're not damned."

"Oh?"

So we drove out of town, back toward the "twin" of Globe, the even less prepossessing town of Miami. Just short of the town, we turned left off U.S. 60 and down the unpaved tracks of Arizona 88 toward Roosevelt Lake and the "back door" to the Superstition range.

"More dirt roads?"

"That's all there is today. This is the Apache Trail, named after the Apaches who built Roosevelt Dam at the turn of the century, the first big reclamation project in this country."

"Yes, Professor."

Since the road down to Piñal Creek Canyon is relatively straight, I took my eyes off it for an instant to make sure she was laughing at me.

She was.

"If you don't like the tour, you can get off and take the stage."

"Stage? You mean one of those horse-drawn things? That would be even worse than your driving."

She was still laughing. Damned but capable of being amused by a foolish boy child.

"They don't use horses anymore. The picture in the hotel suggests a very old motorbus. Before the war it went through to Roosevelt from Phoenix. Now it stops at Tortilla Flat."

"What?"

"Not the place in the novel."

"I'm glad. How far is it to this stage stop?"

"Maybe fifty miles. It's only a few miles beyond Fish Creek, where Clinton is. That's our ghost town. In Lost Dutchman Canyon."

"So I have to stay with the tour till then, Commander?" Now she was chuckling loud enough for me to hear her.

I hunched the old car to the side of the road, turned off the ignition, and took her into my arms. "We seem to have forgotten something last night."

She did not protest or resist, but permitted me to smother her with quick, delightful kisses. "The more you complain"—I paused for breath—"the more I kiss you."

"Maybe I'll complain all day. But then," she said with more laughter, "you won't be able to kiss me and glue your eyes to the next curve, will you?"

"Just watch me."

I was quite sure that there would be no more kissing till Tortilla Flat. If then.

So I tried for a whole day's kissing. This time she returned my enthusiastic affection.

"You like to be kissed," I observed.

"By you."

"Why?"

"You're a good man."

"And a poor kisser."

"No, Commander." She considered me thoughtfully. "A pretty good kisser, too."

Reluctantly I released her, started the car, and lurched back on the highway. The words *I love you* were on the tip of my tongue, but did not quite break free.

We continued through the grass and oak toward Roosevelt Dam.

"It's so much like in the movies," she said, again a little girl admiring the cattle standing patiently in the shade of the trees.

"You haven't seen anything yet."

At the Tonto Monument, I halfheartedly suggested that we climb up to the ruins of the Pueblos where the *salados* (the "salt people," after the Salt River along which they had lived) had moved when unfriendly tribes invaded the flood plain.

"Please, no." She quivered more violently than she had the day before at the Ray Mine. I began to think that, delectable lips or not, I would be happy to get rid of her in Phoenix. She was too odd to run the risk that I might fall in love with her.

I realize now, after four decades, that lost soul or not, I had already fallen in love with her.

We admired the shimmering blue lake ("I could stay here forever," she sighed), inspected the dam, mostly masonry, but impressive for the early part of the century, and turned up 88 toward Fish Creek.

While I would not dream of returning to the Tonto National Forest, one of my kids—the woman doctor— went to Arizona on her honeymoon. She reports that the upper half of the Apache Trail has not changed. It's still a one-lane dirt trail clinging dubiously to blood red, rust brown, and burnished gold cliffs with smooth blue lakes below and soaring mountains above. I was too busy watching the road to enjoy the scenery very much.

"What happens if a car comes in the other direction?"

"There aren't many. We may not even see one today."

"And if we do?"

"One or the other backs up."

"Marvelous." My tourist with the sweet and willing, even eager lips, had turned sarcastic.

"Sorry."

"Why are you going up here?" she demanded impatiently. "I thought you were taking me to Phoenix."

"The Flying . . . I mean Lost Dutchman Mine. Remember, we talked about it yesterday."

"You think you can find in a few hours what others have hunted for decades?" Her lips curled in withering contempt. "You're a bigger fool than I thought you were."

"I want to be able to tell my kids that I looked for it, if

179

only for a few minutes. And saw Clinton, the Dutchman's ghost town."

She did not choose to respond to such foolishness but instead curled into a tight, hard knot, turned away from me, and ignored both the tour and the tour guide.

You wonder if you are still on earth.

The Superstition Mountains earn their name. While the colors and the sweep of orderly ranks of mountain ridges are stunning, the general effect is still to create a feeling of the uncanny—huge rocks poised over the dirt road as though they were ready to plunge down on you; steep, dark canyons; mad hairpin turns; brooding mountains which seem ready on an instant's notice to become dangerous volcanoes again. The foothills of hell, perhaps. Any evil that could be, might be here.

We paused for a picnic lunch on the side of Apache Lake. I carried the thermos of water and the oranges and bread I'd bought in Globe and she brought the cheese and meat and the blanket I had stored in the trunk of the Chevy.

We clambered down the side of the mountain on a steep and barely visible trail.

"It's a good thing I didn't wear my shorts. The cactuses are as bad as rattlesnakes."

"It would be a shame to scar those pretty legs."

"I think you've been a virgin too long, Commander."

It was true enough, but nasty of her to say it.

"After a while you hardly notice. Like being a priest."

"You're not a priest."

"My brother is going to be one."

"Does he know you don't believe in God?"

"No."

He would laugh it off, as my clever, witty younger brother Patrick laughed everything off. I dreaded telling my parents I would not attend Mass with them. But there was no point in being a hypocrite.

We found an oak tree clinging to the side of the lake,

spread the blanket, and settled down for the picnic. She made the sandwiches, with the quick gracefulness which characterized all her movements. We ate them slowly, tasting the water and munching on the oranges. We were alone, the only two people existing in this strange, twisted cosmos of God-made mountains and man-made lakes.

"You'd like him." I nibbled on an orange slice.

"Who?"

"My brother Patrick."

"Priests scare me. I'm afraid that they know. Do you think they do?"

"Know what?"

"That I'm already damned. You know it, don't you? I'm sure your brother does."

"That's silly, Andrea King, just plain silly."

Again I almost told her I loved her. Life might have been very different if I had.

"Is it?"

We sat there for a long time, each of us with our own thoughts, our own fears, our own hungers. I was in no hurry to assault the road again, a more frightening experience than diving into the antiaircraft fire of the Japanese destroyer which was trying to run down some of my ditched squadron mates.

I studied the lovely, slightly bent figure next to me. It dawned on me, unpardonably late, that she was not so much angry at me as frightened. She hated and feared these mountains and had come with me only because she thought I needed protection. A squadron commander with a Navy Cross and Star needed protection!

Well, maybe I did. It had been a couple of years now since the tiff with the destroyer, years in which my imagination had had time to learn how to reflect on possibilities.

No longer did I resent her sarcasm. I felt only tenderness for her generosity. A dangerous emotion, tenderness.

"Is the lake cold?"

"I don't think so. It's probably in the seventies."

"Too bad we didn't bring our swimsuits. It would be nice to jump in. Is it deep?"

"Sure. The walls of the lake are an extension of the canyon walls. I'd hold you."

"I'm sure you would."

"We could swim in our underwear."

"No."

"Why not?" I reached over and opened the two remaining buttons on her sweat-soaked blouse. She remained rigid, neither accepting nor rejecting.

My fingers touched the flesh of her breasts, warm, inviting, reassuring.

Gently she removed my hand and said the same words as at the Tonto Monument. "Please, no."

"No," my wife tells me, means no except when it means yes or maybe. She also insists that a man who knows his woman understands the code.

I didn't know either my woman or the code in 1946.

If I had persisted that day, I might have found that her no meant only maybe. I did not persist, perhaps because the strange mixture of terror and eagerness on her tense face spooked me. I buttoned up the blouse, including the one she had left open in the morning.

"Sorry."

"Don't be. I'm flattered."

Finally, as silent as the watching mountains, we scrambled up the canyon wall to my patiently waiting and overheated car.

I inched past Castle Mountain, away from the lakes and up the walls of Fish Creek Canyon. The eighteen-inch guns of the *Yamoto,* blasting away at us till the bitter end, were less dreadful than the steep drop of thousands of feet which seemed just a few inches outside the window.

"That's Castle Mountain on the left, Miss—oops, Mrs. King," I said through gritted teeth. "Doesn't it look like a blood-red medieval fortress with turrets and towers and battlements?"

"No."

"Well, what does it look like?"

"It looks like a mountain trying to look like a medieval castle with . . . watch out . . ."

I'll admit we skidded a little.

"Nothing to worry about." The sweat was pouring off my forehead like the thunder gods were pouring water on me. Cool Jerry Daugherty, never frightened in combat. Right?

"Are you scared, Commander?" Her fingers dug into my right arm.

"Sure am."

"Good." She sighed in mock relief. "Then I don't have to be."

The turns and curves became a little bit less spectacular as we drew near the side road up Fish Creek Peak to Lost Dutchman Canyon.

And today's batch of ominous thunderheads were already building up—dark, fierce, angry.

Ought I to call the game on account of darkness? Did I want to drive down this mountain goat's trail in a storm? Or after it had turned into an instant river with treacherous waterfalls?

Take her on to Phoenix before dark. Be done with her.

The F6F pilot with his Navy Cross tucked away somewhere, not quite sure where, lose his nerve and turn back?

I would, instead, compromise.

"We'll look at the ghost town for a few minutes and then come back. It's maybe a half mile up from here," I said to my reluctant tourist. "It's called Clinton; most ghost towns have Anglo-Saxon rather than Spanish—"

"Ghost town!" she screamed hysterically.

"Relax, Andrea King, if that's your name; ghost towns don't have ghosts. They're just old abandoned mining towns. Relics of the past."

She changed her tactics. Instead of the hard knot at the

far end of the front seat, she became a soft little girl, clinging to my arm as she had at the worst of the hairpin turns. Notable improvement.

"Sorry."

"What I like is a satisfied tourist."

She laughed and I laughed, too. Contagious enthusiasm.

One glance at the "road" marked on my map, jutting off at right angles from Arizona 88, told me that we could not drive it. I parked the car close to the wall of the mountain, turned to her, and tilted her chin up. "I'm afraid we'll have to walk. Do you want to wait here? I'll be back in an hour."

"I'll come with you, Commander. That's why I'm here."

"Lost Dutchman Canyon," I told her as trudged up the tilting path, "is a long way from Weaver's Needle, where the mine is supposed to be. But a considerable lode of gold was found up here a few years after the Dutchman died. Clinton was founded to extract the gold, and later on, after it closed down, the name was given to the canyon."

"Oh." She accepted my helping hand and held on to it. "Why did it close down?"

"Various reasons. Earthquakes. Rainstorms which flooded the mines, revenge of the thunder gods, if you believe the legends."

"There's still gold?"

"Probably not. The veins were running out anyway."

"Can't blame the thunder gods for that, can you?"

Ghost towns don't have ghosts, right? I mean, you can buy a book even today in any Tucson bookstore and read all about the ghost towns and never read a word about haunting. Ghost towns are so called because they are dead towns, not because they have the spirits of dead people.

Keep that in mind.

If you've ever visited an Arizona ghost town, your first reaction, very likely, is disappointment. Just a few old buildings without any roofs or windowpanes, vegetation growing through the floorboards, an occasional sign tilting at a crazy angle, wind maybe rustling loose clapboard, an occasional small creature darting away in righteous surprise that its haven has been invaded, broken pieces of what might have been furniture littering the land between the buildings.

Not much.

You think to yourself that it's hard to imagine that anyone ever lived here and that Hollywood could build better ghost towns than Arizona has.

Clinton produced exactly that reaction after our long and exhausting pull up the trail. It was nothing more than four broken-down buildings, three small ones, and another larger—a town hall, tavern, and hotel all rolled into one, according to my guidebook.

"It doesn't look very scary." She released my arm, but still snuggled close to me as we stood at the top of the ridge looking at the remains of Clinton.

"It isn't. Do you want to stay here or explore with me?"

She looked up at the sky, now a threatening gray. "I want to stay with you."

Tentatively I extended an arm around her shoulders. Her poor little heart was pounding wildly. She cuddled close to me.

Oh.

"Clinton, Arizona, or Arizona Territory, to be precise. That canyon was a stream fifty years ago." I pointed to a deep gorge behind the pathetic row of fading shacks, Lost Dutchman Canyon. "They came up the mountains on the same road we did, then down the side of that mountain, and pitched their tents and put up these buildings here. They prospected in the stream and in the caves on the side of the canyon. They found a vein of silver and other people poured in. They sank mine shafts all over the place. We're supposed to be careful not to put our foot in any of them. They're not like the coal mines back in the east. Nor the one in the Museum of Science and Industry—"

"What?"

"I'm sorry. You're not from Chicago. I keep forgetting. Where did you say you were from?"

"I didn't."

"Well, anyway, the mines here are mostly narrow shafts sunk straight down into the earth. When the miners left they covered the holes in the ground with boards, most of which have rotted by now. So don't step on any boards on the ground."

"Yes sir."

"Well." I ignored her laughter. For someone who thought she was damned, she could certainly laugh at me. "Although the vein was a good-size one, they exhausted it pretty quickly with modern mining methods, and then everyone left. Whether this was the Dutchman's lode or not depends on which legend you believe."

"How much time did you spend with the guidebook before you left San Diego?" Her eyes glinted briefly with amusement.

"Two weeks." Damn it, she had made me blush again. "I like to be prepared. . . . Anyway, they had a lot of sickness, too. Something like typhoid fever, though a little different. The canyon was supposed to be an ancient Apache sacred place. Couldn't have been too ancient, because the Apache only came here in the seventeen-hundreds, after the Cherokee chased them out of Texas and Oklahoma, where they were herdsmen rather than rustlers. Anyway, one story says that before each new outbreak of the disease, a huge black cloud came to the town at night. Not much regret when Clinton closed down."

"Poor people."

"Any poorer than us?"

"A lot."

"I suppose."

We walked along the creaking remnants of a porch on the front of the main building. She stumbled on a loose board and I held her close.

"You're right. Hollywood could do it better."

I kicked open the loosely hanging door of the main building. A mouse or some other small creature rushed across the floor, stirring up a cloud of smoke behind him.

"Dust," she said, "decades of dust. There must be an inch of it on the floor."

"In the desert, that could be only a year's collection."

"Do you want to go in?" she asked respectfully.

"The commander does not want to go in." I hugged her shoulders. "Not at all, thank you very much."

A bolt of lightning leaped from one of the immense mountains behind us, jumped across the sky, and buried itself in another mountain. In the distance thunder rolled grimly. Andrea threw her arms around me in abject terror.

"Don't worry, Andrea King," I said, trying to sound like the squadron leader of VF 29. "I'll take care of you. Always. If you give me a chance."

I touched her face. It was cold, cold as death, I thought, even though the gray sky and the occasional raindrops had not cooled the air.

"If only you could . . ."

Protectiveness turned without warning to passion. My lips sought hers again, much more violently than earlier in the day, my fingers searched for her breasts, our bodies pushed together. She was mine for the taking. I pushed the blouse off her shoulders.

She pulled away from me.

I stopped. Not this way. Not here.

"Sorry," I said. "I didn't mean to . . ."

"My fault," she replied miserably.

"My fault . . ." I insisted. Then we both laughed and relaxed. "I do love you."

"Don't say that." She laid her fingers on my lips. "Not yet. Not ever."

"Let's get out of here." I readjusted her blouse and fastened the buttons for the second time, realizing that if she had not stiffened, I would have had to unhook her bra and I had no idea quite how that was done.

"Thank you, Commander." Her marvelous blue eyes danced with mischief.

Later in the night, in the midst of the horror, I had the strange feeling that none of it would have happened if I had made love to her at that moment—not in the first wild rush of passion, but in the magic of our eyes dancing happily with one another. Or maybe it was the other way around. Maybe if I had not stirred up our passions as the storm closed in on us, the thunder gods would not have been angry.

Because I didn't believe in God, it did not follow that I did not believe in the thunder gods.

"I think those corsets you swim in would come off very easily, even if they are wet."

"That's because you never had to take off a real corset." She rocked back and forth in laughter. "Though you would enjoy every uncomfortable, frustrating second of it, wouldn't you?" She leaned her head against my chest. "Maybe God did send you, Lieutenant Commander Daugherty. If he did, he has good taste in angels."

"I don't believe in God," I said somewhat testily. "I told you that."

"Maybe it doesn't matter to Him." She jabbed my ribs and discovered I was ticklish.

"I *will* take care of you, Andy." I touched her face gently with my fingers. "Please believe that, at least."

We strolled, arm in arm, back to the Chevy—two strong, happy young people rejoicing in the prospects of life ahead of them, hardly aware of the half mile of rough mountain trail down which they were stumbling.

I must insist on that point. Whatever sense of doom she had felt since Hoagy Carmichael and the train station, and I had felt driving up the far side of the Superstition Mountains, had vanished. Neither of us sensed evil closing in.

I opened the door of the Chevy for her.

"Thank you, Commander, sir . . . no, wait a minute, please, Jerry. Let me apologize for having been so boorish. You're a good and kind and wonderful man. You should never have adopted me the day before yesterday. I should never have come along. Regardless of that, I'm not as bad as I've behaved."

I went around to the other side, noticing that the first torrent of rain was racing along the gorge toward us.

I turned the ignition key over. Nothing happened. The Chevy had its temperament, but it always started. I pulled out the choke, cranked the gas pedal once, and flipped the key again.

"That's funny," I said. "It always starts."

The rain was on us, plunging the inside of the car into midnight darkness.

"It's coming for us," she said calmly. "Don't worry, Jerry, I'll take care of you."

Whatever it was, it came all right.

The doors of the Chevy swung open as though a giant had flipped them open as he raced by us. Wind, I told myself.

It wasn't wind, however, which grabbed the two of us, hurled us out of the car, and carried us through the air, like parachutists in free-fall, back up the half mile of steep trail, as the thunder boomed and the lightning crackled, and toward the main building and through the door, which opened just before we slammed into it.

I must be careful here. That's what seemed to be happening. My images are as vivid as though it all happened yesterday instead of forty-two years ago next week. But they are not like any other memories from a life which has not been devoid of excitement. The images are real enough, but whether they ever had any reality outside my head even during that terrible storm on the side of Fish Creek Mountain, I do not know.

Ask me today and I will say it all happened. Ask me tomorrow and I'll tell you it was just a wild and especially vivid nightmare.

Anyway, we were swept into the main building of the ghost town of Clinton and our hell began.

The thick black cloud was there already, licking its chops in anticipation. We were both slammed against the wall across the room and pinned against it, a couple of feet off the floor. Invisible hands jabbed and poked at us, the way Indians were supposed to torture their victims before killing them. For a few moments I saw Andrea twisting and turning against the wall, then she was lost in the inky darkness. Her screams continued for a long time. Then they, too, stopped.

What happened next seemed like the whole of eternity. In fact, it lasted at the most only a few hours, and maybe only a few minutes. It was like being tumbled down the side of a mountain in a landslide of nightmares, yet the experience was more real than any nightmare and not so much less real than being awake as being a different kind of real.

My nightmares and Andrea's fused and consumed us both. I was being destroyed by these combined nightmares, and even if I could no longer hear her screams, she was being destroyed with me.

My first accusers were the men I'd lost in VF 29—Rusty, Hank, Tony, Marshall, all the others. They circled around me, their dead distorted faces and empty eyes fading in and out in the blackness, screaming curses and accusations. I had cut short their lives, stolen them from their wives and sweethearts and from the children they never knew. I had sent them all to hell.

I shouted my innocence, I had tried to protect all my men, war was hell, casualties were inevitable, I had done my best. . . .

Either they did not hear or they did not care. They were dead and in hell and I was still alive.

And the heat of the wall to which I was pinned became with each accusation more like a frying pan.

Rusty turned into a tiny baby, gurgling helplessly as he was held under water; Tony changed into a sailor half of whose head had been shot away. They, too, accused me of cutting short their lives.

"I didn't kill you," I shrieked. "She did!"

So much for taking care of Andy.

My betrayal did not save me, the screams of outrage continued, my frying pan was now white-hot, the invisible hands tormenting me became more insistent and determined.

Then the new dead were replaced by the old dead—brown-skinned, primitive people from long ago; Spaniards; Apaches; other Indians; Americans; my relatives from Ireland; men and women whom I did not recognize, from her past, not mine.

The Dutchman was there, a horrible grin on his ancient bearded face. And Peralta and Miez and the Mexicans the Dutchman had killed. And the victims of the Apache massacre. And Clara Thomas—all the people in the legend, all come back to judge me guilty of their deaths.

They all died horribly, tortured, scalped, raped, butchered, ravaged by disease; men burned at the stake, women cut into tiny pieces which were then roasted over campfires, children whose heads were smashed against the rock walls of the canyon.

They all accused me, I was the master murderer, the true Hitler of all history. I was the death which had slain them all.

"No! No!" I screamed. "I didn't do it! She did! She is death, not I!"

As I try to recall those psychotic images, an exercise which has fascinated me for forty years (my wife says that I'm the kind who can't keep his tongue off an infected tooth), I think that even then the one or two sane cells that still were working in my brain wondered when the Japanese whom I had undoubtedly really killed in aerial combat would come to accuse me of their murder.

They never showed up, make of that what you will.

The dead and the dying faded into the blackness and the blackness itself slowly lifted, to hover like the threat of pestilence beneath the ceiling. The dead returned to dance.

They whirled and spun, leaped and cavorted, jumped and gamboled like they were celebrating a graveyard Mardi Gras, all the time performing unspeakably lascivious acts on each other. I was pulled off the wall, like a prize trophy, and made to dance with them. Why not? I would soon join them, if I had not done so already.

Did I believe that the horror was more than illusion when it was happening?

Then and now. It was not illusion. It was as real as the Compaq 286 on which I am setting down the story of Andy King, or the first chapter anyway.

Maybe the horror was on a different plane of reality (whatever that means) than my microcomputer, but it was still real. More real.

Why am I alive then? Why did I receive a several-decade—still indeterminate—stay of execution?

I don't know. Not for sure. Anyway, they didn't get me that night in the Superstition Mountains. Or, obviously, I wouldn't be writing this story.

The dead left me, with a strong promise that they would be back in a little while. I was again pinned against the wall in total blackness. I shouted for Andrea, but she did not or could not reply.

Then I heard a clink beneath my feet, coins falling on the floor. Despite the darkness I could see the glint of gold. Hundreds, then thousands of gold coins piled up beneath me, around me, rising rapidly to my throat. I was being buried in gold.

I pleaded with the horror to spare me. I had not come looking for gold.

But you did, the darkness screamed, you wanted to search for the mine of the Dutchman.

Only as a joke.

The clinking stopped.

Then the Dutchman again. Not the Flying Dutchman. The Lost Dutchman, though he did not think he was lost. And he wasn't lost. It was the mine that was lost.

Jacob Walz was only dead.

He was a tall cadaverous old man with a bald head and a dirty white beard. He told me where his mine was. All the searchers are totally wrong about where it might be.

More gold than in South Africa and Russia put together. A mountain, quite literally, of gold. I know exactly where it is.

Why haven't I gone back to get it? I don't need it. I don't want it. And I wouldn't return to the Superstition Mountains for all the gold in the world.

I stayed away from Arizona for thirty-five years. Then, on a vacation to Vegas with my wife, we flew down to the Grand Canyon for a couple of days, both of us hating Vegas. By the end of the trip, the compulsion to drive down to Phoenix was almost irresistible. I barely escaped back to Vegas, which seemed a paradise of sanity and rationality.

No, I'll never go back to the Superstitions, not anywhere near them. The horror is still lurking out there somewhere.

Which is probably why the Dutchman told me where his lost mine was.

Or maybe it's all in my head. Practically speaking, it doesn't matter. Just don't book me anywhere through Phoenix.

The Dutchman disappeared with his horde of gold, and the dead—the other dead—returned for more dancing. The men of VF 29 and Andrea's half-headed husband and drowned baby with them.

I knew I was going to die. The danse macabre was for me. I spun faster and faster as I was passed from one set of obscene hands to another. I teetered on the brink of an eternity of hell, where the torments of my dance of death would endure forever.

Then, made bold by a surge of courage whose origin I did not know, I informed my tormentors that I was very sorry, but I was not about to join them on their return trip to Hades. I didn't belong there. Purgatory, maybe, but not hell. So the bus would have to leave without me.

They didn't like it. The violins screeched more wildly, the dancers whirled more insanely. Jeremiah Gregory Peter Daugherty, USNR, dug in his heels. No. And I mean no.

All right we'll take her. She's the one we want anyway.

Fine. You can have her. She belongs in hell.

They tossed me back to the wall and continued their feverish gavotte. Yes, she is the one we want. We will come for him later.

It's all right with me. I thought she looked like she was dead the first time I saw her. Take her and you're welcome.

Exhausted, burning with heat, terrified, ready to die if only to escape the madness, I thought about my decision.

Coward.

Wait a minute, guys, you can't have her either. Why not? Because she's mine, not yours, that's why not. I have staked my claim on her. The Dutchman can have his damn mine. I'll take her. The matter is not subject for discussion.

The air group commander says so! Pilots, man your planes!

Many years later I wondered if what came next was a war in heaven.

Leyte Gulf on a bigger scale. Between good and evil. Was she that important?

At that moment, despite my pain and fear and near madness, I had no doubt.

Whatever it was, the struggle for Andrea King, if that was her name, was titanic. Not a debate, not a trial, not an argument, but a furious tug-of-war. I wanted her and they wanted her. I loved her and they hated her. We fought all night. Or so it seemed. Sometimes I thought I had won her.

Other times I thought the black cloud had defeated me and carried her off.

Then darkness settled in on me, permanently, it seemed. I was not sure whether I had won or lost.

Much later, consciousness slowly ebbed back into my organism. At first I thought I was in hell. Well, maybe purgatory. Wherever, I was on fire. I tried to open my eyes. The lids wouldn't move. I tried again, hard. Finally they flickered open. Before they closed, I realized that I was neither in hell nor in purgatory but under a blazing sun on the edge of a cliff. Highway 88 on the far side of the Superstition Mountains.

What was I doing here?

Then I remembered the horror.

Andrea!

I struggled to my feet. The Chevy stood mutely next to me. I looked in the window. The key was still in the ignition. I opened the door and turned the key.

My faithful mount purred contentedly.

Where was Andrea!

No luggage in the backseat. No trace of her, not even of the remains of our picnic lunch.

I turned off the ignition and raced, well, hobbled up the trail to the ridge. It took a couple of eternities to make it to the top. Clinton, Arizona Territory, what was left of it, stood serenely at the edge of Lost Dutchman Canyon, as though nothing had happened there since the last miners left.

"Andrea!" I screamed. No response.

I rushed to the main building of the ghost town. She wasn't there.

I searched desperately in every corner of that shriveled old town. Not a trace.

I collapsed on the dilapidated steps of the main building. She had departed, of that I was absolutely certain. I glanced at my watch—1:15 in the afternoon. If she had started at, say, midnight, she would have had time to walk to Tortilla

Flat, which was only a couple of miles away, and catch the morning "stage" to Apache Junction or even to Phoenix. She might have thumbed a ride in the opposite direction, back to Globe—if there were any cars on the treacherous dirt road. Who would turn down a pretty girl, lugging a heavy bag, on a hot, dusty morning?

Improbable? Sure. It was all improbable. Maybe she had been carried off to hell, cardboard suitcase and all.

I stumbled back to the car and, ignoring the dangers, drove as rapidly as I could down to the general store, which was about all there was to Tortilla Flat. Yes, the stage had left several hours ago. No, there was no young woman with dark red hair on it.

I got much the same answer at Canyon Lake and in Apache Junction. No one could remember. Well, there might have been a pretty girl, but, gosh, I can't recollect, young man. Sorry.

She might have jumped on a train in Apache and gone back to Globe or to Phoenix or anywhere in the world.

Or nowhere in this world.

I raced recklessly back to Globe on U.S. 60. No, the woman at the registration desk of the Pioneer had not seen my wife. She regarded me suspiciously. Is there something wrong? Maybe you ought to walk down to the court house and talk to the sheriff.

Back in the car, I realized that I was making a fool of myself and taking a big chance. If the police became interested and asked for an explanation . . . what would I say?

They'd want to send me to an asylum, much to the horror of my poor parents.

What was there left to do?

I would drive as far as the Arizona Biltmore, on the chance I would see her. Then . . .

Then it didn't matter.

What had happened? Had she somehow become a magnet, drawing evil energies down to that sick old place?

Or was she really dead, as I thought the first moment I had seen her? A lost soul seeking her way to hell?

Was she being punished, perhaps, for having murdered her husband and child? Doomed to wander the earth like . . .

Like a Flying Dutchman!

Or had I imagined it all?

Halfway back to Apache Junction, with the gray clouds gathering again, I turned off the ignition once more and, much as I used to overfly the ocean before returning to the Big *E* searching for life rafts, thought about the possibilities.

I'd try the Biltmore. If she wasn't there, I'd fly one more sweep over the ocean to make sure. The hotel was being refurbished, as was everything else in America at that time. The manager responded to my Irish charm by saying that they had not hired any waitresses recently.

Doggedly I filled up the tank of the car and, ignoring the rain, drove back through Tempe, where there is a big university now, toward Apache Junction.

It was dusk when I climbed the trail from the road up to Clinton for the last time.

Flashlight in hand, I strode bravely into the main building. Navy Cross hero at work.

The hero nearly jumped out of his shoes when the glare of his flashlight caused a stirring in one corner.

Only rats. Or some similar desert creatures.

After they left, there was total silence.

Carefully I explored every corner, as though my precision would exorcise the demons. As the minutes slipped away I realized that I was no longer afraid.

The full moon bathed the desert outside in quiet light. Inside, everything seemed peaceful.

Time to return to Tucson.

I swept the room with my beam for the final time. Then I noticed that the dust had disappeared from the floor.

As though there had been a dance the night before.

And I saw in one corner of the room a bit of white cloth crumpled into a loose ball. I picked it up and rubbed it with my fingers. Cloth from her blouse.

It was my turn to shiver. I should call the state police. What could I tell them? A woman whose name I did not know had disappeared I knew not where, because demons out of hell had swept through a ghost town in the Superstition Mountains.

I'd be locked up for psychiatric observation. No one would search for her.

I tossed the cotton rag on the floor, limped back to the Chevy, backed it up, turned around and went down the mountains.

Ought I not return for one more search? Had I not discovered two rafts after the battle we called Marianas Turkey Shoot and saved seven lives?

Yeah, and your tank had a thimbleful of gas when you landed on the *E*.

Fuel is not a problem in this mission.

She's not there. She's not anywhere.

I continued on to Tucson. Arriving after midnight, I collapsed into bed in my old room at the Arizona. The registration clerk had not asked about Andy, thank God. None of the lies I had concocted on the way back from the Superstition Mountains would have been very persuasive.

I slept till noon the next day. If I had any dreams, I don't remember them.

I woke up a with a terrible headache, a thick tongue, a bad sunburn, and an acute fit of depression. Having demanded black coffee and orange juice from room service, I gave the depression my full attention.

Who was she? Or, better, what was she?

A lost soul doomed to wander the earth like a Flying Dutchman?

A demon sent to tempt me? God knows she'd been successful at that.

A creation of my disturbed imagination? So maybe I should see a therapist, as my father had suggested.

A ghost haunting navy flyers?

I would never know.

I soaked a washcloth, put it on my head, and pitched back into bed.

Only to be pulled out of it by room service. The *Arizona Star* headlined WALLACE PROPOSES TRUMAN APPEASE RUSSIA.

A secret letter had been released in which the former vice-president advocated that the United States destroy its atomic bombs because the Russians resented the American monopoly.

Most senators ridiculed the suggestion. Wallace might be a nut, I thought, but how many of those who ridiculed him had seen Nagasaki?

Halfway through my first cup of coffee I had an idea. My contact at the bureau of personnel quickly confirmed what I had suspected: a radar technician named John King had never served on the U.S.S. *Indianapolis*.

Who was I to think (I could hear my sister's voice) that I was someone special? The great war adventure, ugly but exhilarating, was over. There would be no more adventures and I should accept that and settle down. Right?

Besides, this last great romantic adventure with the widow of a radar technician who had never lived had turned into a nightmare, a real-life nightmare, which made the kamikaze attacks seem boring.

Forget it, Daugherty. Go back to River Forest and act like the ordinary human being that you are supposed to be. Marriage, family, career are enough for everyone else, why not for you? Why do you need some special purpose in life?

Your sisters and your mother will find a nice Trinity-grad virgin who will be a good, unexciting spouse.

In fact, get on with it. Since you're horny again, go home and inspect the girls they've lined up.

I drained the coffee cup and filled it again.

Abandon this quixotic jaunt across the continent and fly

home tomorrow. Catch a plane in Phoenix. Who flies there? TWA? They must. What sense does it make to call yourself Transcontinental and Western if *western* doesn't include Phoenix?

I had the money for a ticket, didn't I?

I stretched out on my bed, reached into the pocket of my tattered and soiled jacket, and pulled out my wallet.

Sure enough, the thin stack of bills was still there. I counted them. Eight. Just like there should be.

I replaced the wallet and returned to my coffee.

Eight?

I reflected very carefully, while my heart pounded like a damaged engine on an F6F. I had had ten of them when I drove into Tucson. I used one to pay the charges here the night before last. I had bought nothing else, not even lunch.

There should be nine.

I thought about that. Go on, dopey, count them again.

Fingers trembling, I recovered my wallet. I removed the bills gently and counted. My heart sank. There were, indeed, nine.

Try again.

This time there were eight.

You're losing control.

I spread the C notes out on the bed in pairs.

Four pairs. Four times two is eight.

I felt my painfully burned face cracking into a grin.

I replaced the wallet, set aside my coffee cup, and relaxed on the bed, hands behind my head in complacent satisfaction.

My grin widened as I reviewed the bidding. I whistled "Anchors Aweigh," extraordinarily pleased with myself.

A thief would have taken all nine.

A ghost would not have needed any.

So she was a human girl—lonely, frightened, perhaps in some crazy way possessed. Yet she was out there, still running. Still in the grip of her fierce desire to live.

She was mine. Had I not won her the night before?

Mine. And I was hers, too. Fair enough.

Had she murdered her husband and child?

Had I murdered Rusty and Tony and Hank?

No.

If she were out there, I would find her. And drag her home by her thick red hair. With a stop here for purposes of lovemaking. Honeymoon. Whatever. We'd see about how hard indeed it was for a determined lover to remove a corsetlike wet swimsuit.

Not too hard, surely.

Then River Forest. It would never be the same.

I would hunt down my leprechaun girl with her pot of gold.

My own Holy Grail to pursue, to drink from, to keep, to treasure.

She was somewhere out there. Terrified. I would find her and save her from whatever was causing the terror.

No, with someone like Andrea-King-if-that-was-her-name, you helped her to save herself from the terror. And then you protected her from more terror by loving her passionately and tenderly forever.

There was no room for doubt. I would indeed love her forever.

Pilots, man your planes!

The air group commander called room service again and ordered pancakes.

And steak.

⁂ April Mae ⁂

Monsignor Joseph Meany reached out from the tomb in the spring of 1945 to prevent Rosie from planting the May crown on the head of the Virgin Mary. The monsignor's ghost encountered a grimly determined exorcist—my mother, April Cronin O'Malley.

April *Mae* Cronin O'Malley.

"Unlike the Mercy Sisters," my father would say, looking up from a blueprint or a drawing, "old Joe Meany was well named."

"Vangie!" My mother would protest the irreverence and uncharitableness and then laugh, thus honoring the obligations of respect for the pastor, love for her husband, and truth, with deft economy of effort.

Joseph Peter Meany was a tiny man, a shriveled gnome, not much over five feet three, thin, bald, and like my mother, nearsighted and too vain to wear glasses. He compensated for his height, so my father said, by communicating with mere mortals in a deep bass bellow.

He firmly believed, Dad also said, that within the boundaries of St. Ursula he was God.

At least.

"Everyone," Mom would sometimes protest with little conviction, "thinks he's done such a splendid job as pastor."

That observation was also true. Meany Meany, as we kids called him, was of that generation of Irish pastors who could have counted on the complete loyalty of a majority of his parishioners even if he had been caught committing fornication with Mother Superior on the high altar during the solemn Mass of Easter Sunday.

Incest even.

"Sure," Dad would snort, "it was a brilliant financial decision not to build the new church in 1937 because he thought prices were going down even more. Now we won't have the church till after the war is over. If then."

My father had some interest in the topic. He had designed the long-awaited new church. For free. In the middle of the Great Depression.

I hated Monsignor, mostly because he had, I thought, cheated my father out of payment for his work. I did not feel the smallest hint of grief when he went to meet his maker because of a heart attack. He expired consuming his third scotch in celebration of the death of Franklin Roosevelt.

"God knows the old man died happy," John Raven, the young priest, said to my mother. "But if they assign Joe and the president to the same section of purgatory, he'll ask for a transfer to hell."

"Where he belongs," I added piously.

"Chucky!" my mother protested. And then laughed.

"Like father, like son," Father Raven noted.

I pressed the point. "Look at the way he treated Gold Star families. He won't even come down from his office to tell them that they can't have a priest from outside the parish say the funeral Mass. Instead he makes you do it. And he doesn't even show up for the wake or funeral unless it's a rich family!"

"Chucky!" My mother's tone this time said I'd better shut up. Even at seventeen I had sense enough not to argue with such a tone in the voice of an Irishwoman.

Rarely did any parishioner who was not wealthy speak to the pastor. He immured himself in his suite after Mass each day (at the most a seventeen-minute exercise) and descended only for meals. He would talk to no one in the rectory offices. Rarely did he attend wakes or funerals or weddings and never did he make a hospital visit. His curates had to make an appointment to talk to him, and sometimes they waited for weeks.

He kept, locked in a sacristy safe, a special bottle of wine to be used only at his Masses, a much more tasty and expensive vintage than the wine assigned to the other priests. I speak as one who had sampled both, with more restraint, I hasten to add, than certain other altar boys (who depended on me to open the monsignor's safe).

Monsignor Meany was convinced that John Raven's name was James and called him that, as in "James, that car door ought not to be open. Take it off!"

So great was the power of the pastor's command that John Raven, as he later admitted, without any hesitation or reflection, drove the monsignor's sturdy old LaSalle straight into the offending door and continued serenely down Division Street as the door bounced a couple of times on the bricks before it halted at a stoplight.

"Serves the damn fool right!" the pastor crowed.

No one ever complained about damage to the car.

The other priests called Father Raven "Jim" at the meals which the monsignor attended.

The pastor thought that William McKinley was the last American president untainted by communist sympathies, took the biased news stories in the *Tribune* as gospel truth, insisted that FDR was a Jew, opposed aid to "Bloody England," became a fan of Father Couglin when the "radio priest" turned anti-Semitic (the same time that my father made me stop selling Couglin's paper, *Social Justice* after Mass on Sundays), and firmly believed that Roosevelt had conspired with the Japanese to launch the Pearl Harbor attack. He never spoke against the war exactly, but whenever someone from the parish was killed in action, he would mutter audibly, "Another young man murdered by that Jew Roosevelt."

He would have easily won reelection as pastor if such had been required. His fans pointed to the monsignor's extraordinary personal piety, as evidenced, for example, by his pilgrimage to Lourdes in the spring of 1939. They did not add that the monsignor shipped to France on the same boat which he favored with his presence, both his LaSalle and his housekeeper (I forget her real name, but we kids called her "Mrs. Meany Meany").

My father lamented the fact that he got out of Europe before the war started in September. "Hitler probably would have given him an Iron Cross."

"Vangie!"

"With oak leaf cluster!"

"They don't give oak leaves . . ." I began.

"Enough from both of you."

Wisely we both lapsed into devout silence.

In Joseph Meany's religion there was only one sin: "impurity." It was denounced with great vigor on every possible occasion—with, need I add, not the slightest indication of what it consisted.

Hence his stern injunction to Sister Mary Admirabilis ("Mary Admiral" to us kids and then "Mary War Admiral," after the Kentucky Derby winner) that only "a young woman who is a paragon of purity may crown the Blessed Mother. We must not permit Our Lady to be profaned by the touch of an immoral young woman."

"One with breasts," my older sister Jane snorted. "If Rosie didn't have boobs . . ."

"That's enough, young lady." Mom didn't laugh, but she kind of smiled, as proud of Rosie's emerging figure as though she were her own daughter.

It was the middle of May, a week after VE day and the end of the war in Europe. Monsignor Meany was in his grave—and whatever realm of the hereafter to which the Divine Mercy had assigned him—and Monsignor Martin Frances "Mugsy" Branigan had replaced him. In his middle forties then, Mugsy was already a legend: shortstop for the White Sox in 1916, superintendent of Catholic schools, devastating golfer, ardent Notre Dame fan, genial, charming, witty.

The red-faced, silver-haired Mugsy had been assigned to St. Ursula's with indecent haste.

"Old Joe is hardly cold in the ground," Dad commented as he toasted (in absentia) the new pastor. (There was always something to toast when he came home after the long ride from Fort Sheridan.) "I guess the Cardinal knows that he has a problem out here."

So Monsignor Mugsy was ensconced in the great two-story room in the front of the second floor of the rectory, the part which was covered with white stone. But Mary War Admiral had not yet extended diplomatic recognition to him. In the school the word of the late pastor was still law.

Even though, as John Raven remarked, there is no one deader than a dead priest.

So Mary War Admiral voided Rosemarie Helen Clancy's nearly unanimous election by the eighth grade, in solemn conclave assembled, as May Queen, because she was not the "kind of young woman who ought to be crowning the Holy Mother of God."

She then appointed my sister Peg as Rosie's replacement. Peg would have won on her own—she never lost an election that I can remember—but she had determined that her inseparable friend Rosie was going to crown Mary and that, Peg being her mother's daughter, was that.

When informed by Sister Mary War Admiral that she was to replace Rosie, Peg replied with characteristic quiet modesty, "I'd kill myself first!"

My mother's reaction was that (a) she would go over to the convent and "settle this problem" with Sister Mary Admirabilis, and that (b) I would accompany her.

"I will not visit the parish," she insisted, "unless I am accompanied by a man from my family."

"I'm a short, red-haired high-school junior," I pleaded.

"Your father's in Washington this week at some meeting with the War Department, young man, and you *will* come with me."

"You don't need a man to ride the Central bus with you up to the Douglas plant," I countered.

"That's different. Besides, you're as bad as your father. You're dying to get into a fight. Now go wash your face and comb your hair."

"My hair doesn't comb. Wire brush. Good for scraping paint. Bad for combing."

"TRY!"

"Yes, *ma'am.*"

I kept my opinions on the May crowning to myself. Sister Mary War Admiral, I thought, might have a point. The word from Lake Delevan (alias Sin Lake) the previous summer was that for someone just entering eighth grade, Rosie Clancy was terribly "fast." Admittedly, fast in those days was pretty slow by contemporary standards. But that was those days, not now.

At that time Rosie and Peg were slipping quickly and gracefully—and disturbingly as far as I was concerned— into womanhood.

"They had their first periods the same week," I heard Mom whisper to Dad one night after the Bing Crosby "Kraft Music Hall" while I was supposed to be sleeping in the enclosed front porch I shared with my little brother.

I still didn't know exactly what a period was, but I suspected that it meant more trouble for me.

Standing together, whispering plots, schemes, tricks and God knows what else, they seemed almost like twins—same height, same slim, fascinating shapes, same dancing eyes, same piquant, impish faces. Like Mom, Peg was brown-tinged—eyes, hair, skin—an elegant countess emerging from a chrysalis. Rosie was more classically Irish—milky skin that colored quickly, jet black hair, scorching blue eyes.

Peg was the more consistent and careful of the two. She worked at her grades and her violin with somber determination. Her grace was languid and sinuous, a cougar slipping through the trees. She rarely charged into a situation—a snowball attack on an isolated boy (like me)—without first checking for an escape hatch or an avenue of retreat. Rosie was more the rushing timber wolf, attacking with wild fury, mocking laughter shattering the air. If Peg was a countess in the making, Rosie was a bomb thrower or revolutionary or wild barroom dancer.

She might also, to give her fair credit, have been a musical comedy singer; she had a clear, appealing voice, which, I was told to my disgust when I was constrained to sing with her at family celebrations, blended "beautifully with yours, Chucky Ducky."

Yuck, as my grandchildren would say.

I must give her due credit. If she and Peg tormented me, for example, by putting lingerie ads from *Life* in my religion textbook and stealing my football uniform the morning of a game, they also came to my aid when I was, or was thought to be, in trouble.

Once when I was in eighth grade, two of the more rowdy of my classmates made some comments which indicated that Dad was a "slacker" because he was stationed at Fort Sheridan. In fact, he was the oldest serviceman from the parish. Moreover, neither of their fathers was in the service.

Instead of pointing out these two truths, I made some more generalized comments on their ancestry and on their relationship with their mothers.

And thus found myself on my back in the schoolyard gravel, being pounded, not skillfully perhaps, but vigorously.

Even one of them would have outnumbered me.

Suddenly two tiny fifth-grade she-demons charged to my rescue, kicking, clawing, screaming. My two assailants were then outnumbered—not counting me.

"Where did you guys learn those words?" I demanded.

"From listening to boys," Peg answered, breathless but triumphant.

"Boys like you, Chucky Ducky," Rosie added, her face crimson with the light of battle.

They then, without my knowledge, went to the rectory and enlisted John Raven's support. The two rowdies were put to work sweeping the parish hall, as Father Raven put it, "till the day before the Last Judgment."

Rosie was, or at least claimed to be, broken-hearted at her demotion by the War Admiral, much to my surprise, since I scarcely thought of her as devout. "I feel so sorry for Peg," she told me. "It's not fair to her."

"It's not fair to you," Peg snapped. "Is it, Chucky?"

"My position on Sister Mary War Admiral," I observed, "is well known."

Mom intervened. "Stop talking to the girls. We must settle this silly business tonight."

So we sallied forth into the gentle May night, an ill-matched pair of warriors if ever there were such.

"Now please don't try to be funny." Mom tried to sound severe, always a difficult task with her husband or her first-born son.

"I'll be just like Dad."

"That's what I'm afraid of."

The war in Europe was over. Churchill's "long night of barbarism" in Europe had ended. Some men were being released from the service. Dad expected an early discharge. We were destroying Japanese cities with firebomb raids.

The Japanese were wreaking havoc on our ships with their kamikaze attacks. We had lost thirteen thousand men in the battle for Okinawa Jima. Mom was worried that I would be drafted when I graduated next year and would have to fight in the invasion of Japan, despite my plans to be a jet pilot. (A legitimate worry as it turned out. If it had not been for the atomic bomb, I would surely have ended up in the infantry. They didn't need pilots.) The cruiser *Indianapolis* was about to sail for Tinian (and its own eventual destruction) with the first atomic bomb. Bing Crosby was singing that he wanted to "ride to the ridge where the west commences and gaze at the moon till I lose my senses," so long as we undertook not to attempt to fence him in.

A battle over a May crowning surely did not compare to the major events which were about to shape the new, more affluent, and more dangerous world.

But it was our battle.

The O'Malleys were "active" Catholics as naturally as they breathed the air or played their musical instruments. Mom had been president of the Altar Guild. Dad was an usher, even in uniform. Jane had been vice-president of the High Club. I was sometime photographer in residence, and the always available altar boy to "take" sudden funerals, unexpected wartime weddings, periods of adoration during "forty hours," and six o'clock Mass on Sundays. When our finances improved—Dad's military pay and Mom's wages from the factory—we discussed together increasing our Sunday contribution.

We voted, over my objections, to quadruple the amount we gave. Dad insisted that the Sunday gift be anonymous because he didn't believe in the envelope system or the published list of contributions.

"Why give if we don't get credit?" I demanded, at least partially serious.

"Chucky!" the other five responded in dismay.

Despite the anonymity of our gifts, we were still prominent members of the parish. Even Monsignor Meany almost came to our house for supper one night. So Sister Mary War Admiral must have known she was in for a fight.

I whistled "Praise the Lord and Pass the Ammunition" as we walked up the steps to the convent.

"Hush," Mom whispered, and then joined in with "All aboard, we're not a-going fishin'."

"Praise the Lord and pass the ammunition and we'll all stay free," we sang in presentable harmony as the light turned on above the convent steps.

"You're worse than your father," Mom informed me when she managed to stop laughing.

There was a long delay before the door opened—it is an unwritten rule of the Catholic Church (as yet unrepealed) that no convent or rectory door can be opened without a maddening wait being imposed on the one who has disturbed ecclesiastical peace by ringing the bell.

Sister Mary Admiral did not answer the door, of course. Mothers superior did not do that sort of thing. The nun who did answer, new since my day in grammar school, kept her eyes averted as she showed us into the parlor, furnished in the heavy green style of pre-World War I, with three popes, looking appallingly feminine, watching us with pious simpers.

The nameless nun scurried back with a platter on which she had arrayed butter cookies, fudge, two small tumblers, and a pitcher of lemonade.

"Don't eat them all, Chucky," Mom warned me as we waited for Mother Superior to descend upon us.

"I won't," I lied.

The convent cookies and fudge—reserved for visitors of special importance—were beyond reproach. I will confess, however, that I was the one responsible for the story about the lemonade being sent for analysis to a chemist, who had reported with great regret that our poor horse was dying of incurable kidney disease.

"April, dear, how wonderful to see you!" The War Admiral came in swinging. "You look wonderful. Painting airplanes certainly agrees with you." She hugged Mom. "And Charles . . . my, how you've grown!"

I hadn't. But I did not reply because the last bit of fudge had followed the final cookie into my digestive tract.

The War Admiral hated my guts. She resented my endless presence with camera and flashbulb. She suspected, quite correctly, that I had coined her nickname. She also suspected, again correctly, that I had been responsible for pouring the curate's wine into the monsignor's wine bottle. Finally she suspected, with monumental unfairness (and inaccuracy), that I had consumed most of the monsignor's wine and thus was responsible for the necessity of filling the bottle with lesser wine.

"You look wonderful, too, Sister." Although Mom had blushed at the compliment, she was too cagey to be taken in by it. "My husband is at the War Department this week, so my son has come with me."

Actually Sister Mary Admirabilis looked terrible, as she always did. Like the late pastor, she was tiny and seemed deceptively frail. Her eyes darted nervously and her fingers twisted back and forth, perhaps because she did not bring to the parlor the little hand bell which she always carried "on duty"—the kind of bell you used to ring on the counter of a hotel reception desk.

Most of the other nuns also carried little hand bells, on which they pounded anxiously when the natives became restless.

War Admiral launched her campaign quickly, hook nose almost bouncing against jutting chin as she spat out her carefully prepared lines. "I'm so sorry about this little misunderstanding. Your precious Margaret Mary should be the one to crown the Blessed Mother. She is such a darling, so good and virtuous and popular. I often worry about her friendship with the Clancy child. I'm afraid that she's a bad influence. I hope you don't regret their friendship some-day."

You praise the daughter, you hint at the danger of the friend, you stir up a little guilt—classical Mother Superior maneuvers. And how did my mother, soft, gentle, kindly April Cronin O'Malley, react?

April Mae Cronin O'Malley.

"Oh, Sister, I would be so unhappy if Peg did not graduate from St. Ursula next month, just as Jane and Chuck . . . uh, Charles here did."

Oh, boy.

"But there's no question of that. . . ."

Mom ignored her. "The sisters out at Trinity did tell me that they'll accept her as a freshman with a music scholar-ship even if she doesn't graduate."

"But . . ."

"And, as sad as it would to be break my husband's heart"—Mom seemed close to tears—"I'll have to withdraw Peg from St. Ursula if she is put in this impossible situation."

"She wouldn't come back to school anyway," I added helpfully, licking the last trace of fudge from my lips.

"Shush, darling," Mom murmured.

"Please yourself." The Admiral took off her velvet gloves. "If Margaret does not choose to accept the honor to which she has been appointed, we simply won't have a May crowning."

"Please yourself, Sister." Mom smiled sadly. "My family will have no part of this unjust humiliation of Rosemary."

I began to hum mentally "Let's Remember Pearl Harbor As We Did the Alamo." This was a preliminary scrimmage. Mom was touching a base before cornering Monsignor Mugsy.

"My dear"—the Admiral's voice was sweet and oily—"we really can't let the Clancy girl crown Our Blessed Lady. Her father is a criminal and her mother . . . well, as I'm sure you know"—her voice sank to a whisper—"she drinks!"

"All the more reason to be charitable to Rosemary."

"Like Jesus to Mary Magdalen," I added helpfully.

"Shush, darling."

"Monsignor Meany established very firm rules for this honor."

"Monsignor Meany is dead, God be good to him."

"Cold in his grave," I observed.

"His rules will remain in force as long as I am Superior."

"Time for a change, I guess," I murmured.

"You give me no choice but to visit Monsignor Branigan."

"Please yourself."

The warm night had turned frigid.

"I shall."

"Don't say anything, dear," Mom said as we walked down Menard Avenue to the front door of the rectory. "Not a word."

"Who, me?"

After the routine wait for the bell to be answered, we were admitted to a tiny office littered with baptismal books. Monsignor Branigan, in black clerical suit, appeared almost at once, medium height, thick glasses, red face, and broad smile.

"April Cronin!" he exclaimed, embracing her; unheard-of behavior from a priest in those days. "Greetings and salutations! You look more beautiful than ever!"

"April Mae Cronin," I observed.

They knew each other, did they? Sure they did. All south-side Irish knew one another.

I considered my mother—whom I had always thought of as pretty—a tall, thin, nearsighted refugee countess. Monsignor Mugsy was right. Without my having noticed it, she had, as she passed her fortieth birthday, become beautiful. The worry and the poverty of the Depression were over.

She no longer had to send me to Liska's Meat Market to purchase twenty-eight cents of beef stew ground from which to make supper for six of us. Her husband was safe at Fort Sheridan. The war would soon be over. Her children were growing up. She was earning more money than she would have ever dreamed possible. She had put on enough weight so that curves had appeared under her gray suit. A distinguished countess now.

I glance at pictures I took of her at that time. Yes, indeed, Monsignor Mugsy was right.

"Is this galoot yours?" He nodded at me.

"Sometimes she's not sure," I responded.

"Vangie, uh, John is in Washington," Mom explained.

"What grade are you in, son?"

"I'm a junior at Fenwick."

"Do you play football?"

"Quarterback."

"What string?"

"Fourth."

"I thought there were only three strings." Monsignor Mugsy and I were hitting it off just fine.

"For me they made an exception." I was not about to tell him that I was more mascot than player.

"Where are you going to college?"

"I've seen *Knute Rockne—All American.* Win one for the Gipper!"

"Great," the monsignor exclaimed. "Now, April, what's on your mind?"

Mom told him.

"Dear God," he breathed out, and reclined in his swivel chair. "How can we do things like this to people? Someday we're going to have to pay a terrible price."

"Mary Magdalen . . ." I began.

"Shush, darling."

"I hear that Old Man Clancy is something of a crook." The monsignor drummed his stubby fingers on the desk.

215

"A big crook," I said.

"You two are willing to vouch for the poor little tyke?"

"Certainly." Mom nodded vigorously. "She's a lovely child."

"You bet." I perjured myself because I thought my life might depend on it.

"Well, that settles that . . . ah, Jack, don't try to sneak by. I suppose you know the O'Malleys?"

"I think so." John Raven, golf clubs on his shoulder, grinned. "The kid has a reputation for switching wine bottles; watch him."

"Calumny."

"I hear," the pastor said, peering shrewdly over his thick bifocals, "we have some trouble with the May crowning. Why don't you talk to Sister, Jack, and . . ."

Father Raven leaned against the door jamb. "The smallest first-grader has more clout with the War Admiral than a curate has." He chuckled. "It's your fight, Mugsy."

"And your parish," I said.

Everyone ignored me.

The monsignor threw up his hands. "See what's happening to the Church, April? Curates won't do the pastor's dirty work for him anymore. Well, go home and tell Peg—I know which one she is, she looks like you did when you crowned the Blessed Mother at St. Gabe's—that her friend will do the honors next week."

When we arrived back at our tiny apartment three blocks south of the rectory on Menard, Peg hugged me enthusiastically. "Oh Chucky Ducky, you're wonderful."

Rosie, her face crimson, considered doing the same thing but wisely judged from the expression on my face not to try. Instead, tears in her vast eyes, she said, "Thank you."

"It was all the good April," I replied modestly. "I just carried her bowling shoes."

Parish reaction to Monsignor Branigan's intervention was mostly positive. The Clancy kid was too pretty for her own good and a little fast besides. However, it was time someone put Sister Mary Admirabilis in her place.

Was there any complaint that April O'Malley had gone to the new pastor to overrule Mother Superior?

Certainly not. If you are April O'Malley, by definition, you can do no wrong.

The Sunday afternoon of the May crowning, in the basement gym which had been Meany Meany's bequest to the parish, the blue and white plaster statue (pseudo-Italian Renaissance ugly) of the Mother of Jesus was surrounded by a circle of six early-pubescent girls dressed as though they were a wedding party and one pint-sized red-haired photographer clutching his Argus C-3 and flash attachment.

The ceremony had begun with a "living rosary" in the gravel-coated schoolyard next to the church. The student body was arranged in the form of a rosary, six children in each bead. At the head of the cross stood the May crowning party, Rosie in a white bridal dress, her four attendants in baby blue, and two of the tiniest First Communion tots in their veils carrying Rosie's train.

The recitation of the Rosary moved from bead to bead, the kids in the bead saying the first part of the Pater or the Ave and the rest of the school responding, accompanied with not too much enthusiasm by parents who had come to the ceremony with about as much cheerfulness as that which marked their attendance at school music recitals.

I lurked on the fringes of the "living rosary," automatically reciting the prayers and capturing with my camera the most comic expressions I could find. It wasn't hard to discover funny faces, especially when a warning breeze stirred the humid air and the bright sky turned dull gray.

The voices of the seventh and eighth grade hinted at the possibility of adolescent bass. The younger kids chanted in a singsong which might have been just right in a Tibetan monastery. The little kids piped like tiny squeaking birds.

The spectacle was silly, phony, artificial, and oddly, at the same time devout, impressive, and memorable.

As we moved from the "Fourth Glorious Mystery, the Assumption of Mary into Heaven" to the verses of the Lourdes Hymn, which would introduce the "Fifth Glorious Mystery, the Crowning of Mary as Queen of Heaven," the first faint drops of rain fell on the crowded schoolyard. The voices of mothers gasped in protest.

It was decision time. John Raven drifted over to the War Admiral, nodded toward the sky, and then towards the church. Fingers caressing her hand bell, she shook her head firmly. We would finish the Rosary. God would not permit it to rain.

Father Raven raised an eyebrow at Mugsy, resplendent in the full choir robes of a domestic prelate.

"Looks as pretty," my father had remarked of the robes, "as doctoral robes from Harvard."

Mugsy peered at the sky through his thick glasses, as if he really couldn't see that far, and nodded.

John Raven shrugged. You're the pastor, pastor.

Mugsy stepped to the primitive public-address microphone and said, "I think God wants us to go inside."

Obediently the altar boys in white cassocks and red capes—cross bearer and two acolytes with candles long since extinguished by the stiffening wind—began to process toward the church. The girls in the crowning party fell in behind.

The War Admiral's bell rang out in protest. Several other bells responded. A couple of nuns rushed forward and pushed the kids in the first decade of the rosary into line behind the altar boys; the rosary would unlink itself into a straight processional line with the crowning party at the very end, like it was supposed to be, instead of at the beginning.

In which position it was most likely to be drenched, since the rain clouds were closing in on us.

I snapped a wonderful shot of the War Admiral twisting a little girl's shoulder so that the child resumed her place in line and another of her shoving Peg to a dead halt as my sister challenged the ringing of the bells and began to cut in front of the procession and dodge the raindrops, which were even now falling rapidly.

Irresistible force met immovable object.

The standoff was resolved by the push of parents, who were not bound by the wishes of Mother Superior and rushed for the church door—despite the outraged cries of the hand bells.

Peg simply ducked around the War Admiral, snatched up one of the First Communion tots, and followed by Rosie, who had seized the other tot, raced for the church door in the midst of a crowd of parents.

I still have the prints—on my desk as I write this story. Peg was not to be stopped.

God may not have been sufficiently afraid of the War Admiral to hold off the rain. But He (or She, if you wish) was enough enchanted by Peg to stay the shower until the crowning party had pushed its way into the shelter of the church.

Peg reassembled her crew in the vestibule at the foot of the steps leading to the basement church, waited till everyone was inside and then led the crowning party solemnly down the aisle toward the altar.

The nuns were too busy pushing and shoving kids and glaring at parents in a doomed effort to restore the "ranks" to cope with a determined young woman who knew exactly what she intended to do.

Peg would have made a good mother superior in her own right.

Doubtless given a signal by John Raven, the organ struck up a chintzy version of Elgar's "Pomp and Circumstance," an exaggeration if there ever were one for this scene.

Only about half the school kids were soaking wet when

they finally struggled into their pews. The War Admiral's determined efforts to restore order had deprived the kids of the "sense to come in out of the rain!"

If S'ter says you stay out in the rain, then you stay out in the rain.

The nuns all had miraculously produced umbrellas from the folds of their black robes and had stayed dry, if not cool.

When the Admiral and her aides could turn their attention to the crowning party, Peg had herded them safely to the front of the church, where they waited patiently under the protection of Monsignor Branigan and Father Raven—and naturally in the presence of your and my favorite redhead photojournalist.

I still laugh at the pictures of the nuns turning misfortune into calamity.

Monsignor nodded to the younger priest, who strolled over to the lectern which served as a pulpit and began, "To make up for the rain, we will have a very short sermon. My text seems appropriate for the circumstances: 'Man proposes, God disposes'—I almost said 'Sister proposes, God disposes!' "

Laughter broke the tension in the congregation and drowned out the clanging hand bells. We were no longer wet and angry; we were wet and giddy.

I could imagine Mom and Dad arguing whether Father Raven had gone "too far." Mom would giggle and lose the argument.

The air was thick with spring humidity, girlish perfume, and the scent of mums, always favored by the War Admiral because, as I had argued, they reminded her of funeral homes.

The crowning party fidgeted through the five-minute-and-thirty-second sermon. Eighth-grade girls were too young for such finery, some of them not physically mature enough to wear it, and all of them not emotionally mature enough.

Peg, however, looked like a youthful queen empress, albeit a self-satisfied one.

And Rosie?

She was shaking nervously and deadly pale.

And, yes, I'll have to admit it, gorgeous.

She kept glancing anxiously at me, as if I were supposed to provide reassurance.

I ignored her, naturally. Well, I did smile at her once. I might even have winked, because she grinned quickly and seemed to calm down.

The sanctuary of the "basement church" was in fact a stage. The statue of Mary had been moved for the event to the front of the stage on the left (or "epistle") side. A dubious stepladder, draped in white, leaned against the pedestal. Of all those in church, only the statue was not sweating.

After the sermon it was time for the congregation to belt out, "Bring flowers of the rarest from garden and woodland and hillside and dale," as I remember the lyrics. Rosie bounded up the shaky white ladder, still the rushing timber wolf. The ladder, next to my shoulder, trembled.

Anyone who attended such spring rituals in those days will remember that the congregation was required to sing two times, "Oh, Mary, we crown thee with blossoms today, queen of the angels, queen of the May!" During the second refrain, much louder than the first (which itself was pretty loud), the ring of flowers was placed on the head of the statue.

I had been charged to take "a truly good picture, darling. For her parents, who won't be able to come." Given the state of flashbulb technology in those days, that meant I had one and one chance only.

Just as Rosie raised the circle of blossoms, I saw an absolutely perfect shot frozen in my viewfinder. I pushed the shutter button, the bulb exploded, the ladder swayed, and Rosemarie Helen Clancy fell off it.

221

On me.

I found myself, dazed and sore, on the sanctuary floor, buried in a swirl of bridal lace and disordered feminine limbs.

"Are you all right?" she demanded. "Did I hurt you?"

"I'm dead, you clumsy goof."

"It's all your fault," Peg snarled, pulling Rosie off me. "You exploded that flash thing deliberately."

I struggled to my feet to be greeted by an explosion of laughter.

What's so funny? I wondered as every hand bell in every nunnish hand in the church clanged in dismay.

Then I felt the flowers on my head. Rosie had crowned not the Blessed Mother, but me.

Even the frightened little train bearers were snickering.

I knew I had better rise to the occasion or I was dead in the neighborhood and at Fenwick High School.

Forever and ever.

Amen.

So I bowed deeply to the giggling Rosie and, with a single motion, swept the flowers off my wire-brush hair and into her hand. She bowed back.

She may have winked, too, for which God forgive her.

These days Catholic congregations applaud in church on almost any occasion, even for that rare event, the good sermon. In those days applause in the sacred confines was unthinkable.

Nonetheless, led by Monsignor Branigan and Father Raven, the whole church applauded.

Except for the nuns, who were pounding frantically on their hand bells.

Rosie looped the somewhat battered crown around her fingers and joined the applause.

Then someone, my mother, I'm sure, began, "Oh, Mary we crown thee with blossoms today. . . ."

Rosie darted up the ladder just in time to put the crown

where it belonged. As she turned to descend, the ladder tottered again. I steadied it with my left hand and helped her down with my right.

She blushed and smiled at me.

And owned the whole world.

There was, God help me and the bell-pounding nuns, more applause.

Rosie raised her right hand shyly, acknowledging the acclaim.

The monsignor stepped to the lectern.

"I think we'd better quit when we're ahead."

More laughter. Oh Lord, we were giddy.

"Father Raven, who has better eyes than I do," he continued, "tells me that the rain has stopped. So we'll skip Benediction of the Blessed Sacrament and end the service now, with special congratulations to the May crowner and her, uh, agile court. First, we'll let you parents out of church, then our bright young altar boys will lead the schoolchildren out, then, Chucky, you can lead out the wedding—uh, crowning party. It won't be necessary for the children to go to their classrooms. We want to get everyone home before the rains start again."

It was a total rout for the War Admiral. To dismiss the kids from church without requiring that they return to their classrooms was to undo the work of Creation and unleash the forces of Chaos and Disorder, indeed to invite the gates of hell to triumph against the Church.

The clanging hand bells displayed a remarkable lack of spirit.

Afterward, back in our apartment, the sun shining brightly again, Mom insisted that I was hero of the day. Peg did a complete turnaround, a tactic at which she excelled, and told everyone that "Rosie would have been badly hurt if Chucky hadn't caught her"—a generous description of my role.

Dad, returned from Washington in time for the show, affirmed that at last St. Ursula's had a real pastor.

"Joe Meany is now in his grave permanently."

"And War Admiral has been put out to stud," I said.

I was old enough to know vaguely what that meant.

My prediction was accurate. The following year Sister Angela Marie, even older, it was said, than the War Admiral, appeared at our parish and governed with happy laughter instead of a hand bell.

In the midst of the festivities I wondered whether in my eagerness to freeze what I saw in my viewfinder I might have brushed against the ladder.

And what was the instant I captured on my Plus-X film?

That night, when the apartment had settled down, I crept off to my makeshift darkroom in the basement of our building. After developing the film and exposing the paper, I watched the magic instant come up in the print solution.

What I saw scared me: two shrewd young women, one of them recognizable as a marble statue only if you looked closely, making a deal, like a buyer and seller at the Maxwell Street flea market. Rosie was about to offer the crown in return for . . .

Well, it wasn't clear what she expected from the deal. But she expected something. No, she was confident she would get it.

I hung the picture to dry, thought about claiming that the film had been ruined, and then reluctantly decided that I wouldn't get away with it.

"You could call the picture," Mom would say, "the way *Time* magazine does, Rosemary and friend."

None of them would see the deal being consummated in the photo. They would say that it was all in my imagination.

After the ceremony that afternoon, my friends from Fenwick had demanded to know whether I had "copped a feel" when "Clancy" was on top of me.

"Nothing to feel," I insisted, with notable lack of both honesty and loyalty.

"What was she like?" they demanded with horny insistence.

"Heavy," I told them.

Now, as I watched a second print materialize in the solution, I admitted in a deep, untended, and secret sub-basement of my brain that the sensation of Rosie's body on top of mine had been so sweet that if the ever-vigilant Peg had not pulled us apart, I might have been content to remain there always.

❧ Brigid ❧

I knew we were in for trouble when Biddy, my youngest, announced at the dinner table the week before Christmas, "I don't care, I think Willie Gault is cute!"

The other three kids were never quite your classical stereotypical teens. Fifteen- year- old Brigid Elizabeth made up for them.

"Is he a rock star, dear?" I said absently, thinking about a teenage client I had listened to for a sick fifty minutes earlier in the day, a frustrated rock groupie.

"Mo-THER! He is a wide receiver!"

"Along with Dennis MacKinnon and Ken Margerum," her aunt Trish, an inseparable ally, who is also fifteen and was "eating over," explained. "They're all cute, but Willie Gault is the cutest."

"Chicago Bears, dear," whispered my husband Joe (alias "the pirate" because he looks so fierce when he wears a beard). "You know, the football team."

I should have seen the possibilities for acute family crisis even then. But I was still preoccupied with my would-be groupie.

226

"Of course I know the football team."

Joe is a psychiatrist, too; though there's nothing wrong with that. Necessarily.

"Willie Gault," Brigid Elizabeth went on implacably, "is responsible for the Super Bowl Shuffle."

She and Trish are often thought to be twins, black-haired, black-eyed pixies, with cute little teenage figures, and lovely faces when they're not in motion, which is practically never. The complexity of our family structure confuses people because, of course, Biddy must call me "Mom," or when she's impatient with me, which is practically always, "Mo-THER," while Trish, as my half-sister, addresses me as "M.K." or "Mary Kate" as in "M.K., you don't know what the Super Bowl Shuffle is!"

"I am not unaware that the Bears are in the play-offs," I said with as much dignity as a decrepit square, 'cuse me, geek, can muster.

"Along with the Foxboro Patriots," said my husband. "And the Anaheim Rams and the Irving Cowboys and the East Rutherford Giants."

Joe and I met a couple of centuries ago when he was a resident at Little Company of Mary Hospital and I was a medical-school clerk. We did not get along from the first second we met and fought furiously every hour of my six weeks in the program.

"Miss Ryan," he shouted on my last day, just a week before Christmas, "you create the kind of sexual tension which can only be resolved on the marriage bed."

"All right, Dr. Murphy." I gulped.

"That was an acceptance?" He backed off warily.

"That was a proposal?"

"I can't believe my good fortune." The poor dear sweet man was so terribly flustered that I knew I'd love him forever and ever.

"I'm the lucky one," I said. It was the first nice thing I ever said to him. And the wisest thing I have ever said.

We didn't kiss till after dinner (at The Club—the Beverly Country Club, of course) that night.

So here we are, a silver anniversary later, and we're still resolving that tension and Christmas is coming and Biddy is complaining that I don't know about Willie Gault, and damn fool Irish Catholic sentimentalist that I am, I wanted to cry.

"I'll go next door and get Daddy's tape." Trish was putting on her St. Ignatius jacket. "You *gotta* watch it, M.K. *Really!*"

"When Ned Ryan buys videotapes of football players," Joe observed, "we may be witnessing a phenomenon."

"But the kid's too young—"

"Archetypical."

Joe is a Jungian and I'm a Freudian, which makes for an interesting relationship, not to say an interesting love life.

So, Joe's arm around me, I watched, with, I admit, some interest, Willie Gault, Jim McMahon, Sweetness Payton, and the rest of them cavort before the camera with notable lack of talent. My half-sister and my daughter explained who each of these players was, including such characters as "Otis" and "Samurai."

"Who is that poor fat boy without the teeth?" I asked. "The one they call the Fridge."

"Mo-THER!" screamed my daughter.

"Mary KATE!" yelled my half-sister.

They endeavored to explain.

"But if they have a, uh, running back like Mr. Payton, who is the best ever, why would they need that poor boy to score touchdowns?"

The kids hooted.

"You haven't seen him in the McDonald's ad?"

"Or with all those Cokes."

"But can't he afford to get his teeth fixed?"

"Poor," my pirate said, "he no longer is."

We were, I began to suspect, about to experience a phenomenon.

I suggested that on the phone the next day to my youngest full brother, the Punk. Who is a monsignor. There's nothing wrong with that. Necessarily.

"The possibilities are awesome," he intoned solemnly. "The capacity for madness in this city, if they make it to the Super Bowl, is beyond estimation. The last time we won a World Series, to which the Super Bowl can be fairly compared, was, as you may remember, 1917. They have taken away from us Chicagofest, the World's Fair, a doomed stadium, and almost everything else of which an urban populace may be proud. We can barely hold on to an overage submarine. Mark my words, good sister, Thermidor is coming."

"I may be your older sibling, but I was not here in 1917. But then, neither were the kids. Biddy and Trish."

"Appalling." He sighed with relish and approval. "Fridge as Bruce Springsteen."

"It goes like this." I began to sing.

> *"This is Speedy Willie and I'm world-class*
> *I like runnin' but I love to get the pass,*
> *I practice all day and dance all night,*
> *Now I'm as smooth as a chocolate swirl,*
> *I dance a little funky, so watch me, girl,*
> *There's no one here that does it like me,*
> *My Super Bowl Shuffle will set you free."*

"Brigid, Patrick, Comumcille and all you holy saints of Ireland preserve and protect us," my brother prayed.

> *"So please don't try to beat my hustle,*
> *'Cause I'm just here to do the Super*
> *Bowl Shuffle."*

"You perceive the problem, of course." Blackie was now being really serious, a rare enough event. "With the old fella, I mean."

"No, I don't. What problem? Ohmygod, Punk, you don't think he would, do you? We've kept it a secret for so long."

"He has a streak of stubbornness which I alone of the eight offspring seem to have escaped."

"But the grandchildren." I ignored his falsehood. "And poor Trish. They all adore him. We can't let them find out."

"None of us is perfect."

"They think Grandpa Ned is perfect. We can't let them know about such a terrible character defect."

Blackie sighed noisily. "It may be out of our control."

"You talk to him. He identifies with you."

"It might make him worse."

"There's that."

Our father, Ned Ryan, is one of Chicago's grand old men, though he resolutely refuses to act like he's old. An apparently quiet little lawyer with snow-white hair, leprechaun blue eyes, and a gentle bass voice, he has mellowed a bit through the years, but he's still the kind of person who, when blown off the *Arizona* at Pearl Harbor, swam back to help rescue his gun crew, and then at Leyte led a group of pathetic destroyer escorts in a charge against Japanese battleships, which scared the Japanese admiral into turning tail and running. As my mother, Kate Collins Ryan, God be good to her, would say, "Your father may have backed away from a fight once or twice in the years I've known him, but I can't quite remember when."

It was said that even Dick Daley at the height of his power was afraid to make him angry. Only my mother and my stepmother (who is only two years older than I am and was handpicked by Kate Collins as her successor) have dared to face him down.

But to the kids he is kindly old "Grandpa Ned" who tells stories and works magic tricks and provides candy and ice cream and beer and video movies and drives the boat when they water-ski. And to the three Helen has borne him—

Chantal, Sean, and Trish—he is "Papa Ned," whom they have kept permanently young. "Second childhood," he says, grinning ruefully as Trish explains Springsteen lyrics to him.

How could we let them know about this terrible character flaw?

"He restrained himself this summer," Blackie said hopefully. "And there was ample opportunity."

"Was there? I'm afraid I didn't notice. But the children were not so involved then."

"We will have to see what happens. By the way, have you considered the possibility of further problems if New England should, through some miracle, survive to do battle with our stalwarts in the Super Bowl?"

"New England?"

"The quondam Boston Patriots."

"Oh my God!"

Our poor family might be in for real trouble.

I settled the Patriot thing with my pirate that night in bed.

"What if the Patriots play the Bears in the Super Bowl?"

"You make the most interesting pillow talk, Dr. Murphy."

Joe thinks he understands me completely. Through our quarter century and more together, I have insisted that I am five pounds overweight and will not look presentable until I lose those hated eighty ounces, a point which he refuses to concede, he says on the basis of expert knowledge of the subject matter. Then, when the new standards came out last year which put me smack dab in the middle of "normal," the pirate freely predicted that I would promptly add five more to preserve my self-disrespect.

"Wanna bet?"

He did, and of course I won. Two decades and a half and he hasn't figured me out.

"That's irrelevant and possibly chauvinist," I insisted, snuggling closer to him because it was a cold December night—though I don't need excuses. "We're going to have enough trouble as it is."

"The Pats won't make it out of the Meadowlands."

"Yes, but . . ."

"And I'm a Chicagoan, by marriage and voter registration."

"But that basketball team, whatever they're called . . ."

"The Celtics!" He drew away from me as though I were in the grip of a dangerous infectious disease.

"Whatever . . ."

"That's different. And they have deserted good old Boston for Foxboro anyway."

"You'll be suspect because of your accent."

"You're terrible, woman." He reclaimed me with obviously prurient intent.

"This is all going to get out of hand," I predicted.

"I think it has already."

"No, I mean the Bears."

I could not have been a better prophet.

On January 6 we assembled next door in Dad's house: my brother Packie, who is a politician, and his Tracy, the only non–Irish Catholic in the clan, my sisters Eileen (a judge) and Nancy (who writes science fiction), and assorted spice and children and boyfriends and girlfriends of children and even my brand-new son-in-law Kevin, God help us all. The last one to arrive, looking like the permanent adolescent cherub he is, was Monsignor Punk, wearing a Chicago Bears jacket, scarf, ski hat, and sweatshirt, and twirling, rather ostentatiously, I felt, a Chicago Bears keychain. He favored us with an improvised stanza from the Super Bowl Shuffle which he claimed to have recited at Mass that morning in the Cathedral (much to the dismay, I daresay, of Cardinal Sean Cronin, who long ago gave up trying to reform his gray eminence: Blackie gets along so well with teenagers because, Ph.D. on Whitehead or not, he will always be one):

> *"I'm Father Blackie and I say the Mass*
> *I preach and sing, without much class,*
> *The cardinal will tell you I'm A-okay*
> *So long as I do whatever he say;*
> *I've cheered the Bears all my life,*
> *If they don't win for me, they're not nice.*
> *I promise God that She'll get no trouble*
> *'Long as the Bears take the Super Bowl Shuffle!"*

A priest would never do that, you say? Certainly not a cathedral rector?

You don't know the Punk. Apples don't fall far from their trees. And the Punk is the apple closest to Ned Ryan's tree.

Which is why all of us were worried about the character flaw.

Dad was well behaved. He had replaced the large-screen TV with an even larger one (almost as big as the Mitsubishi they later put in the Daley Plaza—temporarily the Chicago Bears Plaza—on Super Sunday), produced an enormous amount of popcorn, potato chips, diet Coke, french fries, beer, chocolate-chip ice cream, and other health foods, and promised that he would show *Streets of Fire,* a rock film nearing cult status, after the game.

The kids sat on the floor around his chair like he was King Arthur and the big old house was Camelot. The wall was lined with framed Chicago Bears posters, drinks were served in Chicago Bears tumblers and cups, a Chicago Bears telephone was on the table next to his easy chair ("the same as Mike Ditka uses," he told the worshipful Trish and Biddy), and Dad wore a blue sweater with a Chicago Bears helmet emblazoned on it. I heaved a sigh of relief and winked at the Punk. The old fella would behave.

"All you'd need to be Santa Claus is a beard." Helen, who has mastered the art of giving him the needle, gave him his daily glass of Jameson's—straight up. First glass anyway.

233

"Santa Claus, poor man, drinks scotch. Single malt, of course."

He explained to his adoring descendants that blue and orange were the Illinois colors, chosen for the Bears by "George" because that's where he went to college and won letters in track, baseball, basketball, and wrestling, as well as football. The *C* was the University of Chicago *C* because he didn't want to use the same *C* as the Cubs did. The title "Mighty Monsters of the Midway" was applied to the University of Chicago back in the days of Pop Stag and Jay Barwanger and was transferred to the Bears when the university folded up its football program, "not a minute too soon."

During commercial breaks and at halftime, he told stories about the Canton Bulldogs and the Decatur Staleys and the great Bear teams of the thirties and forties (leaving out, thank God, the game which was being played when he was blown off the *Arizona* by a Japanese bomb—that would have meant trouble) and about Red Grange, and Bronco Nagurski, and George "One Play" McAfee, and Marshal Goldberg (the Punk rolled his eyes at that name, but nothing came of it). The crowd of kids, even Kevin, listened in mute adoration.

Well, poor Ken O'Brien got pounded into the turf and Joe Morris was stopped cold—appropriate word for Soldier Field of a January Sunday, and the Bears roared on. The younger generation screamed like they were permanently institutionalized at each sack and each McMahon-to-Gault pass, the girls worse than the boys. Katie Kane and Cat O'Connor and Trish gave a fair imitation of the knitters in the Place de la Révolution. But our Brigid Elizabeth was the loudest of all.

"Bring on Eric Dickerson," she screeched. "We'll kill him!"

"Who's he?" I whispered to my Joe.

"Running back for the Anaheim Rams."

"Poor man."

That night I thought I saw the social significance of it all. "The difference is the girls?"

"Huh?" my sleepy husband responded.

"If Blackie is right and there is a groundswell of celebration . . ."

"'Liturgical celebration' was his exact phrase."

"Whatever . . . It's the young women who are at the center of it. This play-off season may mean more to them than anyone else. Every girl child in that room was wearing some kind of Bears emblem."

"There was a lady shrink," he said as he took my hand in his, "who was talking about Shaun Gayle in the nickel-forty-six defense."

"Regardless."

The city warmed to its January as the temperature rose. It was disastrously warm when the Rams came to Soldier Field. John Robinson, Anaheim's charming coach, admitted that he was a Chicago native; Biddy and Trish denounced him as a geek. Blackie appeared on the ten o'clock news to speak of "collective representations," which demonstrate the power of a city's liturgical spirit. He also observed that God had two choices, either permit the Bears to win (which "ought to be easy for Her") or send a hundred thousand angels to protect the city from despair. Stores on Michigan Avenue blossomed with orange and blue displays, Fields played the Super Bowl Shuffle in their main lobby. Mayor Harold made periodic confident predictions with "Fridgerettes" bouncing around him, and Coach Ditka allowed as how the Rams were a Smith team and the Bears were a Grabowski team. Nick Curran, egged on by his wife, my cousin Cathy (who is CRAZY), redesigned the stationery of his staid, prestige-laden Loop law firm so that instead of being "Minor, Gray and Blat," it became "Minor, Grabowski and Prat." Some of his senior colleagues were not amused.

Richard Dent hinted that he might not play in the Super

Bowl if his contract was not rewritten. Jim McMahon was fined five thousand dollars for wearing an Adidas headband. The *Sun-Times* appeared on Friday with a twenty-page "wrap-around" about the Bears and was snatched up as soon as it appeared on the newsstands.

I took counsel with my other siblings. They were all aware of the problem, and as Eileen put it, most uncharacteristically, "All we can do is pray."

Sunday, January 12, was indeed L.A. weather—record warmth. Nonetheless Eric Dickerson was stopped cold as my youngest had confidently predicted, Jim McMahon wore a "Rozelle" headband, and he and Willie Gault (actually a very attractive young man) had another splendid day. McMahon, who did not learn his manners from his Mormon mother, poor woman, celebrated by sticking his tongue out on national TV.

New England, unaccountably, knocked off the hated Dolphins; my Joe took a permanent oath of loyalty to the Bears—at Biddy's insistence—"unless the Sullivans move the team back to Fenway Park"; Trish allowed as how it would be "unlucky" to have to play the Pats after they had won three upsets; Katie worried about the Pats' ability to cause fumbles; Cat frowned heavily and announced her fears that Jim McMahon had been hurt again.

My Biddy pounded a coffee table upsetting a mostly empty popcorn bowl. "No one can run against the Bears!"

"Too many teams moving around these days," Dad muttered ominously.

"Remember," Packy rushed in, "when Halas threatened to move to Arlington Heights and the mayor said that they would be the Arlington Heights Bears, not the Chicago Bears!"

"No one even argued." Dad chuckled. "They thought that Dick owned the label!"

Enormous sigh of relief.

On TV Virginia McCaskey kissed Walter Payton, presented the Halas Trophy to her husband and son, and assured the national audience, in what the Punk praised as classic Catholic doctrine, that the Old Man was still with us.

John Madden—who Biddy insisted was "adorable"—had already suggested that the Old Man had turned on the snow which came at the end of the game.

The next two weeks the mania grew like a plague. Catholic grade and high schools had "Bear Days" and even "Bear Weeks." GO BEAR! signs sprang up everywhere. Flowers appeared at the Halas graveside. (One said, "Somewhere he's doing the shuffle.") A Bears helmet, stolen and recovered, was displayed once again on an Art Institute lion. A headband was attached to the Picasso sculpture in the Daley Center Plaza, which had been renamed—in a touch of genius from someone in the Washington administration —the Chicago Bear Plaza. T-shirts and sweatshirts vanished from the racks of drugstores and dime stores and Marshall Field's; I encountered two young matrons on Michigan Avenue with small punks in strollers, both of whom were wearing "Rozelle" headbands. They waved cheerfully at me, doubtless because of my long orange and blue scarf and vast Bear's button, which, when stroked, appropriately played "Bear Down, Chicago Bears!"

Speaking of which, at the symphony on Thursday night, regular series C for the pirate (who is cultivated as well as sexy), Sir Georg Solti, wearing a Chicago Bears cap, directed the world's greatest orchestra in "Bear Down, Chicago Bears!"

"I doubt that it has ever been played quite so elegantly." Joe took my arm as we flowed with the crowd (most of whom were sporting Bears colors) into the Monroe Street parking lot.

"We're entitled," I sniffed.

The Punk was affronted because Margaret Hillis and the Symphony Chorus were not on hand to sing the sacred verses. He was also less than happy when he learned that the Lyric Opera, getting into the act, too, had dressed the three little messengers in the Zauberflöte in Bears jerseys. "None of them were black!" he protested. "Not fair to Samurai Mike!"

"Or Willie Gault," Biddy protested. "Totally gross!"

"Punk," I told him, "you're worse than the teenagers."

He smiled as though I had paid him a great compliment.

Jim McMahon suffered from his bruised rear end, an acupuncture specialist was brought to New Orleans, McMahon was accused of insulting New Orleans women, then exonerated. Brigid was nearly speechless with outrage, even when I explained to her that Jim was skillfully taking pressure off the rest of the team and building up the quasi-paranoia that the Grabowskis needed to stay angry.

"Really," was my youngest's only comment.

On the ten o'clock news, the Punk was interviewed by a wide-eyed young woman who did not know an end zone from a third-base line.

"It's a grass-roots revolt against neo-puritanism." The Punk was his most professorial. "Chicagoans are fed up with the national image of a second city, distinguished only by the 1968 convention, the Council Wars, and teams that don't win. We know, despite the self-hatred of some of our journalistic elites, that we are a great city. Somehow we receive no credit for our art museum, our orchestra, our writers, our universities, our splendid architecture. So now we are going to get even."

"You don't think it's all hype, Monsignor? Or Bear mania?"

Blackie sighed, his west-of-Ireland, asthma-attack sigh. "The only hype that can produce this phenomenon is a twenty-yard run by the ineffable Walter Payton or a touchdown pass from Jim McMahon to Willie Gault or—"

"You don't think there's a touch of commercialism?"

"—a two-yard plunge by William Perry."

"Are you going to New Orleans, Monsignor?"

"Oh, no. The cardinal will represent the Church at the Superdome. He's much older than I am, you see"—

blinking eyes—"and hence has been a Bear fan much longer."

"Uncle Punk is right!" Brigid trumpeted. "We're number one!"

"Really!" Trish bellowed.

"We're number one! We're number one! We're number one!"

A battle cry we would hear many times in the next couple of days.

In the relative quiet of our connubial privacy, while I brushed my hair and noted that the silver was becoming ever more common than the gold, we returned to the Problem.

"Did you talk to Helen?" Joe asked.

"I did. Of course. She is convinced, as I am, that the best thing to do is to say nothing. You know how stubborn Dad can be. . . ."

"Only one in the family."

"That remark is uncalled for. And stop looking at me that way. I don't feel like being ogled tonight."

"And the pope is no longer Polish. And if you don't want to be ogled, put your dress back on. . . . What did Helen say about the exhibition game?"

"It was just as you and the Punk predicted. It was only the two of them, of course, and they were in the house up at the lake, but he cheered for the Big Red from beginning to end."

"Oh my God!"

"Can you imagine what it will do to Brigid—and poor dear Trish—if they find out that he was and still is *a Chicago Cardinal Fan*!"

"Disaster!"

I'm not sure that Joe took the crisis as seriously as he might. In his heart of hearts he was probably pulling for the Pats. A terrible sin, but not enough to order him from the marriage bed!

Since the subject was undiscussable, we had never

learned the reason for this strange aberration in Dad's personality. Cardinal fans were few and far between to begin with. And when the Bidwells moved them to St. Louis, only a few did not abandon them for the Bears.

The diehards, however, persisted in their folly. The Big Red were still their team. And, worse luck for all of us, they were proud of their folly.

But, dear God in heaven, don't let him tell the kids on Super Bowl XX Sunday.

On Super Bowl XX Friday, Joe and I joined the O'Connors at supper over in Hyde Park. Typical University of Chicago dinner party. Narcissism rampant. Nancy and Steve learned long ago to bring in some of us so that they would preserve their sanity. The other guests usually seemed to think that Joe was a surgeon and I was a nurse.

They were disgusted with the "Bear hype."

"I'll be glad when it's over," someone said.

"Typical mass-media hype."

"Commercial exploitation."

"Most people are losers. They like to identify with winners."

"Terrible waste of money on all those gimmicks."

"Someone is getting rich."

I was a little offended because I was wearing a blue dress with orange trim.

"It's a University of Chicago *C*," I said tentatively.

The pirate swung into action. "Jung would have described the phenomenon as an affirmation of our community links with the forces of nature. Consider how many of the teams are named after totemic animals. Bears, of course; Lions, Rams, Dolphins, Cardinals, Eagles, Colts, Falcons. He would have seen it as the anima's effort to remind us of our ecological relationships. There are primal urges at work here which my clinical experience would lead me to believe are more healthy than not."

Horse manure, of course, but Joe learned long ago that academics are (a) inclined to view analysts with the same respect for the uncanny that more primitive types reserve for witch doctors, and (b) you can pile the horse manure up to the roof and no one notices, so long as you attribute it to Jung.

And, having learned a few things in twenty-five years of marriage, I didn't ask what totem the Patriots represented.

Brigid had not slept a wink on Super Bowl XX Saturday night. Katie Kane slept over at our house because her parents had to go to New Orleans (her father is a columnist and, like Fitz and Mike Royko, took a dim view of the recent converts to Bear mania: "Like all converts, they should be given collection envelopes and holy water!"). Trish, of course, joined them. They played the shuffle all night.

The sportswriters were optimistic on Sunday morning. The *Tribune*'s computer said Bears by three points, which seemed kind of scary. Brigid, who had pored over a chart most of Saturday, emerged at breakfast with her official prediction:

"Bears by thirty-five!"

Her brothers and her boy cousins hooted and hollered. She stomped out of the room in furious tears. I almost followed her, torn, as usual, between my mother instincts and my shrink skills. The latter won and I left her alone. Why spoil the fun!

Besides, despite the Punk's pessimism ("In our deepest hearts all Bears fans anticipate disaster"), I figured five touchdowns was about right. The Patriots had a very weak pass defense and McMahon would pick them apart. And no one scores much against the Bears!

The family party started at Dad's house at three o'clock and dragged on interminably while we all fretted nervously. Biddy and Trish, white-faced and silent, lay on their stomachs as close as they could get to the TV, as though their presence would reassure the team in far-off New Orleans.

They didn't listen even to my stanza of the Ryan Family Shuffle:

> *"I'm Mary Kate, the lady shrink,*
> *I read the unconscious, know what you think,*
> *Sure you all want the Bears to win,*
> *Even this hunk with the Boston grin,*
> *We haven't had a champ in a long, long time,*
> *And we're not gonna wait to eighty-nine.*
> *No Foxboro team can burst our bubble,*
> *We're just gonna claim the Super Bowl Shuffle!"*

"Really, Mo-THER!" Brigid sighed, sounding much like her monsignorial uncle.

Finally the game started. On the second play, disaster: Payton fumbled. I was certain Biddy would go into hyperventilation.

Instead she was as cool as Mike Ditka.

"They're a little tense. Give them a play or two to settle down."

She proclaimed that the New England field goal was decisive. "They couldn't gain a single yard from scrimmage! They're finished. Like totally."

Well, I won't bore you with the game, which for anyone not from Chicago was a bore after Matt Suhey's first touchdown. We blew them out.

I began to relax. In another few hours it would all be history. There'd be a big celebration in the Bear Plaza, a lot of Bears souvenirs would be purchased, and our family would have survived a major crisis. No revelations about the Big Red.

The family secret blew up at halftime.

"Poor Walter Payton," I said sympathetically. "They're all keying on him. No records today."

"Who holds the record for NFL championship game running?" Dad wondered, a little grin playing on his lips.

Blackie rolled his eyes in horror. I didn't know why, because I wasn't that much of a historian of the NFL. Yet.

"Do you mean the most yards per carry?" Brigid cocked her eye at her grandfather. "Everyone knows that, Grandpa Ned."

"Well, who?"

"Elmer Angsman in 1947 when the Chicago Cardinals won the championship from the Philadelphia Eagles, twenty-eight to twenty-one. I don't know why they're not mentioned when people talk about the other Chicago champs. Their title is more recent than either the Cubs or the Sox."

If I had false teeth to swallow, I would have swallowed them. The Punk looked like he was going to choke on his Perrier. The rest of the room lapsed into dead silence.

"Called them the Big Red." Dad was grinning broadly.

"They had a wonderful backfield," Biddy continued, as though she had been in Comiskey Park in 1947 to watch them. "Pat Harder, Charles Trippi and . . ." She hesitated.

"Paul Chrissman at quarterback."

"Right."

"God be good to him, he was the best announcer till John Madden."

"Before my time." Brigid returned her attention to the screen, where the teams were forming up for the second half.

"I think they've won, dear," I said, changing from shrink to mother.

"The game isn't over," Dad began, his pale blue eyes glinting.

"Till the fat lady sings," Brigid finished for him.

What can I tell you?

That night I woke up in the small hours.

"Did they really win?" I asked the pirate.

"Who? The Patriots?"

"Silly. No, I mean it really happened?"

"Yep, the Bears really won. . . . Hey," he said, remem-

243

bering an unsolved puzzle like you do in the small hours. "How did Biddy know about the 1947 Cardinals?"

"She's been devouring books about pro football for the last six weeks. I wish she'd pay as much attention to her schoolwork."

"You don't think the old fella put her up to it?"

"Of course he did. He's been laughing at us all along."

"Oh." Yawn. Puzzle solved.

"You know what worries me?"

"What?" He was almost back to sleep.

"Suppose the Bears play the Cardinals in the NFC championship next year."

"I think I might move back to Boston."

He wouldn't dare.

❦ Caitlin ❦

You don't expect your family to be denounced at Mass the Sunday before Christmas. Not even if your family is like mine. I mean, if you and your husband are both psychiatrists, the family is bound to be a bit odd. Right?

But still, the week before Christmas?

Father Rick Neenan was the celebrant—oops, president of the Eucharistic Community. Rick is tall, blond, lean, a sort of underweight ecclesiastical Nick Nolte, till you see the harsh light in his eye and the thin line of his lips. Then you think of Dominican friars with thumbscrews.

"We cannot be Christians in the modern world," Rick informed us, "unless we identify with the poor and the oppressed. Those who seek revolutionary justice in the third world are the true followers of Jesus, the greatest of all revolutionaries. If we do not make common cause with them, we have no right to claim to be Christian."

On one side of me my husband, Joe Murphy, sighed. On the other side my oldest, Caitlin, giggled. Joe is one of the few Catholic laity left who actually listen to sermons. Rick could have suggested the sacrifice of twenty maidens to Astarte and Joe would have been practically the only one in the church to have noticed. Your typical parishioner goes into such a profound trance at the beginning of the sermon —oops, homily—that even if something worthwhile is being said s/he doesn't hear it.

Caitlin, well, let's just say that she has a highly developed sense of the ludicrous.

"Christianity is a harsh, demanding challenge, particularly to those who live in a neighborhood like this and are therefore guilty of the terrible sin of exploitation. You are able to gorge yourself with food and drink and presents at Christmas because your feet are on the necks of the oppressed of the earth."

Rick is not all that bad, actually. He's from the neighborhood, of course; home for Christmas with his mother and father before they leave for the family condo on Maui. ("Should go to Molokai," Caitlin whispered into my ear. "I didn't know your generation learned about Damian," I whispered back, a little snidely perhaps.) There's nothing wrong with him that getting out of school into the world wouldn't cure. Twelve years in the seminary, another four years studying theology in Holland, two years of postdoctoral work at Union Theological—before you know it, a priest is in his thirties and never done a wedding rehearsal or policed a High Club dance.

"Poor Rick," my brother Blackie said recently, and sighed, "is infected with a bad case of German idealism. The prognosis in such cases is guarded." Blackie is a priest, too. A monsignor even. Though, as Caitlin says, we do not hold it against him. "In any confrontation between American empiricism and German idealism, the American loses because he is required to listen."

Our pastor is a dear sweet man who has not taken a stand on anything since 1970. The week before, a priest from some right wing group had ranted in the parish hall against the Marxist danger. Now we had Marxism from the altar the week before Christmas. A few people write the chancery every Sunday afternoon to complain. The rest just go into a self-induced hypnotic trance.

"In the years to come," Rick droned on, looking, if I do say so, incredibly handsome, "the Church will undoubtedly respond to the pleas of the poor and the oppressed of the world and abolish Christmas, because it has become a culture feast which only confirms people like us in our slothful complacency. Christmas has deteriorated into corrupt, cuddly, commercial capitalistic complacency. It cannot be saved."

"Alliteration," Dr. Murphy murmured in despair next to me.

"Definitely cute." Caitlin giggled on the other side. "I think I'm going to be a target."

"Shush," I said to both of them.

The pastor would no more notice Rick's diatribe than would any of his parishioners. "I enable and affirm," he says. "I don't take stands." Which led my brother the monsignor to remark that the pastor would make a wonderful archbishop.

"We must take Christ out of Christmas," Rick continued, "and free Him from the comforting, sticky, saccharine sentimentality which has dechristianized the holiday season. We must return to the early-Christian custom of celebrating His Coming on the Feast of the Epiphany and experience that Day as an occasion for rededication to the cause of the liberation of the third world from capitalist and imperialist oppression."

People around us were beginning to glance at their watches. Your Catholic laity will sit through total nonsense in sermons—oops—homilies, if the nonsense doesn't take more than ten minutes. After that they go into prerevolutionary agitation.

"Moreover, women will come to understand that the Madonna as we see her in Christmas cards and department-store displays is a symbol of male chauvinism, totally unrelated to the oppressed woman in the cave at Bethlehem. The woman in the typical crib scene is a symptom of false consciousness."

"My God," I said.

"Shush," my spouse and oldest replied in unison.

Hey, I'm the vice-president of the Women's Caucus in the American Psychiatric. I know chauvinism and false consciousness when I see them; and I get plenty of chance to see them. Moreover, I'm a liberal Democrat like my mother before me. I'm for justice to the poor and oppressed, too. But Christmas . . .

"The Madonna has become a figure of sentimentality, a symbol of exploitation and oppression. She reassures us that Jesus is on our side when in fact He is on the side of those we oppress."

"Here it comes." Caitlin leaned forward expectantly.

He wouldn't dare, I thought without much conviction.

What can I tell you about Caitlin?

There's no point in being a mother unless you can worry about your kids. Right? Try as I might, I've never been able to worry much about Caitlin, which is enormously frustrating. I think she worries about me more than I worry about her. When I'm worn and battered but not enough to go to my training analyst, I talk to her. I'm the only mother in the country who calls her daughter at college because she needs a shoulder to cry on.

Even when Caitlin was a teenager, which she stopped being two years ago, her principal form of adolescent revolt was laughing at me. She's a tall, strikingly beautiful honey blonde with impish blue eyes in a delicate face that is a photographer's delight. If Bo Derek is a "10," my Caitlin is an "11," at least.

She's in her last year at Notre Dame and, instead of being a model for photographers, plans to be a photographer herself and has been taking courses in photography at the Art Institute for the last couple of summers. She is also into gymnastics, body-building, and karate. A sweet, loving, thoughtful, party-saving girl. Until you push her too hard. Like the boy did at the Gamekeeper's (a bistro on Fullerton) last summer. He pawed her once and she told him to stop. He pawed her a second time and she told him that if he did it again, she'd break his arm.

He did and she did.

That's my Caitlin.

"You admired those pictures in the vestibule of the church when you came in for the Eucharist, did you not? You told yourselves how cute the little babies were and how pretty all the colors were. You told one another how nice it was to have such a sweet display at Christmas." Rick was rising to his peroration. "If Jesus of Nazareth were here today, he would tear them from the wall just as he overturned the moneychangers' tables in the temple. The women and children in those pictures are false symbols. They hide misery and injustice. They confirm you in your sick, sentimental complacency. They should be torn out of this church just as this phony season should be torn out of your lives."

"Mary Kate!" Joe pulled me down. "Not during Mass!"

"Mo-THER!" Caitlin whispered in mock horror. "Everyone is *looking* at us."

Which they were.

Rick strode back to the altar like he was Jim McMahon going into a huddle after completing a thirty-five-yard pass to Willie Gault. The congregation rose to its feet, engaged in the ancient Christian ritual of looking at the watch, and struggled heavily through the Nicene Creed. We then sang "O Come Emmanuel" while I told myself that the child was old enough to take care of herself. If she wasn't humiliated, why should I be?

Break the so-and-so's arm, Caitlin.

Besides, hadn't her exhibition of "Ethnic Madonnas" won the Art Institute prize for students last summer? Hadn't there been an article in the *Sun Times* about the show? Didn't Caitlin explain to the reporter, tongue in cheek, I fear, how she had sought out the young mothers who best portrayed the experiences of the black, Hispanic, Asian, Native American, Appalachian, Italian, German, Polish, Hungarian, Croatian, and oh yes, Irish heritages?

What did I care what some smartmouth young priest with a Ph.D. said?

Actually Caitlin had searched for the cutest mothers and the cutest babies she could find. "What else do you think Raffaello did?" she demanded.

No, I didn't care what Rick Neenan, the spoiled only child of rich parents, said about my daughter's prize-winning exhibition.

Still, break his arm anyway.

"Calm down before Communion," my Joe insisted. It was typical of the Boston Irish Jungian that he is. From him, my Caitlin gets her sweetness. Not from me, as you've probably guessed.

So I calmed down. More or less.

More less than more.

My husband and my oldest steered me toward the door of the church at the opposite end of the vestibule from Father Neenan, who was smiling broadly and accepting the praise of the older women of the parish. He nodded gracefully, as if he had just won his fourth Olympic gold.

Poor dear man, he didn't realize that he could have preached in Ugaritic (a language to which Blackie refers frequently, though he doesn't know any more about it than I do) and the same women would have showered on him the same praise.

If the empty niches in the vestibule of our church (emptied by an earlier and highly ecumenical pastor who felt that they would offend the Protestants who occasionally dropped by to see what was new in popery) were filled with rotund nudes, the place would remind you of the curved lobbies of the old Balaban and Katz theaters in Chicago. While Rick was receiving the adulation of his court, Caitlin set up shop at the other end of the vestibule and played archduchess to those who admired her exhibit.

Our receiving line was a lot bigger.

"None of them have mentioned the sermon," Joe said, his arm firmly around me.

I don't mind Joe's arm, even when it's there for purposes of restraint. Mostly.

"None of them heard it," I replied, not exaggerating all that much.

Then Rick, towering over the heads of his fans, saw us. Slowly he comprehended that the crowd around us was related to the color prints which decorated the marble walls. At first he seemed hurt; the women who had praised his homily (got it right finally) were now in line to praise the very sticky sentimentality he had condemned.

They had not heard a word. He had preached in vain. Jesus ignored by those who came down from the Mount of the Beatitudes with Him.

Then he recognized who the central figures were at our end, and he began to look faintly sick. He was, after all, a well-brought-up young man; the Ryans and the Neenans had been neighbors since he was a baby. If you're a Neenan, even a Neenan revolutionary, you don't insult a Ryan granddaughter. If she's young and radiantly lovely, you look like an even bigger fool.

When the congregation had left the vestibule to fight the parking lot and Sunday-morning papers, he sheepishly walked over to the three of us, his face about to turn the same color purple as his Advent scapular.

I didn't want to break his arm any more, poor embarrassed boy.

"I didn't realize . . ." he stumbled, groping for words.

"Hi, Father Rick." Caitlin brushed her lips lightly against his cheek. "Don't they feed you anything in New York? My mother will give you some of her fruitcake. Instant calories!"

"I . . . uh, the technique is excellent, Caitlin. . . ." A

crimson wave rose above his Roman collar and swept up his face to the roots of his curly blond hair.

"Oh, *these*? Nothing really, just a project I did for the AI last summer."

"First prize," I said fiercely.

"Mo-THER!"

"Article in the *Sun Times*," Joe added gently.

"Fa-THER!"

"The color composition is excellent. . . ."

"I want you to look at the eyes, Father Rick." Caitlin took his arm and guided him to the pictures. "See how fierce each of these mothers is? I tried to catch the passion they feel for their little boys. I didn't do it very well, but . . ."

"Very interesting." If the Lord God had appeared with an offer to carry him off in a flaming chariot, poor Rick would not have hesitated a second.

Joe rolled his soft gray eyes, a gesture which said, "She is her mother's daughter, no doubt about it."

"I think that's the way God feels about us, don't you, Father Rick?" The naive student willing to learn from the great theologian. "I mean, She loves us with the same sort of protective intensity that you see in a young mother's eyes. Right?"

"Right," he agreed weakly.

Was she making it up on the spur of the moment or had she thought that way all along? With my Caitlin, who can tell? Right?

"So that anyone who causes us to suffer is going to be in as much trouble with God as a person who hurts a baby would be with the baby's mother, don't you think?"

"Of course." He picked up a little confidence. "St. Bernard says—"

"Yes." Caitlin nodded her agreement. "We should suck the milk of grace from the breasts of Christ. I was kind of imagining a series next year on nursing mothers. Do you think the pastor"—all sweet, diabolical innocence—"would let me exhibit them in church? I mean, isn't God happy when She's feeding us sort of like a mother is when she's nursing a little baby?"

"Certainly." He was now searching for an excuse to flee to the safety of the sacristy.

"My madonnas' breasts would have to be beautiful," she mused. "Because they reflect God's beauty, don't they?"

"That's sound theology," he gasped, now the color of Cardinal Cronin's best robes.

"Theologians should use pictures in their books, don't you think, Father Rick? I don't mean pictures of women. Necessarily."

"An interesting idea."

"I mean God uses pictures when he makes us. Right?"

"Uh . . . I suppose so. Right."

"Then you think the pastor wouldn't mind? Bare breasts in church . . . I don't know. 'Course, the hungry baby sort of represents the hungry people of the world, doesn't he?"

"Lots of churches in Europe have nursing madonnas," he mumbled. "I really have to get ready for the next Mass. Nice to see you again, Joe, Mary Kate, Caitlin." He smiled faintly and blundered into one of the glass doors. "Have a . . . a happy Christmas."

Caitlin fired her parting shot as he fled up the aisle. "Merry Epiphany, Father Rick!"

"Witch," I said proudly.

"Well." Caitlin sighed contentedly. "*At least* I didn't call him Father Grinch, poor dear man."

⚘ Laura ⚘

"**Y**ou've never liked me, Ray." The gorgeous, suntanned blonde considered me with her cool, aloof blue eyes, glacial ponds glistening in the midmorning light, facsimiles of the lake next to which we sat on rainbow-colored deck chairs. "Why not?" She gestured submissively toward herself, a novice asking for a mother superior's judgment. "What's wrong with me?"

In our house, above the sun deck, my little sister's radio was announcing that diamonds were a girl's best friend. Laura Hurley was wearing her diamond, but unless I misread the signs, it was not just now her best friend.

"I don't like you?" I pretended to look around to see if she was talking to someone else. Our red and white prewar Higgins, smelling as always of ancient lubrications and dry rot, rocked uneasily next to its bleached and battered pier. Laura Jane had invaded my dreams in fifth grade. Dislike her? I adored her.

"You," she said, distinctly not amused. "You and Michael both. Neither of you have ever liked me. Why? I'm not too old to change."

Twenty was certainly not too old to change, not in the summer of 1950 with the warm sunlight on Lake Geneva promising you, if you are beautiful enough and smart enough, a life of happiness and excitement. Laura was model beautiful and scholarship smart, if by reputation shallow and "stuck up." Why worry about an inoffensive seminarian and a loudmouth navy veteran turned college freshmen? Why even think about them when you are engaged to the scion of an important west-side medical family?

"You're wrong, Laura." I sipped some of my mom's lemonade and shifted my chair so I was looking directly at her finely cut face, fine as Irish lace. Michael, not Mick. No one called him Michael. Except maybe someone who was in love with him. The phonograph switched to *"C'est si bon."*

In those days a priest or a would-be priest enjoyed a certain security in the man/woman game. He was mostly dismissed from the flirtation/pursuit/seduction ritual which is built into the relationship between the sexes. He could hide behind the mask of ecclesiastical wisdom, and a woman could be more relaxed and trusting with him. It's a useful custom that still persists, though some of the lads messed it up badly during the chaos of the late sixties, when, in the name of self-fulfillment, they turned predator.

"The little Hurley girl is here to see you," my mother had said fifteen minutes before. I was on the deck above our boat house, partly reading Abbot Marmion on the love of God and partly thinking of Janet Leigh in *The Red Danube* the night before (those were in the pre-*Psycho* days).

"She's not little." I put the Abbot aside. Lovely women on the screen (black and white) were much less disturbing than lovely women in flesh and blood (full color and stereo sound) on a humid summer day by the side of a lake studded with bouncing diamonds lapping against our decrepit old pier a few feet away.

"She's not in that two-piece swimsuit," Mom said reassuringly. My mother, who had never announced a visitor before, was about ninety-five-percent respectable upper-middle-class Irish matron. The other five percent was leprechaun waif. She rolled her eyes. "Not that it matters much. I'll bring lemonade."

"You'd better."

Mom was right; it didn't matter what Laura was wearing. Her light blue shirt, pleated white slacks, red belt, and red sandals did nothing to obscure her radiance. Lithe and willowy rather than voluptuous, tall, a slender, brisk, self-possessed athlete with pale blond hair (contained by a light blue ribbon which matched her blouse) and a porcelain-figurine face. Who needed Janet Leigh?

"Have some more lemonade." I filled her glass. "Have one of my mother's chocolate-chip cookies."

"Do you like chocolate-chip cookies . . . um, not as good as mine." She smiled slightly, a rare enough event, and Lake Geneva disappeared. "I'll make you some so you can compare. And you haven't answered my question. I'm serious, Ray. I won't leave here without an answer."

The phono switched to "Mona Lisa."

"I'll take the cookies, but only by the barrel." Cookies from Laura Hurley. I bet she'd never offered to make them for the Mick.

"Let me count the ways that I love her," he had said to me the other day. He had slipped away from summer school to take me on at the Commodore Barry Golf Course at nearby Twin Lakes. I bumped over to meet him at the train in our prewar LaSalle, which could have served as a Sherman tank. The Mick was out of shape. I beat him by nine strokes.

"I like school," he said. "Can you imagine what Sister Lourdes would say? Mick Breen likes school."

We were sitting outside the Red Barn, a publike place near the first tee of the course. Mick was drinking Coca-Cola.

He was, in those days, your Tyrone Power kind of Irishman: wavy black hair, skim-milk skin, dimpled jaw, thick eyebrows, low forehead, haunted eyes, half pirate captain, half poet. The son of a cop, he had joined the navy as soon as he graduated from high school (barely, because of time spent on mischief and beer drinking) to make it under the wire on the benefits of the GI bill. He'd spent three years scraping paint off ships in the San Diego navy yard (avoiding the shore patrol and the brig, much to the astonishment of the neighborhood) and was now working as a runner at the board of trade while he struggled through college, starting just as the rest of us were about to finish.

"I particularly like English literature." A deep flush spread over his dark face; Mick needed a shave every couple of hours. "This guy Browning . . ."

"What's that got to do with pork belly futures?" I wiped the sweat off my forehead.

"There's a trader in the corn pit who can quote whole passages from *The Ring and the Book*."

"*The Ring and the Book?*" I choked on my beer. "The only other person I know who's read that is Laura Jane Hurley."

"You see her?" he asked with elaborate casualness, his face so gentle that you'd have thought he was holding a six-month-old child in his arms.

"Her family still owns the house over in Glenwood Springs. She comes to my sister's parties."

"Still stuck up?"

"Surely not. Did we say such things about her, Mick?"

"Kids are cruel, aren't they?" He jammed his hands into his dirty navy fatigues and began pacing again. "I can't stop thinking about her. She haunted me every night for three years in San Diego. How do I love her . . . let me count the ways. . . ."

"That's Elizabeth to Robert," I pointed out.

"I know that." He sank to the ground and leaned against

257

the tree, holding his Coke glass in front of him as though it were a chalice. "I'm not a complete dummy, Ray. Just an incorrigible romantic who has fallen in love with an inaccessible woman."

The Mick was now up by four strokes in a much more intricate game than golf. He was reading the Brownings, he admitted he was an incorrigible romantic, he had confessed that, like me, he was obsessed with the lovely Laura, and he was prepared to grant that the obsession might be directed at a fantasy woman instead of a real one.

"Don't turn her into a goddess or a statue, Mick," I said, ducking behind priestly wisdom. "She's a flesh-and-blood person."

"Yeah." He stared dreamily at the whipped-cream clouds marching across the blue Wisconsin sky. " 'I love her freely as men strive for Right;/I love her purely, as they turn from praise./I love her with the passion put to use/In my old griefs, and with my childhood's faith.' "

This was, you must remember, 1950, and the west side of Chicago (in its summer mode). Our generation didn't quote Victorian poets. For that matter, we didn't know Victorian poets existed.

In one tiny corner of my brain there was the persistent thought that maybe she was not lost to either of us. You don't like to be ruled completely out of the game before it starts.

"I don't think she loves Tim Scanlan."

"How do you know that?"

"My sister says so. She knows everything." What Irish sister doesn't?

"How can I compete with Tim?" He spread his hands abjectly. "What could I offer her?"

"You don't need four or five drinks in you to be funny and fun. You can make her laugh; that's all she needs."

"Yeah, Mick Breen the clown." He hit the hard sand of the golf course like he wanted to start an earthquake.

"You gotta figure out whether you're Robert Browning or Pagliacci."

"Come on." He shook it all off with a laugh, typical Mick reaction. "I'll play you another nine."

I beat him by five strokes.

I had had some time to think about Mick and Laura before she showed up two steps ahead of my mother's lemonade and chocolate chips. What was I supposed to do?

She sat in the shade against the hill and slipped her sunglasses into the pocket of her blouse. We talked first about school. How did I like the seminary? I was surviving. How did she like Manhattanville? Wonderful. She was excited about the plays of Christopher Fry, especially *The Lady's Not for Burning; The Masters* by C. P. Snow, and the *Cantos* of Ezra Pound. She didn't like Henry Morton Robinson's *The Cardinal* and simply adored Thomas Merton's *Seven Story Mountain,* was terrified by but loved the film *Rashomon.* What did I think?

Laura had become a blossoming intellectual, careful and modest in her opinions, but articulate and willing to stick to her guns, chin resting on hand, long, distracting legs elegantly crossed, when I disagreed about Thomas Merton. (In retrospect, she was obviously right.)

After she graduated, she might enroll in a program in creative writing at the University of Iowa. Tim, however, disapproved. Why did a woman need creative writing to be a good wife and mother?

I was dazzled, awed, overwhelmed. What had brought this challenging goddess/genius to our sun deck? Then she asked, long fingers, nails burnished a pale red, resting defenselessly on solid, white-covered thighs, why I disliked her.

We both knew that wasn't the issue at all. Opportunity for treason to Mick appeared on the horizon, no bigger, as the Bible would say, than a man's hand. But getting bigger.

"You're wrong, Laura." I repeated my protest. "We don't dislike you."

Her skin tightened over those incredible facial bones. "You both think I'm stuck up. You both hate me."

Hey, don't break down and cry on me. I have no idea what to do with that.

My sister, in her role of music director, now provided "Good Night Irene."

"We both respect you a lot," I tried again. "Just the other day over at Barry we agreed that you weren't stuck up."

"Thanks," she said, bitter and unappeased. I filled her lemonade glass and offered her another cookie.

A mask had slipped away from Laura Hurley during our intense conversation about books and films and politics. Her eyes danced with pleasure that someone cared what she thought. She even laughed twice, once mildly and at me when I said I did not know who Ezra Pound was, and once enthusiastically and with me at herself when I said that she probably identified with the heroine of *The Lady's Not for Burning.*

Ah, lovely Laura, I can make you laugh more than Mick can.

Mick who?

Body and mind, sex and ideas, breasts and thighs and brain, vulnerability and strength, surrender and aggressiveness; if the spiritual director at the seminary could picture you and this conversation, he would be properly horrified. Not without reason. My "vocation" was in jeopardy.

What vocation?

Even today, the poignancy of that moment stings at my eyes, not for the pain of what would come later but for the beauty of the moment itself. It was a heady, dizzying quarter hour, like drinking too much of my father's prewar sparkling burgundy, which coexisted in our garage with the prewar LaSalle.

She would be well matched with Mick, my gentle roughneck mystic, my sweet-tempered roustabout saint. Only just now he was second in line to me, a golden-tongued precinct captain—well, silver-tongued anyway. A distant second.

Those were the most grace-drenched minutes of my life. Later, when I doubted the wisdom of my response, I complained to God that S/He shouldn't have permitted me to face a turning point in three lives with so little preparation. Still later I learned that grace has a timing of its own. You're never prepared for it, and you must always prepare for it.

"You avoid me. You despise me. Do you have any idea what it's like to be beautiful? Everyone hates you." Tears were replaced by fury tinged with despair. "Women because they're envious and men because they want you and you won't let them have you. It makes me feel foul and dirty and worthless. Why don't you like me?"

"Let me count the ways."

"You're quoting Elizabeth Browning out of context," she sniffed. "She was talking about love, not hatred."

I was now running on pure west-side Irish political instincts. "So am I."

"Huh?" She placed her lemonade tumbler carefully on the deck.

"I love you, Laura." I spoke very slowly. After this, I told myself, the subdiaconate with its commitment to celibacy would be a snap, if I ever arrived at that turning point. "I can't remember not loving you. Certainly from third grade on. I've always been about eighty percent in love with you. I avoid you partly because it takes boys our age a long time to get over their shyness with dazzling women and partly because I'm afraid of you."

"Afraid?" she stammered. "But I wouldn't . . ."

"Afraid." I plunged on; now it was sink or swim and I thought I would sink in the next couple of seconds. "That I'll fall the other twenty percent; that wouldn't be good for either of us."

Tiny circles of perspiration appeared on both sleeves of her blouse. Laura was shedding disguises with a more disconcerting effect on me than if she were shedding her clothes, a fantasy which at that moment seemed less troubling than what was actually happening. Gather 'round, you angels and saints; Ray Casey is in trouble.

Years after that morning I would read in Buber about what happens when an "it" becomes a "thou." Laura was in those precious seconds my first "thou," no longer merely exquisite breasts and quick wit blended into an appealing package, but a person like me, with fears and hesitations, hopes and anxieties, dreams and terrors. That made her all the more challenging, all the more mysterious, and therefore all the more delectable, all the more in need of me.

I wanted to reach across the few inches which separated us and touch her face with my consoling fingers.

"Why do you love me, Raymond?" Water was welling up in her eyes again.

I told her why I loved her. Not very poetic or romantic sentences. Straight pragmatic facts—all the time pretending to timeless priestly rationality and thus able to speak words otherwise impossible at the beginning of courtship. She was smart, beautiful, personable, honest, loyal, virtuous, everything a woman should be. She didn't laugh enough—we both laughed uneasily—but that could be cured. I even stumbled through some stuff about her own anguish and the desire to heal it. I added, as an inspired afterthought, that she was not only graceful but grace.

I felt that as a neophyte lover I hadn't done too badly. Dear God, how I loved her that morning in 1950.

"I know what you are saying, Raymond." She leaned her head back against the fabric of the deck chair and closed her eyes. "It's not the way my parents see me."

"If someone says such things to you often enough, you'll begin to believe them." Now comes the hard part, Ray Casey. Let's see how the golden-tongued orator copes with this one. Mick no longer exists. God? Who's He?

She loves me as much as I love her. A thin line of moisture was beginning to appear above her upper lip. "Tim thinks I'm a pretty nitwit."

Laura, as I'm sure you understand, did not need my

advice to give Tim his walking papers. She had made up her mind to that and was now testing other waters. Nonetheless, ducking behind my mask, I gave advice.

"Get rid of him."

She tore away my mask. "You're sure you're going to be a priest, Raymond?" She opened her tundra eyes and examined me curiously, respectful but still appraising.

There it is, you angels and saints, we all knew it was coming, didn't we? Make your decision, Casey.

"Yes."

I couldn't quite believe I said it. I still can't.

She nodded again. "I've always loved you, too, Raymond. I never could make up my mind between you and Michael." She blushed and grinned impishly. "I took turns with my crushes. Still, I'm glad you're going to be a priest."

"So am I. I think."

"Does Michael love me, too?"

Aha. That was the question, which at some not completely unconscious level of her personality she had come to ask. So . . . So why should I feel offended? So, she asked about me first, didn't she? So I wasn't an also-ran, was I?

"You don't expect me to answer that, do you, Laura? Ask him yourself."

"He doesn't intend to be a priest, does he?" The fingers of her right hand touched the back of my left hand, lingered for a few seconds, and then quickly pulled away, as if I were a hot oven.

"I think you can count on that. Here, swallow this chocolate chip while you're digesting the canary."

We both laughed, easily this time. Almost home.

"Then . . ." She wore a puzzled frown, an intellectual woman with an intractable problem. "Why be afraid of me? I'm only Laura."

"You didn't listen to me." I was as exhausted as if I had sailed our dory all day in a brisk wind. "If Laura is who I say she is, any man in his right mind would be afraid of her, especially a shy young man without much money who has only begun to discover himself."

She stood up crisply. "Well, I have my assignment." She considered me again with clouds over her glacial eyes. "Thank you, Ray."

"Don't mention it." I was entitled to my share of good, honest self-pity.

She kissed my cheek, hesitated, and then moved her lips to mine. Oh boy, I thought, I'm going to have to make that decision all over again.

"I'll always love you, Raymond. Always."

"Oh?" I said intelligently, for lack of something else to say. "Why?"

Her turn, "Count the ways." More tears. "'And if God chose, I shall but love thee better after death.'"

Then something happened—hormones in youthful animals, I suppose. Our arms encircled each other, our bodies pressed desperately together. If you're going to have only one skyrocket passionate kiss in your life, it might as well be with someone like Laura. She was as ethereal as the first shaft of light after a summer thunderstorm, as magical as the aurora on an August night, as solid and substantial as the noonday sun in the sky above us.

I was immersed, submerged, drowned in a soothing, gentle caldron of grace. Whatever the resident angels and saints might think, I resolved I would remain there always, even if she did taste strongly of lemonade and faintly of a post-toothbrush cup of coffee. We were betraying God and the Mick, but it didn't matter.

I know now that love between Laura Jane Hurley and me would not have betrayed anyone. I think I knew it then, too. Grace did not calculate obligations. It offered options.

I would still be there if she had not broken away, tears cascading again, and dashed up the steps. No, that's not true: if I had clung to her, she would not have broken away. On the lawn she turned, waved in a glorious, devastating gesture, and shouted, "Thanks, Ray, I'll never forget this morning."

The image of her waving to me, hand raised, magic figure extended invitingly against the cloudless sky while the phonograph played "Good Night Irene," is burned in my memory, never to be exorcised. Venus du lac. Deeply but, I must confess it, pleasantly shaken, I returned to the good Abbot Marmion. The song now was "Tzena, Tzena, Tzena!" No one had the right to be that vigorous on a humid Wisconsin summer day, not even a Sabra warrior.

"Who won?" my mother asked maybe ten minutes later.

"God, I guess."

"He usually does."

"Yes." Actually I was beginning to feel pleased with myself. I had not behaved brilliantly, but I hadn't booted it completely either. Laura had learned that she was loved. So had I.

"And the Mick?"

"Unless he's a complete idiot." I turned the page in Marmion, quite unaware of what the man had said on the last ten pages.

It's worked out, I guess. They seem happy together. There have been troubles: a leukemia death; conflict in 1968; a son, an ROTC officer, wounded in Nam; a daughter, a peace activist, arrested at the Democratic convention; parents torn between them, blaming one another. Now all reconciled. A number of fierce battles; they both walked out twice, though never for longer than forty-eight hours. ("My fault all four times," Laura insists, but her husband claims it was his fault at least three times.) Five healthy kids now, four marriages, six grandchildren. One son, a blond-bearded giant, is still in graduate school in comparative literature at Harvard. Laura smiles and laughs more than the Mick (still "Michael" to her, save on comic occasions when I think the nickname is a secret erotic invitation) and he smiles and laughs even more than he did in high school.

He's the only trader on the floor with a Ph.D. in English

literature. She's published two books of short stories and a book of poems and has won some prizes. To my prejudiced eyes she is more beautiful now than she was then.

Do I regret my decision? Every day. It was the right choice for all of us. If you go north and are happy there, you regret that you did not go south and mourn for all the lost joys that may have been yours in the south. If I had gone south, I would now have even more regrets. The luminous Laura's soul blended much better with the spirit of a roughneck mystic than it would have with that of a silver-tongued precinct captain.

Do I believe that? Sure. Usually ninety percent. Sometimes fifty percent. Occasionally, hardly at all.

We have never spoken about the humid summer morning in 1950 when to the music of "Good Night Irene" I held her in my arms, her breasts firm against my chest. Maybe I should ask her how she remembers it. I guess I'm afraid she won't remember it.

I dream of her often. I still love her and always will. A grace forever and ever.

Amen.

Does she still love me?

I don't know. You'll have to ask her.

However, I never suffer from a shortage of chocolate-chip cookies.

❧ Maggie ❧

It happened ten years ago and I still shiver when I think about it.

Usually I don't think about it, if I can avoid the subject. And when I do remember what happened, I try to persuade myself that it didn't happen or that it was a dream or that I have forgotten all the details.

Then I remember that I heard the doorbell. There can be no doubt about that. I heard the doorbell.

I'm afraid to talk to Maggie about what happened that day. I tell myself that she probably doesn't remember it at all. She was only twelve, going on thirteen. Kids don't remember, I tell myself. Why upset her?

The truth is that I fear she will remember perfectly. Then I'll be deprived of my treasured half conviction that it never happened.

I shiver as I set down these sentences. *Shiver* is the only word I can use to describe the reactions of myself and the others involved, so you must excuse me if I use it often toward the end of the story.

Like, as poor Mom used to say, someone walked over

your grave. A touch of the uncanny, like being afraid of the dark in the middle of the night when you were a little kid.

I got over shivering in the dark. If it has lasted ten years now, I don't think I'll ever be cured of the shivers when I recall that beautiful spring afternoon.

If it really happened. Maybe it was all a dream.

Anyway, with Maggie's marriage at hand, the memories of that afternoon are strong these days. Maybe if I set the story down on paper, I'll realize how absurd they are and I'll stop shivering.

The four of us did not exactly react enthusiastically when we heard that my father intended to remarry. Mom's slow, brave, agonizing death eighteen months before had been a shattering experience for three teenagers and one preteen. A stepmother we did not want or need.

Especially one like Maureen. She was much younger than Dad, a junior partner in his law firm. Short, pretty, even sexy in an intense blond way, she was as different from Mom as anyone could possibly be, the cool, competent, ambitious young professional woman to the tips of her well-manicured fingernails.

Why her? we all thought.

She tried to be cautiously friendly with us, doubtless because she had read somewhere about the problems of resentful teenage stepchildren. She was, however, in a no-win situation. If she had been more friendly, we would have resented her presumption. As it was, we resented her aloofness.

In theory we knew that Dad would remarry eventually, but we were not happy that he had not waited till we were all firmly out of the way—till after Maggie was married, for example.

So Christmas that year was not much fun. Melissa came home from Miami of Ohio, where she was a freshman, with that terrible eagerness for home and family and old friends that only a freshmen can feel—to find Maureen waiting for her. She cried herself to sleep the first night.

I arrived home from Stanford the next day to encounter Lissa, Tommy, and Maggie in a hysterical fight over the cars. It took me hours to find out that the real cause of their rage was *her*.

Tommy, a high-school senior at the "no big deal" stage, insisted repeatedly that Maureen was no big deal. Maggie told me between weeping jags that she hated Maureen and always would. Lissa took the position that it was all right with her if Daddy had to take a woman to bed with him, but "why such an incredible drip?"

"Don't be crude, Lissa," I protested.

"I don't care. I think it's disgusting."

So did I, to tell the truth. Kids and young people can be horny, but not parents.

I should add that they were not living together and, for all I knew, not sleeping together.

I disliked her at first meeting; she was just too much well-dressed, funny-talking Ivy League for me; arrogant, I told myself, and frigid. I also felt a tiny bit sorry for her. We scared the living daylights out of her.

And she had lots of reasons to be scared.

Mind you, we were perfectly civil. We had been brought up to be polite to strangers and we were polite. Unassailably correct. We communicated our feelings about Maureen to her—Dad was too out of it to perceive our signals—by silence, by body language, and by conversations from which she was excluded because she didn't know the contexts.

We never mentioned Mom, of course; a much more effective technique than if we had talked about her all the time.

I suspect that we sent her home in tears more than one night during that holiday season. The party for us at her (elegant and tasteful) apartment was a total disaster, largely because Maggie came down with what she alleged was the "stomach flu" in the middle of the meal and didn't quite make it to the bathroom.

Maggie was a strawberry blonde poised temporarily on

the border of radiant young womanhood, smart, lively, funny, and model beautiful, enough to threaten any stepmother.

Mom had been a Maggie, too, when she was growing up—short for Margaret Mary, of course. Dad always called her Margaret. Our sister was a namesake and, like all youngest children, acquired her nickname without anyone realizing. As Mom used to say of her, "She's a Maggie, all right, not a Peggy or, God help us, a Megan."

She was also diabolically clever at practical jokes, a cleverness which was now being turned to deadly serious purpose.

Daddy was immune to everything. We were one big happy new family and everyone would love Maureen as their "new mother." Maureen, to give her credit, winced whenever he said that and tried to pull back discreetly from an instant intimacy that she saw we did not want. She tried subtly to hint to Dad that he should cool it for a while, but he was so much in love, poor man, that he didn't hear her.

"This marriage will be the best thing that has happened to our family in a long time," he announced cheerfully as we rode home from the debacle at Maureen's apartment near Lincoln Park.

"I wish you wouldn't say that, Daddy." Lissa was not a drama major but she had a fine sense of how one should deliver a carefully prepared dramatic statement. "It may be the best thing that's happened for *you*, and of course we are happy for you. But it's not the best thing that's happened for us."

Before Dad could ask for an explanation, almost as though she were reciting a line, Maggie retched again. Dad had to stop the car on Lake Shore Drive so she could vomit.

The next day I went over to the rectory and talked to the young priest.

"Of course you resent her," he said. "So what else is new?"

"What do you think of her?" I demanded.

"What does it matter what I think?"

"I don't trust what I think."

"Ah, Johnny, you *are* growing up. What a pity. We lose one of the great all-time teenage hardheads. Let me try your maturity further. What if you met Ms. McNulty at a party and there was no prospect of her marrying your father?"

"Well . . . I'd size her up, figure she was pretty cool, and feel disappointed that she wasn't a few years younger."

"Precisely."

"A nice, intelligent, attractive, even very attractive young woman."

"Ah?"

"I'd probably wonder a little what she'd be like in bed and kind of envy anyone who was going to find out."

"Now we get down to cold, hard, clinical male judgments. She's not what you would call voluptuous?"

"There's different ways to be sexy." I felt my face grow warm, because I was both defending my intended stepmother and admitting that my own criteria had changed in the past several years—as the young priest had cheerfully predicted. "And she paints and plays the piano and reads a lot. . . ."

"And?"

"Well, I wouldn't mind seeing what she looks like in a bikini." Which was true enough, but more important to maintain a little of my rectory image.

"You may then eventually come to accept her as your father's wife?"

It was a clever way to put it. I knew all along that I would eventually make my peace with Maureen—probably on the day I called her "Mau."

"It's not me I'm worried about. It's Maggie. She can be a bitch on wheels when she makes up her mind."

"That, John, my newly wise friend, is an understatement."

So I called a family meeting.

"I like her, you know." Tommy astonished us all. "She likes hard rock, too. Not just that classical stuff she played for us. She's not bad-looking, either."

"Don't be infantile," Lissa sniffed.

"I hate her, hate her, hate her." Maggie clenched her fists in somber determination.

"Cool it, you guys," I ordered, in my role of senior offspring. "Dad loves her and wants to marry her. In a few years we will all have left home. I don't want to have to worry about his being lonely."

"I'll have to put up with her till I go to college," Maggie sobbed. "Five years! I can take care of him as well as she can."

Even then I was smart enough to know that was the issue. Maureen was taking Dad away from Maggie, who had seen herself as both daughter and wife all through her high-school years.

"A daughter is no substitute for a wife." Lissa agreed tentatively with my position. "But why did he have to pick someone so *weird*?"

"What's weird about her?" I asked.

"Well . . . those yucky paintings . . ."

"You like the ones Jan Crowley does."

"That's different. She's my friend. Anyway I don't think Maureen is marrying Daddy because she loves him. She just wants to stay with the firm."

"Oh, she loves him all right." Tommy changed the station on the FM radio which was always by his side. "She's goofy about him. Worships him." He sighed. "Probably figures that with him as a husband to take care of her, she can relax a little and enjoy living."

"She does *not* love him," Maggie screamed. "She's marrying him to keep her job."

"No, she's not," Tommy continued doggedly. "She will leave the firm and go somewhere else after they're married.

I heard Mr. Clarke kid Daddy that they were losing the best young lawyer he'd seen in the last ten years."

"What do you think, Johnny?" Lissa turned to me.

"Well . . ." I spoke slowly and carefully. "I agree with Tommy. She's like a teenager who has fallen in love for the first time. If Dad does that to women, we have to figure that he's going to come home with a new wife eventually. We could do a lot worse than Maureen. She'll be good to him, and that's what he needs. It's up to him, after all."

Lissa seemed relieved, positively eager to accept my judgment. "I suppose you're right." She brightened. "If Dad likes her, it doesn't matter that I think she's weird."

There was a hint in her conclusion that Lissa's dramatic role had ended and that her judgment about Maureen's weirdness was subject to later review.

As in, "I *never* said she was weird."

"She's afraid of us." Maggie's jaw jutted sharply, her blue-green eyes turned the color of alloy steel. "She knows Dad loves us more than he loves her. He would choose us if he's *forced* to."

An ominous threat if I ever heard one.

"I'm not going to put him in that position," I said. "You have to give her a chance, Mag."

"No way."

The three of us argued with Maggie for another hour without budging her.

"She'll be all right," Lissa said to me as she was waiting for her date that night. "You know how dramatic kids her age have to be."

"I hope so." I didn't feel much confidence.

So Lissa and I returned to our respective colleges for the long hard time between Christmas and semester break; gray cold, hectic, lonely days. Well, they weren't gray or cold at Leland Stanford Junior Memorial University, but that was another matter. Dad phoned occasionally. He sounded harried and uncertain. He put Maureen on once. She asked me in a very timid and uneasy voice how school was.

"No problem." I couldn't believe I'd let the cliché slip out.

First thing I did when I got home in March was check with Tommy, Maureen's only true ally among the family.

"I don't think there will be a wedding," he said in his best no-big-deal tone. "Probably they shouldn't get married now anyway."

"Why not?"

"Would you want a stepdaughter like Maggie bugging you every day for the next five years? What if you have a couple of kids of your own and she hates them, too?"

"She might love a little sister or brother."

"I wouldn't bet on it."

"Has Dad talked to her?"

"Dad and Maggie fight all the time. Which is what Mag wants, of course. It worries Mau and then she and Dad fight."

"Mau?"

"That's her name, isn't it?"

Like a coward I took off for Florida with only a quick conversation with Dad. He looked beat out and depressed. Maggie was winning.

The wedding was scheduled for the last week of May. I came home before exams at the end of April to interview for a summer job. The wedding was kind of on hold. Maureen did not appear at our house and I had the impression that she and Dad were in the middle of a long and bitter fight. Maggie seemed triumphant.

It was on a Friday, the last day of April that it happened. I had postponed my return to Palo Alto till Sunday night because of what seemed then a very problematic blind date. So I was in my room studying for my Latin American history final, trying to make up for the time I'd lost on the subject with the seductive argument that I always did well in history.

It was a glorious afternoon, the kind we don't normally have in the Middle West because they passed a law against spring here in the days before Daley was mayor and could have prevented it. Green lace had begun to appear on the trees, Mom's bulbs were blooming in the garden, the neighborhood was quiet, the sky clear, the air still and pure with a touch of lilac scent floating lightly in it—a Chaucer April day instead of a T. S. Eliot April day. I thought about writing a poem on the strength of life and then dismissed the idea because after Chaucer and Eliot, who was I to try April?

Even if the date turned out to be a dog (which I fully expected) I was glad I'd stayed to enjoy the day.

See how clearly I remember the details after ten years? Believe me, I don't want to remember them.

A little before three I heard Maggie trudge up the stairs, home from seventh grade.

"Johnny?" she shouted. "You home?"

"Yeah, where's Mrs. Finnerty?"

Our silent and patient housekeeper.

"Day off." She sounded sullen. "I have to go to volleyball at the park at four."

"I'll drive you."

Not a word of thanks. When Maggie was stonewalling the world, no prisoners were taken.

Fifteen or twenty minutes later the doorbell rang. I determined to ignore it. It rang again and then again.

"Mag, would you answer the door, please. I'm studying."

"Answer it yourself."

"*Please,* Maggie."

"Oh, *all right!*"

As she clumped down the stairs, sounding like a platoon of fully equipped combat infantry, the bell rang again.

"Answer it, *Maggie!*"

"*Okay!*"

I continued to study.

Sometime later, five, maybe ten minutes, maybe less,

Maggie bounced up the stairs and down the corridor to my room. I didn't turn around. No point in worrying about the Brazilian empire on my blind date.

"John . . ." She sounded excited.

"Did you answer the door?"

"Yes!"

"Who was it?"

"Mom!"

I wheeled around in my chair and almost fell on the floor. Maggie was still wearing her plaid school-uniform skirt and white blouse. She was glowing with such ecstatic happiness that at first I thought she was standing inside a halo.

"Mom's dead. . . ." The first hint of the uncanny, the first hint of many shivers.

"Oh, I know *that*. Only she isn't, not really. She even bawled me out for not answering the door the first time, like she used to. Anyway, she says we should all be really good to Mau"—her words bubbled out like Chaucer's cheerful brook—"and that she understands why we don't like her, but she likes her a real lot and that she and Dad need each other and she's happy for them both and that I should stop being gross and love Mau a whole lot because it's hard for her to come into a family that's already going and I should make up for all the times I made her cry, poor woman, and that everything is going to be all right and—"

"Maggie, who was it at the door?"

"I told you it was Mom, silly." She was weeping but because of ecstatic joy. "Would I make something like that up? And she says you're going to like your date tonight a real lot and that Mau and I will be great pals . . . remember how Mom use to say *pals*? And—"

"What did she look like, Mag?"

"Like she always did. I mean, how else would she look? Pretty and happy, with her white dress, you know, like before she was sick. . . . Now will you drive me over to volleyball? I'll change my clothes real quick."

She bounced down the hall to her own room.

In the car I tried to persuade her that she had either imagined it or made it up. She dismissed my arguments as not worth considering. "'Course she was real. You heard the bell, didn't you?"

I then told her that maybe it would be a good idea to keep what happened to ourselves. She agreed readily. "They might not understand, huh?"

"That's right."

"Okay, I won't tell anyone else."

At least I wouldn't have to worry about Maggie being shipped off to a shrink.

Was that all I did?

I'm afraid so. I was only twenty. Faced with the inexplicable and the uncanny, I chickened out. If Maggie was having a nervous breakdown, Dad would notice soon enough.

So I pretended to myself that whatever had happened did not happen and reflected on the joys of the blind date on the flight back to San Francisco on Sunday night.

Ten days later I came home for the wedding, the summer, and the pursuit of the blind date, in the reverse order of importance. The Friday-afternoon event had been stricken officially from my memory.

I had not put my duffel bag on the floor of the front room before the phone rang. The young priest. Would I mind dropping over to the rectory for a few minutes? Now?

Maureen was in the rectory parlor with him, gorgeous in a light blue dress. I kissed her on the lips—in love with one woman, in love with them all—and said brightly, "Nice dress, Mau, you're looking great!"

They were perfectly agreeable lips, fun to kiss, tasting just now of very recently administered mouth spray. I must make a point to kiss them often. How better to let an appealing and vulnerable stepmother know she was accepted?

"Uh, thanks, Johnny." She blushed and tried to gather her emotions together. "You're very sweet. . . ."

Only then did it impinge on my consciousness that she and the young priest had both looked pretty grim when I barged in on them.

"Everyone is being sweet to Maureen these days." The priest lifted his eyebrows. "Including Maggie."

"A complete turnaround, John." Maureen seemed breathless. "She couldn't be more loving or supportive or helpful. She really is a marvelous little girl. I thought I would never like her, and now I find that I love her dearly."

"Well, that's the way Mag is. I figured she'd turn around like that."

I had started to shiver, terrified and at the same reveling in the taste of Mau's lips.

"But Maureen is now worried sick about her."

"Really?"

Here it comes.

"She claims"—Maureen hesitated, flustered and baffled, and shivering a little, too—"that your mother came up to the door of the house and, well, sort of endorsed me."

"She wasn't supposed to tell anyone that." I pounded the young priest's desk.

"In other respects"—he rearranged his notebook and calendar which I had disturbed—"she seems perfectly normal and healthy. Sister tells me that she is no more hyper than any of the other seventh-grade girls with vacation coming. It is natural that she would feel, uh, some unease about your father's forthcoming remarriage, and search for the sort of approval which would legitimize a change to a more positive attitude, one in keeping with her normal enthusiasms. . . ."

"I asked her why she had changed her mind." Maureen was, quite unconsciously, wringing her hands, poor dear bikini-appropriate woman. "And so she told me. She said you'd made her promise not to tell anyone, but she didn't think it applied to me."

"Of course not." The young priest rolled his eyes.

"I'm so terribly concerned about her. She said you were there. . . . Did you see. . . ?"

"No, I didn't see anyone."

"My position"—the young priest tapped his fingertips together—"is that it was a harmless hallucination and that there is no cause for concern unless her behavior becomes disquieting in other respects. We take grace where we find it and with gratitude. . . ."

"Did you. . . ?" Mau, my glorious stepmother-to-be, groped for words.

I knew that I had to tell the truth.

"I heard the doorbell ring."

There was the stillness of the graveyard in the rectory parlor, maybe the stillness of "very early in the morning, the first day of the week."

"You heard the doorbell?" the young priest asked, very tentatively.

"Yes, I heard the doorbell."

"As I say, we take grace wherever we find it. . . ."

"You heard the doorbell?" Mau's jaw dropped and her wondrous blue eyes opened into huge circles.

Then, despite the terror of the moment, or maybe because of it, I made explicit in my head an observation which had been implicit for a long time: she'd be great in bed. Simultaneously, I also finally admitted my father into the male half of the human race along with all the rest of us.

His delectable future wife and the young priest both shivered slightly.

"I heard the doorbell. Four times, the last just before Maggie opened the door."

And now, ten years later, there is no escaping that point: I did hear the doorbell.

Four times.

❧ Marge ❧

At supper on Christmas Eve my mother and father began another argument. I was delighted. If his first Christmas at home turned into a brawl, he might start drinking again. Then he would leave and we would be rid of him.

"You don't know what you're talking about, Pat." Mom poked furiously at the haddock which she had cooked because she knew he liked it. (In 1947 Catholics ate fish on Christmas Eve.) "The Depression is over. We're going to have prosperity that will make the 1920s look dull."

We were eating in the dining room, the table covered with Irish linen and laid with the best china and silver and Waterford crystal. Mom believed in elegance, especially at festivals. Dad did, too, as far as that goes. The Christmas tree in the living room was already lighted. It had been turned on for Uncle Ned, Aunt Kate, and their kids, who had stopped by earlier. A faint aroma of evergreen contended at the table with the lush thick smell of smoked haddock.

"Those who don't heed the lessons of history are doomed

to repeat its mistakes." Dad jabbed the tablecloth with his knife. "There's always a depression after a war. It's your money and your company, Margie, but building a new plant is inviting trouble."

"You're damn right it's my money," she shouted at him. "And I'm not putting it in government bonds either."

"I didn't say you should," he shouted back. "All I said was that I would do it if I were you."

My parents could not disagree about the most abstract issue without it turning into a personal quarrel. At grace before we ate, Mom offered thanks for the good year her firm, which had changed to making television parts, had enjoyed. Dad, who was skeptical that television would ever replace the radio and the newspapers, murmured that it would take extra effort by God to protect firms that expanded when a depression was about to begin.

They were off to the races.

The night before, they had argued about communism. Dad knew European politics as well as our precinct captain knew Cook County politics. There would be trouble with Russia; the Truman doctrine and the Marshal Plan were the beginning of the confrontation. Domestic left-wingers would be in serious trouble. Mom was sensitive on this issue because her brother's wife, Kate Collins Ryan, had been a communist in the 1930s for a couple of years. Another raging quarrel.

My father, Patrick Michael Casey, was one of the finest journalists in America. He knew world politics as well as anyone in Chicago. My mother, Margaret Ryan Casey, was as shrewd a business executive as you could find in the United States. She had turned a decrepit family company into an immensely successful corporation during the war. They both were right, as you've noticed, in their own field. But they both had to be right in the other's field, too. So they fought.

They had battled in the early years of their marriage, but I was too young to know what the fights were about then. Now they were fighting at every possible chance in their second try together. Soon, I thought happily, that will fail, too.

Looking back on their life together, I seem to see clearly the reasons for the arguments were irrelevant. They fought because both of them had to be right all the time. Their need to be right and my grandfather's contempt for journalists and my father's drinking had broken the marriage up once. Dad had stopped drinking; Grandfather was dead; but the fights went on.

When Dad left to cover the Italian invasion of Ethiopia for the *Chicago Daily News* in 1935, the marriage was for all practical purposes finished, much to the satisfaction of Mom's family and, I think, much to Dad's relief. Fighting the Ryans was hard work.

My uncle, Monsignor Thomas Canfield Ryan (who was the cardinal's secretary), tried to obtain an annulment, but in those days they were hard to get even if you had ecclesiastical clout like we did.

So between my fifth birthday and my sixteenth birthday, I saw my father five or six times, usually for a day or two while he was passing through Chicago on the way to Spain to report on the civil war or to China to write about the Sino-Japanese War. (He escaped from Nanking a half hour before the Japanese killed everyone they could find in that hapless city.) He was in Chicago, staying at the Stevens Hotel (now the Conrad Hilton), the day Pearl Harbor was bombed. Only once during the war did he stop by our modest bungalow in St. Ursula's parish on the west side, traveling from Australia to Europe to be on the scene at D-Day.

That was the only time I saw him, after the marriage ended, when he wasn't drunk. In those days it was said that all Irish reporters in Chicago were drunks. Dad's reply, according to Uncle Ned, the only one in the family who liked him, was that the statement was malicious calumny. Only the good ones were drunks.

He was a little man, shorter even than Uncle Ned, who was five nine, and barely as tall as Mom, with thin delicate features, a dimpled chin, silver-blue eyes like mine, and curly brown hair. "If he wasn't so sensitive about being pretty, he wouldn't drink so much," my uncle Tom remarked contemptuously when he advised Mom not to take him back.

"He's the one that's taking me back," Mom said firmly, to my annoyance and dismay.

Dad was born in 1900, the son of the editor of an Irish nationalist weekly. He graduated from St. Ignatius in time to lie about his age and fight in the marines at Belleau Wood in the First World War, and learn perhaps even then to prefer the grimy simplicities of combat to the subtle conflicts of ordinary life. When he came home from France, his father, who did not let his Irish politics interfere with making a little money on the board of trade, sent him to Notre Dame. When he graduated, he went to work as a copy-boy for the *Chicago Examiner*. He covered crime in Chicago during the days of Al Capone, Elliot Ness, Anton Cermak, Barney Ross, Frank "The Enforcer" Nitti, and such crooked journalists as Jake Lingle (who betrayed both his paper and the Mob and was gunned down in broad daylight) and such gifted journalists as Ben Hecht.

He was a witty and eloquent man, more witty and more eloquent, as I remember, drunk than sober, but still, stone sober, he talked like a college professor or an Oxford graduate in an English novel. Even when he was drunk, he was fastidious about his personal appearance—a stuck-up little dandy, Grandfather sneered; sailor straw hats, spats, French cuffs, cigarette holder. Drunk or not, he was clean-shaven and sweet-smelling. Except in combat, of course; there was no cologne on Guadalcanal.

Before that Christmas Eve he had had his last drink in

Southampton on June 5, 1944, the day preceding his forty-fourth birthday, which was also D-Day. "Omaha Beach," he told me after he'd come home and was trying to befriend me, "sobered me up in a hurry."

I responded with the cold silence with which I habitually deflected his efforts at friendship and penitence.

"I'd been in other tight spots," he stumbled on, like a man trying to dig himself out of a ditch which is collapsing on him. "The Ebro River, Nanking, Henderson Field . . ."

I resolutely refused to ask how Omaha Beach in Normandy on D-Day was different, knowing that he would tell me anyway.

"I never doubted that I would survive those. That morning in Normandy, I was convinced I was going to die. So I made a promise to God." He cocked an eye in my direction, a skilled raconteur expecting a response. "So far I've kept it."

If he expected my approval, much less my praise, he'd come to the wrong person.

Mom had been aware that he was a heavy drinker when she married him. He was not quite an alcoholic then, but he knew the inside of all the speakeasies in the Twin Lakes/Lake Geneva area of southern Wisconsin, and there had been a lot of speaks in that part of the country.

He wasn't the only drunk who hung around the Knights of Columbus Country Club at Twin Lakes, Mom had argued to Uncle Tom when Dad was in the Solomon Islands.

"He was the only one you married."

She was twenty and movie-star beautiful, with a gorgeous figure, big blue eyes, and long brown hair. She was easily dazzled by his charm and courtesy, since her father and Uncle Tom were rough-hewn men who believed that women were simpleminded innocents whom one protected with stern discipline. Pat Casey sent her flowers every day, listened carefully to her opinions, praised her intelligence and taste, and respected her feelings. Even that Christmas Eve he'd brought a big poinsettia home from the *Tribune,* where he was working.

"It was bad enough," Uncle Tom snapped at her, "to let him take you in once. Why make the same mistake again?"

"I went after him the first time because I wanted him," Mom replied tersely. "I still want him."

"He seduced you both times." Uncle Tom paced the room like an angry grizzly bear.

"Please, Tom; not in front of Michael."

Even at sixteen I was not so dumb as to think that I had been born three months prematurely. Like most kids, I could not believe that there was passion between my parents, ever, and certainly not when he was in his middle forties and she in her late thirties after a decade of separation.

Yet I found out after they were dead that she had written him every week while he was away pursuing wars and that he wrote back. You could not exactly call their correspondence love letters. They shared diaries of daily events. But why bother, unless they still felt something for one another, despite the pain and the anger?

"Your mother," he said to me when he came home, "is the rare woman who is more beautiful at thirty-seven than at twenty. We are both blessed men."

I had not particularly noticed that my mother was attractive. I could not, however, disagree with him. So I continued to say nothing. I was a tall, stringy, morose kid; strong but awkward. I had left the seminary because I liked girls too much to follow Uncle Tom's path into the priesthood, much to his chagrin, but I rarely talked to girls. I had left the Church, or so I thought, because I didn't believe in it anymore, but I was profoundly shocked and angered at the picture, portrayed vividly by Uncle Tom, of my mother and father having a love affair in a shabby hotel in Berlin.

"The Kepenski is not shabby," Mom contended stubbornly.

"Everything in Berlin is shabby." He tugged at his starched clerical cuffs. "Don't you have more control over your baser emotions?"

"They're not base." She reached for her handkerchief.

Mom took a lot from Uncle Tom. Her parents were both dead, her brother Ned was married and away in the navy, Tom's approval was important. She needed his acceptance of her decision.

"I love him, Tom. I always have," she pleaded through her tears. "My government work was finished in Bonn. I flew to Berlin because I wanted to see him."

"Lust, not love." He reverently touched the swath of purple underneath his white collar, the discreet hint of monsignorial office.

"It was so cold in Berlin . . . and I was cold. I'd been cold ever since he left."

"Then you should have turned up the heat in your hotel room." He pulled on his overcoat in abrupt disgust. "The cardinal is waiting for me at St. Ferdinand's. If you take that drunken bum back into your house, I will never set foot in it again."

My uncle did not make such threats lightly. He did not speak to Mom after Dad came home. Uncle Ned's reaction was the opposite. That Christmas Eve afternoon he and his wife Kate and their four little kids, the oldest a skinny eleven-year-old hoyden, traveled on the Rock Island and the L and the Austin Boulevard bus from their south-side home to visit us and bring presents. Dad was in his element. He and Uncle Ned talked about the war; he told stories to the kids and worked magic tricks which made their eyes bulge. Mom relaxed and smiled, rare enough reactions since Dad returned.

"Your mother and father are certainly happy together, aren't they?" Uncle Ned said to me as I drove them in our old Packard to the L station. "Sometimes I think I ought to leave Aunt Kate for ten years or so, so she'll love me that way."

"If you leave again for ten days, I'll break your neck," Aunt Kate said cheerfully. "Right, kids?"

The kids were accompanying "How Are Things in Glocca Mora?" on the car radio. After the chorus, they echoed her enthusiastically, "Right!"

The loudest agreement came from the youngest kid, three-year-old Blackie, an elfin little creature already looking like one of Santa's gnomes, who would later follow Uncle Tom to the priesthood, but become, God knows, a very different kind of priest.

I turned off the car radio as soon as I had left my relatives at the Lake Street L station. I had heard more than enough *Finian's Rainbow* songs that year.

Returning home through the slowly falling snow, I wondered. I thought I knew what love was. I was in love with Ann Blyth in *A Woman's Vengeance*. I was in love in a different way with Annie O'Brien (and still am, I suppose) but her terrible grief over the death of her boyfriend in the Hurtgen Forest and her parents in a bus accident outside Lourdes frightened me away from her. I didn't see how these emotions applied to what Uncle Tom called an "illicit tryst" in a dirty hotel in Berlin.

Between my parents there was nervousness and tension and anger and resentment. Whatever had happened in Berlin last winter, and despite Uncle Tom's denunciations, I exorcised from my imagination any pictures of it, and it did not survive the journey back to Chicago. On the contrary, their new life together seemed to confirm Uncle Tom's parting shot: "You've sinned, Margaret." He squared his broad, carefully tailored shoulders. "Sinned terribly. You have betrayed your family and your God. Now you have condemned yourself to even more suffering to expiate that sin."

If it were love which bound them together, I wanted no part of that kind of love.

The tension had returned to our bungalow before I did. It exploded at supper.

"I don't understand, Marge." My father continued like a schoolteacher correcting a term paper. "Good fish, incidentally."

"Thank you." Mom was wearing a dark green "new look" dress with ruffles and a long skirt and looked, I must admit, both beautiful and fragile. "What is it you don't understand?"

"Hmm? Oh yes . . . I don't understand why you must take everything I say as a personal assault on you and your family." He gestured with his fork, like the late FDR with his cigarette holder. "Can't I have an opinion about the economic situation without being perceived as challenging your undeniable competence?"

"Sure." Her eyes glinted fiercely. "You can have such opinions, but you don't. You always have to think of yourself as smarter than we are."

"That's not true." He rose from the table. "Your parents and your brothers treated me with contempt. I was not good enough for you. Despite the fact that my father was an educated man and your father did not graduate from high school."

Same old fight.

"Sit down, please. Patrick. A bite of fruitcake doesn't violate the Christmas fast, does it, Michael?"

I didn't say anything because the script never called on me to say anything.

"Good cake. *Very* good. I don't know how you run a major company and cook such wonderful meals."

"Thank you. Hard work. Ned never treated you with contempt. He's a conceited war hero just like you."

"Your parents and your brother tried to destroy his marriage," Dad crowed triumphantly. "Even before they were married. Because Kate was a communist. And I was a reporter. Both of us college graduates from well-educated families but neither one good enough for their children."

"Leave my parents out of it." Mom was crying. "They're dead, poor people. Can't you forgive the dead?"

So it went.

Dad did not throw on his overcoat and prepare to storm out of the house over the question of dead parents or the future of the economy.

The straw that broke the camel's back was midnight Mass.

Cardinal Mundelein had forbidden the ancient custom, allegedly because there was too much drinking after Mass. Archbishop Stritch reinstated it. Dad wanted to go to midnight Mass to hear the sermon of our new pastor, Monsignor Mugsy Branigan, who had played for the Chicago White Sox in 1916. Out of loyalty to Mundelein, who was Uncle Tom's patron, the Ryans had steadfastly avoided midnight Mass. "A pagan custom," Uncle Tom dismissed it contemptuously.

Mom repeated his judgment over the fruitcake.

"I don't understand why the hand of a dead cardinal should weigh so heavily on us," Dad shouted.

"You never did respect the dead," Mom shouted back. "First my parents and now the poor cardinal."

"Jesus said let the dead bury the dead." He rose from the table again, this time really angry.

He's going to leave, I thought. At last he's going to leave. He'll tie one on. Christmas is a bad time for reformed drunks. He'll have a lost weekend like in the film. Then we'll be rid of him.

"I'm proud of my family. I won't repudiate them." She rose, too. "Not for you. Not for anyone."

Behind her I saw the Christmas tree, which they had decorated the day before with much laughter and good spirits; its lights formed a kind of multicolored halo around her head and shoulders.

"Who wants you to repudiate them?"

"You do!" She began to sob. "You have since our first date. I thought you'd change or I would never have taken you back!"

She buried her face in her hands. A runty little angel on top of the tree, just over her head, watched blandly.

"Who took whom back? As I remember, you started the seduction, not me. Both times."

"Get out of here," she wailed. "I never want to see you again."

"With pleasure!" He stomped out of the dining room toward the front hallway.

An electric candle, burning in the window next to the tree, welcomed the traveler to Bethlehem. Beyond it the snow was falling heavily. The light of the candle shone on the tinsel of the tree.

Oh hell. I would have to do something.

"Good-bye," Dad yelled from the front door.

I bolted from the dining room, dashed to the doorway, and grabbed him.

"No."

"Huh?" He paused, more astonished than offended by the determined lock on his arms.

"I said no. You're not leaving. That doesn't help. You tried it once and it didn't work."

"Let me go, Michael." He tried to struggle free.

"No."

"We seemed to have produced a son, Marge, who is stronger than he looks," Dad observed ruefully, as if he was considering a lead for a story.

"Let him go, Michael." Mom, her eyes red from her tears, stood at the other end of the front hall. It was a pretty weak order.

"No."

"I said let him go."

"He's your husband. It's your job to keep him here."

She looked at me as though I had suddenly grown a second head.

"I suppose that's true," she agreed thoughtfully. "The boy did say no, Pat." Her arms imprisoned him, too.

"I see." His voice choked. "Should we let this young hellion decide which Mass the family will attend? Give him the swing vote, so to speak?" He stopped struggling.

"Why not?"

They were talking about me, but I might as well have been on Guadalcanal for all my presence mattered. I released my father. There were stronger bonds tying him to us than my arms. I understood for the first time as my parents clung to one another like a young couple on their first date, what love really is, an unruly, difficult, irresistible power binding and repelling, a storm, a fire, a flood. It scared me.

Was that what Christmas was supposed to be about? Then Christmas scared me, too.

"How does the swing vote decide?" My mother laughed, not at me but at him.

I tried to hate him and could not.

"I like Monsignor Mugsy."

"Traitor." She laughed again. "Serves me right for having a son."

Actually she seemed rather proud of me.

Dad picked up a package of tinsel from the hallway table, an extra one which was supposed to be stored in the attic for next year. He began to arrange the strands of silver in Mom's hair.

"Did you know, Mick"—the first time he called me by that name—"that your mother is really an Irish countess in disguise? A warrior queen like Grace O'Malley, of whom I'm sure you've heard?"

I had not.

"Countesses should have strands of jewels in their hair," he continued. "Should they not, Mick? Alas, at the moment my supply of strands of jewels is a little on the low side. However, Christmas tinsel gives the same kind of effect, if you sort of squint your eyes and don't look too closely."

He laced the bits of foil through her hair like he was

dressing a bride for her wedding day. Mom submissively accepted his efforts as if she were indeed a warrior countess, accustomed to such delicate service.

"You're mad, Pat," she said weakly. "And this big, good-looking kid, standing here grinning at us, is mad, too."

"Our prison keeper, do you mean?" He rearranged a strip of tinsel. "Do you mind, Mick, if I borrow your mother for an hour or so of serious husband–wife conversation?"

"Pat . . ." She was flustered and blushing.

"She's your wife," I said. They were going to make love. I should have been shocked. Parents don't do that sort of thing. But I wasn't shocked. I understood them now. They couldn't help themselves. He could borrow her as often as he wanted.

"Indeed she is," he agreed.

They went off to the bedroom in the back of the house. I read Anne Frank's *Diary of a Young Girl* by the light of the Christmas tree.

They both glowed at midnight Mass. Monsignor Branigan congratulated them on how happy they looked as we left church.

"Is that tinsel in your hair, Marge?" He peered through his thick glasses. "Decorate the tree just before you came over? That's the way it ought to be. The light of the world should not be lit until the time of His coming."

Mom blushed but she didn't remove the strip of foil from her hair.

It was a turning point, I guess. They did stay together, and in fact became quite gentle with each other through the years. It was a long time before Dad and I became friends—after I returned from the Korean War, in fact.

They're both gone now. As is my wife. I have three daughters and as many grandchildren. I've made a lot of mistakes in my life, some of them terrible mistakes. Yet every time I put tinsel on the tree at Christmas time—and I always insist that it's my part of the job—I think of the scene in our hallway.

At least I didn't make a mistake that night.

To this day I don't understand why I wouldn't let him leave us again.

❧ Rosemarie ❧

"**H**alf price?" The young woman, a rather hefty artificial blonde, looked at my five-dollar bill.

"Pardon?"

"I *said*"—she chomped harder on her gum—"are you over twelve?"

Behind me, my two charges chortled gleefully. "Hurry up, Chucky," Peg badgered, "We've already missed the cartoon."

It was a comic beginning for a day in which three surprises would provoke my first religious crisis, one which has not been resolved even now, four decades later.

I hesitated at the ticket booth. I was already humiliated. Could I turn defeat into victory by gaining admission to the State and Lake Theater for half price, and as the Irish would say, myself just turned seventeen?

The prohibition against lying was absolute in the O'Malley house. Mom was, as she put it, not raising a bunch of little fibbers. "If you don't tell the truth just once, who will ever believe you again?" she would demand.

"An honest person chokes on a lie," she would add,

setting up a conditioned reflex in me from which I have never been able to escape.

The world, however, was complicated. There were situations in which grayness ruled. So I would run to Father John Raven for clarification and instruction in the principles of casuistry.

It was not a lie to give the streetcar conductor three cents or the woman in the ticket booth at movie houses ten cents. If they accepted such half-price offerings, then it was their decision. On the other hand, if they asked how old I was, I was under obligation to tell them the truth.

"There ought to be some compensation," John had said, laughing, "for being as youthful looking as you are."

He meant short.

I did not burden Mom's conscience with these delicate matters.

But the situation was different today. I was five years older than the half-price barrier, if only just five years. Moreover, I was being humiliated. Finally, while I dearly desired revenge on the State Lake for humiliating me in the presence of the two brats, the achievement thereof would require a lie.

"Three full price," I said, mustering as much urbanity as I could with two thirteen-year-old girls guffawing behind me.

It was Saturday afternoon in September of 1945. The war was over and quickly forgotten. Around the world the armed forces were demobilizing themselves with demands to return home which were close to mutiny. The Cubs were lumbering toward a World Series with two pitchers named Claude Passau and Hank Borowy and a bunch of minor leaguers and 4-Fs, the last World Series they would see—forever, as I would hold. The Fenwick football team was sweeping all before it in a drive for the city title.

On the day before a crucial game with our old rivals from St. Philip's (a high school, now lamentably defunct, behind

Our Lady of Sorrows Church, where the Sorrowful Mother Novena had begun), Charles E. O'Malley, crucially important to a Fenwick victory, had been constrained to escort his sister and his foster sister on their premier solo trip to the Loop.

At first they both opposed this plan. "If Chucky goes with us, then we won't go by ourselves, so it doesn't count."

"Right," I agreed on Friday afternoon when this adventure was being planned.

But they changed their tune when it was clear that if I didn't chaperon their transition, they wouldn't go at all.

"Okay." Peg sighed noisily. "If that's the only way we can see *State Fair,* I suppose he can come with us."

"I won't have you two riding into the Loop without someone to take care of you," Mom repeated her relevant principle, "especially not on Saturday."

"Much good Chucky would do," Rosie sniffed.

"I have a game Sunday."

"Your practice is on Saturday morning, dear."

"Yeah, but I have to prepare mentally."

"Fourth-string quarterback," Peg sneered.

"Holds kickoffs, big deal!" Rosie added contemptuously. "Won't even look at the big palooka when he kicks the ball."

It was an astute observation. I could hold the pigskin against the turf with my forefinger until Vince booted it only if I closed my eyes.

Then I had to struggle to my feet and rush down the field toward the receiving team as though I intended to tackle the ballcarrier. Fortunately, no one ever broke through the charging Fenwick line and made me the only player standing between the opposition and a touchdown.

Nonetheless I had nightmares about such an eventuality. My plan was to do all I could under such circumstances to make it look like I was attempting to tackle the runner without actually making physical contact.

At practices I was required to tackle only the tackling dummy, a pretty strong dummy, I might add.

"You can prepare mentally on Saturday night, can't you?"

"Especially since you won't have a date," Peg taunted me.

"I could find one. . . ."

"Besides," Rosie pleaded, "you like Rodgers and Hammerstein."

"I don't think I'll like this one."

Mom began to strum chords on her harp for *Oklahoma!*

" 'Where the wind comes sweeping down the plain . . .' " A soprano and an alto joined her.

My fate was sealed.

My family's love for music was not limited to the classical. Our tastes were catholic—classical, jazz, big band, show tunes. We could do Mozart or Handel and then turn immediately to Romberg or Kern. Rodgers and Hammerstein were made for our propensity to belt out tunes at the top of our lungs.

Once my sister and my unofficial foster sister had made up their minds that we were to see the first Rodgers and Hammerstein film, all I could possibly accomplish was a brave rearguard action.

Late Saturday morning when I came back from practice, on a windless Indian-summer day with the air a golden haze that smelled of burning leaves, Dad was working on plans in the dining room. "Twelve years without a commission," he murmured, "and now more than I can handle . . . April, where is that letter again?"

"Here it is, dear. You really need larger working space."

"We may be able to rent an office soon if the money keeps flooding in."

Flood?

"Speaking of that," I interrupted, "I have been shanghaied into taking the two brats to a movie downtown. Do I have to pay for it?"

"Certainly not, dear." Mom reached in her purse and removed two five-dollar bills. "Now I expect what is left over to come back in change. You may not retain any surplus for your bank account."

"Me?"

"And you go down on the bus and the L." Dad peered over his glasses at me. "Don't take the streetcar just to save a few pennies."

"Eighteen!"

The streetcar was seven cents; the motor coach and L would cost ten cents. Back and forth for three people times two was twenty-four cents.

"Dear," my mother said patiently. "We can afford two dimes."

"I know that. It's the principle."

"What principle?"

I couldn't quite remember.

I must add, in defense of my younger self, that I was joking.

Four dimes and I might have been serious.

As I made clear when the ticket woman returned two dollars and three tickets in exchange for my five-dollar bill.

"Isn't there more?" I said, shocked and dismayed.

She gestured at the price list affixed to the glass. Full price was a dollar? So that was what they meant by inflation?

"You're embarrassing us, Chucky," Peg hissed as I tumbled into the lobby of the State and Lake, still traumatized.

I compensated for their embarrassment by spending another dollar on three large bags of popcorn and three cherry Cokes.

They had overdressed for the event as high-school freshwomen do—fall knit dresses (maroon for Rosie, gold for Peg), precious nylons, spiked heels, makeup suitable for a formal dance, military purses slung over their shoulders. They managed to carry off the pose except when they wobbled on their heels.

In my grubby black Fenwick jacket I was partly proud of my attractive companions and partly ashamed of the possibility that those who turned their heads to look at them would think I was the perhaps handicapped little brother of these two autumn Dianas.

State Fair was the first of the three surprises that day.

The war was over. This was the first of the great postwar musicals made as if the war had never been. It was produced in vastly improved Technicolor and directed with imagination, verve, and skill. Moreover, it hit us with its most powerful weapons at the very beginning.

Play your videotape again, if you have one, ar   agine that you had never seen Jeanne Crain and never heard "It Might As Well Be Spring." The opening song, "Our State Fair," is a lively bit of nonsense set against a makebelieve Iowa backdrop. Then, almost at once, Margey leans out of the second floor window in response to her mother's call.

"Oh my God!" Peg exclaimed.

"Wow!" Rosie agreed.

Before I could close my mouth and attempt comment, Ms. Crain began "It Might As Well Be Spring."

> *"I haven't seen a crocus or a rosebud,*
> *Or a robin on the wing,*
> *But I feel so gay*
> *In a melancholy way,*
> *That it might as well be spring."*

Jeanne Crain singing "It Might As Well Be Spring" was a knockout punch from which none of us recovered. Although the movie did not and could not live up to its opening moments, it was still pure delight.

Whispers flew back and forth.

"Look at that maroon dress! I want it!"

"She looks like you, Rosie."

"She does *not!*"

Actually she did.

"Why don't you say something, Chucky?"

"I'm eating my popcorn."

"You haven't eaten a bite since that girl came on the screen."

"Nice music."

I tried to nibble on the popcorn.

By the time the story progressed to its second song that was destined to become a "standard," I had given up on my popcorn.

> *"It's a grand night for singing*
> *The stars are bright up above*
> *The earth is aglow*
> *And to add to the show*
> *I think I am falling in love!"*

I had fallen in love completely.

Jeanne Crain would have become an important component of my fantasy life even if the other two surprises of that Indian-summer day in 1945 had not happened.

If you play your videocassette, you'll note that Ms. Crain, who was just twenty at the time, could not act at that early stage of her career. It didn't matter.

Even then I must have realized that her eye movements were abrupt, her facial makeup was too obvious, and her breasts could point as sharply as they did only if they were imprisoned by a rigidly constructed and oppressive cylindrical bra. None of these reservations mattered. She was a stunning promise—she had to be to make me stop eating popcorn.

A promise of what?

Love, passion, life, beauty, goodness . . . whatever a young man seeks in a young woman. That she became my Indian-summer virginal Venus probably shows a lot about my tastes. No Rita Hayworth for Charles E. O'Malley's libido.

And, as we all agreed later, it was not unimportant that she was indisputably Irish.

"Isn't she beautiful, Chucky?"

"Too fat!"

"Chucky!"

"Look at that rear end!"

"You're the one that's staring at her, Chucky Ducky! Doesn't she look like Rosie?"

"No. Hey, give me my popcorn b   "

"You're not eating it!"

While I reacted to the movie by not eating, my charges reacted by devouring everything. They tried to make me return to the lobby to buy more popcorn. Naturally I refused.

When the movie ended, they whimpered in satisfaction at the happy ending, in which romantic love was rewarded; I, still keeping my licentious emotions to myself, withdrew to buy popcorn.

We had missed the "selected short subjects" at the beginning (because my two young women were tardy in their last-minute rearrangement of their faces in our apartment), so we stayed for the cartoon and the March of Time. I returned with the popcorn and more cherry Coke halfway through the cartoon, of which I have no recollection at all, and settled down to make up for lost popcorn.

Then Westbrook von Vorhees, in a voice appropriate for Gabriel announcing the Final Judgment, shouted, "The March of Time!"

It was a Final Judgment edition of the March of Time—a film about the Nazi death camps.

My second surprise.

I had seen pictures of the camps when they were liberated on the back page of the *Daily News,* but they had made little impression on me. My two charges did not read the papers, so they were completely unaware of Belsen, Buchenwald, Dachau, Auschwitz.

The film, perhaps made to stir up support for the Nuremberg war trials, showed the camps with exquisite attention to their horror—gas chambers, crematoria, mass graves with bodies stacked like cordwood, haggard faces of survivors, pictures of little children who had died, lamp shades made out of human skin, bars of soap made from human flesh.

Need I say the three of us stopped eating our popcorn?

If we had seen the twenty-minute documentary before *State Fair,* it would not have affected us the way it did. But after so much life, we now saw so much death.

Why did the film distributors combine the two in one package? Probably they did not even think about the combination. If they did, they must have assumed that the romance of the feature would quickly erase the images of the grimly realistic documentary.

A single stark question branded itself on my brain to remain there until this very moment: which was real—the magically beautiful young woman or the mass graves?

One had to be an illusion, either the delectable autumnal virgin or the gas chambers.

We left the State and Lake, climbed slowly up the steps to the L tracks, crossed to the north side, and boarded the lumbering old wooden Lake Street local in total silence.

On the ride downtown, I had sat in a seat by myself behind the two girls. There was only room on this train, leaving the Loop late on Saturday afternoon at a time when many businesses worked all day, for the three of us to sit together on one of the lengthwise seats.

Then came the third surprise.

"Dear God, how terrible!" Peg, tears in her eyes, broke the silence. "Those poor people!"

"They were only Jews," Rosie said grimly, almost automatically.

"Rosie." Peg's eyes were wide in horror. "What a terrible thing to say!"

"They're as good as we are." I blew up and quoted my mother, "Maybe better. Do you think they didn't suffer just because they were Jews?"

Then, carried away by my own rhetoric and my own personal horror at the film, I launched into a fierce diatribe. "Are they less human than we are? Why didn't the same thing happen to us? What about Joanie Fineman? Would you want someone making a bar of soap out of Mr. and Mrs. Fineman's cute little granddaughter?"

"He's right, Rosie." Peg nodded slowly.

She looked from one to the other of us, astonished, shattered, frightened.

"I'm sorry," she whispered, "I really am. . . . Chucky *is* right. I don't know why I said that. It was terribly dumb."

"Evil," I added.

She bowed her head solemnly. "Yes, it is. I'm an evil person."

Her face froze in a somber, withdrawn scowl. Her blue eyes turned hard, as if she were looking at herself through a microscope and was disgusted at what she saw.

Peg and I remained voiceless, not knowing what to say.

"I should have died in one of those gas chambers instead of them. I wish God would permit me to exchange my life for one of those poor girls. . . ."

I now understand that her reaction to our complaints was exaggerated, inappropriate, perhaps even dangerous. Her words were stupid, but only the repetition of a vile and hateful expression of bigotry she had heard from a parent (then, I thought her father; now, I suspect her mother), a mechanical attempt to respond to the horror of what we had seen.

When we had protested, she had become conscious of the meaning of her words and realized instantly that they were damnable. She retracted them and the sentiment behind them.

303

Shame and regret were appropriate. Even then, however, I comprehended that there was something wrong with her reaction.

What was going on inside her lovely head?

What was I supposed to do now?

Since I didn't know the answer, I did nothing. Not a word was said on the rest of our trip to Austin Boulevard.

"Who can I apologize to?" she asked as we waited at the corner of Austin and Lake, across from the Chateau Hotel, for the bus. Appropriately the golden Indian-summer haze had been replaced by a cheerless gray overcast. "They're dead. You are both too easy on me. And God must hate me."

"God doesn't hate anyone," Peg said promptly, sounding exactly like her mother.

"You really didn't mean it, Rosie." I groped for the right phrase. "It just kind of slipped out."

"Only a monster would let words like that 'just slip out,' Chucky. I don't deserve to live."

"Don't say that, Rose," Peg pleaded. "Don't ever say that!"

The green bus huffed up to us; we did not speak until we had boarded it and walked to the back, where high-school kids always sit.

"Shall we get off at Division and have something to eat at the Rose Bowl?" I asked fatuously.

The Rose Bowl was an ice-cream emporium on Division Street, an institution second in importance in my life only to another Division Street establishment, Fred's Pool Hall. It was owned by a Greek family—which proved, according to my reasoned opinion, that Greeks made the best ice cream and bred the most sensuous-looking young women in Chicago, if, as I explained to Vince, you like your sensuous young women dusky.

"*Chucky!*" Peg reprimanded me. "How can you think of food at a time like this?"

I did not reply that I could think of food, especially ice cream, at almost any time.

We left the bus at Thomas and walked the four short blocks to Rosie's house at the corner of Thomas and Menard.

"Why doesn't God destroy me now and get it over with?" Rosie shattered the stillness as we stopped in front of her house.

"Rosie . . ." Peg pleaded.

"I'm damned, Peg, I really am."

"Maybe you ought to go over to St. Ursula"—I glanced at my watch—"and talk to Father Raven. I think he's probably still in the confessional."

Her bitter eyes swiveled toward me. "That's a very good idea, Chucky," she said as though she were surprised that I were capable of such. "Thank you."

"You're welcome."

"Take a raincoat," Peg suggested. "You don't want to ruin your dress if it rains."

"It's not important. . . . Thank you for the movie, too, Chucky."

"What was that all about?" I asked as Rosie almost ran down the street toward the church.

"I don't know." Peg was disconsolate. "Sometimes she's awfully mean to herself."

I walked home with Peg and then slipped away to return to the Rose Bowl. It seemed legitimate to charge Mom for my chocolate malt, part of my payment for my efforts of the day. I studied very carefully the slim outline of the young Greek woman behind the counter and concluded that (a) I had a slight preference for Irish over Near Eastern loveliness, and (b) I was entitled to a second malt.

Why couldn't one eat and agonize at the same time?

How come, you ask, that I was such a paragon of religious understanding at that still early age of my life?

It was no merit of my own. My mother had made up her mind that I would not be a bigot. That was that.

My mother's snobbery, like everything else about her, was amiable and kindly. "Foreigners" was a term applied to anyone who was not Irish, with the sometime exception of the Germans. (Protestants did not figure in the calculus because they were not important folks in the lives of the Chicago Irish at that time.) They were not bad people; you would never treat them unkindly and certainly never exclude them from your house. Given enough time, they would become as American as anyone else—meaning as American as we were. Indeed, Mom found "foreigners" fascinating, puzzled as she was by the fact that anyone would choose to be a foreigner.

"They really are," she would assure us with a benign smile, "very nice people."

When I was in fourth grade in 1938, I came home from school one night during the week before Halloween and announced proudly, "We waxed that dirty kike Fineman's windows for him. He'll never get them clean. Serves the Hebe right."

"Don't ever say those words again in this house." She took off her glasses and stared at me. "I won't tolerate them, Charles Evans O'Malley. I am not raising any bigots, do you understand?"

"I'm not a bigot," I pleaded, near tears because Mom almost never shouted at me.

"Yes, you are. Now you go right back to that little dry-goods store and apologize to Mr. Fineman and clean every last bit of wax off his windows."

"Why?" I wailed.

"Because Jews are every bit as good as us, aren't they, Vangie?"

"A little better, maybe. They work harder."

No help from him, that was obvious. "Jesus was Jewish." Mom was still angry at me.

"So was his mother," I said brightly.

"The Finemans are his relatives. Now go clean their windows."

Mr. Fineman, a little man with a gray face and dark, dark brown eyes, accepted my apology graciously. "So"—he waved his hands—"boys will be boys. You're a good boy, you apologize. Why should you clean it up?"

"I didn't know those were bad words," I said, honestly enough.

"You're a sweet child," said his plump little wife, "such cute red hair You go home and tell your mother that I said so."

"Mom won't let me back in the house unless I clean the windows." I was beginning to understand what we later called ethnic diversity. "You know what Irish mothers are like."

They both thought that remark was much funnier than I did. So they let me clean the windows.

So they gave me chocolate ice cream with chocolate sauce and chocolate cookies and a chocolate candy bar.

"Eat them," Mrs. Fineman said. "Chocolate is good for you. It gives you energy."

"Yes, ma'am." I slurped up my reward. "May I wax your windows tomorrow?"

"Such a cute little boy. Isn't he a darling?"

"Your mother"—Mr. Fineman pointed his finger at me—"is the classiest lady in the neighborhood."

"Yes sir," I agreed. "She says you're God's relatives."

They both laughed joyously at that.

"So we have clout?"

"You sure must."

I went back often to their store after that to volunteer to run errands for them. They wanted to pay me, but I would accept only one Hershey bar.

Well, sometimes, maybe two.

The memory of the Hershey bars constrained me to order a third malt at the Rose Bowl on that September day in

1945. I needed some consolation while I continued to agonize over good and evil.

Good and evil and Rosemarie Helen Clancy in between, the battleground on which the war was being fought.

I did not like that image at all.

It rained around midnight. The next day was murky and much colder. My mind churned all night long as I tried to sleep, and continued to churn at Mass.

Like most Catholics, I enjoyed the Mass, even when it was in a language I didn't understand and even when it is badly performed in English. Many years later, even after most Catholics decided it was not really a terrible sin after all to miss Mass (or the Eucharist, as it is called now) occasionally, they continued to attend just the same.

I protested once to my parents when we were on vacation that according to my brother Mike, by then a student for the priesthood, we didn't have to attend on Sunday if the trip required more than a half hour's ride. So we wouldn't sin if we excused ourselves from a forty-minute ride.

"It's not sin, dear; I like to go to Mass."

"It opens up our lives to the sacred," Dad commented. "That's why people stay Catholic."

They were right. Back in 1945 I didn't understand the phenomenon, but I still enjoyed praying in church with everyone else from the parish.

I went to the eight o'clock Mass so that there would be plenty of time to ride up to Hansen Park for the game. It was the Holy Name Sunday Communion Mass for "the men of the parish," designed to persuade a generation of Catholic men, older than my father, that they should go to Mass once a month instead of once a year. Typically the church was crowded with more than eight hundred men and boys, a robust refutation of the notion that religion was only for women. The men entered together in procession led by a color guard of Boy Scouts carrying the American flag, the yellow and white papal banner, and the bright red

Holy Name flag. Because Father Raven insisted, they sang "Holy God We Praise Thy Name," a hymn normally reserved for the end of the Benediction of the Blessed Sacrament.

"It's the only hymn they know," Father Raven explained in answer to my question.

Before Mass they repeated the "Holy Name Pledge," a promise against blasphemy, which, to tell the truth, was not one of the more serious temptations for Catholic men of our neighborhood in those days.

My father did not participate. Rather, he would attend ten o'clock Mass every Sunday with Mom, who sang in the choir.

"Your mother has special clout with God. I don't think He'd listen to my prayers if I dared show up without her."

That Sunday my prayer was a wordless plea for understanding. How could *State Fair* and Auschwitz be in the same world, the beautiful body of a young actress and the cordwood piles of corpses?

Were the death camps finally what life was all about?

And what did the horror in Rosie's eyes mean?

These were not questions about which I wanted to think. They were questions I could not drive out of my mind.

I felt a little better after Mass, but the contrasting images of make-believe Iowa and all too real Dachau continued to struggle inside my head, with Rosie's doomed face somehow in the balance. She was, or would be, as beautiful as Jeanne Crain, but the ugliness of the death camps was in her eyes.

We routed St. Philip's in the mud of Hansen Park 42–0. I held the ball eight times, so obsessed by my questions—a form I suppose of the only religious question which is worth asking—that I didn't bother to close my eyes when Vince's massive shoe crashed into the pigskin.

The next day, walking home from the bus after school, I encountered Father Raven in his old Ford.

"Give you a ride home, Chuck?"

"Sure."

"Nice game yesterday."

"Yeah."

"You made a tackle."

"An assist. Vince really stopped the guy."

A point which Peg and Rosemarie had made with customary vigor, lest I get a big head.

Rosie had added, "You did help, Chucky."

I kind of assumed that this unexpected touch of graciousness was evidence that her conversation in the confessional had provided her with a temporary respite and that I was being given credit for an assist there, too. Not yet would she destroy herself.

"Why so cheery?" The young priest glanced at me as the car turned down Menard.

"Father, does good win or does evil?"

He turned the corner at Augusta and Menard, by Clebak's Grocery, where we shopped now that we had a little more money.

"Tough question, Chuck. The answer we believe is that good does, but only on the last play of the game."

The luminous beauty of my Indian-summer virgin wins out in the last play over the death camps?

It's the answer I endorsed then. "That makes sense."

It's the answer I still cling to, sometimes by my fingertips. I can understand, however, that others don't buy it.

As my senior year at Fenwick continued, peaceful as it seemed, I still pondered the question.

I also tried to figure out how the terror in Rosie's eyes fit Father Raven's answer. I didn't believe she was damned. What, I wondered, must it be like to think you're damned?

I suspected uneasily that I would have to do something about her terror. Despite my veneer of cynicism, I was, even at seventeen, an incorrigible romantic. In the deep sub-basements of my character there existed a notion, which I would have denied vigorously should anyone have suggested it, that to rout Rosemarie's terror would be high adventure and great joy.

Eroticism or death—not an original dilemma for me, surely: part of the human experience. Which ought one to believe, the promise in the beautiful body of a young woman or the fate in the rotting body of a corpse? The balance seemed to tip in favor of the latter because the young woman would surely someday be a rotting corpse.

Yet as John Raven told me during that autumn of 1946, "Like that crazy German Nietzsche said, only where there are tombs are there resurrections."

My dreams, wild, violent, and terrified, were obsessed with the problem. The women I had known, my mother included, became corpses in those dreams, and then returned to life.

Sometimes.

Sometimes in my dreams I wished they would stay dead—the ultimate terror was the return of the beloved. I can't remember the images of those frenzied, turbulent dreams. If I still have them today, and I think I do, I can't recall their content the next day. I must suppress them. However, I do know their "feel." My unacceptable and unaccepted wish to escape from the demands of the beloved are caught perfectly by Samuel Beckett in one of those poems in which, with precise words and orderly cadences, he celebrates chaos and anarchy:

> *I would like my love to die*
> *and the rain to be falling on the graveyard*
> *and on me walking the streets*
> *mourning the first and last to love me.*

Very morbid and very Irish. Escape from the young woman to the crematorium?

Surely I don't believe that.

One deep cellar of my being, however, understands.

That was in my dreams. In my conscious life in those days, my body, if not my mind, wanted the body of a young woman for my own (to cherish with tenderness and respect while I was enjoying her, I quickly add). Her wonders would blot out for a few moments the grinning skull.

My mind told my body that it would have to wait a long time for that pleasure.

My body replied that it couldn't wait.

❧ Patricia ❧

Patricia could have done almost anything well. Therefore she did nothing at all. Or as Sister Claire Marie, Patricia's last defender in the parish, would put it, "She has done nothing yet."

She was, she would explain to you if you asked why she had given up a project, "not ready for that yet."

Sister says that if we give her time, she will be ready. Most of us think she'll be ready the day after the Last Judgment.

Patricia is a fine teacher, a presentable writer, a superb administrative assistant, an efficient organizer, a charming salesperson, a decent singer and pianist, a fine student, and a wonderful mother.

Unfortunately she couldn't choose all of these roles and activities. Therefore she chose none of them, except the mother role, which, if you marry and make love and do not prevent conception, is forced on you by the natural processes of the species.

If Patricia had been programmed like an ant, so that her choices were made by instincts directing the natural processes, all would have been well. Unfortunately our species, the most protean of those we know, must program itself by choice. That Patty would not or could not do.

Patricia is sweet and pretty, sexy in a fragile black-Irish, pale-skin, blue-eyed way. It is hard not to like her even though half the time she is likely to cancel out of a dinner or a date or a project or a commitment at the last moment, pleading some prior or overriding obligation, usually of the most intensely moral nature.

You understood that half of the time, she would show up anyway, having been miraculously absolved from the obligation or having concluded that her obligation to you was even more overriding than the other obligation.

You learned to expect such predictably unpredictable behavior from Patty, and because she was pretty and lively and fun to be with, once and if she did appear, you gritted your teeth and allowed for it.

Rarely did she try to account for herself. To one of her friends, a lot of the drink having been taken, she once said, "I hope I never become an alcoholic. You don't know what it's like to have an alcoholic mother. You have to guess at what is real."

You never knew what her husband thought about her peculiar behavior. He was attentive and affectionate when they were together (which wasn't too much, given his obligations as a high-priced corporate lawyer) and tolerantly supportive of her eccentric behavior, which he seemed to dismiss as appealing, if childish. When the multiple obligations became overwhelming, she would retreat into a "poor pathetic Patty" posture and win sympathy for herself from husband and friends.

It was the last line of defense against adulthood.

Sister Claire Marie, who is a psychologist, argues that Patty's responses are typical of a child of addictive parents. Some of us who knew a bit of psychology point out that she did not marry an addict, as so many such children do. To which Sister replies briskly that Patty's husband is a classic co-dependent—addicted to his work for a change of brain chemistry just as surely as her mother was addicted to the "creature."

"He's like most men in the parish," Sister insists, "a work addict. It's so common that no one thinks it's abnormal. Patricia is the child of an addict, the spouse of an addict, and an addict herself."

Not everyone agrees, though few dare to dispute Sister.

When the Poor Pathetic Patty response was too overwhelming, she would depart with her husband on a vacation (often with agonized last-minute confusions about whether the kids would come or not). Oddly enough, in the totally unstructured environment of a vacation, she would relax and let the flow of the vacation world direct her life.

That should have been a hint that she was capable of adulthood. Indeed, a lot of folk who would never be termed indecisive could not let go of control during a vacation, while Patty relinquished control in those circumstances enthusiastically and reverted to the style of a carefree, happy teenager.

If the kids, four girls and two boys, thought their mother's behavior odd, they never said so, though they would complain, as all kids do, of the "geeky" or weird things their mother expected of them.

That they were not unaware of their mother's indecisiveness can be gathered from the certainly not-apocryphal story of her elder son's response when she criticized his inability to select a college major or decide what he wanted to be in life.

"You're twenty-two years older than me," said the young man, "and you haven't decided what you're going to be when you grow up. Why should I?"

The legend does not recount her reply, though it is unlikely that she laughed.

Vacations with other couples, however, were disasters, and once they became widely known as such, no one in the parish would be available when Patty suggested that they "really ought to spend some time together on a vacation" (nothing, but nothing, could ever be proposed to others save in terms of obligation). The memory of their trip with the Kearneys up the Inside Passage to Glacier Bay had become a parish myth not to be forgotten.

The trouble with cruise ships is that they offer a smorgasbord of activities to while away the essentially boring business of covering large spaces of water in an uncomfortably rattling ship jammed with affluent but elderly (for the most part) strangers.

The passengers, especially if they have had previous experience, quickly sort themselves into the various categories to which the cruise staff is prepared to minister—the drinkers, whose morning grapefruit juice is laced with bourbon as a prelude to the rest of the day; the card players, who are at the bridge tables before the ship eases away from the dock; the gamblers, who stand in line waiting for the casino to open; the shoppers, who spend much of the waking day pawing over bargains in the ship stores (which cost on the average only twenty-five percent more than they would in a shop in the hometown of your choice); the partygoers, who make every entertainment act available on the ship every night and sleep most of the day; the exercise freaks, who walk, or better, jog around the promenade deck with determined and virtuous vigor (and little regard for the safety of the more sedentary types who might be lounging by the rails); the loafers, who do nothing at all and enjoy it enormously, even though such an attitude is thoroughly un-American; and the sightseers/picture takers, who peer eagerly through the fog, hunting for a vista to immortalize forever on Kodachrome (a discouraging enterprise in the Inside Passage because there is just so much mountain and forested island that the human brain can absorb; after a while you begin to imagine schools of whales); and finally the landing parties, who live from port to port and from one shabby portside tourist-trap row of souvenir shops to the next.

Having paid your enormous price for a week or so on a cruise ship run by mysterious foreigners whom you suspect despise you, you're entitled to whatever mix of the above life-styles you want to choose.

It's hard to do all of them. Even if you're Patty. But you can give it the old obsessive-compulsive try, to use the adjective that Bill Kearney finally used when Patty tried to drag them away from the spectacular ice fields at Glacier Bay (worth the trip, perhaps) so that (a) they wouldn't miss the new bargains in the ship stores, and (b) they might see the Barbra Streisand and Robert Redford film that they had all missed.

It is not clear whether the sheer magnitude of options drove Patty round the bend on that cruise or whether the presence of the other couple was the cause. Or both. Having talked the Kearneys, who were new in the parish (and hence unprepared for what happened and unimpressed by the demands of the Poor Pathetic Patty reaction) and younger, into the trip, Patty assumed total responsibility for their enjoying every minute of it.

It was at Glacier Bay that Liz Kearney, a normally circumspect and soft-spoken young matron, told Patty, if excellent sources are to be credited, that she should "fuck off," and that Bill Kearney, himself a psychiatrist, used the words *obsessive* and *compulsive* and—it is reported—"anal-retentive bitch": striking evidence of how distraught this normally quiet couple had become. It is also reported on good authority that Bill suggested five years of classic analysis as the only hope for Patty.

Actually she had seen a therapist for years without any positive result.

Her husband's reaction is not recorded in the received version of the adventure. However, some of the more cynical women of the parish argue that he doubtless did what he always did when "Patty flakes out" (their words): "Not one damn thing."

In any event, the friendship was over, definitively. According to the aforementioned parish harpies, it served the Kearneys right for getting mixed up with Patty in the first place.

It is generally believed that upon returning, Patty dispatched a vicious and outspoken letter to Liz Kearney, describing in considerable detail what was wrong with her as a human being and as a wife and freely predicting that her husband would leave her if she did not mend her ways. Liz, reverting to type, had the good sense not to answer, though she did indulge herself to the extent of showing the text to some of the aforementioned harpies. Which was the equivalent of publishing it in Kup's column.

Patty's letter illustrates an unfortunate aspect of her indecisiveness, one that grew worse with time: she would explode with anger against any available target when the strain of choice became unbearable. The clergy and the religious were excellent targets, especially since their behavior often made them suitable inkblots and because they were usually in a poor position to defend themselves.

Patty's anger was fearsome, especially when she put it on paper. Heaven knows she had reason to be angry—at her parents, who had shortchanged her in her preparation for life, and at her husband, who tolerated her flakiness, but she was unable to direct the anger at appropriate targets. So God help the surrogate targets.

Since she was durably attractive, the major, if discreetly asked, question in the parish was, of course, about sex: what was Patty like in bed? One school thought that someone as flaky as Patty would surely be frigid. Another, more sophisticated view was that once she was properly stirred up, Patty would be spectacular as a bedmate. She was good at everything else, why not sex, especially since beyond a certain point, that activity requires very little in the way of decision making. Getting her started, according to this opinion, might be hard work, but after that, the rewards would be substantial.

Certainly this perspective would explain why her husband so readily accepted her decision-making daffiness.

Patty was born thirty years too late. In the 1950s a matron of her age—careful homemaker, excellent mother, faithful and helpful wife of a successful professional man, arguably a skilled lover—would have been entitled to relax, accept the accolades her accomplishments had merited. She might have consumed a few too many martinis, played bridge a little too much, flirted more than was acceptable, and eventually worn too much makeup, but there would be no denying the achievements of her life.

Two social changes intervened—feminism and physical fitness. Together they caused Patty's downfall.

Patty was of the first generation which came out of college with the conviction that a woman ought to be something besides a wife and a mother. She was ambivalent about this point, severely criticizing most of the successful working women of the parish for neglect of their children, but envying their cool professional competence.

Hence the terrifying question which had plagued her since she dropped out of college after her sophomore year (unable to decide whether the final two years were worth the money it would cost her parents): what should I be?

She could no more dismiss the question and accept the carefree answer of her mother's generation (nothing else besides a wife and mother) than one can avoid jamming one's tongue against what might be a sore tooth.

The problem, as noted above, was that she might have done a score of things well. If her abilities were limited to secretarial work, she might have moved into her husband's office (though whether he wanted her around during the day was problematic) or that of some other lawyer—part-time at first and then full-time as the nest emptied.

Or if her abilities were limited to teaching, she could have taught religion in the local Catholic boys' high school, where she was a great success as a temporary substitute. (And as evidence that she was not a prude, one may cite the fact that she rather enjoyed the students' attentive admiration.)

But the Lord God, something of a trickster, it is to be feared, gave her a long menu from which to choose and no obligations outside herself to impose choice.

So she tried everything—she did part-time secretarial work in our suburb, abandoned that to return to school, quit school to take up real-estate sales, left that to teach at the high school, and departed from the school when they offered her a full-time job with pay for finishing her college and M.A. coursework. Then she turned to volunteer work, first with the parish women's society as vice-president (she turned down the presidency, which she could have had without opposition), then with the local community organization. She left that to sell women's dresses in a tony shop in our local mall. She quit that to take up piano lessons and abandoned them to return to school, since a degree was more important than music, should she ever need to go back to work.

Each time she abandoned a project, Patty would get on the phone and tell all her friends, "I'm just not ready for that yet."

No one ever asked her when she would be ready.

So it went, a charming and graceful woman in an awkward and seemingly frivolous dance step, not light-hearted enough to be musical comedy and not tragic enough to be serious ballet.

The parish took Patty's dance for granted and watched each new movement in her waltz with sympathy and amusement. "Have you heard what Patty's done now?"

The kids were the final excuse for her twirling away from one position to another. She quit the community organization because it would have interfered with the family summer vacation—which by now the kids looked forward to as they would to a case of mono. She abandoned her real-estate job (at which she was reportedly making astonishing amounts of money) so that she could devote all the Christmas season to her children returning from college, a presence which did not particularly enthuse the kids.

Such amusements would have been relatively harmless if Patty had lived in a world in which there was no time to slip through your fingers. But the kids grew older, the nest emptied completely, life forged beyond the most generously estimated halfway mark, and Patty saw time running out on her. If she didn't become something, then she wouldn't be anything. Her waltz became panicky, frantic, and her outbursts of anger more frequent.

In a few years, as she saw it, instead of having too many choices, she wouldn't have any.

That's when physical fitness intervened.

Patty leaped from fad to fad as she had from career to career. There had been a meditation phase, a biofeedback period, a health-food kick, a yoga interlude. She soon found that she "was not ready" for those activities.

Then came running.

While her body continued to be appealing at an age when many women would have longed for such an attractive figure, Patty gave it little heed. Indeed, she condemned those women whose preoccupation with physical fitness caused them to neglect their children.

Then one of her friends persuaded her to accompany her on her training runs for the Chicago Marathon.

As the pastor of the parish remarked, it was a good thing that she turned to running instead of to cocaine, because the result was instant addiction.

She had found in the runner's high (whose existence she denied) another biological imperative, another irresistibly imposed external demand which became a life-shaping program for her. To her husband's astonishment and her kids' delight, they were no longer the most important elements in her life. She missed a graduation to compete in a race and refused to accompany her husband to a bar association dinner at which he was being installed as an officer, because she might break training.

The family loyally supported her efforts, returning the favor for all the basketball and volleyball games she had attended in earlier years. The kids cheered, made banners, celebrated with victory parties. Her husband was inordinately proud to be married to a woman who won the Chicago Marathon in her class after less than a year of running.

She was good at it, you see. Patty was good at everything. And in the world of runners and her running team she was praised for being good at it, praise which she had never permitted herself to receive for anything else in her life.

Her husband was also pleased with Patty's physical transformation. Poor Pathetic Patty disappeared, to be replaced by self-possessed, self-reliant Patty. Her slumped shoulders straightened, her bent head tilted up, long unused and flabby muscles became firm. Habitually a little underweight from her expenditure of nervous energy, Patty put on ten well-distributed and solid pounds because of compulsive care about her "training table." In a running suit, she caused cars to slow down, and in shorts and T-shirt during the marathon she attracted the lingering, if chauvinist, attention of TV cameras from two different channels. If she minded the replays on the ten o'clock news, she certainly did not protest very loudly.

Those of us who care about Patty were delighted. Marathon running might not be exactly high-level intellectual or religious activity, but it gave her something to live for and to keep her happy, so why knock it? The dance from career to career to career had ended, thank heaven. Patty had found her identity in the deepest biological constraints of our species: she was a runner.

Moreover, perhaps just to prove that She can plant grace anywhere, God managed to slip Sister Claire Marie into Patty's story.

There are not many Catholic college presidents who run

in marathons, and Sister is probably the only one with a D.Phil. from Oxford. Those who know how anticlerical Patty had become insist that she and Claire had become friends before Patty discovered that she was a college president and a nun.

"Poor woman needed someone her own age to talk to," Sister later said. "I listened and we became friends. She didn't hold my religious vocation against me. Furthermore, hope is never over till it's over."

When asked if running is not an addiction for her like it is for Patty, Sister snorts, "Problems I have but addiction isn't one of them. I run because I like to. Poor Patricia runs because she has to."

Sister looks like Patty, a little less sexy perhaps and a little more determined, but same slender, fragile Irish-linen sort of woman. She's one of those brilliant, gifted, sensitive women who make you regret that the religious life is fast disappearing. Those of us who were pulling for Patty thought that Sister's intervention in her life would turn everything around.

As it turned out, we had misread the situation. Patty's increasingly confident self-awareness was the first step in a belated construction of her own identity. She attempted no second steps.

The women who raced with her were not just runners. In addition to Sister, they were lawyers, doctors, accountants, teachers—and mothers, too, if not always wives. As fellow runners—members of the sisterhood, so to speak—they were immune to the charge of neglecting their offspring. Some of them must have staged informal consciousness-raising sessions, which brought Patty's only occasionally expressed rage boiling to the surface.

Sister wasn't part of these sessions. As she is said to have commented, "There's nothing wrong with my consciousness." You'll never persuade her to break any of Patricia's confidences. Women from the parish who were still close to Patricia at that time, however, insist that Sister was keeping her sane and forcing her to face reality. Some of them contend that if her husband hadn't been so stupid, Sister would have eventually presided over a reconciliation. Others will tell you that it was too late even for such a vessel of grace as Claire Marie.

As someone in the parish remarked after the event, when a woman's midlife anger finally explodes, it almost always turns on the nearest target, her husband, regardless of how little or how much he is to blame. Patty's husband had tolerated her flakiness, supported her various ventures into career and education, and never, as far as anyone knew, insisted that she ought to settle down and act like a good housewife. Compared with most husbands, he was a model of nonchauvinism.

"A model addict, if you ask me," Sister Claire Marie will tell you if you give her half a chance.

But, poor dummy, he didn't perceive that Patty was changing, that her new self-confidence had cleared a path for long-suppressed rage, and that he was the obvious target. He did not tread lightly, nor did he prepare to duck.

Instead, in a model of male stupidity, he complained about her plans to travel, by herself, since he was on trial, to Los Angeles for the marathon there. He didn't want his wife to be alone in that dubious and sinful city. Besides, wasn't she pushing this running business a little too far? Why did she need national competition anyway?

Well, that did it. All his life, he was told, he had used her to further his professional career, to maintain his house, and to raise his children. He had cheated her of the chance to become someone in her own right. She was sick of being known only as his wife. She wanted a life of her own, free from his exploitation and domination, he disgusted her, she did not care if she never saw him again.

She stormed out of their bedroom that night and informed him that if he were in the house when she returned from Los Angeles, she would find herself an apartment "downtown."

She won in the thirty-five-to-forty class, competing defiantly with women who were often ten years younger than she was. Channel 7 sent a team to cover her. At the end of the race, looking exhausted, happy, and quite fetching with her sweat-drenched running shirt pasted against her chest, she was asked by the gushing woman reporter how her husband would react to her emergence as a successful national competitor.

Patty smiled sweetly and said, "I don't care how he reacts."

The few LaSalle Street lawyers who didn't hear the remark on the ten o'clock Sunday-night news were informed about it before 8:30 the next morning.

Her husband did not move out of the house. On the contrary, he was waiting for her when she returned from L.A. a week later, hoping for reconciliation, compromise, a new beginning, anything.

He blew it, of course, as macho men do. "Where have you been," he demanded sternly, "and what have you been doing?"

Her answer, which he refuses to repeat, seems to have been obscene.

There are two possible satisfactory closures to the story of Patricia, two reasonably happy endings.

In one she leaves her husband and, strengthened by her athletic accomplishments, builds a new life for herself that is undeniably her own.

In the other, perhaps with Sister's help, she and her husband are reconciled and he actively supports her in her career choice; the two of them grow together, sharing strength instead of weakness.

Unfortunately reality does not always opt between such neat closures. In fact, neither occurred.

She did not move out of the house, but rather withdrew to the guest bedroom, where she still remains. She rejects all suggestions from her husband that they seek family counseling or talk to the parish priest or do something, anything, to save their marriage. "I'm not interested in that," is her stock reply.

She has stopped going to church and rarely speaks to her old friends in the parish. She evinces only mild interest in her children's education, careers, loves. Running has become her life.

She refuses to decide for separation or divorce or on a career which might provide her with income and financial independence. She earns some money from endorsements of running equipment and has had a couple of modeling offers, about which she refuses to decide, so they slip away.

One of the modeling offers, engineered by a friend in an ad agency, was from a famous national modeling agency which was desperately looking for "older" models. The guarantee for her first year was enormous.

Patty replied that she wasn't ready for that yet. Those who are down on her say that she never even told Sister about the offer before she turned it down. Another version is that she did and that Sister strongly urged her to accept the offer.

"But, Claire, they might want me to model lingerie."

"You can always say no to that, Patricia; anyway, you'd look great in lingerie. It would be a great boost to your self-esteem."

There is some conviction that no nun would ever make a comment like that. These days, however, you can't be sure what a nun might say.

In any event, Patty rejected the offer without learning any of the details; her friendship with Sister seems to have waned after that.

Patty seems quite content to accept her husband's money as a matter of right and live in the same house with him. But she repudiated all obligations of a wife. "I'm finished with that," she told him.

Addiction to running gave her an outlet for her rage, but rage provided no further direction for her life or even the motivation to seek direction. She was content to be angry and to run. Everything has changed and nothing has changed. She still can't or won't make decisions.

Occasionally she moves out of the house for a few days to visit a college friend or to stay at the apartment of a fellow runner (always female) who is out of town. She returns to her house after a few days, without apology or explanation. If she has any love affairs they are with men she meets on the marathon circuit; the parish, for all its intense curiosity, has been able to learn nothing about them.

There is parish folklore about a conversation which occurred between Patty and her husband, either—depending on the version you hear—right after her Los Angeles triumph or much more recently. Since no one was present besides the two of them, we have two strains in the tradition about the conversation, hers and his, more or less passed on by the women and the men respectively. If you follow the usual principles of reconstruction and combine the two accounts, you can put together a conversation which in its essentials went something like this.

"I'm proud of you, Patty, for your success in running. I don't want you to think that anything I might have said in haste diminishes my pleasure at your success or happiness."

"Thank you."

"And, if I may say so, you have never looked so beautiful."

"That's an objectification."

"It's objective truth."

"You have no right to say that."

"Who does if I don't?"

"Those who have earned the right by respecting me as a person."

"I do respect you as a person, Patty."

"You never have and you never will. What is the point of this conversation?"

"The point is that we cannot go on this way. If you want a separation, I will agree to that, even a divorce. But if you don't want to leave me, then we should try to act like husband and wife again. For the kids and for the neighbors and for ourselves."

"I don't want to do that."

"You want a divorce, then?"

"I won't seek one. You can if you want to."

"But, Patty, we can't continue like this. It's a contradiction."

"No more than our life used to be. The difference is you see a contradiction now."

"You cannot go on this way. You must decide about the rest of your life."

"I'm not ready for that yet."

When asked about the accuracy of this version of the conversation, Sister Claire Marie says that it's basically fair, but misses some of the nuances of hope. Sister sees hope everywhere.

Some of Patricia's friends think that she is beginning to look haggard, not with age or sorrow but with that curious lean, ascetic look, a suggestion of a stern monastic cloister, which marks the addicted runners.

Her husband goes on as before, though he looks worn out and thin these days. He pushes neither for divorce nor for steps toward reconciliation but waits patiently. No one is quite sure how he survives.

So she runs and rages and refuses to decide.

And grows older.

She continues to talk with Sister Claire Marie, though not as often as she once did.

She can't go on this way forever, her friends tell themselves.

No one dares to ask why she can't.

❧ Ms. Carpenter ❧

"The next appointment," announced Father Muratori implacably, "is a certain Ms. Mary Carpenter."

"Ms?" said the archbishop. "Of what vintage is this Ms. Carpenter?" He emphasized the *Ms.* both times he used it.

His secretary shrugged. "Her term, Archbishop. I'd say she has at least a year to go before she's twenty."

"Do we know her or what she wants?"

"What she wants is 'personal,' she says, and she looks vaguely familiar to me, but I don't think I know her."

The archbishop sighed. He prided himself on his accessibility, but it was Muratori's job to screen out the nuts from the people who really had something to say to their spiritual leader. He must think this Mary Carpenter was worth seeing, so there was no point in arguing with the dutiful but inscrutable young man about it. It was such a soft May morning with flowers in bloom outside his window. Tulips, he thought. He wasn't up to another confrontation with a feminist today.

Mary Carpenter was shown in. The archbishop realized

that Muratori was probably right. The young woman did not look like a nut. Dressed smartly in a gray suit with a plaid scarf at her neck, she seemed a presentable and sensible late-adolescent girl. Still, there was something slightly "foreign" about her. Her skin was almost olive in color, and her long black hair and deep brown eyes seemed to suggest the eastern Mediterranean. Carpenter was not a Greek name, but maybe it was a translation of something more clearly Levantine.

"Good morning, Ms. Carpenter," said the archbishop, emphasizing the *Ms.* ever so lightly, as he rose from his desk to greet her.

"Good morning, Archbishop," she replied, bowing to kiss his ring—an old Church custom he found embarrassing. Her brown eyes sparkled, and she showed a row of even, white teeth in a quick and somewhat impish smile.

Then he recognized her. The world spun around him. He was on a crazy cosmic roller coaster. He quickly went back to his seat behind the desk and sat down, badly shaken. Ms. Carpenter sat down across from him, a friendly grin lighting up her face. "You recognized me, didn't you?" She spoke delightedly, as if they were playing a wonderful game. Her voice was rich and deep, as though somewhere in the background there was breaking surf.

"Yes. Do you read minds?"

She laughed. "No, not really, but I'm pretty good at reading faces."

"What I want to know is why you look exactly like I always imagined you to look."

More laughter. "But, Archbishop, how else did you expect me to look? Admittedly, if I were going to China— to cite the old example—I would have had to make certain other changes. . . . " Her laughter hinted at wisdom which teenagers didn't have. But then she really wasn't . . .

"How many changes did you have to make for me?"

"Surprisingly few. That's one of the advantages of dealing with a scholar who specializes in the area." The laughter was still in her eyes and smile. What deep dancing eyes. He amused her; she felt no constraint to hide the fact.

He was still shaken. "Would it be proper to offer you some tea?"

"Why not?"

He poured her a cup of Lapsang souchong from the pot on the warmer. She smiled with surprise and pleasure when she sipped it.

"First time?" he asked.

"Only for this brand. You are surprised that I would drink tea?"

"No reason why you shouldn't, actually. We have a doctrine that says you should be able to. But please spare me the shock of asking for one of my cigars."

Now the laughter was explosive. "Well, it wouldn't give me a cancer at any rate!" They laughed together. This was not a dream. Nor was he suddenly out of his mind, but reality was slipping away, like a fading TV signal on a rainy night.

"Uh, what is the proper title that I should use?"

"Oh, I have lots of them, but I think Ms. Carpenter is fun. We had a lot of laughs over that. 'Course, you can always use my first name if it doesn't scare you too much."

It did. "Well, would it be out of order, Ms. Carpenter, to ask what you want—other than to sample my brand of tea?" Get down to business; yes, that was the thing to do.

Her eyes widened. "A favor, Archbishop. What else have I ever wanted? I think my record on that is quite clear."

"A church?"

"Come now, Your Grace, you and I really ought to be beyond that sort of thing. Besides, they have already built one for me here in this country."

"A beautiful church then?"

"I have heard the joke, too, you know. Heaven forgive me, I laughed at it."

"Heaven forgive you? Surely that's an inappropriate phrase?"

"Archbishop, you are a literalist, aren't you?" The same impish grin spread across her lovely face. She looked like he thought she should, but there was a hoydenish quality about her that did not fit his expectations.

"There was a time when you seemed to need beautiful churches."

"Not I, my lord. People wanted to build them, and that was all right. But I never needed them."

"They put up some fine ones, though."

"Yes, and I'm proud of them; but not many after the fourteenth century, don't you think?"

"Quite."

"Do I shock you, Archbishop?" Her voice was frank and unassuming.

"To be honest with you, you do surprise me."

"I don't seem to fit the image of an age-old human symbol."

"Oh, I'm not arguing with the symbol, Ms. Carpenter. If what you reflect is like what you are, then the cosmos is a better place than I thought it was. . . . "

She actually blushed. "A very pretty compliment . . ."

"Yes"—he continued his thought—"better if a little wilder and more unpredictable, and—"

"Better make it good," she murmured.

"—and more filled with playful wonder." Grand larceny with someone else's phrase, but under the circumstances . . . He was on the roller coaster again.

She clapped her hands like a child at a circus. "Oh, very good indeed! May I have more tea?"

He poured the tea. "Now, as to that favor you wanted?"

"So businesslike—just when we were having such a nice conversation. Well, you don't need to look all that serious and solemn. I won't affect your budget at all." She was now a pretty fishwife in a marketplace, promising him a bargain. Oh Lord, he was in trouble. . . .

He put down the teapot with a clatter. "You did read my mind!"

"I told you that's out of bounds for me. I'm just a shrewd bargainer and a good reader of faces. You know my ethnic background." She leaned over his desk, every inch the confidential negotiator.

"You know the cloistered convent up at Docksville?"

"Sure, there's three old nuns in it and one postulant. The order is being suppressed by Rome because it doesn't have more than a score of members all over the world."

"Don't close it down. Leave it open. I told you it wouldn't cost much."

"But why?"

"Now, my lord, you ought to know better than that. People don't ask me that kind of question." In her dizzying spin from mood to mood she now was playing the part of an Italian cardinal.

"To quote yourself, Ms. Carpenter, you and I ought to be beyond that sort of thing."

"Ah-ha, you catch on to the game too quickly. You also ought to know that my kind tend to make up the rules as we go along. Anyhow, I just know that it's very important that the convent be left open."

"Very important, to judge by the status of the messenger."

She shrugged in the ancient gesture of the Near Eastern negotiator. But her answer was twentieth-century New York. "What can I tell you?"

"I've got rules I've got to keep."

"Bend them."

"Orders from Rome."

"Ignore them. The Romans won't know the difference."

"That sounds slightly seditious."

"I'm sure you won't tell on me." She winked. He wouldn't mind the conversation if she wasn't enjoying it so much.

"You do remember the story about the leper from the Hebrew scripture, don't you? I think we improved on it in ours, but you know the lesson. If I asked you for something

333

big, you would cheerfully do it, so I ask for something small and you hesitate."

"I'm not hesitating; I'm just saying I don't understand."

"That's the whole point. You're not supposed to understand. Besides, if I hadn't come, you certainly would have closed it."

"I certainly would have. I can think of no good reason to keep open an expensive and useless convent. Neither can Rome." It was his most archiepiscopal tone, reasonable but firm.

"Keep it open as a favor for me, please?" There was a tone of pleading in her voice.

"How can I say no?"

"I don't take away people's freedom. You can say no by saying no. You can even make a good case that I have no authority to release you from Roman regulations. I am not, as you surely realize, a member of the curia."

"I can't." He sighed, looking at his hands as he always did when he had to say no.

"You won't keep the cloister open?" She wrinkled her nose in disbelief. "Not even for me?" The girl was used to getting her way.

"I'm afraid I can't. I've got the Congregation of Religious in Rome on one side of me and the pastoral council here on the other side. And they both have decided to close it. If I had my way . . ."

Her small hand tightened, the knuckles turning white. Sparks flashed from her eyes. "Don't I have any vote?"

"I'm sure you do, but as you well know, there are legitimate channels of authority in the Church. We all have to go through them. I could arrange for you to talk to the chairman of the priests' senate. . . . "

She rose from her chair and paced back and forth in front of his desk. "Fine chance I'd have with them. They think I belong in a medieval monastery." She was angry . . . but she wasn't supposed to . . .

"Or a Portuguese basilica." He didn't know what made him say that, but it was a mistake.

She turned on him, her face grim, her jaw set, her eyes now blazing. "Archbishop, you're a fool and a coward. You're not really a bad man, as canon lawyers go, but you've balanced so many forces for so long that you've forgotten what you're supposed to be. You don't really want to close that cloister down. You never did. . . . " Her dark skin flushed a dusky rose in anger.

"How do you know that? I thought you didn't read minds."

She dismissed the quibble with an imperious wave of her hand. "Someone who does told me. You like the old nuns, you even believe that cloisters are a good idea. You have compromised so often that you can't follow your own instincts anymore." She stamped her feet impatiently. "Why don't you wake up before you waste your whole life?"

Shock and dismay must have begun to show on his face. She smiled faintly. "You're scandalized because I'm angry. I'm not supposed to get angry, right? Just a plaster statue to light candles for?"

"I am a little surprised," he mumbled.

"Sure, I should not have any human emotions at all, no strong feelings, no concern; you want to make me the kind of person who would be a good archbishop."

"That's not fair. . . . I . . ."

"It is too fair. I may grow angry, but I'm not unfair. You know that."

"Ma'am, you have me trapped."

She sat down in her chair again. "That, my lord, is the general idea. To clear up this point: you don't think someone would have been given my job unless she had powerful feelings, do you? You don't think that I would lose those feelings ever, do you? What kind of a theologian are you?" Her anger seemed to be rising again.

"I just wish I could sign you up for a talk with some of my theological advisers. You'd blow their minds."

"No thanks. Archbishops are bad enough."

He played with his episcopal ring as he always did when making decisions. The flowers were still blooming in the garden outside. The sun was still shining. He could hear Father Muratori's typewriter. It was not a dream. Ms. Carpenter's theology was impeccable. He had never thought the principles should be taken that literally, though. If people like her . . . strange way to put it . . . really cared desperately, then . . .

"Would you have really preferred me, my lord, without passionate concern?"

"No . . . but the force of it surprised me. . . ."

The same impish grin. "A lot of people are going to be surprised. Now tell me that you are going to fend off the Congregation and the senate and follow your own good instincts about those poor nuns. . . ."

"Woman, you are used to having things your way."

"Solid scriptural grounds for that, too, Excellency." She knew she had him. "Well . . ." She stood up. "It's been a pleasure to do business with you, Archbishop. Now I really must be going."

"Don't try to tell me that you haven't enough time."

"I've already taken too much of yours. You have so many administrative responsibilities." Now she was just plain making fun of him.

As he walked around his desk to see her out he said, "May I be so bold as to point out that having persuaded me to break Rome's rules, you're in no position to say anything about the responsibilities of my office."

The laughter was like an old bell pealing across a French countryside. She knelt to kiss his ring. "I've enjoyed this conversation."

"I guess I have, too, though it will take me a while to get back down to earth."

"A nice pun, if unintentional. Good-bye, Archbishop. Till we meet again."

"We will meet again, Mary?" He finally got out the name.

She beamed. "I don't know the future any more than I can read minds. But, yes, Archbishop, I have a feeling we will meet again."

Father Muratori came into the office after Ms. Carpenter had left.

"Not a kook?"

"Oh, no."

"Didn't look like one. She want anything important?"

"Depends."

Muratori got the signal. He wasn't supposed to ask.

"I can't help the feeling that I've seen her someplace before. Anyone I ought to know?"

The archbishop looked at him steadily. "George, you wouldn't believe it if I told you. Who's next on the visitors' list?"

❧ Rita ❧

The priest used to think that if he were married to Rita, he would have found it difficult to keep his hands off her. He would never forget the night he said just that to the two of them.

He had learned soon after ordination that the oils of orders did not immunize you from fantasies about what it would be like to undress an attractive woman, fondle her until you both were mad with desire, and then make love all night long.

Only death eliminated such dreams. Perhaps. On the whole, in fact, he hoped that it would not.

The problem with such automatic and involuntary fantasies was not that you might replace her husband in bed or would even, on reflection, want to.

The problem was that the fantasies distracted you in the exercise of your priestly role. They made you forget that superb physical suitability as a bed partner does not by itself guarantee anything, not even that the woman will let you take off her clothes on your wedding night.

Or want to take them off herself.

So you don't think at first that sex could possibly be the problem in a troubled marriage in which that kind of woman is the wife.

"We have a good intellectual relationship," Brian, her husband, said at the beginning of their conversations with the priest. "A few years of marriage taught us that sex isn't very important in our relationship."

"It has taught us only that we can get along without it," she contradicted him, "if we have to."

It was, the priest told himself, unimaginable that one would lie next to such a magnificent woman in bed and not touch her for months.

He knew better, even in those days. The fires of human passion may be fierce, but during its long existence, the species has developed ingenious cultural and psychological mechanisms which easily extinguish the flames, not unlike the methods by which one caps a burning oil well.

Rita was classically beautiful, not voluptuous, certainly not anything as cheap as "sexy," but rather the kind of well-proportioned woman whom it would be easy to picture in a long and elegant Roman or medieval dress, with a face so perfect that you imagine it as having been copied from a Bayeux tapestry. She would have been ideally suited for a model on the cover of *Bride,* a chaste and prudent virgin in transition to a chaste and loving wife.

An instant transition, of course, accomplished on a single day without experience or preparation, from a status in which not even brief fantasies were permitted without the obligation of confessing them, to a status in which total sexual abandon became an act of virtue.

You leaped from the high dive of perfect virginity into the pool of passionate married chastity. Cold pool or warm? You didn't know till you jumped.

She was also a delicious blend of talent and timidity, gifted enough to have had two poems published in poetry journals before she graduated from college and vulnerable enough to hint that she needed reassurance and protection against critics who did not understand her poetic vision.

At their wedding Mass, flushed and happy, they seemed to everyone in the parish, including each other, the perfectly matched couple. Well educated, handsome, devout, serious, passionately idealistic and intensely intellectual—as those latter two adjectives were defined in the Catholic community just before Pope John and his council changed the meaning of lots of adjectives.

"There was nothing in Paul Claudel," Rita said bitterly later, "to prepare me for pregnancy sickness on our honeymoon."

Nor was there anything in Thomas Aquinas (read in *The Companion to the Summa*) to equip Brian to protect his masculinity from an apparently indefinite term of indentured servitude to his father's construction company in which, despite your law degree and title of vice-president of the company, you were paid a semiskilled laborer's wage and your lifestyle was supported by weekly bonuses you had to ask for every Friday afternoon.

Intellectualism for them was constituted by the "Neo-Thomists," who found in the text of St. Thomas almost all the answers to the problems of the modern world, by Henry Adams's *Mont St. Michele and Chartres,* which suggested that the thirteenth might after all have been the greatest of centuries, and by the English Catholic convert writers a generation older than them—Waugh, Greene, Chesterton, Eric Gill—and the conservative French Catholic authors like Bernanos, Mauriac, Bloy, and Claudel.

"There is but one tragedy," they would quote from the ending of Bloy's *The Woman Who Was Poor:* "that is not to be a saint."

That quote served as a transition between their intellectualism and their idealism: Brian's visited Dorothy Day's Catholic Worker Center in New York and worked in the soup kitchen in Washington during his last year in law school; Rita's served in the Catholic inner-city tutoring program in Chicago during the evenings after her English M.A. classes at Northwestern.

The models for idealism which their "sophisticated" Catholic college–educated religion provided were Waugh's Julia, who gave up her love to be true to the Church's marriage teachings, Manzoni's Betrothed, who remained faithful to each other even though it seemed likely they would never see each other again, and Bernanos's Country Priest, who offered his own soul to be damned to hell in order to save the soul of another.

Or, if one did not find literary models appealing, there were always the standard retreat master's Catholic husband and wife who practiced celibacy because another pregnancy would risk the wife's health and they would not "pollute" their marriage with the "mutual masturbation" of birth control; or the college "marriage course" instructor's Catholic wife—"still in her twenties"—who, deserted with her seven children, by a brutal drunken husband, refused to marry a "wealthy Protestant" who would have been a good father to her children, because she did not want to be deprived of the Church's sacraments.

The "marriage course" was, naturally, always taught by a nun or a priest.

They had both thought about "vocations"—Brian to the Dominicans and a life of intellectual contemplation, Rita to the BVMs and a life of poetic creation. But they decided, separately before they began to date one another, that their "vocation" was to the "lay apostolate," she representing the Church in the world of creative writing, he in the world of Chicago politics.

They had to be the best, they would tell you, eyes shining brightly, at what they did, to reflect Jesus and the Church in their respective worlds. One now transmitted to others the Catholic "answers" by example rather than by indoctrination. The deep love of their marriage relationship and their dedicated activity in the parish would provide them, they said confidently, with the spiritual resources they needed for their contribution to the secular world.

Seemed reasonable, the priest thought, and envied Brian, ever so lightly, his gorgeous bride.

They courted during a sunny era when issues and solutions were clear and clean; Pope John was alive on the banks of the Tiber, John Kennedy on the banks of the Potomac. It was to be their age and they approached it with graceful confidence, heads up, eyes glowing, hand in hand, looking, as another Catholic cliché of the time put it, not at one another but together in the same direction.

"I can't figure out where it went wrong," Brian told the priest. "Everything seemed neatly put together. We had our ideals and our ideas. Then a month after our wedding, it all fell apart on us."

"I knew we shouldn't have stayed in the same parish with our families," she said. It had become an automatic response from Rita to explain how Brian's mistakes had blighted their dreams.

Their sexual relationship would have been much better, she would then insist, if Brian had only bothered to read the "little book about women" that she had put on the bedstand at his side of the bed. Brian would reply that he didn't need to learn about women from a book. When she was especially angry, she would end this bit of dialogue with the emasculating crack that then he'd better learn about them somewhere.

They were two medieval figures—a tall, broadshouldered, dimpled-chin blond knight (former captain in army intelligence at the Pentagon) and a black-haired, ravishing maiden. Cathedrals and plainsong seemed to leap from Rita's angelically passionate poetry. Brian's commitment to decentralized political power (which in Chicago actually existed in the corrupt ward organizations he despised) was sound medieval "organic" social theory, worthy of an enlightened feudal aristocrat.

Later, friends would joke, meanly, to the priest that Rita

and Brian were the last ones to leave a party because they wanted to put off entry into their bedroom as long as possible. They would gleefully quote Rita advising her unmarried friends to purchase twin beds for their first apartment.

When he was finally summoned to provide help, the priest realized almost at once that they needed better counseling skills than he possessed. But Brian and Rita would never dare seek professional help as long as they lived in a community in which both families kept a close eye on every move the couple made—much as they had watched them ten years before when they were teenagers. Like many other Catholics in those days Rita and Brian sought bargain-basement clerical therapeutic help because it was unthinkable that they should need anything more, and besides, psychiatrists cost "twenty-five dollars an hour."

"Where would I get that kind of money?" Brian asked querulously. "And what would Pa say if I told him I needed more money so I could pay to have my head shrunk?"

The priest had been trained at the seminary never to turn his back on people in need. So once every week, after he was finished in the rectory office, he would tramp over to their apartment (not yet called a town house) and struggle against the harassed, irritable frustration which had become the climate for this, the parish's "perfect marriage."

It was required that he come to their apartment—and thus lose his own professional base and some of his professional status—because they had to economize on baby-sitting expenses.

The priest felt like a doctor who was forced to fight infection without antibiotics.

If he had been more confident of his own skills, he would have bluntly accused them of taking turns in their efforts to sabotage his efforts. He would have insisted that he would not visit their apartment again unless he was assured that their angry, irritable three-year-old was put to bed first and kept there so she could not disrupt any more sessions.

"We were certain we'd be different from our parents," Rita said one night through her tears. "Now we fight as much and are as unhappy as they are."

"Just a minute, honey." Brian raised his hand as though he were flagging down a car on the expressway. "I think my parents are happy."

"How long have they slept in separate bedrooms?" she fired back.

"Well, they don't cut each other up in public all the time like your parents do."

Their "real" world was not Virginia or Northwestern, not degrees or publications or prestigious LaSalle firms or Capitol Hill offices. That world was a game, like basketball or volleyball, to be played so long as it didn't get in the way of the important elements in life—the neighborhood, the country club, Brian's father's construction company, Rita's mother's never-ending litany of worthy charities, grandchildren for their parents, what neighbors might say or think, settling down to the "serious responsibilities of life."

Once, when the two children had been particularly disruptive (the three-year-old teasing the one-and-a-half-year-old), Brian said just as the priest was putting on his scarf to venture into the winter night, "I suppose Rita has told you about our sexual program?"

To protect his own male image, Brian pretended that the counseling was for his wife and he was an occasional participant in order to keep her happy.

"No, she hasn't."

"We have not made love much in the last two years." She turned her face away so that the priest would not see her embarrassment. "We tried rhythm after Norine. I was pregnant within six months. We're good Catholics and we didn't want to violate the Church's law. So we've been on abstinence ever since."

"It's kind of hard sometimes," Brian complained. "It's not an important part of our marriage but . . . well, it's Rita's fault that we're still on the program."

"It is *not*! I was the one who suggested we try the pill. Lots of priests say . . ."

"And then you forget to take them . . ."

"Once the spring benefit is over and I get organized . . ."

"You've been saying that about your book and your M.A. paper for the last four years. Do we add sex to the list?"

"You're usually not interested, so why should I remember to take the pills?"

On his walk home, the subzero cold a painful wall against which he bent his head, the priest wondered what would happen if the pope's commission should approve a change in the Church's birth-control teaching? What other excuse would Catholics like Brian and Rita have for the disappearance of passionate love in their marriage?

The brave knight as impotent, the fair bride as frigid. A pair of romantics dying of an overdose of realism.

Rita had argued that they should not be living in the same neighborhood, where his parents could watch every move and ask foolish and embarrassing questions. ("I heard you had morning sickness again the other day, darling.") And Brian, she said, ought not to be working for his father. He should take one of the jobs offered him in the Loop. Sure, his father had used the construction company as a step to political influence, but it was not the kind of influence that Brian wanted anyway, was it?

Brian argued that Rita was too "overcommitted" to give him the "encouragement" he needed. The priest could not figure out whether he meant good sex or help in resisting his father. Probably, the priest finally decided, Brian didn't think that the two were different. If their marital sex became suddenly satisfying—without any change in his approach to it—he would be sufficiently assured of his manhood to resist his father.

Rita was always a little breathless and a little late—a busy woman rushing desperately to keep up with will-o'-the-wisp responsibilities which receded ever further into the distance.

"What's worth doing at all," she frequently quoted her mother, "is worth doing well." So everything—a dinner party, a benefit dance, a one-class-a-week poetry course in the parish school, natural childbirth, breast-feeding, a surprise party for her father—all had to be solemn high productions which frazzled and exhausted her. She enjoyed none of these projects. They were things which had to be done.

At first, the priest thought that they ought to move as far away from the neighborhood as possible.

After Rita's outburst about their "program," he added another goal: they should resume, no, begin a normal sex life.

Whatever that was.

"Sex isn't the only thing in marriage, not even the most important thing," Brian protested when the priest, as delicately as possible, tried to return to the subject of their intimacy the week after Rita forced the topic into the open. "Sometimes I think you celibates overrate its importance. There's more holding my wife and myself together than sex."

"Certainly it's not the most important aspect of marriage." The priest hoped he could remember the points he wanted to make. (He had outlined them carefully at the rectory before he trudged over to their house.) "But if it wasn't for sex, we wouldn't have marriage. And without sex to smooth over the frictions and bind a man and woman together when their relationship is troubled, most marriages would be difficult, if not impossible."

"Maybe we ought to try it." Rita laughed.

Then Brian took a deep breath. "I've been offered a job with a new organization that is committed to building low-cost private housing—foundation money. I'd be general counsel and vice-president. Three-year contract."

"Then we'll be able to move out of the neighborhood!"

"Well, I haven't accepted yet . . ."

"You have to accept it, Brian, you just have to."

"I'll see what Dad thinks; we have a busy summer. Maybe they'll give me till autumn to decide. . . ."

Then, better late than never, she changed her tactics, threw her arms around her husband, and became the proud medieval matron embracing her hero husband, returned maybe from the Crusades.

"I'm so proud of you, Brian, and so happy. It's exactly what you've always wanted. Now I'll have to finish my book of poems to catch up with you."

"It'll all work out," he agreed, nestling her close.

They parted quickly, but the hormones were already gushing through Brian and Rita's bloodstreams, at their timeless task of driving man and woman toward one another, despite the anger and the fear which resisted intimacy.

When the priest was leaving to walk back to the rectory in the falling snow, Brian tentatively extended his arm around Rita's waist, let it slide a little lower. She leaned against him.

"Didn't I tell you things would work out, Father?" He was again basketball captain who had made a game-winning free throw and was reassuring the coach.

What the priest said next was pure instinct: "If I were married to her, I couldn't keep my hands off her."

"I can't either." Brian drew her closer. "She's a terrible distraction."

They all blushed and laughed happily. Thus did they seal their tripartite friendship and love. The priest walked back to the loneliness of his rectory oblivious to the blizzard.

He had said something totally outrageous and they had not been offended. It had worked.

He'd won.

Both families campaigned to prevent the rebirth of

married love between Brian and Rita. The group which was hiring him was a communist front. Didn't it have Ford Foundation money? What about the June dance at the club? Did they realize what people would say? What about his father's heart condition? Couldn't it wait till next year?

Brian wavered and vacillated, changing his mind every day and sometimes several times a day. Rita, however, was unshakable: she shoved aside the piles of lists on her "secretary" and began to edit her poems. She called real-estate companies about apartments near Lincoln Park. She announced that though Brian's new job would start April 1, he was quitting his father's company on March 10. She called a travel agent and made reservations for two and a half weeks in the Caymans. She persuaded her older sister Kate to take the kids while she and Brian were on their "second honeymoon."

"It's really going to be the first, Father," she told the priest, to whom she spoke on the phone for moral support every day.

Brian, attracted more by the transformation in his wife and the prospect of a couple of weeks alone with her on a deserted beach than by the new job, finally stuck to his guns and walked out of his father's office on Friday afternoon, despite the elder man's accusing silence (and despite his mother's last-minute tearful telephone plea, "Do you want to kill your father? Can't it wait six more months?").

Rita called the priest from the airport on Sunday morning to thank him for all his help.

"It will be so wonderful down there in the sun. We're all looking forward to it."

"All?"

"Brian and the kiddies and I."

"I thought the kids were staying with Kate."

"Oh, I couldn't do that to her." A tone of voice that implied that the second honeymoon was an adolescent fantasy which no one had taken seriously. "Besides, Brian won't have much time for the kiddies in the next six months. So I think it's only fair to give him a chance to enjoy them now."

Too much intimacy, the priest thought. She's lost her nerve.

And I've lost them.

❦ Stranger ❧

S he was almost too thin. Maybe naturally slender, more likely underweight. Worry, perhaps. There was anxiety in her dark brown eyes. None of his business. He'd already had enough trouble with lovely, lonely women for a couple of lifetimes.

Yet he couldn't take his eyes off her. She walked with the confident grace that hinted at professional training, well aware that her form-fitting black swimming suit revealed a superb figure, however much a few extra pounds might have marginally improved it.

He forced himself to look away. He had not come for romance, nor for a vacation, but for a lecture at the university. A Sunday afternoon under the sun was not intended to exorcise the middle-western cold but rather to give him time to finish the talk. Virtuously he put a red pencil mark through an obscure paragraph of his text.

The pool was in a grass courtyard formed by a newer horseshoe-shaped ring of motel rooms, each with a sliding-glass door opening on the lawn. The room was more expensive than it should have been; there was no view save of the line of pink bungalows across the canal. He was willing to pay his hosts' money for it because he assumed it would be more private than a fashionable resort; and privacy was what he wanted this hot Sunday afternoon. The management had gone out of its way to correct for the poor view. The court was filled with flowering plants and citrus trees. The sweet smell of blossoms assaulted his sinuses. It made him look at the girl again.

Twenty-seven or twenty-eight probably, no rings on her fingers. Not a native. Her pale skin would have tanned quickly if she were. Why stay at this obscure if comfortable hotel by the canal away from the lights of the city? She had come from a room directly across the courtyard from his. What was she doing here?

Virtue yielded to curiosity. She was in a poolside chair next to the canal, sufficiently far away to indicate that she desired no conversation with him. The old couple at the other end were the only other ones at the pool. She wanted to be alone. She slid the straps of her suit off her shoulders, anointed herself with oil, and settled back to read. What do mysterious strangers read?

He went back to his paper. It had to be good. There would be just enough skeptical and influential people to make trouble if he should fumble. The tone of the paper was far too pompous.

The easiest way to find out what she was reading was to swim by her in the pool. Besides, he needed to cool off. He noted that she did not even look up when he dove into the pool—I could have been an Olympic diver, young woman, do you realize that?

He peeked quickly at the books as he swam by her. *Sense and Sensibility*? Were the other paperbacks next to her also Jane Austen? Who reads Jane Austen at the side of the swimming pool on a Sunday afternoon? Was she part of the university? No. If she were, she would be reading Kurt Vonnegut or John Gardner.

She wasn't all that beautiful, he told himself as he

climbed out of the pool, hurt that she seemed unaware of his existence. Just the typically well-engineered young American woman. The country was filled with such types— curly brown hair, standard measurements, nice legs, muscles firmed as was fashionable now by Nautilus or some equivalent torture machine, fine wrinkles around the eyes. But why such fear in those eyes?

None of his business at all, he insisted mentally as he wrapped a towel around himself and relaxed in his chair. Perfectly ordinary woman, even if she did read Jane Austen and even if her breasts were lovely.

"Why do men always check out a woman's breasts?" Monica had demanded.

"We're programmed to do so," he had replied promptly. "By evolution or, if you want, by God. It keeps the species going."

"It's embarrassing to women."

"If men ever lost interest in women's breasts, humankind would not last a generation."

"That's bestial."

He had given up on the argument. Later he would give up on Monica. The cost of making his contribution to the continuation of humankind with her would have been too high. Maybe with anyone. Maybe he was not suited for mating.

He pried his eyes away from the breasts of the girl at the side of the pool. He had played knight errant rescuing troubled damsels once too often. There were more important things which had to be done in his life. Even it if were the time for another romantic fling, it would have to be with someone sensible and down to earth. No more great adventures.

She put the straps back on her shoulders, stood at the edge of the pool for a breathtaking moment, then dove gracefully into the water. All right, she had a good kick. All-American girl. Still, she and her problems were none of his business. He excised another ponderous paragraph.

He didn't count the number of lengths she swam. So, she's in good condition, too. She climbed out of the pool, shook her curly brown hair, and wrapped a towel around her shoulders. Actually it was quite an excellent body. The first twinge of desire embarrassed him. Back to the paper, this time seriously. Poolside pickups were for teenagers. Why did she seem so preoccupied? Of what was she afraid? Marvelous shoulders, too . . .

The sun was scorching hot. Not a leaf in the palm trees moved. The only sound was the hum of traffic on the highway the other side of the motel. Sunday didn't seem right without *The New York Times*. He was thirsty . . . a beer . . . no, not in this state on Sunday. He walked to the Pepsi machine at the other end of the pool. She was wearing large sunglasses, reading again, absorbed in the problems of tough-minded Ninteenth Century. Was the worried frown for their problems or hers? He warned his imagination to put her swimsuit back on. He had work to do.

She had certainly given no sign of awareness of his presence. He was not, after all, that unpresentable. Damn . . . he was too old to be thinking like a high-school sophomore.

A large white cabin cruiser, thirty feet at least, eased into the pier beneath the motel. Skillful seamanship. The *Dora May*. Who was Dora May? He was glad of the distraction. There were two men on the boat, one white-haired, slight, unshaven, the other much younger, big, noisy. A former pro-football player going slightly to seed in the business world?

There was conversation on the patio next to the dock. He could hear it but not see the participants. A successful fishing expedition. Hooray for them. The big man was called Tony.

Tony came up the steps, beer can in hand, dirty white windbreaker over his trunks. He put the beer can on a table near the young woman and plunged like a comic porpoise into the pool, splashing water dangerously close to the morrow's precious paper. The girl with the brown hair ignored Tony just as definitively as she had ignored him.

Tony managed only a few lengths before he was back to the security of his beer can. Then he saw her. He stood watching her like a critic in an art museum, tenderly evaluating a masterpiece, untroubled by any doubts that the masterpiece wanted to be evaluated. He sat on the chair next to her. They were too far away for him to hear Tony's soft, persuasive words. The girl paid no attention to him. Once she shook her head decisively. Tony took her hand. The low intense tone of his voice just barely carried to the other end of the pool.

He felt his fingers tighten on the red pencil. Neither the girl nor Tony cared about his presence. The old couple was gone. It was still none of his business. Tony must have considerable success with women. The girl withdrew her hand, picked up her purse, suntan oil, and books, and walked calmly back to her room across the pool. The Christian princess coolly walking away from the overawed barbarian. From the rear she was just as attractive as from the front—still a little too thin, though.

Tony tossed his beer can in a trash container and returned to the *Dora May,* shaking his head in disbelief. The heavens were being told that such an astonishing event didn't happen often.

All would have been well if it had not been for the look of pain in the girl's eyes when she walked by him. He put aside his paper and furiously attacked the waters of the pool. While he swam, she appeared in a short white robe to hang her swimming suit on a table by the sliding door of her room. Extremely nice legs. He imagined how smooth they would be to touch, how soft to stroke. Intolerable fantasy. He abandoned his backstroke for a fierce crawl.

He didn't like air-conditioning in resorts. Why come to a warm place only to cool off? But he shut the sliding door of his room, drew the blinds, and turned the air-conditioning on full blast. Just to make sure of himself, he locked the door. By four o'clock, he had revised half the talk and thought of those pain-racked eyes and slender white legs no more than he had lamented a Sunday afternoon without *The New York Times*.

The problem was loneliness. He had resolved after his foolish adventure with Monica had collapsed into low comedy that he must work on his career for several years before risking involvement again. He would stay away from lovely women who needed help. It worked. In the year and a half he had finished one book, got well into another, and published four major papers. If you kept busy enough, you hardly noticed the wrenching vacancy in your life. Not having someone with whom to share your achievements was much worse than not having someone with whom to share your bed.

You lost yourself when you began to be tender to someone else. You only realized the pleasures of such a loss when you didn't have them. Most of the time you could pretend the loneliness wasn't there by keeping busy. It caught up with you occasionally like someone had hit you in the head with a brick. Sunday afternoons at almost-empty resort motels turned out to be very lonely situations. He should have known better.

So you went to bed and slept heavily. Then you dressed for supper and took only one covert look at the drawn drapes of her room on your way to the dining room. Was she, too, killing the pain of loneliness by sleeping? How did he know it was loneliness which caused her pain? Empty resort motels on Sunday afternoons were only a danger if you had a hyperactive imagination.

The motel had been elegant and exclusive once, probably in the forties just after the war when its location between the highway and the canal was thought to be desirable. It had faded, but the nearness of the university had saved it from collapse. The dining room was impeccably clean, the Cuban hostess and waitresses neat and prim, the flowers on each white tablecloth fresh. The prices of the meals left no

355

doubt the old girl was still a paragon of respectability. He chose the indoor dining room because it was empty. The older couples on the patio in the fading light of day would make him feel sad. He turned to the second half of his paper. The clean, cool air of the dining room was a reassuring contrast to the steamy poolside.

He did not look up from his paper until the young Cuban girl brought him his salad. His poolside companion was sitting only two tables away, dressed in an expensively simple white dress, her hair carefully combed, her makeup precise. She still seemed unaware of his existence. The eyes were still anxious, the brow still frowning. Her chin was propped up by delicate fingers. What was on her mind? He felt a quick rush of desire, then returned to the final pages of his paper.

She came to his table with the main course, speaking only after she was already seated. "Do you mind if I join you for supper? Our friend from this afternoon is in the bar, and I would like to have him think I made other arrangements."

He felt as if his boat had just gone over the edge of a waterfall—an elegantly scented waterfall at that. "Be my guest," he stumbled.

There were freckles on her nose up close, an imperfection which made her even more attractive. There was one more button open on her dress than was necessary. He restrained his urge to stare. She was old-fashioned enough to be wearing a bra, even if it was something less than opaque. He had to finish the paper, he told himself, banishing the spasm of pleasure which a quick thought of undressing her produced.

"A lecture at the university?" she asked. A light pleasant voice. Again, standard American-girl voice with only faint hints of something more mysterious. So she had been watching him this afternoon as closely as he had been watching her. Damn women, they were so much better at it than men.

"I've got to get it revised tonight," he said apologetically, pulling his boat back up the waterfall and avoiding her eyes. He preferred the previous pain to the laughter which was lurking there now.

"I won't distract you," she said softly, and began to eat the sole which the Cuban girl had brought to the table.

He munched on his roast beef and continued to make red pencil marks until Tony showed up. A lot more beer had followed the contents of the can discarded at poolside.

"Honey, you could do a lot better than this creep," he began ingratiatingly.

"Please," the girl said. There was terror in her eyes, more terror than a pig like Tony justified. There was something wrong with this whole scene.

"Why don't you go away, little fella?" Presumably Tony was talking to him. In a fair fight Tony would smash him to pieces. Of course, he had no intention of letting it become a fair fight. He hoped Tony would not make it too difficult. He did not want to kill him. He looked around the room. Three witnesses: the girl (probably unreliable) and the two Cubans (intelligent but frightened on the witness stand). It had to be clear beyond any doubt that Tony struck the first couple of blows. The university wouldn't appreciate the publicity at all.

"You'd better go away, Tony," he said firmly, his eyes locking hard on Tony's eyes. "The woman has made her wishes known. There's no accounting for taste."

Tony muttered a few obscenities about the two of them and slunk back to the patio bar outside. He mentally sighed with relief. The look had worked on other occasions. No reason to let the girl know he had been scared.

"You frightened him away." Her smile was soft and warm with affection. For a moment he thought of her naked body in bed with him. Then he quickly banished the lovely image. "If I could frighten him off, he scares easily."

The girl was certainly sensitive to signals. She was silent until he finished his meal, signed the check, and picked up his paper. "Thank you very much." She rose with him. "If we just go out the door together . . ."

They did. The humid air was like a solid wall. The glare of the sun made them both squint. The *Dora May* was no longer at the pier. Tony had withdrawn from the scene of his defeat. She thanked him again as he entered the inside corridor to his room. He smiled. "Any time." She would be very good in bed, shy and modest at first and then a real challenge. . . . He had to go over the paper again.

The light was not on in her room across the courtyard. He turned off his air conditioner, opened the drapes and the sliding-glass door, and with a Coke in one hand and the protective red pencil in the other, he lay on the bed in his shorts, working through the manuscript for the final time. He did not look out the door once.

It was a few minutes to ten when he finished. As he turned on the TV he permitted himself a glance across the courtyard. Orange lights like Chinese lanterns around the swimming pool. The bushes created grotesque shadows. The pool glowed invitingly. Only one other room seemed occupied . . . hers, of course. The door was open, the thin sun drapes were stirring in the night breeze. He turned off the TV and strode out onto the soft, wet grass. The air was cool, too cool to be crossing the lawn in your shorts, but to hell with it. The scent of flowers seemed to scream at him.

She was sitting at a table, her back to the window, writing rapidly with a maroon-colored pen. A sheaf of papers was at her elbow. So she was left-handed. Her thin nightdress was cut low in the back. His heart did a slow, lazy spin. Her thin shoulder blades moving in rhythm with the pen looked weak and vulnerable. He could almost feel the back of her neck. The door was wide open in invitation, the translucent curtains heightening the mystery of the invitation.

It was the curtains, fragile cloth that they were, which stopped him. It was all too easy. Beautiful women like her, however lonely, do not offer themselves that easily to strange men on a Sunday evening at a resort motel. Was Tony part of the stage setting? Or was he a helpful accident? The woman had troubles. That was too bad, but he wanted untroubled women for the rest of his life.

Still he hesitated. A strap had fallen off her ivory shoulder. A man might touch and caress and kiss that shoulder for the rest of his life and never grow weary of it. He knew that she was his for the taking—no, his for the asking—and might be for the rest of his life if he wanted her that long. Demanding lust and tender affection fought within his soul. Tenderness won. He would take care of her always, just as he had done in the restaurant.

He told himself that the emotions he was feeling were nothing more than shallow lust. Might they not, however, mature into love? Love sufficient to bind him to her for a half century? She seemed to be the sort of woman who would wear well in every respect, did she not?

How could anyone live with the same woman for a half century?

You think too much, Monica had told him. Maybe I do. I was capable of action once, Monica. No, he had not said that. He had told no one about that era in his life.

I'm thinking now. I'm thinking about spending my life with a woman I don't know. That's a crazy thought.

The bed near the desk where she was furiously scribbling had been slept in. Her afternoon nap? As lonely as his? Her sleep tonight would be equally lonely. He turned around and with unaccountably sinking heart walked back to his own room. It was surprisingly easy to go to sleep. He found no need to explain intellectually why he had refused the invitation.

He awoke later in the night, his body hungry for a woman. She must have haunted his dreams. This time he ran by the pool and across the lawn. The door was still open, but the bed was made. She was gone. Only the maroon pen on the table and melted water in the ice container showed that she had ever been there.

The next morning the early sun was already searingly hot. The black maids were making up her room early as he went to breakfast. The Cuban clerk insisted that no woman had been registered in that room. After his tea and English muffin, he walked back through the garden. The maids had left the room. The maroon pen was still on the desk.

She was not an illusion after all.

Impulsively he darted into the room and picked up the pen. Helmsley Palace Hotel. New York. A clue if he wanted another chance.

He put the pen in his jacket pocket and slipped out of the room. The image of her delicious shoulder would not fade from his memory.

You don't get second chances, he told himself as he packed his flight bag. Virtuously he threw the Helmsley pen into a wastebasket.

He collected his papers and left the room. Halfway to the motel office, he turned and sauntered back. The pen was where he had thrown it. He picked it up and balanced it in his hand.

Maybe long searches were better than short ones.

Carefully he put the pen in his flight bag.

He took a cab over to the university for his lecture, still uncertain whether he would return to his own school or fly to New York after the lecture.

❧ Gilberte ❧

When fact, he reflected, begins to model itself after fiction, it should stick to the script.

"Aren't the Bears wonderful this year?" she said, a line that he would never write.

She wasn't supposed to be an enthusiast for the Chicago Bears. Neither in the treasured memory of his adolescent admiration nor in the paradigm of the woman who flitted through his stories in various shapes and guises was there any room for the Mighty Monsters of the Midway (whose headquarters were in Lake Forest, about as far from the Midway as you could get and still vote in Cook County). He was the Bears expert; he remembered Clyde "Bulldog" Turner and George "One Play" McAfee; he knew that the 1942 Bears had been unbeaten until the play-off game, the only unbeaten team before the Miami Dolphins of 1972.

Yet the handsome upper-middle-class grandmother, marked by age indeed but hardly ravaged by it, who sat across the table from him in the slightly baroque splendor of the Arts Club—a wall of windows, polished black floors, infinitely polite waiters—could match him story for story. She knew that Jim McMahon was the best quarterback since Sid Luckman and that Ray "Scooter" McLean had once drop-kicked a point after a touchdown in 1940.

"Who would have thought," she continued, "that Mike Ditka could handle the Refrigerator story with such grace? Remember when he was tight end? He sort of invented the role, didn't he?"

What bothered him about this story in which he was one of the two principals (the less important, in all candor) was that he couldn't quite figure out what metaphor the Storyteller had in mind.

"He and John Mackey."

"Of the Colts, wasn't he? Before they moved to Indianapolis?"

Fair enough. Despite endless autumn Sunday-afternoon agony in front of the TV screen, he'd been to one Bears game in thirty years. She seemed hardly to have missed one.

At first he had felt like he was in a Hindu myth, an author caught up inside one of his own tales in which he and another person recite lines that he has already written, all part of the dream of some medium-caste god. Three, maybe four videotapes, playing at the same time.

The Hindu myths, however, stick to their scenarios. Mike Ditka does not intrude, Refrigerator in tow, to disconcert and unhinge.

"I knew you would reappear in our lives." She eased her fruit salad to one side. "I wasn't surprised at all when you wrote at the time of Tim's death."

"Really?" In his stories he would ask why. Love never dies, even distant and unspoken love, even when the loved person becomes a myth and invades your stories.

Still, in the myth in his head, as distinct from the myth in his stories, the fascination was supposed to be one way.

"I phoned your sister's house a few years ago. Did you get the message?" she asked.

"They said you'd call back."

"You've changed. You were so quiet we hardly knew you."

He was talking to three different women, a past, a present, and a dream, the last of which had become a myth. The boundaries separating the three faded and then reappeared. She was a story become real, perhaps so that she might become a story again.

"You've changed, too."

"Not as much. But what happened to make you change?"

He tried to explain that when you find yourself a pariah in the Church because there is a new administration, you discover that freedom has been thrust on you whether you want it or not. Since you have no intention of leaving, you use that freedom, first gingerly, then with increasingly reckless leprechaun flair. The quiet rule-keeper had been an unperceived mask all along.

"I kept all the rules till I was thirty."

"My daughters"—she laughs at herself—"say that I never broke a rule in all my life."

He sensed that he had explained poorly, but she nods quickly, seeming to understand. In all the versions, her intelligence was decisively quick.

The young waiter carefully offered the plate of roast lamb from which they were to help themselves. The Arts Club was like home—you ate what was put before you.

"You've had an interesting priesthood, haven't you? Exciting even?"

"Not what I'd expected. Things changed." The male in his stories had much better lines. "The excitement I could often do without."

"I suppose so." She nods again, once more seemingly to understand his cryptic responses. "Any regrets?"

As she nibbles at her roast lamb she is exploring the boundaries, making sure she understands the geography.

"No. I'd do it all again." This is the time to define the boundaries sharply. "I wouldn't even leave if they tried to throw me out. Stay and bother them."

She laughs for the first time in the conversation. "As in marriage, I'm sure faithfulness has something to do with it."

"I had a hard time understanding those who left until I was forced to put myself inside the soul of one of them in a story. It's not my path."

The waiter clears away the dishes. Outside, traffic is already backed up on the crowded street which feeds the hungry Kennedy Expressway.

"Blueberry cobbler? With ice cream? I'd love it. I've always had a sweet tooth. And weight isn't my problem. Just the opposite. My daughters are always on my case because I'm too thin."

The woman in the story had sweet teeth, too. He did not know the past woman well enough to have learned her tastes. So quickly had she been transformed from a beautiful girl to a lingering myth. Now reality was imitating the myth again. Or maybe he'd made a good guess.

Before lunch, he had tried characteristically to order his thoughts and emotions for the drama with models of Marcel Proust's Gilberte and Jim Farrell's Lucy Scanlan. Why not start with two of the most shimmering young loves in all of storytelling?

Neither one of whom is as beautiful as she was.

Unlike Marcel Proust he had recognized his Gilberte at a dinner party after forty years. Instantly.

Proust's metaphor was Gilberte's daughter. The daughter of his "Gilberte" was dazzling, too. But "Gilberte" was the metaphor. Whatever the metaphor was.

"You stared all evening," his companion said.

"Can you blame me?"

"Not the first time."

Did Jim Farrell ever think of the real-life counterpart of Lucy Scanlan as anything more than an object for Studs's doomed dreams?

Very young love is an illusion; intense, preoccupying, unbearably sweet, but finally shallow, transient, and deceptive. Right?

Maybe not.

An author who tried to peddle the plot of *À la recherche* today would be laughed out of the offices of any self-respecting New York publishing company. Similarly a writer who suggested that young love might be revelatory, sacramental, a hint of what life is finally about, would find himself dismissed as an incurable romantic.

Which doesn't mean necessarily that he is wrong.

It all depends on your Gilberte, doesn't it? Or your Lucy Scanlan? Or the god, possibly Hindu, in whose dreams you live?

What if you were lucky? Or had enormously good taste? Even in first grade?

Okay, lucky. Either in your Beatrice or in the god into whose dreams you have managed to intrude.

"It's hard to express in words," she begins, her eyes, always the sparkling blue of a pretty Wisconsin lake stirred by light summer breezes, smiling even if her face is serious. "Or it is for me anyway, how I feel when I read a book by someone I knew long ago."

"It must be."

"It's not that I don't like them"—she hastens to dispel any thought of criticism—"and I'm astonished by your memory. You don't forget anything, do you?"

"The images and memories come back"—he knows that he must have written this exchange in one of his books—"when the story requires them. Nothing happens in the stories quite the way it did in life—not even that spelling bee between two people, both of whom we might think we know." His face becomes warm. "And no one in the stories is drawn from life exactly either. It's all what didn't happen but might have happened."

"Or should have happened?"

"Not necessarily."

"I've read them all. I think we all have. Looking for ourselves"—a quick, shy blush—"shocked if we recognize ourselves and disappointed if we don't."

He had wondered when his stories became popular whether those whom he hadn't seen in four decades would read them. He had assumed that they would not. Then it turned out that they did indeed read them—as quickly as they could grab them off the stands. How come, my own people in my own country?

"They're not exactly autobiographical. I mean, a storyteller—this one anyway—rewrites it all to make the story. It's not a video replay. Even the great autobiographical novelists, Proust and Joyce, retold their lives to fit the story."

Lit 101. She probably hadn't read either *Portrait* or *À la recherche,* not that it mattered. She should read Studs, however. It was about their own kind, the incorrigible Chicago Irish.

"Are you the narrator in the first book?"

"My sister says twenty percent of the time and I'd like to have been forty percent of the time."

"No Ellen?"

"That's what the cardinal asked me once. No, no Ellen."

"That's too bad, in a way."

"He thought so, too."

"But you know a lot about women."

"I'm a male member of the human race, with all the hormones that accompany that."

"That doesn't always make much difference."

"Thank you then for the compliment. I'm still trying—in the process of learning."

Why do you fall in love with a little girl when you're both in first grade, worship her from a distance for eight years, see her once or twice after graduation, and hold her in a place of honor in your memory ever after? So much so that your childhood and adolescent images of her survive for four decades and explode in your stories, almost every one of them?

Because you are an incurable romantic, that's why.

All right, but even for a romantic she must have been someone special.

She was pretty, she was smart, she was good, she was self-possessed, she was a resilient academic rival. Are those not enough good reasons?

Still pretty, still smart, still resilient—tense and nervous as she fought off pain and grief and adjusted to life alone, yet determined to survive and survive well, a burden to no one. No, not all that different. From a distance, and not much of a distance, in skirt and sweater, she made it 1942 again.

But what's the metaphor here? What does this mean in the dream of a god who loves surprises? No Hindu god, that.

"The stories bring back a lot of memories for me, too. You were so smart. I think I was probably envious of that."

His temptation is to say that to her alone envy is permitted. Instead he tells the truth: "You had reason to be angry. You were a girl, you were too pretty, and you weren't going to a seminary. No way you could win."

She laughs, not convinced. "I never thought I'd become as much a feminist as I have in the last five years." She folds her glasses and puts them in her purse. "There really is terrible discrimination against women."

"Women priests?"

"I don't know."

"There's only one reason to exclude them. If they're inferior human beings."

"They're *not* inferior." The feisty rival once more. "But I do think of God as a mother. I mean, if you've had a mother and been a mother and loved and been loved both ways, how could you not?"

He hadn't written that line. But unlike talk about Mike Ditka and Jim McMahon and the Fridge, he wished he had.

Certainly no medium-caste Hindu god was writing this story. It was Yahweh, Good Old. And Lady Wisdom, God's self-disclosure in the order and charm of the cosmos. Lady Wisdom, whom he'd once told a reporter was an Irish comedienne.

"If God is a mother as well as a father, why not women priests?"

"I suppose." She was thoughtful again, slipping up to a big question perhaps. "None of us thought you would be a novelist."

"I didn't either and I'm not sure I am."

"I am the girl in this book?" She held it in front of her, like a shield, or maybe a prayer book. "Kind of?"

"Bits and pieces." He swallowed much too large a piece of blueberry cobbler.

"My daughters didn't recognize me. So I didn't tell them. They all say it's their favorite." The same magic smile from first grade. Special indeed. "I know you much better after reading these books than you know me." She opens the book tentatively. "Yet you know a lot about me that you couldn't possibly know."

The God in whose dreams he lived, perhaps not at all the God who dreamed Proust and Farrell, is a God who enjoys surprises, twists and turns, kinks and ironies, and happy endings. Ultimately anyway.

Nonetheless, it was excessive of Her to write him into the kind of story into which he had written his own characters.

"A lot of the girl in the book is based on my imagination of what you might have become. Some of it was pretty thin. . . ."

"And some pretty accurate, too. I can't understand how you did it."

"All the people are composites. I dream up the story line and then the characters come rushing out of my imagination, fully grown." He omits any reference in this writer's workshop lecture to Venus from the sea. "Only afterward do I realize that bits and pieces of people I've known through the years have been incorporated."

"Am I in the other women?"

"Most of them, I guess."

"That's nice. . . ." She reaches for her glasses again, as though to reread the book. "I like the books. And I like the women, too."

"I was half-afraid that you might read this one especially, recognize yourself, and be angry."

Another quick blush. "Certainly not angry. Surprised. Maybe flattered. Anyway"—pointing at the girl on the cover—"*she* wouldn't be angry, would she?"

"*She* would love it. Maybe I should have trusted my imagination."

Neither of them says what they both know. To have so influenced stories after forty years, she must have occupied an enormous place in his imagination.

A new Cadillac is becalmed outside the window beneath their table. Not at all like the startling Studebakers of 1946. He imagines a Study on the street and thinks that Proust, genius that he was, erred. Time is neither lost nor found, but given.

"You wrote that poem, the 'rival' one, about me, too? The one that ends, 'We shall be young again, we shall laugh again'?"

"Who else fits it?"

"Thank you for that, too."

As someone else remarked when she heard about this tête-à-tête at the Arts Club, no one is anything but pleased to discover that they've been loved for fifty years.

Or, for that matter, to say that one has loved for fifty years and is fully prepared to love for fifty more.

Which is certainly true, though it doesn't help much in the search for a metaphor. He ought to be depressed. No one could live up to his residual adolescent fantasies. Only somehow she went beyond them, not as a two-dimensional fantasy, but as a three-dimensional person.

Is the Author trying to tell him something?

"Do you think the Bears will go to the Super Bowl?" She nods at the waiter for more coffee.

Is that what the Author had in mind? He thinks this story is being changed into a comedy.

"No doubt." He crosses his fingers and together they laugh with the hollow cheer of the dogged Chicago sports fan.

"None at all. Will you watch it at our house?"

Forty years—the span of a woman's adult life: falling in love, courtship, marriage, the difficult early days of parenthood, struggle against initial economic problems, life for a while in a strange city, marvelous but contentious kids (in the nature of the creature), sorrows, disappointments, failures, difficult decisions, intense if all too transient joys, unexpected surprises, pride of accomplishment, interludes of contentment that slip through your fingers, tragedy, the somber realization that most of the joys are in the past and were not embraced as fervently as they might have been, grim awareness that the end is now much closer than the beginning. Life too quickly almost done before it has even begun.

By all odds and according to all conventional wisdom, he ought to be disappointed with the impact of such a life on her, either with a sense of lost opportunity like Studs or painful disillusionment like Marcel.

In fact, she delights him, as much as in first grade if for different reasons. Better ones, come to think of it.

There's a metaphor there someplace if he could only find it.

"I should begin the drive home before the rush hour."

"I'll walk you to the parking lot."

"Thanks for lunch . . . and thanks for the books." She gestures with one of them. "And thanks for coming back into our lives."

"The gratitude should be the other way around."

If he had walked a different path in his life, there would never have been romance between them. They were not star-crossed lovers. Whatever metaphor the Author had in mind, it did not involve sadness over what might have been, nor joy over what might yet be. They will continue to walk different paths in the years ahead, though not nearly so far apart. The metaphor is not about that sort of issue.

It was somehow more subtle or maybe more simple—like our dreams are never grand enough. No, that wasn't it either. Close perhaps, but with metaphors, close didn't help.

It's all right, fella, the Author seemed to be saying, for you to use those images in your story. I play a different game, because I'm not only into surprises, but offbeat surprises. You yourself called me a comedienne, right?

Right.

He kissed her good-bye at the parking lot and promised indeed that on January 26 he would watch the Super Bowl with her family.

Go Fridge!

A wind off the lake had swept the clouds away from the Michigan Avenue skyline. As he walked east the tall buildings, framed in deep blue, shone silver and gold in the late-afternoon winter sunlight.

Life goes on, not in Gilberte but her daughter. Lucy Scanlan is the lost angel of light for one whose life does not go on.

Come on, guys, don't try to give me those clichés!

His Author, a Hindu god turned Jewish and then turned Celtic, had a much better metaphor, not in a woman who

371

had lost her vitality but in one who had kept it. Nor in a woman who was less than imagined but, in intricate complexity, more.

It was surely an excellent metaphor, but he didn't quite know how to interpret it.

He might have to write another story.

About the Author

Andrew M. Greeley is the author of *VIRGIN AND MARTYR*, *THY BROTHER'S WIFE*, *THE CARDINAL SINS*, *GOD GAME*, *THE FINAL PLANET*, and *LORD OF THE DANCE*, among other bestselling novels. He lives in Chicago and teaches sociology in Tucson.

BESTSELLING BOOKS FROM TOR